how to walk away

Katherine Center is the author of six bittersweet novels about love and family. She lives in her hometown of Houston, Texas, with her husband, two sweet children, and their fluffy-but-fierce dog.

ALSO BY KATHERINE CENTER

Happiness for Beginners

The Lost Husband

Get Lucky

Everyone Is Beautiful

The Bright Side of Disaster

how to walk away

Katherine Center

MACMILLAN

First published 2018 by St Martin's Press, New York

First published in the UK 2018 by Macmillan
an imprint of Pan Macmillan
20 New Wharf Road, London N1 9RR
Associated companies throughout the world
www.panmacmillan.com

ISBN 978-1-5098-5897-2

9 8 7 6 5 4 3 2 1

A CIP catalogue record for this book is available from the British Library.

Printed and bound by CPI Group (UK) Ltd, Croydon, CR0 4YY

For my mom, Deborah Detering,
who is my personal superhero.

And to the memory of her brother and friend,
my uncle, Herman Detering.
We will always miss you, Bubsie.

You get one life, and it only goes forward.

—Wesley Branch

There are all kinds of happy endings.

—Eve Lapin

how to walk away

One

THE BIGGEST IRONY about that night is that I was always scared to fly.

Always. Ever since I was old enough to think about it.

It seemed counterintuitive. Even a little arrogant. Why go up when gravity clearly wanted us to stay down?

Back in high school, my parents took my big sister, Kitty, and me to Hawaii one year. I dreaded the flight from the moment they told us until well after we were home again. The phrase "flying to Hawaii" translated in my head to "drowning in the ocean." The week before the trip, I found myself planning out survival strategies. One night after lights out, I snuck to Kitty's room and climbed into her bed.

I was a freshman, and she was a senior, which gave her a lot of authority.

"What's the plan?" I demanded.

Her face was half buried in the pillow. "The plan for what?"

"For when the plane hits."

She opened an eye. "Hits what?"

"The ocean. On the way to Hawaii."

She held my gaze for a second. "That's not going to happen."

"I have a bad feeling," I said.

"Now you're jinxing us."

"This is serious. We need a survival strategy."

She reached out and patted my bangs. "There is no survival strategy."

"There has to be."

"No." She shook her head. "Because if we don't crash, we won't need one. And if we do crash . . ." She paused so I could catch her drift.

"We won't need one?"

A nod. "We'll just be dead." Then she snapped her fingers.

"You make it sound easy."

"Dying *is* easy. It's *not dying* that's hard."

"Guess you have a point there."

She closed her eyes. "That's why I'm the brains of the family."

"I thought I was the brains," I said, nudging her.

She rolled away. "You know you're the beauty."

Impossibly, we survived that trip.

Just as impossibly, I survived many more trips after that, never hitting anything worse than turbulence. I'd read the statistics about how flying was the safest of all the modes of transportation—from cars to trains to gondolas. I'd even once interned at an office right next to an international airport and watched planes go up and come down all day long with nary a problem. I should have been long over it.

But I never could lose the feeling that "flying" and "crashing" were kind of the same thing.

Now, years later, I was dating—seriously dating—a guy who was just days away from getting his pilot's license. Dating him so seriously, in fact, that on this particular Saturday, as we headed out to celebrate my not-yet-but-almost-official new dream job, I could not shake the feeling that he was also just about to ask me to marry him. Like, any second.

Which is why I was wearing a strapless black sundress.

If I'd thought about it, I might have paused to wonder how my boyfriend, the impossibly fit and charming Charles Philip Dunbar, could be one hundred percent perfect for me in every possible way—and also be such an air travel enthusiast. He never thought twice about flying at all—

or doing anything scary, for that matter, like scuba diving or bungee jumping. He had an inherent faith in the order of the universe and the principles of physics and the right of mankind to bend those principles to its will.

Me, I'd always suspected that chaos was stronger than order. When it was Man against Nature, my money was on Nature every time.

"You just never paid attention in science class," Chip always said, like I was simply under-informed.

True enough. But that didn't make me wrong.

Chip believed that his learning to fly was going to cure my fears. He believed that he'd become so awesome and inspiring that I'd have no choice but to relax and enjoy it.

On this, we had agreed to disagree.

"I will never, ever fly with you," I'd announced before his first lesson.

"You think that now, but one day you'll beg me to take you up."

I shook my head, like, *Nope.* "Not really a beggar."

"Not yet."

Now, he was almost certified. He'd done both his solo and his solo cross-country. He'd completed more than twice his required hours of flight training, just to be thorough. All that remained? His Check Ride, where a seasoned pilot would go up with him and put him in "stressful situations."

"Don't tell me what they are," I'd said.

But he told me anyway.

"Like, they deliberately stall the plane, and you have to cope," he went on, very pleased at the notion of his impressive self coping. "Or you do a short-field landing, where you don't have enough space. And of course: night flying."

The Check Ride was next week. He'd be fine. Chip was the kind of guy who got calmer when things were going haywire. He'd make a perfect pilot. And I'd be perfectly happy for him to fly all he wanted. By himself.

But first, we were getting engaged—or so I hoped. Possibly tonight. On Valentine's.

I can't tell you how I knew, exactly. I'd just sensed it all day, somehow, the way you can sense it's going to rain. By the time I buckled in beside him in his Jeep, I was certain.

I'd known Chip a long time. We'd been dating for three years. I knew every expression in his repertoire and every angle of his body. I knew when he was faking a laugh, or when he was bullshitting. I could tell in seconds if he liked a person or not. And I certainly knew when he was hiding something—especially something he was excited about. Even though this date seemed exactly like every other date we'd ever had, I just knew something big was about to happen.

I figured he'd take us to the Italian place with the twinkle lights where we'd had our first date. But, instead of heading for downtown, he turned toward the freeway and ramped up.

The top was off his Jeep. I clamped my arms down over my hair. "Where are we going?" I called.

He called back, "It's a surprise!"

My stomach dropped at that. Once again, I knew Chip's intentions without his even hinting. This was kind of a problem with us. I could read him too well. He wasn't taking me to dinner. He was taking me to the airport.

TWENTY MINUTES LATER, we had left the city of Austin far behind. He pulled up the parking brake beside an airplane hangar at a private airfield in the middle of nowhere.

I looked around. "You can't be serious."

He leaned in. "Are you surprised?"

"Yes and no."

"Just pretend. Just once, I'd like to surprise you."

"Fine. I'm shocked. I'm awed."

"Don't pretend that much."

He came around to my side and took me by the hand, and then he pulled me behind him, bent over all sneaky, around to the far side of the hangar.

I followed him in a state of cognitive dissonance—knowing exactly what he was doing while insisting just as clearly that he couldn't possibly be doing it. "Are you sneaking me in here?" I whispered.

"It's fine. My friend Dylan did it with his girlfriend last week."

I tugged back against his hand. "Chip. I can't!"

"Sure you can."

"Is this—illegal?"

"I just want to show you my plane."

"It's not your plane, buddy."

"Close enough."

I had zero interest in seeing his plane. Less than zero. I was interested in wine and appetizers and candlelight. I almost had the job of my dreams! I wanted to be celebrating. I was in the mood to feel good, not bad. "Can't we just go to dinner?"

He peered around, then turned back to me. "*Anybody* can go to dinner."

"I'm cool with being anybody."

"I'm not."

Then, with a coast-is-clear shrug, he pulled me out across the pavement and stopped in front of a little white Cessna. It looked like the kind of plane you'd see in a cartoon—wings up high, body below, and a spinny little propeller nose. Very patriotic, too. Red, white, and blue stripes.

"Cute," I said with a nod, like, *Great. We're done.*

But he took my shoulders and pointed me toward the cockpit.

I took a step back. "What are you doing?"

"Let's go for a ride."

"I'm afraid to fly. Remember?"

"Time to get over that."

"I'll throw up. I'll be motion-sick."

"Not with me, you won't be."

"It's not about you. It's about flying."

"You just need the right pilot."

I was shaking my head—half disbelief, half refusal. "You're not even certified."

"I'm as good as certified. I've done everything there is."

"Except take the test."

"But the test is just to see what you've *already learned*."

"Chip? *No*."

"Margaret? *Yes*. And right now before they catch us."

The force of his insistence was almost physical, like a strong wind you have to brace against. He wanted to do this. He wanted *me* to do this—to show faith in him, to believe in him. It wasn't a test, exactly, but it was still something I could fail.

I wasn't a person who failed things.

I was a person who *aced* things.

It felt like a big moment. It felt draped in metaphorical significance about bravery, and trust, and adventurousness—like it would reveal something essential about who I was and how I'd live the rest of my whole life. Saying no to flying right now suddenly felt like saying no to every possibility forever. Did I want to be a person who let minuscule statistical risks undermine any sense of bravery? Was this a challenge I couldn't rise to? Was I going to let fear make me *small*?

I'm not sure I ever really had a choice. Chip was Chip. He was my perfect man, and I'd thought so ever since his parents moved in next door to my parents, back when we were both in college. Our mothers became best next-door-neighbor friends, drinking wine on the patio and gossiping, but I only saw him on vacations. In the summers, his dad made him mow the lawn, and I'd stand at our window and watch. One time, my mom urged me to take him out a bottle of water, and he glugged the whole thing down in one swoop. I still remember it in slow-mo.

But I really didn't know him at all until we both wound up at business school together back home in Austin by accident. I was team leader of our study group, and he worked under me, which was good for him.

That's how we fell in love.

I'd have married him that first night we kissed, if he'd asked me. He was that kind of guy. Tall, clean-shaven, blond, all-American, high-achieving, confident. And dreamy. People did what he wanted. I felt lucky to be with him, and I'd doodled "Margaret Dunbar" more times than I'll ever admit. I once Googled dog breeds for our future pet. And one night, when shopping for something else—I swear—on the Home Depot website, I clicked on a little pop-up box for wood fence pickets. Just to see how much they were.

Now we were both out of school with our brand-new MBAs, both about to start our new jobs—Chip as an entry-level financial analyst at an investment bank, a job he found through a friend of his dad, and me as a business development manager for an oil and gas company called Simtex Petroleum. His job was good, but mine was far better, and I thought it was sporting of him, and rather gallant, to be so happy for me.

In truth, I wasn't even qualified for my new job. It required "five years of experience in the sector," "advanced knowledge of bidding for commercial contracts," and actual "international experience," none of which I had—but my B-school mentor had gone out on a limb for me, calling in a favor from a friend and writing a stunning letter of recommendation that called me a "fiercely energetic forward thinker, a problem solver, an excellent communicator, and a team player with strong business and financial acumen."

I'd laughed when he'd showed me the job listing. "I'm not remotely qualified for this."

"People get jobs they're not qualified for all the time."

I stared at the description. "They want 'demonstrated strategic and higher operational level engagement with the logistics environment.'"

"You're a shoo-in."

"I'm a joke."

"Now you're just thinking like a girl."

"I *am* a girl."

"We need to remedy that."

I gave him a look.

"When you go to this interview, I want you to pretend to be a man."

I closed my eyes. "Pretend to be a man."

"A *badass* man," he confirmed. "A man who's not just qualified, but overqualified."

I shook my head at him.

"Qualifications," he said, "pale in the face of confidence."

"If you say so," I said. Though I didn't believe it for a second. I went into the interview that day fully expecting to be laughed out of the room. But I did what he told me to. I pretended like hell—if nothing else, to prove him wrong.

Then they offered me the job. Or, at least, as the HR guy walked me to the lobby, he touched my shoulder and said, "It's not official, but you've got it."

My starting salary was going to be 50K higher than Chip's—but my mother told me not to tell him that. The important thing was: We were beginning our lives. Things were falling into place.

And here, at the airfield, I didn't want to be the only thing that didn't.

Chip squeezed my hands. "You trust me, right?"

"Yes." Sort of.

Then he pulled me into a kiss—a manly, determined, all-this-can-be-yours kiss, digging his tongue into my mouth in a way that he clearly found powerful and erotic, but that I, given how the sheer terror of what I was about to do had iced my blood, was too numb to feel.

Then he swatted me on the butt and said, "Climb in."

What can I say? I did it.

But I'm telling you, my hands were shaking.

As I worked on hooking the shoulder strap, I gave myself a stern talking-to: This was the right thing to do. Wasn't that what love was, after all? Saying *yes*—not just when it was easy, but also when it was hard?

Of course, any analyst worth her degree could have easily made the exact opposite argument: that I should trust my gut, and I shouldn't let Chip push me into doing things I didn't want to do. That his lack of respect for my genuine discomfort in the face of his *Top Gun* fantasies did not bode well for our long-term prospects.

But I wasn't going there.

I was going flying.

Then he was next to me, buckling up and handing me a set of black headphones. I had that feeling you get once you've picked a roller coaster seat and clamped yourself in.

Chip immediately shifted into character as the pilot. He slid his aviator sunglasses on and pressed the headphone mic so close to his mouth that his lips brushed against it, and started speaking a language to the control tower so specialized, it was basically nonsense: "South Austin Clearance Delivery—Cessna Three Two Six Tango Delta Charlie with information Juliet—VFR to Horseshoe Bay cruising three thousand three hundred."

It sounded to me like he was pretending. Who talked like that? But the tower didn't agree. Crackling through the headphones came "Cessna Three Two Six Tango Delta Charlie—South Austin Clearance—squawk two three one four, departure frequency will be one two zero point niner."

Oh, shit. This was happening.

Chip checked instruments and dials, looking them over like a pro. He looked at ease. Capable. Trustworthy. Macho, too. And, dammit, yes: super cool.

"I already went through my safety checklist before I came to get you—twice," he said. His voice was crackly through the headphones, but he took my hand and squeezed. "Didn't want to give you time to change your mind."

Smart.

But I was all in by this point. I'd made my choice. For better or worse, as they say.

So Chip turned his attention to bigger things.

Still in sexy-pilot mode, he spoke into the mic and gave another nonsense message to the tower, confirming that we were waiting for the runway. I'd never been in the cockpit of a plane before, and this plane was all cockpit. Technically, there were two seats behind us, but it felt like we were in a Matchbox car.

Another plane had to land before we could take off, and I studied the dashboard with all its knobs and dials and 'ometers. I pointed at it. "Isn't this kind of tall?" It was higher than my head. I could barely see over.

He nodded. "It's not like driving a car," he explained, "where it's all about what you see. Flying's more instrument based."

"You don't look out the windshield?"

"You do, but you're looking at the instruments and gauges just as much. It's half looking, half math."

The other plane touched down, slowed, and trundled past us. *See?* I said to myself. *They survived.* We revved up, Chip announced us again over the radio, and he started working the pedals to bring us into position. The blades on the propeller spun so fast they disappeared. The plane vibrated and hummed. I sat on my cold hands so I wouldn't squeeze them into fists.

"Please don't do any loop-de-loops or anything," I said then.

He glanced over. "Loop-de-loops?"

"Spins or flips. Or whatever. Show-offy stuff."

"I don't have to show off for you," he said.

"You sure don't."

"You already know how awesome I am."

I gave a nod. "Yes. And also, I might throw up."

We sped up, casting ourselves forward. As we lifted off, I decided it wasn't that different from going up in a regular plane. A little bumpier, maybe. A smidge more front-and-center. A tad more *Out of Africa*.

The ground floated away beneath us. Easy.

Chip was focused and calm, and it was so strange to think he was making it all happen. Once we were airborne, he started narrating everything he was doing, as if he were giving me a lesson. He told me the Cessna 172 was the most popular plane ever built. A classic. We would level off at 3,000 feet. We'd be traveling 125 miles an hour, speeding up as the air thinned out so we didn't stall. He had to scan the sky for other planes, as well as watch the radar on the screen for towers.

Then something disturbing: He mentioned that the fuel was in the wings.

"That seems like bad engineering," I said. "What if the wings break off? You'll get doused in fuel."

"The wings don't break off," Chip said. "That's not a thing."

"But *if they did*."

"If they did, you've got bigger problems than a fuel spill."

I put my hands in my lap and deliberately arranged them so they would not look clenched.

The plane was loud—hence the headphones—and we vibrated more in the air than we had on the ground, especially when we passed under a cloud. Chip explained that clouds actually sit on columns of rising air, and that turbulence happens when you cut through those columns. I had never thought of clouds as sitting on anything—just floating—but once he said it, it made sense. The more sense he made, the safer I felt.

He grinned over at me. "Awesome, huh?"

Kind of. "Awesome."

"Still scared?"

Yes. "Nope."

"Glad you came?"

"I'll be gladder once we're back on the ground."

"I knew you'd enjoy it. I knew you could be brave if you tried."

Such an odd compliment. As if he'd never seen me be brave before. As if my capacity for bravery had been up for debate.

But I did feel braver now, as we rose above the subdivisions laid out like a mosaic below us.

The hardest part was over, I remember thinking.

Before long, the suburbs beneath us thinned out, and I realized I had no idea where he was taking me.

"Where are we going?" I asked.

"I'm just going to show you one quick thing," Chip said, "and then we'll turn back around and go home."

I could see that up ahead, dark and jagged, was a body of water.

"Is that Horseshoe Bay?" I asked. My grandparents had a house there. I'd been there a million times, but I'd never seen it from this angle.

Chip nodded. "You guessed it."

We were approaching the far shore. "What do you want to show me?"

"Wait and see."

Chip angled us back to circle over the lake, brought our altitude down a bit, and maneuvered us closer to the water. I could see houses and little cars below, but it was hard to recognize anything from this bird's-eye view. We dipped a little lower, close enough to see little waves breaking against the shore.

"Keep an eye on the beach," he said, taking us lower still.

I peered out my window. A thin strip of sand, and people, and picnic tables on the grass nearby. Now I recognized it. The public beach on the far shore.

After a few minutes, he said, "There!" and pointed.

I looked. "Where?"

"Can you read it?" Chip asked.

"Read what?"

He peered down, out his side window. "Shit. We're too high."

But any lower made the towers on the radar turn red.

Chip turned my way. "There's writing in the sand down there."

I didn't see anything. "What does it say?"

"It says, 'Marry me!' "

My heart gave a little jolt, but I played it cool. "It does?" I couldn't see any writing in the sand.

"I saw it on the news yesterday. A guy proposed by writing the words in giant letters in the sand with rocks, then taking his girlfriend for a picnic by the lake to surprise her. "

"Cool," I said, like it was just empirically interesting. What were we talking about?

"I really wanted you to see those words."

"You did?"

"I did." He glanced over again. "Because I've been wanting to ask you the same question."

It's one thing to expect something to happen, or root for it, or hope— and it's another thing entirely to live the actual moment. I put my hand to my mouth and pressed my head to the window one more time for a better look.

"And there's something else. Open the glove box."

Sure enough, there was a little storage compartment in front of me. Inside, I found an emerald-green velvet ring box.

I was so glad I'd forced myself into this plane. Sometimes, terrifying, nausea-inducing risks are worth it. I turned to Chip. "You're asking me to marry you?"

His voice crackled out through the headphones. But I knew the answer was yes.

So I gave my own answer. "Yes!"

"You haven't even opened the box."

"I don't need to. Just: Yes!"

Chip turned toward me with a big smile full of perfect teeth. I could see myself reflected in his sunglasses, and my hair was a mess. I fought the urge to straighten it up. I also fought the urge to climb over and kiss him. It seemed strange not to kiss at a moment like that, but no way was I unbuckling. I couldn't even remember how to unhook the shoulder strap.

Instead, I gave him a thumbs-up.

"It's not official till you put on the ring," he said.

I opened the box to find a very ornate gold-and-diamond engagement ring.

"It was my grandmother's," he said.

I pulled it out and slid it onto my finger. It was a bit big. Big enough, actually, that when I held out my hand to admire it, the diamond slid to the side and hung upside down.

"It's perfect," I said.

"Do you like it?"

"Yes!" I said. Not my style, but who cared?

"Are you surprised?"

Yes and no. I nodded. "Yes."

"Are you glad you came flying with me?"

"Very," I said. And that answer really was one hundred percent true. For a little while longer, at least.

WE NEVER FOUND the letters in the sand. But it was okay. We didn't need them.

It was about twenty minutes back to the airfield, and we filled those minutes by arguing adorably about the wedding.

We agreed we should have the ceremony on that very beach, and then started listing bridesmaids and groomsmen. Most people were shoo-ins, like his brother, and his buddies Woody, Statler, Murphy, and Harris from undergrad—but then, of course, the question of what to do about my sister, Kitty, came up and stumped us for a while.

I hadn't seen or talked to Kitty in three years. Her choice.

"You have to invite her, though," Chip said.

But I wasn't sure I wanted to. When she first went away, she announced she was "taking a breather" from our family. She'd be in touch, she said. Then she never was.

We knew she wasn't dead. Our dad had kept in occasional contact, and he could verify that she was living in New York, alive and well—just unwilling, for some reason she would not share, to come home. Even for a visit.

At first it had been a little heartbreaking, losing her like that—being *rejected* by her like that. But by now, after all this time, I just felt cold. She didn't like me? Fine. I wouldn't like her, either. She wanted to pretend like her family didn't exist? No problem. We could pretend the same thing right back.

Chip thought we needed to invite her to the wedding, at least. If not make her the maid of honor. But I disagreed.

"First of all," I said, "she won't even come. And second, if she does, she'll ruin the whole thing."

"You don't know that for sure."

"Just her being there will ruin things for me. Just feeling weird about seeing her again will suck the joy right out of the day. Instead of looking forward to the most joyful day of my life, I'll dread it. Because of her."

"Maybe you could see each other beforehand and get the weirdness out of the way," Chip said.

I was in no mood for reasonable suggestions. "Even," I went on, "if I manage to get past the weirdness, having her there would still mean *having her there.* Which means a ninety percent chance of her getting drunk and climbing into the punch bowl. Or getting drunk and biting a groomsman. Or getting drunk and grabbing the microphone for an Ethel Merman impersonation."

Chip nodded. I wasn't hypothesizing. Kitty had actually done each of these things in the past. He shrugged. "But she's your only sister."

"That's not my fault."

"It would seem weird for her not to be there."

I went on. "And it's not my fault we're not close anymore, either."

"No argument there."

"*She* created that situation."

"I agree."

"And now she gets to spoil the only wedding day I'll ever have."

My luck. I'd throw the most exquisite wedding in the history of time, and the only takeaway would be my drunk, black-sheep sister trying to ride the ice sculpture.

If she deigned to come.

Actually, that summed up our dynamic exactly. I was always trying to get things exactly right, and she was always hell-bent on getting them spectacularly wrong.

UP AHEAD, THE airfield came into sight.

Chip was especially good at landings, he mentioned then. He just had a knack for them, kind of the way he had a knack for parallel parking.

That said, the sky up ahead was quite different from the sky we'd seen on the flight down. Darker, stormier. "That's unexpected," Chip said, taking it in.

"Was it supposed to rain?"

"Not last I checked."

"You can fly in the rain, though, right?"

"Not really. You avoid it. Or wait for it to pass."

"I'm fine with either," I said. So agreeable with that ring on.

"The thing is, though," he said then, "we're going to need to land sooner rather than later."

"So we don't miss our fancy dinner reservation?"

"So we don't run out of fuel."

I studied the horizon. The sky behind us was bright blue, but up ahead it was grayer and grayer. And a little purple. With a smidge of charcoal black.

"That's definitely rain—but way past the airport. Right?"

He nodded. "Right."

Off on the horizon, there was a flash of lightning.

Maybe the storm was affecting our air. The ride back had become quite a bit bumpier, and soon I was motion-sick.

As we approached, Chip called in our coordinates in that official pilot's voice, which was a little deeper than his regular one, and then he maneuvered us into the flight pattern for landing. We pulled around to the left, then turned to run along the length of the runway, then U-turned to descend to the ground. Chip was all concentration. I felt, more than saw, the ground getting closer. A welcome idea.

And then a funny thing happened. As we were nearing the runway, the wings did a thing I can only describe as a waggle—dipping sideways a little and then popping back up—that gave me a physical sting of fear in my chest.

It was over in a second, but that second changed everything. Something was wrong.

I looked over at Chip. His face was stone still.

"Chip?" I said.

"The wind's shifted," he said.

"What?" I asked. "Is that bad?"

"It's a crosswind now" was all he answered.

A crosswind? What was a crosswind? It didn't sound good. Chip was checking dials, and working the pedals with his feet. His face was expressionless.

He seemed to be holding us fairly steady. I kept quiet, concentrating on willing us some good luck.

We were maybe twenty feet above the runway now, coming in straight. And then, suddenly, the tarmac just slid off to the side. It was below us, and then it shifted away, like someone had tried to do a tablecloth trick—and failed—putting a grove of trees in front of us instead.

"Shit!" Chip said, and he hunched closer to the yoke.

He maneuvered us back into position, lined up over the runway again.

"Chip?"

But he was talking to the radio tower. "Cessna Three Two Six Tango Delta Charlie. Failed approach, strong crosswind." Then his pilot-speak seemed to fail him, and he fell back into plain English. "Pulling up to try the approach again."

A blast of static on the headphones. "Roger that, Cessna Three Two Six Tango Delta Charlie, proceed on course."

And then the earth dropped away from us again. The engine sounded suddenly extra loud, like a lawn mower on steroids. We rose up in the air and repositioned to start the descent pattern over. To the south, blue skies. To the north, purple. Another flash of lightning.

"Is the crosswind because of the storm?" I asked.

Chip didn't answer. A bead of sweat ran down behind his ear and soaked into his T-shirt collar.

For the second try, he started farther down the runway, as if giving himself room to course-correct if he needed to. Which he did. Twice the runway beneath us rotated out to the side, and twice Chip manhandled the plane into lining up over it again.

"Nice!" I said, wanting to encourage him, hoping like hell he didn't pull up again and make us start all over. It was the least of my worries at this point, I guess, but I was right on the edge of throwing up.

I wanted nothing more than to touch down on that concrete.

It felt like the longest descent in the history of flight. Chip made one more course correction, and then we were lowering closer, and closer. I could see the concrete of the runway welcoming us down. I willed us to touch.

Then we came to a section of the runway with an airplane hangar right beside it. The size and width of that hangar seemed to provide a little windbreak. We were maybe ten feet above the runway as we passed the hangar—so close—and I could feel the wind ease off as we moved into its shadow. Everything seemed calmer somehow. Even the engine sounded quieter. Chip eased off his struggle with the controls. The ground was so close.

We made it, I thought.

And then we passed out of the wind block, past the corner of the hangar, back into open air again, and as we did, a blast of wind hit, so concentrated and fierce that it scooped up under the wing on my side and punched us into a type of spin that folks in aviation call "cartwheeling."

I remember it in slow motion. I remember slamming hard against my seat belt—so hard, it felt like a wooden post—as my wing jerked up and the plane rotated on the tip of the other. I remember that wing scraping the tarmac with an eardrum-ripping, metal-against-concrete shriek. I remember Chip's shocked voice shouting, "Hold on!" though I had no idea what to hold on to. I remember screaming so hard I felt like nothing but the scream—and Chip doing it, too—the two of us holding each other's shocked gazes, like, *This can't be happening.* I remember some tiny tendril of my consciousness veering off to a funny little philosophical moment in the center of it all—marveling at the pointlessness of the screaming since we were so clearly beyond help—before arriving at the bigger, more salient picture:

This was the moment of our death.

There was no arguing with what was happening, and there was certainly nothing either of us could do about it. We were the very definition of helpless, and as I realized that, it also hit me that everything I'd been looking forward to was over before it even began. Chip and me—and the lakeside wedding we'd never have, and the rescue beagle we'd never adopt, and the valedictorian babies we'd never make. They say your life flashes before your eyes, but it wasn't my life as I'd lived it that I saw. It was the life I'd been waiting for. The one I'd never get a chance to live.

My future slid past my fingers as I fumbled for it—and missed.

I felt suddenly coated with anger like I'd been dunked in it. I didn't think about my parents in that moment, or my friends, or how hard my death would be on anyone else. I thought only of myself—and how I just couldn't fucking believe this was all the time I got.

I couldn't tell you how many full rotations we completed as we blew across that runway like somebody's lost kite, but there's a reason they call it cartwheeling. The wings were the spokes of a giant wheel, and we were the axle in the middle on a spinning carnival ride from hell. At a certain point, I lost all sense of spatial orientation, and it stopped feeling like we were spinning—more like rocking back and forth. I remember focusing all my energy on not barfing because there was nothing else to even hope to control.

I was maybe three seconds from spewing vomit like in *The Exorcist* when the passenger-side wing mercifully broke off with an unearthly, bone-rattling *crack*. A spray of jet fuel hit the windshield with a *clomp* sound like we were at a drive-through car wash, and we collapsed at last in a ditch, with my side—the passenger side—wedged down in it, and Chip's side angled up at the sky.

We stopped.

Everything was still.

Then I vomited onto the window below me.

Two

A THOUSAND YEARS later, I heard Chip, out of breath: "Margaret? Are you okay?"

"I threw up," I said, not quite catching his urgency.

"Margaret—the fuel—we have to get out. Are you hurt?"

"I don't think so."

Chip was moving around unhooking and unbuckling and trying to work his door open like a hatch. His side didn't seem to be crumpled like mine was. It was stuck for a second, so he had to brace against his seat to kick it, but then it popped easily out with a satisfying *ka-chunk* and fell open wide, squeaking at the hinges for a second as it bounced.

He climbed up and out, then reached back down for me. "Come on!"

I hadn't even unbuckled yet. Everything seemed to be moving in slo-mo and time-lapse all at once. My hands didn't seem like they even belonged to me. I watched them reach to unhook the shoulder strap, and that's when I realized that it was already unhooked. Next, I tried for the lap belt, and discovered that, in ironic contrast, it was jammed.

It might not have mattered anyway. My side of the plane was crumpled. I was not exactly *sitting* in my seat anymore—more like sandwiched in between it and the dash.

I tried to wriggle out, but I was wedged in. I tried to move my legs, but they were pinned and didn't budge.

Chip was up on the outside now, peering down through his window like a hatch. "Come on! Margaret! Now!"

"I can't!" I said. "I'm stuck!"

He reached his arm down for me to grab. "I'll pull you."

"I can't. My legs are pinned."

Chip was silent for somewhere between one second and one hour—hard to tell. Then he said, "I'm going for help."

For the first time, at the prospect of being alone, I felt afraid. "No! Don't leave me!"

"This thing could blow at any minute!"

"I don't want to die alone!"

"We need the fire department!"

"Call them on your cell phone!"

Chip's voice was high and strange with panic. "I don't know where it is!"

"Don't go, Chip! Don't go! Don't go!" My voice, too, sounded odd—like someone else, someone I might not even like or feel sympathy for. Some screaming, hysterical, pathetic woman.

Chip was still leaving. "I have to get help. Just hold on. I'll be back in two minutes."

And then he was gone.

I WAS ALONE, in a crumpled plane, breathing air thick with jet fuel fumes. The air was so sour, and toxic, and corrosive, it felt like it was melting my lungs.

"Two minutes," I whispered until the words turned into nonsense. "Two minutes. Two minutes. Two minutes."

Next, a crack of real thunder that rattled the instruments in the dash.

Then it started raining.

The drops sounded frantic against the metal shell of the plane. Chip's door was still wide open, so the water sheeted straight in on my bare shoulders, cold and mean.

More than two minutes went by, but I can't tell you how many. Ten? Thirty? A hundred?

I wondered if it the rain was a good thing or a bad thing. Would it prevent a fire—or make it worse? I just wanted the entire world to hold still until I was out and away and safe. It was dark in the ditch, like the rain had put out the lights, too. Soon I was shivering. The raindrops pinged like gravel hitting the metal shell of the plane. I could hear a ticking noise. I could hear my own breathing. I wondered how long before the ditch filled up with water and I died by drowning in a plane crash.

I kept trying to unwedge myself. Nothing.

I've felt alone plenty of times in my life—in both good ways and bad—but I have never felt alone like this. "Come back," I whispered to Chip. "Come back." But the words were lost in the noise of the storm.

Then, over it all, I heard the most beautiful sound I've ever heard—before or since.

First far away, then closer: a siren.

The fire department.

Chip had not come back, but now I had something better. I was so glad I'd bought that firefighter calendar last year. Best twenty bucks I ever spent.

Just like that, almost as if it had heard them coming, too, the rain slowed and thinned out to a sprinkle.

The acoustics in the plane were pretty good. After they cut the siren, I could hear the firemen outside, maybe five or six, talking and calling orders to each other. I heard noises I couldn't decipher: clanking, squeaking, twisting. One guy called another guy a knucklehead. Minutes passed, then more. I wondered why no one had come to get me yet.

Then I heard a new sound—something different: A *whoosh*. Just like when your gas stove burner finally catches and leaps up into flames.

It came half a second before the flames themselves. Just long enough for me to lean a tiny bit closer to the ground and put my arms over my face.

Then: noise, wind, heat. I kept my head down because it was the only thing to do. I felt a flash of white heat sting my neck, but then it went away. Seconds later, the fire was gone. The cockpit was smoky and smelled like barbecue and burned hair.

THE NEXT SOUND was the clanking and gonglike pounding of metal. I heard banging, men's voices, a motor and a buzzing sound. Then, in what seemed like a second, the roof of the plane—which, given how we'd landed, was more like a wall—was peeled away. Kneeling next to me was a firefighter in full gear and a mask. And all behind him was snow. There was snow in the cockpit, too, now that I noticed.

He took off his mask, and he turned out to be a lady.

That struck me as very novel. A lady firefighter! She told me her name, but I have no idea what she said. Sometimes, even still, when I can't sleep, I try to remember what it was. Karen? Laura? Jenny?

"We have a live patient," she announced.

I wondered if I heard surprise in her voice.

She kneeled down beside me, while another two other guys continued cranking off the roof. "Tell me what hurts the most."

"Nothing hurts," I said, as she leaned in to check my pulse.

She looked doubtful. "Nothing at all?"

"I'm fine," I said. "Just stuck." Then I asked, "Why is it snowing?"

"It's not snow," she said. "It's foam. For the fire."

Foam! For the fire! I'd forgotten the fire for a second! Now I realized my neck and arm were stinging. "I might have some burns, actually," I said.

She smiled at me. "You're very lucky. The fire broke out just as we cranked up the hoses. We had it out in under a minute."

"That does sound lucky," I agreed.

"Plus," she went on, waving a tiny flashlight back and forth in front of my pupils, "facedown in a ditch is the best place to be when the flames roll over."

"So, double luck," I said.

"Are you kidding? Quadruple. I'm amazed you're not a charcoal briquette."

"Me, too," I said.

"We're going to put you on a backboard," she said then, "to hold your body still while we transport you to the hospital."

"I think I'm really fine," I said. "Just wedged."

But now she was pulling out an oxygen mask and cupping it over my face. "We're going to give you some vitamin O. Just to help you breathe easier."

Vitamin O. Cute. "I'm really fine."

"Just to be safe," she said, winking. "Just procedure. You don't want me to get in trouble, do you?"

I didn't. Lady firefighters probably had the deck stacked against them anyway.

And so I held still, breathing in cool vitamin O while she attached me strap by painstaking strap to a long backboard. She also put me in a C-collar, even though it seemed perfectly clear to me that I didn't need one. The last step, once I was secure, was also the longest: prying apart the crumpled front of the plane to free my legs. This project involved three different firefighters—who took their sweet time.

I was grateful for their care, though. Nobody took shortcuts. Nobody seemed eager to get off shift. They did things right. My nameless lady firefighter stayed right by me the whole time, asking me over and over to wiggle my fingers and toes and making chitchat to keep me calm. She told me if this had been a jet crash, they'd be calling in heavy rescue—but "these little planes are like tin foil."

Before they had me out, I heard a helicopter. "There's your ride," my new friend said.

"I'm really fine," I tried again.

"You'll like it. It's fun."

"Where is Chip?" I asked.

"Is that your boyfriend?"

"Fiancé," I said, for the first time ever.

"He's back by the truck."

"Is he hurt?"

"They're doing an evaluation," she said. "But I'd say there's not a scratch on him."

Once they finally had me out, and had loaded me onto a rolling stretcher, they wheeled me to an ambulance, where they cut off all my clothes with shears ("Life Flight likes 'em naked") and started an IV with morphine.

The storm had blown off in another direction, and now the sky was remarkably cloudless. I could see a million stars up above, and I thanked them all. I thanked them for luck, and firefighters, and sirens, and flame retardant, and ditches, and bolt cutters, and good timing, and vitamin O, and hope, and miracles, and not being burned to a crisp.

The paramedics worked hard. Every time I told them I was fine, they shrugged and said, "Procedure."

Another procedure: I had to ride in the ambulance two hundred feet to the Life Flight chopper. They wouldn't let Chip come with me, either, even though there was plenty of room.

"I need you to stay with me," I told him, as they rolled me away.

"I can't," he said.

"Do it anyway!"

"I'll meet you there," he called after us, arms at his sides.

If we were flying and he was driving, I thought, he was going to have to hurry up. But he didn't hurry up. I grabbed one last glance of him as the team hustled my gurney into the chopper. He was still in the same spot, standing like a statue.

I could not believe all this fuss. Honestly. Over nothing.

Well, maybe not nothing. A brush with death. A worst nightmare come true. The crash, the rain, the fire. I might never stop shaking.

But we'd survived.

By the time I was loaded, I was pretty sleepy, though. I wondered if being afraid could do that. Or maybe it was the morphine. Or maybe just too much vitamin O. The last thing I remember before conking out was wondering if I'd have to spend the night in the hospital. I hoped not. If I could get out early enough, maybe Chip and I could still make it to a late dinner.

Crash or no crash, we still had a lot to celebrate.

Three

I WOKE UP as all hell was breaking loose in the trauma bay—but that's not the first thing I noticed. The first thing I noticed was my back hurt like fire. And as soon as I noticed it hurting, I realized it had been hurting all along—since back at the crash site, even.

It sounds completely crazy, I know, but it wasn't until I *noticed* the pain that I *remembered* it.

"My back hurts," I said, to no one in particular—and I wouldn't have even known *who to say it to* because there were at least twenty people moving in and out of my peripheral vision in utter chaos, calling to each other in words so fast they just sounded like noise. I recall sounds and sights in little pinpricks of memory from that room—noises and images I can't even put into the right order. People in aqua scrubs moving with purpose, arms and bodies in motion, machines beeping. An unearthly light rained down from the fluorescent fixture above and blurred out the edges of my vision. Someone changed my IV fluids. Someone else asked for a catheter. I heard the words "x-ray" and "CT scan."

My neck was uncomfortable in the collar, and I asked a plump male nurse with a kind face if we could take it off.

"Not until the C-spine is cleared" came a voice across the room.

"A little longer, sweetheart," the nurse said.

Was I allergic to medications? *No.* Did I have any preexisting conditions they should be aware of? *No.* Was I pregnant? *God, I hoped not.*

"Healthy as a horse," I said.

A guy I later came to recognize as the neurosurgeon paused to tell me that they were evaluating me for pressure and sensation with pinprick tests, and they were starting me on a steroid to prevent swelling because the benefits of its use outweighed the complications.

"Okay," I said. But it didn't occur to me until after he'd stepped away to ask, "Swelling of what?"

I said it to the room, but I got no reply.

After the evaluation and CT scan, the neurosurgeon popped into view again and began to talk nonsense. "Your scans reveal a burst fracture to your L1. We're sending you to surgery to clear out debris. Your evaluation shows some deficits, but there appears to be some sacral sparing. The good news is that your iliopsoas seems to be functioning, and we believe at this time it's an incomplete injury. Of course, we'll know a lot more once we get in there."

"Incomplete injury of what?" I asked at last.

He blinked, like he thought I already knew. "Your spinal cord."

I held my breath a second. "Is that why my back hurts?"

But he'd turned away to a nurse with a question. When he turned back, he said, "You're lucky. The L1 was good and crushed, but it didn't sever the cord. Now we just need to get in there to stabilize and clean up."

"Now?" I asked.

He nodded. "We're heading to surgery. And while you're there, we'll have a plastic surgeon evaluate your face and neck and the area above your trapezius—maybe debride what he can. But that'll be a second surgery. After you've stabilized. First things first."

"What will be a second surgery?"

"The skin grafts. For the burns."

The skin grafts. For the burns.

The surgeon was ready to get moving. "Do you have any questions for me?"

I wanted to nod, but I couldn't. Yes, I had questions for him. A thousand, at least. I just couldn't figure out what they were.

Instead, I asked the only question I could come up with. "Could somebody please find my mother?"

NORMALLY, MEMORIES HAVE a chronology to them. Even if you've lost pieces of the story, you usually have a sense of order, at least—*this led to this*. What I recall from the ICU is just a pile of images, sounds, and feelings so jumbled, it's like a game of pick-up sticks.

They say everybody loses time in the ICU. It's basically Vegas in there, minus the showgirls and slot machines. No windows, for one. Bright fluorescents humming at all hours of the day and night—dimmed, sometimes, but not much. Doctors, nurses, techs, residents, physical therapists, occupational therapists, social workers, case managers, administrators, family members, and just about anyone else who feels like it walking through at all hours. Machines beeping and hissing. Rolling carts with computers. Shoes squeaking the floor. Phones ringing.

It annihilates your circadian rhythms, to say the least.

Plus, you. You're asleep, then you're awake. The world is blurred with drugs and pain. You're woken at all hours—to take medicines, to be turned to avoid bedsores, or even just because someone, anyone, has a question for you. You're a passive, drugged-out element of an unearthly ecosystem that churns day and night to keep you alive—but you're about as far from alive as it's possible to be.

Short of being dead.

I know from my mother, who arrived with my dad just after they wheeled me off to surgery (and found Chip in the waiting room looking "devastated—absolutely devastated") that the surgery took about two hours and they screwed rods to either side of my lumbar vertebrae to stabilize my spine.

I was stable enough the next day to go back in for a second surgery to skin-graft the burns. I heard all about this later from my mom as well. Ever the overachieving student, she took copious notes in her tidy cursive, and used them not only to tell me the story of my life but to teach me many new vocabulary words, as well.

She explained that I was lucky, in a way, that the burns were so bad. Third-degree burns don't hurt because all the nerves have burned away. She explained that the spinal surgeon met the plastic surgeon in the OR to arrange me on the table so they could get at the burns on my neck without more damage to my spine. She explained, too, how he shaved off the black, crispy, burned skin with a "weck blade" (I imagined it like a carrot peeler), and then harvested skin from two donor sites just under my collarbones (the "superclavicular" area) for "full-thickness skin grafts" on my neck. They sewed the new skin down with "Prolene sutures" in crisscrosses, like quilting.

I was in recovery for both surgeries in the ICU for seven days, and the entire time, I had a dressing over my neck attached to a suction tube sucking the moisture from the skin grafts as they waited to see if they would take. My mom took a picture with her iPhone before deciding it was in bad taste. She let me see it many weeks later before erasing it entirely. I looked like I was being attacked by a giant albino lamprey.

Apparently, the first person I asked for after both surgeries was Chip. He came in after the first (though I have no memory of it), but after the second, he'd gone home to sleep, and they sent my mom in instead.

Other things I know but don't remember: I had an "indwelling Foley catheter" draining into a bag, and my bowels apparently had to be "manually evacuated" by some hospital tech with a very unfortunate job. What was left of my hair kept getting caught in my dressing, and so someone had trimmed it, unceremoniously and without asking—possibly while I was asleep. I took more drugs in one week than I'd taken in my whole life put together—massive doses of acetaminophen, Valium, Cipro, nizatidine, OxyContin, Clonis, Maalox, and a blissful little substance that makes you forget everything called Versed. Visitors were only allowed in for ten minutes at a time. Mostly, I was alone, surrounded by machines—and herds of strangers.

One of the painkillers made me throw up a lot. That I do remember.

I also remember flashes of faces. My mother, leaning down, her face puffy from crying. My father, pursing his lips to be tough and holding out a little thumbs-up gesture at me over and over, like he was giving a toast. Chip, still as a statue, right by the bed but seeming miles away. The weirdest memory I have is of various physical therapists in navy-blue scrubs coming by at all hours to move my legs and feet around for me—bending them, stretching them, turning them. I could see what they were doing, but I couldn't feel it.

It was just like a long, strange dream. With vomiting.

Four

IT WASN'T UNTIL I moved out of the ICU that I started to wake up. And it wasn't until I started waking up that I began to realize how bad things really were.

On the day they moved me out of the ICU, it took all morning to get me into the wheelchair, for example. A nurse called Nina arrived to crank the bed up in slow increments to get me sitting. I'd been lying down for so long, my blood pressure was at risk for crashing, which could cause me to faint or even have a heart attack. You lose muscle mass amazingly fast when you are immobilized and unconscious, and I had lost twenty pounds in one week. I was like a tiny, frail old lady.

I remember worrying about how shocked Chip would be to see me—and feeling kind of glad he wasn't there. Like if I had a few days, that might be enough time to pull myself together.

But that didn't stop me from asking where he was. "Where's Chip?" I asked my mother at least three times before she answered.

"He's not feeling well today, honey," she said.

"Not feeling well?" I asked.

"A touch of the Irish flu," my dad said.

"Cliff!" My mother slapped him on the shoulder.

Nina could easily have lifted me and placed me in the chair, but that's not how they roll at inpatient rehab. It's all about getting you to do things—impossible things—by yourself and before you're ready. So there I was, not even out of the ICU, enduring a three-hour teachable moment, one slow inch at a time.

"Can't you just lift me?" I asked.

"I can help you lift yourself," she said, making her "no" sound a little bit like a "yes."

My parents were nearby, standing shoulder to shoulder, tilting in toward me in sympathy. Cliff and Linda. I'd seen them shoulder to shoulder many times, but never perched so anxiously. They were itching to step in and give me a hand, but Nina body-blocked them. She had a board, and I had to edge my way onto it in my gown, with my weird hospital panties on—still catheterized, by the way. With all the tubes and bandages and light-headedness, it was a miracle I even sat up at all.

And my legs? I still couldn't feel them—or move them. They were like mutant Japanese udon noodles hanging dead from my knees. Nina edged them over the side of the bed. I watched them dangle.

"How long till the feeling in my legs comes back?" I asked.

"That's a question for the doctor," Nina said.

By the time I was in the chair, and Nina had pulled the little foot flaps down and propped my feet up on them, I was as out of breath as if I'd sprinted a mile.

"Attagirl!" my dad shouted, when I made it—the same shout he'd always used when I crossed the line first at track meets.

I didn't look over.

Nina took my chair handles and wheeled me out, trailing after. We traveled miles through the labyrinth of hallways of the building to find my new room two wings over. It was a double room, but both beds were empty, which meant I got to pick—except my mother really wound up picking, which is kind of her signature move. She asks you what you want to do, waits for your answer, tells you why that won't work, and then makes you do what she wanted all along.

I picked the bed nearest the bathroom, but then my mother said she'd read an article in *Reader's Digest* that looking at nature was "very healing" and didn't I think it might be good to stay near the window?

As usual: I chose one and wound up in the other.

At my new bed, we did the whole wheelchair rigmarole in reverse to get me in. It took an hour, and I was panting and nauseated by the end. My parents stood at the foot of the bed the whole time like statues, watching.

"Where's Chip, again?" I asked.

"Sleeping off his hangover," my father said. This time, my mother let it be.

I turned to Nina. "How long until I get this catheter out?" I asked, as she pulled up the sheets at last, and I leaned back against the crackly hospital pillow.

"That's another question for the doctor."

I got the feeling she said that a lot.

As soon as Nina was gone, my father went for coffee downstairs, and my mother started decorating the room. This was part of her job. She and my dad ran a contracting business together, and he generally handled the construction end of things, and she did the design. So it was both her professional and personal responsibility in almost any situation to make things look better.

She'd brought a blue-and-white-checked quilt from home and a fuzzy throw blanket. She'd been collecting get-well cards all week from friends and relatives, and she'd brought some Scotch tape to affix them to the walls. She'd bought magazines, which she arranged in a fan shape on the side table, and she'd found my favorite stuffed animal from childhood in the attic (a fuzzy bunny named Fuzzy Bunny) and brought it with her. When she ran out of things to do, she took a seat on the reclining side chair and criticized the décor.

"I don't know what they're thinking with this God-awful mauve on the walls. It's like the 1980s threw up in here."

I'd just survived a plane crash, so of course this was what we talked about. Nothing pissed Linda Jacobsen off like bad décor.

"Mauve and gray," she went on. "It's toxic. They're poisoning you visually."

"It's not that bad," I said, like, *Come on*. "It's a hospital room."

But she lifted her chin. "The person who decorated this hospital," she announced, like a woman claiming her dignity in the face of unspeakable horror, "should be in jail."

I took a slow breath.

"You could open the curtains," I suggested at last.

She turned toward the window, as if she'd forgotten it. "Of course. Yes." She clicked right over, her heels making the same noise they'd made my entire life, and yanked the curtain back.

I don't know what either of us had expected to see, but the window overlooked an airshaft to a parking garage.

My mother turned to me. "It's worse open."

Indeed it was.

Just then, the heavy door to the room swung in, and a doctor I'd never seen before walked in, straight toward my bed, grabbing the computer cart on the way and pulling it behind him. He said, "How's everything feeling?" as he leaned in to check the dressings over my neck.

I didn't know how to answer. "Weird. Surreal. Bleak."

"Pain?" he specified.

Oh. "I'm not sure."

"That's the drugs. They're disorienting. But we're weaning you off them, so you should get a better read on the pain tomorrow."

"I'm not sure I want a better read on the pain."

It was a weak, embryonic joke. But he gave me a shrug. "Point taken."

He stepped back to the computer, swiped his ID badge, and started checking my charts. "The good news is," he said, "everything we grafted is working. No rejection of tissue."

Oh! He had operated on me. I guess we had met before.

"We took two full skin grafts from just under your collarbones," he pointed at the large dressing that was taped there, and I noticed it, really, for the first time. "You'll keep that dressing on about five more days, and then we'll just let it air dry. It'll scab up and heal. It'll leave a scar, of course, but once the skin has grown back, there are ointments to help it fade. In ten years, you won't even see it."

Ten years! If I'd been drinking a beverage, I would have spit it right out.

He went on, unperturbed. "We used full skin on the front of the neck, and partial over the back trapezius area, so there will be more scarring there. Partial leaves a more mottled appearance. But you can cover some of that with hair." He smiled. "No more ponytails."

"Why is there no bandage on the graft?" I asked.

"Once it 'takes' we like to let it air, and just keep Silvadene ointment on it. It doesn't need to be covered. But you will have to go sleeveless on that side for a good while. Just buy some cheap T-shirts and cut the neck and left sleeve off." He chuckled. "Kind of Tarzan and Jane."

My mother was not amused. "What about the face?"

My eyes widened. *The face?* I didn't remember anything about 'the face.'

The doctor looked over at my mom like he hadn't noticed she was there. Then, to me: "Bet it's nice to have your mom here."

"Sort of," I said.

She went on, in a stage whisper, "I can't even look at her," and now that she mentioned it, I noticed that was true.

"The face is all second-degree," the doc said. "It's going to blister and scab and itch like hell—but if she doesn't scratch, there should be minimal scarring. Should heal up in about three weeks."

My mom was a stickler for details. "Does 'minimal scarring' mean *no* scarring?"

But she was being too greedy. "I never make promises," the doctor said, finishing up on the computer and rolling the cart away. "We'll do our best, and we'll hope that's enough."

After he left, it was dead quiet. This room had nothing of the mind-vibrating cacophony of the ICU. Just the white noise of the A/C vent, and the uncomfortable echoes of everything my mom had just said. Then, suddenly, the shuddery breaths of her crying.

I looked over. She had turned toward the window, arms clutched tight at her waist.

"Mom, stop it," I said.

"You're going to be just fine," she told me, like the opposite.

"Pull it together, please, Mom." I closed my eyes again. So tired.

"You were *perfect,*" she said then. "No wonder Chip is too sick to come."

My mom had a remarkable talent for making things worse. She could always find the downside. And she had no filter, so once she found it, everybody else had to find it, too.

"You know what?" I said then. "I'm pretty exhausted."

But she wasn't done. "You had your whole life ahead of you."

So. The opposite of comforting, really.

"I've read the statistics," she went on, "about what something like this does to a relationship."

"Mom—"

"Guess what? Women don't leave men, but men do leave women."

"Chip is not going to leave me, Mom." Ridiculous wasn't even a big enough word for how ridiculous that was.

"No," she said, turning to face. "No, he's not. Because we are going to fix you."

I knew that look on her face far too well.

"God did not give me all this strength for nothing," she went on. "You'll recover, darling girl. We will put you back as good as new. I've already got a file folder as fat as a brick with articles on miraculous recoveries and people who've defied all their grim diagnoses."

Was my diagnosis "grim"? Something told me not to ask.

My mom turned around and fixed her gaze on the blanket at my feet. "You're going to bounce back from this and show them all," she said, going just the tiniest bit Scarlett O'Hara. "We'll find the best cosmetic surgeons in the world. We'll scour the earth. We will not rest. If Daddy and I have to spend every cent we've ever saved—*Cash in our life insurance! Sell the house!*—we'll do it."

I should have just let it go. I should have let us lapse back into silence. But something in me needed to convince her. "Chip is not going anywhere," I tried again. "He loves me."

"The old you, maybe," she said. "But now?" She frowned. "But we're not going to let that happen. I've been online every night, researching people who've faced this type of thing and overcome it, and I know that more than anything, it takes determination. One girl I read about dove into a too-shallow swimming pool at her bachelorette party and broke her neck. She should have *died*—but she fought her way back and now she teaches water ballet. Another woman? Crushed by a truck! Broke every bone in her body and then some. Now she's an aerobics instructor in San Bernardino. Another girl was just crossing the street when a drunk driver mowed her down. Now she's an underwear model."

"I get it, Mom."

But there was no stopping her. "What do all these people have in common? Gumption. Grit. Strength. And you've got all that in spades—you always have. And you've literally got extra, too, because you've got me."

It wasn't uninspiring. It was good to know she had my back. Plus, she wasn't wrong—the woman was strong as an ox. But somehow the sensations it was leaving in me—hazy as they were to identify—seemed equal parts worry, inspiration, and panic. As was always true with my mother, you never could get exactly what you wanted. I wanted the strength without the fear-mongering. I wanted the determination without the control. I wanted the pep talk without the underwear model.

Mostly, right now, I just wanted to close my eyes.

Lucky for me, my dad walked in next with a tray of coffees. He knew in an instant just from the vibe what kind of conversation we were having. "Look at this room," he said, attempting to redirect. "Linda, you've worked your magic."

But Linda wasn't having it. "The doctor came in. He says there's no guarantee that her face will recover."

"I believe he said there should be minimal scarring," I volunteered.

"You know what?" my dad said, reading us perfectly, "I think our girl needs some rest." He'd been with my mom for thirty years. He was an expert on damage control.

"What about the coffee?" she protested.

"We'll take it in the car."

He came to me, looked me right in my burned face, and crinkled his eyes into a smile while he squeezed my hand. "Get some rest, sweetheart."

"Dad?" I asked.

"Yeah?"

"Where *is* Chip?" Now she kind of had me worried.

My dad just chuckled. "I'm sure he's just sleeping it off, sweetheart. We could all use some rest. This'll be your first quiet night's sleep in ages." Then he noticed me frowning and patted my hand. He knew what I was asking. "Sometimes, when you really need your man to be big and strong for you the most—that's when we go to pieces."

"I've never seen you go to pieces," I said to him.

He gave my mother a sideways glance. "I'm saving it all up for later."

Okay, I thought, after they left. *Okay. A good night's sleep. I can make that happen.* That was something to look forward to, at least, if nothing else. Rest. Recuperation. A restful sleep in a quiet, dark room.

EASIER FANTASIZED THAN done. Nurses were still in and out quite a bit, checking monitors, emptying catheter bags, and turning me over. I was not wearing a brace—surgeon's orders—so I was extra laborious to turn. I had just fallen asleep when I got a visit from the surgeon, checking in, and had just dozed off again when a hospital social worker woke me to see how I was feeling.

"Fine. Good," I said.

"Any depression?"

"Depression?" I wasn't fully awake.

"Depression's pretty common for situations like yours. It's nothing to be afraid of. And there's medication, if you need it."

"Oh. No."

"Suicidal thoughts?"

"Um," I said, like I was thinking. "Not yet."

I did keep wondering where Chip was, though.

In truth, I wasn't feeling anything yet—at least, when my mother wasn't around. It was like my emotions had gone offline. It was like I wasn't fully there. Things were happening around and to me, and there was pain, discomfort, exhaustion, but it was like I was witnessing it rather than experiencing it. I was across the room, watching somebody else's life unfold, and not even fully paying attention. Even if I'd tried, I suspected, I couldn't make sense of the pieces and how they fit together. There was no story of what was happening. I took each moment as separate from the others and did not try to piece together what those moments meant or where they were headed.

This was probably some kind of feature of emotional shock. I'm sure it had a protective quality: my brain just refusing to grasp what it knew it couldn't handle. But as the pieces of my situation came together, I received them all with detached interest. Like, "Oh? My face is burned? Huh." And, "I can't use my legs right now? Okay." And, "My mother is going to town on my hospital room like Shirley MacLaine in *Terms of Endearment*? It *is* actually kind of nicer now."

No understanding at all that my life would never quite be the same.

Until I fell asleep.

The worst thing about sleeping, after something terrible happens, is that sleeping makes you forget. Which is fine, until you wake up. That night, I had my first nightmare about the crash, and in the dream, I was the pilot—in a wedding dress with a veil—and I steered us straight for the ground at full speed, sure to kill us both, as Chip shouted, "Pull up! Pull up!" But the controls were stuck. I woke just before we hit, breathing hard, tears from nowhere all over my face, thinking, *Thank God, thank God. We didn't crash.*

But we *did* crash.

The dream receded and I was left alone in the dark with real life—which was worse, by far—my heart pounding with panic, my eyes wide.

I stared at the ceiling and tried to take deep breaths—but they were great, heaving, scraping ones instead of anything close to calming. I hadn't died, I kept telling myself.

But what if this was worse?

Now I tried to put the pieces together—but I couldn't. My life as I knew it was over, and that was more than enough to keep me awake all night. I didn't know what was left, or what to expect, or what it might be possible to hope for. I lay there in the dark, breathing deep, terrified breaths for endless hours. I thought about calling the nurse, but what could she do? I needed to talk to someone, but who could I even talk to? My brain raced and spun and searched for avenues of comfort—but there were none. And, for several endless, black hours, through the deepest part of that night, I fought to keep from drowning as comprehension breached the hull of my consciousness and filled it to the top.

Five

I WAS STILL awake at 6:00 A.M. when Nina the nurse and a tech came to turn me.

I was so immobile at that point that I still ran the risk of bedsores. They flipped on all the lights and talked to me about the traffic and the weather as if nothing had changed in the world. They gave me pain meds, and changed the bandage on my donor sites, and smeared the burns with Silvadene ointment using a spatula. They were almost aggressively cheerful and jocular with each other and with me. Nina liked to call me "lady"—like, "Hey, lady, how'd you sleep?"

I didn't know how to begin.

"You start OT and PT today," she went on. "In the rehab gym."

"What's the difference?"

She was fussing with my chart on the computer. "OT is like working on day-to-day tasks, and PT is like strength training."

"Oh," I said.

"You've got Priya for OT, and—uh-oh."

That got my attention. "What?"

"There's a mistake here."

"What mistake?"

"They gave you the wrong PT. I'll talk to them."

I started to ask "What's the wrong PT?" but before I could, the door pushed open and Chip stumbled in.

We all stared. His blond hair looked greasy. His face was covered in stubble. His polo shirt had a brown stain—*Soy sauce? Worcestershire? Blood?*—all down the front, and his pants were ripped. One of his shoes was untied.

He made straight for me and shoved his face down on top of mine in a slobbery kiss that tasted like beer. And dirt. And sleep deprivation.

I held my breath until he finished, and as I did, I realized what this moment was: a simple, clear, all-purpose answer to that question I kept asking.

Where was Chip? At a bar.

I pushed him off. "Are you drunk?"

Chip blinked at the question. "I think so. Probably."

"It's six in the morning."

But he was studying my face. "You used to be so beautiful—and now you look like a pizza." He made himself laugh with that one, and Nina and I stared as he doubled over for a second and hung from his waist, his shoulder shaking with chuckles. Then he stood up. "But I just kissed you anyway! Because you"—here, he held up an imaginary glass for a toast—"are the love of my life."

I looked over at Nina, who lifted her eyebrows to see if she needed to stay.

I waved, like, *No big deal.* "I've got it." Whatever he was about to say, I certainly didn't want her hearing it. I didn't even want to hear it myself.

Nina set the nurse buzzer next to my hand before going. "Call if you need me."

I turned back to Chip. "Where have you been, Chip? I've been waiting for you."

I hated the way my voice sounded. I'd learned many boyfriends back that desperation never works. You can't ask someone to love you or be there for you or do the right thing—and you certainly can't guilt them into it. Either they will or they won't. I'd have sworn that Chip was a guy who *would*—up until the crash, at least.

Suddenly, I wasn't so sure.

"Do you know I escaped that crash without a scratch?" Chip said then. "The plane is totaled. You"—he let out a bitter honk of a laugh—"are totaled. But me? Nothing. I didn't even get a Band-Aid."

"Chip, what are you doing?"

At the question, he crumpled down beside the bed—literally fell to his knees on the hospital floor, his hands in fists around the bedrails—and he broke into sobs.

It was a shocking sight. I'd never seen him—or any guy—cry like that. My father never cried. He got wet eyes at funerals sometimes, but always quietly, stoically—nothing like this. This was shoulder-shaking, full-body sobbing. I poked my hand through the bars and stroked Chip's hair.

"Hey," I said, after a while, as he started to quiet. "Maybe you should go home and get some sleep."

"I can't sleep," he insisted. "I don't sleep anymore."

I made my voice tender. "I bet you could, if you tried."

He broke away—pushed off from the bed and paced to the far wall. "Don't be so nice to me."

"You're overwhelmed. You need some rest."

Now he was mad. "Don't tell me what I need!"

"Chip," I said. "It was an accident."

But that just made him madder. He stared straight at me. "I ruined your life."

"You didn't. It was the weather! It was the wind!"

"You're blaming *the wind*?"

But who else could I blame?

"You're better at self-delusion than I thought. Have you seen yourself? Have you seen your *face*?"

I hadn't, actually. My mother had covered the mirror in the bathroom with a pillowcase. Not that I could have stood up to see into it anyway.

"You're like something out of a horror movie! Because of me! I did that."

Wow. Okay. "The doctor said there'd be minimal scarring."

"Not on your neck. Those are *third-degree* burns. They're never going to heal right. They will look like Silly Putty until your dying day. You've got me to thank for that—me and my ego and my insecurities—" He shoved his hand into his hair. He looked a little green, like the alcohol was catching up with him.

"It was an accident," I insisted.

He looked up—right at me. "I broke your back. You understand that, right? They told you? You didn't want to go up in that plane with me. It was the last thing on earth you wanted to do, but I fucking forced you. You trusted me. And now—because of me—you will *never, ever—*"

Maybe for the first time ever with Chip, I didn't see his next words coming:

"*—walk again.*"

For a second, I thought I'd maybe heard him wrong.

Then, just like that, I knew I hadn't.

It was like the oxygen had been sucked out of the room. My lungs seemed to flatten. I tried to take a breath, but I couldn't make it work. All I could manage was tiny little flutters.

Chip sobered, reading my face, and peered in closer. "They haven't told you yet?"

I felt dizzy, I still couldn't catch my breath, and then I got that salty tingle you get in your mouth right before you throw up.

Chip took a step back. "Oh, my God! They didn't tell you you're paralyzed!"

Didn't see "paralyzed" coming, either.

Next? I threw up. All over the floor, and the bedrail, and my hospital gown, though my mother's nine-patch quilt from home was miraculously spared.

Right then, as if on cue, the door pushed open and my father walked in, carrying a box of French pastries over his head like a waiter's tray and announcing, "We've got—" But he stopped short when he saw us, and then finished under his breath, "Croissants."

Chip rounded on him. "Nobody's told her?"

My dad shifted into action, leaning back out into the hallway—"Can we get some help in here?"—then tossing the pastry box on the side chair and leaning over the bed to check on me. I stayed draped over the railing in case I puked again. Plus, now I was afraid to move my back. Had leaning over hurt it? Had the heaving made things worse? Could I have accidentally just made myself *more* paralyzed?

My father grabbed a towel and reached around to wipe my face off.

Chip's outrage seemed to exempt him from caretaking duties. He stayed safely across the room. "She's *paralyzed*—and nobody told her?" Chip demanded of my dad again, slurring a little.

"Sounds like you just did," my father said, tucking my hair back behind my ear.

"She has a right to know, doesn't she?"

"Of course," my dad said, his voice tightening, turning to face him. "But not like this. We were waiting for the right moment."

"Like when?" Chip demanded. "Over Thanksgiving turkey? On Christmas morning?"

"You self-righteous little clown—"

My dad was a big, bearlike guy—a former marine—and Chip was more in the "wiry" category. Everyone knew my dad could crush Chip if he wanted to—and I suddenly understood that maybe that was exactly what Chip wanted.

"Dad!" I called. "He's drunk. He's been out all night drinking. Just take him home."

"I can't leave you."

"I'm fine."

"You don't seem fine to me, sweetheart."

"Just get him out of here, Daddy." I hadn't called him "Daddy" in years. "Please."

My dad let out a long sigh, and as he did, Nina bustled in with a fresh gown and new sheets. An orderly followed her with a mop cart and spray bleach for the floor.

I let Nina fuss over me, and get me changed, and reposition me in the bed. I watched the orderly mop, wondering if he'd notice the far splat in the corner. The room seemed to fill with a wispy, numbing fog. It was like the real world was too much, and so my brain was going to blur it out. There were noises, there was talking—I heard my dad and Chip muttering and hissing at each other—and the door opened and closed and opened and closed, but the moment seemed to break into puzzle pieces scattered across a table.

For a long time after Nina got me settled, I tried to hold very still, afraid to move and make things worse. When I finally lifted my head to look around, the only person still left—still stuck—in the room was me.

THAT FOG LASTED for a good while.

Never walk again. What did that even mean? How did they know? How could they be certain? Who were they to make predictions about the rest of my life? Wasn't the human body full of mysteries and miracles? Could they just announce something like that about me and then leave me to live with it?

Of course they could. I'd broken my back, apparently. That was what happened to people who broke their backs. They spent the rest of their lives in wheelchairs. I'd watched a documentary about it last year—a team of invincible teenage boys who'd crashed their cars or their motorcycles or dived into shallow water only to spend the rest of their lives in wheelchairs. But now they'd formed a championship wheelchair basketball team. Which might have been inspiring to think about, except that I'd always sucked at basketball.

Paralyzed. Trying to work that idea into my brain was like trying to suck a bowling ball up through a drinking straw.

Impossible.

Not possible.

And yet Chip accepted it. My dad hadn't argued with him. It was apparently already an established fact about my life—one everybody knew but me. On some level, of course, I wasn't surprised. I'd been contending with my dead, pendulous legs for more than a week now. But things heal. Things *always* heal. I'd never had any injury—and I'd had plenty—that didn't mend itself eventually. *Paralyzed.* I couldn't fathom it. How would I drive a car? How would I cook dinner? How would I take a shower? Go to the bathroom? Buy groceries? Go out with friends? Have a job? Be the boss of whatever I was supposed to be the boss of? My brain was short-circuiting. I could feel it throwing sparks and smoking.

I tried for calming breaths, but I accidentally hyperventilated instead.

That's when the physical therapist arrived—while I was basically doing self-Lamaze.

He wore pale blue scrubs and sneakers, and he had short, clean-cut hair that spiked up some in the front. He walked in and said, "I'm Ian Moffat. Your physical therapist."

Except it didn't sound like words to me. Just a bunch of syllables.

He swiped his badge in the computer and looked at my chart a second, before he said, "So. You're Margaret."

But again. Just syllables.

When I didn't answer, he waved a little and said, "Hello?"

That I understood.

"It's time for your physical therapy," he said.

"What?" I asked.

"What what?"

"I can't understand you," I said, shaking my head a little, as if to shake water out of my ears.

"Nobody can understand me. I'm Scottish."

Wow. That explained it. Yes, he certainly was. I thought my brain had shut down—but it wasn't me, it was him. He was super Scottish. So Scottish he sounded like he was talking through a mouth full of pretzels.

"You'll get used to it," he said. "Ready to go?"

I wasn't. I wasn't ready to go. I shook my head.

"Not ready to go?" He held that last *o* with his lips, and I was forced to notice his lower teeth were a little crooked, but in a good way.

I shook my head.

"Why not?" he asked, with no *t* on the end.

My drunk fiancé just told me I'll never walk again. "It's been a tough morning."

"Lots of mornings are tough. We still have to do this."

"No."

"No what?" Later, I would decide that it wasn't just the consonants that were exaggerated—it was the vowels, too.

"No," I explained, "I can't do this right now."

"Look," he said, putting his hands on his hips and narrowing his eyes. "Every day—every hour—that you lie in that bed, your muscles are atrophying. Nothing will make you sicker than lying motionless all day. You have to get out. Whether you feel like it or not. You have to come with me to the physical therapy gym every day, always—not because you want to, or because you feel inspired, but because *not going* will put your health in genuine peril."

I had to work to mold all those syllables into meaning. His words seemed to sit on top of each other, stacked in columns instead of laid out properly in sentences. And for a grand finale, he clacked his *r* on "peril." I wondered if an American could pull off a word like that in conversation. But I got his gist.

"Thank you for the inspiring pep talk," I said. Then: "No."

"You're coming."

"I'm not."

"You are."

"I won't."

I don't really know where we would have gone from there. He didn't much seem like the type to give in, and I was—suddenly—just spoiling for a fight.

But that's when Nina walked in—a last check before she went off shift—and I don't know if she'd been listening at the door or what, but without skipping a beat she said, "Oh, this one's not starting till tomorrow. It was a typo in the chart."

Ian looked back and forth between us.

"Ask Myles, if you want. She's still got one more day."

He eyed us—suspiciously, like we might be in cahoots. Finally, he said, "Tomorrow, then."

He walked out.

"No, no, no, no, no," Nina said then, typing into the computer at the same time. "They are not giving you that guy for PT. I already told them to switch you out."

"What?" I asked. "Is he bad?"

"He's not bad," she said, "but he's not for you."

"Not for me?"

She kept her eyes on the monitor. "He's just not kind. He's relentless. Merciless. Thoughtless. That works for some people. Not you. We'll get you someone else. You've got enough going on."

On a different day, I might have asked more about him. But who cared about that heartless guy, really? Who cared about anything?

"Nina?" I asked then.

She kept typing. "What is it, sweetheart?"

"My drunk fiancé came in here this morning and told me I was never going to walk again."

Nina looked up.

"Is that true?" I asked.

From her face, I could see that it was.

Still, I waited for more—some words of encouragement, or some little crumb of hope to pick up. But she just let out a long sigh, and paused longer than could possibly be good news. "That's—"

And then I knew exactly how she was going to finish, and so I said it with her: "A question for the doctor."

Six

SO BEGAN THE strangest day of my life—one of them, at least. Top five.

What I wanted most all day was exactly what I wanted least.

I desperately needed time alone to process the news that Chip had just given me, and I just as desperately did not ever want to process anything—or be alone—again. I needed to take an emotional breath, but I was petrified to do it. So I spent the day mentally panting, light-headed and oxygen deprived, with my soul crying for air but my brain refusing to breathe it—and also dreading the night, when I'd have no distractions from every impossible thought that would rush in without my permission.

My parents startled me by arriving with lunch—Tex-Mex takeout from my favorite spot—before I realized any time had gone by. They had big, anticipatory smiles, as if fajitas might make everything okay for me.

I didn't touch the food—too nauseated from the meds—but I thanked them. Not even the idea of the food was comforting. My dad gave me the report on driving Chip home: He'd thrown up twice on the drive—"kind of a motif today"—once out the window, and once all over the dashboard. His parents were waiting in their driveway, and they steered him inside to sleep it off.

"Poor Chip," my mother said. "I hope they offered to pay for a detail."

Poor Chip? Was Chip the one we felt sorry for?

"He's not handling this well," my dad said.

My mother gave me a pointed look. "Sometimes I think people are more worried about him than about you," she said, as if we were making chitchat.

"I don't need people's worry," I said. I was worried about me. That was enough.

"He shouldn't have said what he said to you today," my father went on.

"He told me I look like a pizza," I said. "Is that true?"

"No, sweetheart," my dad said. But my mother looked away.

"I'd like to get a look," I said then, catching my mother's eye. "Can I borrow your compact mirror?"

But the headshake she gave, I knew from a lifetime of experience, meant *no way in hell.* "You're not ready."

Okay. Maybe she was right. Maybe I'd learned enough today. On to the next question—the one I didn't want to ask. But I paused a long time. I took a low breath. "He also said I was paralyzed," I said at last.

My mother sat up a little straighter.

"Is that true?"

My father gave me a sad little shrug. "Let's just say it's a good thing you're still on our insurance."

My mother had insisted that I stay on the plan they kept for their employees until I was settled in my career, even though the premiums were higher. We had argued about it more than once.

I hated it when she was right.

"What does that mean?" I asked, turning to my mother, who was braver.

She let out a big sigh. "From what the doctors have told us, only time will tell. It takes about six weeks before the bone heals and all the swelling in your spinal column clears out and we can see what kind of damage is left. Right now, the swelling itself could be blocking nerve signals. It's possible that once everything has healed there will be no blockage at all, and all normal function will come back."

I read both of their stoic faces. "Possible," I said, "but not likely."

"Not very likely, no," my dad said. "The doc is very encouraged by some parts of your nerve responses and less encouraged by others. But he also says there's real mystery involved in these kinds of injuries. He said there are people you think will never take another step who wind up running marathons."

"Or becoming underwear models," I said, my voice like a robot.

"Exactly," my mother nodded, like that would be a good thing.

"So we're waiting," my father explained. "Doing everything the docs tell us, and waiting."

My mother still couldn't look at me for more than two seconds at a time. "The point is," she chimed in, eyes on her taco salad, "it's all about attitude."

I squinted, like, *Really?* "Sounds to me like it's all about swelling and nerve damage."

She pushed on. "You have to believe you can get better. You have to work hard and never give up. I saw Chip's mother in the yard this morning, and I promised you'd be good as new by summer."

My dad and I both stared at her.

"You didn't," he said.

My mother sat up straighter. "I saw a video just this morning about a young BXM racer—"

"BMX racer," my dad and I both corrected.

"—who simply refused to let his spinal cord injury hold him back. He broke his neck, Margaret!" She reached up and tapped at the spot on her own neck, still averting her eyes from my face. "They told him he'd never feed himself again! Now, he's riding his bike from coast to coast raising money for charity—and he's about to record a country album."

"That's very inspiring," my dad said. "But it's not just mind over matter, Linda. If you break your leg, you can't just tell yourself it's not broken."

"But the human body *does* heal," my mom said, pointing at him.

"Yes, but the spinal cord is different," my dad said patiently. "Remember what the doctor said? When those nerves get damaged, they don't grow back."

"Well, I don't see why not."

My dad looked at me. We both imperceptibly shook our heads. "But they might not be damaged," he emphasized to me. "They might just be compressed. Your job is to get lots of rest, take your medicine, and do whatever these folks tell you. For five and a half more weeks."

"Five and a half?" I asked.

"That's what insurance covers," he said. "One week in the ICU, and five and a half weeks in the hospital afterwards."

"That's awfully specific."

"Yep."

"What happens at the end of five and a half weeks?"

My dad shrugged. "They stop paying. You move home and start outpatient therapy at a gym."

"Move home? Which home?"

My dad smiled. "Any home you want."

I took all this in. I was going to be here for five and a half more weeks.

"The point is," my dad went on, "to make the most of your time here while you have it. We'll just see what happens when we see what happens. That's all we can do."

"And have the right attitude!" my mom added, like he'd forgotten the most important thing. "And believe two hundred percent that you can beat this."

My mom had gone to my apartment and picked up my laptop, and the novel I'd been reading, and some fuzzy socks, and my pale blue chevron-print pillowcase, and some ridiculous, strappy high-heeled sandals that she thought might "cheer me up"—but, of course, did the opposite.

I didn't want to use my laptop or read that novel or even look at the sandals. I didn't want to see anything from before.

"Your cell phone was destroyed in the crash," my mom said next, "along with everything—burned to a crisp—and so I stopped by the store and got you a replacement. They were really very understanding."

She handed it to me and pulled out a charging cord for my dad to plug in. We watched my dad hunt for the plug.

"They never found the ring, either," she added, after a bit.

"What ring?" I asked.

At that, my mother took a good look at me for the first time all day. "Your engagement ring!" she said, like, *Duh!* Then, "Chip gave us the good news while you were in surgery."

The good news. I looked down at my naked hand. I'd forgotten a ring was ever there. "Oh."

"It must have come off in the crash."

I nodded. "It was enormous."

"Too bad," my mom said, bending back over her bag to root out some other things. "It was his grandmother's. Irreplaceable."

She pulled out some framed photos. She'd grabbed two of the three that I kept on my dressing table: one of Chip and me on a hike in the Rockies, and one of me with my parents the day we'd gone zip-lining. The third picture on my dresser was of me and my sister, Kitty, when we were little, dressed up like cowboys with hats and bandanas, back when I used to adore her. That one, my mom left behind.

My mother and my sister did not get along.

Like, really did not get along.

Like, I suspected my mom was the reason Kitty had been ignoring us all for three solid years.

In fact, my mom was the last of us to see Kit before she took off and didn't come back. My parents were hosting a Fourth of July party three summers ago. Kitty had been drinking that night, as she often did, and she'd been loud and boisterous and causing trouble, and at one point, she accidentally-on-purpose pushed my mom into the swimming pool. Kitty laughed so hard at the sight, she collapsed onto one of the chaises and stayed there until my mother climbed up the pool steps, gushing water onto the patio, and dragged Kitty inside and upstairs to have it out.

I took up my mom's hosting duties while they were gone, keeping an eye out for them all the while, but when my mom came back much later, fully dried off and wearing a whole new outfit, Kitty wasn't with her.

"Where's Kit?" I asked, but she wouldn't tell me.

In fact, she never told me. To this day, I had no idea what they fought about that night. All I knew was, it must have been bad. Kitty sent me an email the next day, to tell me that she was moving to New York. Immediately.

I tried to get her to come home and talk to me about it, but she wouldn't. I tried to get her to tell me where she was, but she wouldn't. I didn't think she'd really leave, but she did.

I didn't think it would last, either, but it did.

She left, and she didn't look back. She stayed away from all of us. My mom never tried to contact her, but I did, and my dad did, even though emails went unanswered and texts and phone messages were ignored.

The whole situation bewildered me at first. My mom and Kit had never really gotten along, I knew. I also knew my mom had always been harder on Kit than she was on me. But just disappearing? Ignoring everybody? No Thanksgivings, no Christmases? No birthdays? It seemed like a bit much.

After a year and a half of trying and trying and getting nowhere, I stopped trying so hard. I stopped wondering what we'd all done to push her away, and I just found myself feeling resentful of the fact that she'd gone. You can only reach out so many times before you stop trying. After a while, just the fact that somebody is mad at you can make you feel mad at them. The longer she stayed away, the more defensive I became, and without even noticing, I drifted into an alliance with my mother—steadily resenting Kitty for disappearing without ever even saying why.

At this point, my sweet dad was the only one of us still hoping she'd decide to get in touch.

"No picture of Kitty?" I asked—not because I was surprised, but as a way of calling attention to our allegiance, a way of reinforcing a little closeness when I could.

My mom gave me an eye-roll that was just as reinforcing. "Please."

But the mention of Kitty did raise a question. "Has anybody called her about this?" I asked.

"No," my mother said definitively, just as my father said, "Yes."

My mother and I both looked at him. "You did?"

My dad nodded. "I sent her an email with the subject URGENT FAMILY EMERGENCY."

My mom looked away. "I'm surprised she replied."

"Well," my dad said, "she did. And then she hopped on a plane and came home."

"She's *here*?" my mom asked.

My dad nodded. "She came to the ICU several times." Then he glanced at my mom. "When you were out."

I shook my head. "I don't remember seeing her."

"You were on a lot of medication."

My mother gave my dad the look she gives him when he's been very bad. "We didn't *pay* for that plane ticket, did we?"

He ignored her. "She'd like to come see you," he said to me, "but she doesn't want to upset you or make any trouble. Can I tell her it's okay?"

From his expression, he clearly expected me to say *fine*. But I found myself shaking my head. The idea of some big, delayed, years-too-late confrontation with her felt like way too much right now. I couldn't face it. I had enough going on. Even just thinking about seeing her again made me exhausted.

"Okay," my dad said, nodding. "I get it. I'll tell her you're not ready."

"Just tell her to go back to New York," I said. "I won't be ready anytime soon."

My mother had that look she gets when she wants to yell at my dad, but she holds it in for the sake of the children. I did not envy his car ride home.

"Thank you for going to all this trouble to grab my stuff," I said to cheer her a bit.

"No trouble," she said, shrugging in a way that let me know *yes*, it had been trouble, but that's the kind of self-sacrificing mother she was.

Also, she was going to make another trip later to bring her folding bridge chairs "so company would have a place to sit."

"No company," I said then. "I don't want any visitors."

My parents looked at each other. My estranged sister was one thing—but *no visitors at all*?

"A few close friends, at least?" my dad asked, in a *be reasonable* tone.

"No friends. No one."

"Sweetheart," my mother said. "The phone's been ringing off the hook. The front hall table is covered in cards. People want to see you."

It was my moment to reflect graciously on how kind it was of people to think of me. But I just said, "I don't really care."

"We can't barricade the hospital," my mother said.

But my dad said, "We might talk to the nurses. Say she's not ready."

My mom frowned. "But all the literature says not to let them get isolated."

Oh, God. She'd been reading "the literature." It was worse than I thought.

"I just need some time," I said, trying to get her on my side.

Truer words were never spoken. If I had to make a list of things I wanted to see right now, old friends who would pity, judge, and gossip about me would be the last things on it. I didn't want anyone else thinking the things I was thinking. I didn't want anyone else privy to the specific horrors of my new situation. I did not want to be the topic of anyone's phone chats, or get-togethers, or status updates. I didn't want to be the reason other people counted their blessings.

I would see them—*might*—when and if I could do it of my own accord.

Which left my mother with nothing but decorating. After capitulating at last to the No Visitors policy, she made us both weigh in on whether or not the hospital might let her bring some floor lamps. Her next stop, she said, was Bed, Bath & Beyond for a tension curtain rod and some better window treatments. Maybe a throw pillow.

This was my mother's method for loving people: through décor. She glared at the mauve-and-gray-swirled curtains as if they actually might try to harm us. "Doesn't that fabric make you want to cry?"

I tilted my head. "I'm not sure it's the fabric."

"That fabric," she went on, pointing at it now in accusation, "is a crime against humanity."

My dad and I knew better than to argue. If my mother ruled the world, its prisons would be crammed full of nothing but citizens with bad taste.

AFTER THEY LEFT—taking the morning's sad croissants to donate to the nurses' station after I declared I'd never eat them—I decided to close my eyes for just a second, and I fell dead asleep. You wouldn't think being confined to a bed would be so tiring.

I slept until my new occupational therapist, Priya, came in and wanted me to try to wiggle my toes. She also wanted to work on transferring from the bed to the wheelchair, saying the sooner I could get into the chair on my own, the sooner I could wheel myself to the bathroom—and the sooner I could do *that*, the sooner we could remove my catheter to see if, God willing, I could pee on my own.

We practiced an extra transfer, just for good measure.

I kept expecting to see Chip. All day, every time the door swung open, I expected it to be him—carrying flowers, at least, and full of apologies and encouraging words. But he never did show up. Maybe he was still at his parents' house, sleeping it all off. For his sake, I hoped so.

All of this bustling busy-ness seemed oddly cheerful on the surface. Every professional I interacted with had a pleasant, just-another-day-at-the-office demeanor, and yet I strongly suspected they were faking. I know for sure that I was. I kept things calm, I stayed pleasant, I took my medicine—but the truth is, I had woken up in a dystopic world, one so different that even all the colors were in a minor key, more like a sour, washed-out old photograph than anything real.

It looked that way, and it felt that way, too.

I couldn't imagine the future, and I couldn't—wouldn't—even think about the past. And by "the past," I mean ten days earlier. My past hadn't even had time to fade: It had been severed from me—the whole history of who I'd been, what I did, anything I'd ever dared to hope for—gone.

That kind of thing puts quite a spin on your perception.

By that evening, I was so tired, I had hopes I might actually sleep through the night. Exhaustion is a friend to the grieving. I was the kind of tired where sleep just reaches out and tugs you into its gentle sea without you ever making a choice. Just as I was giving in and closing my eyes, the door opened again.

And it was my sister, Kitty. With a suitcase.

Seven

KITTY HESITATED AT the door. “Hey, Mags,” she said.

When I didn’t respond, she held her hand up in a little wave.

“I know you said you didn’t want me to come,” she said. “But I came anyway. Obviously.”

I just stared.

She didn’t step in. She waited for permission that I wasn’t prepared to give.

Three years. Three years of unanswered emails and phone messages. Three years of nothing, and now here she was.

She looked utterly different from the sister I’d last seen. She had short, spiky hair now, bleached a bright yellow, instead of the shoulder-length brown I’d always known. She had little hoop earrings going up the sides of both ears. She had no makeup except for bright red lipstick. She had a ring in her nose like a cow.

But of course, I knew her at once. Even after all this time.

“Nice nose ring,” I said.

“So—can I come in?” she asked.

“I don’t know,” I said. I wasn’t sure I was up for it.

"Just a quick minute," she promised.

"I'm super tired."

"I just want to say hi." There was a nervous energy to the way she stood, as if she were standing on the edge of some tall building's flat roof rather than just in my doorway.

I felt that same energy—a little bit of that same stomach-dropping feeling. Plus, so many different things all at once—surprised, uncertain, annoyed. She could have *called,* right? She could have let me know she was coming, at least. Did I really need some weird stealth attack from her right now? She'd had three years to get in touch, and she'd waited until I literally couldn't escape. It felt like too much. My instinct was to send her away.

But I couldn't.

Part of me wanted her to stay. A bigger part than I'd realized.

"Fine," I said, and I kept my eyes on her face as she walked closer.

She set down her bag as she stepped to the side of my bed.

"Hi," she said.

"Dad said you were in town."

She nodded.

"Have you seen him?" I asked.

She nodded again.

"Have you seen Mom?"

She shook her head.

"Are you going to? Before you go back?"

She gave a half-smile. "I'm gathering up my resolve."

I didn't know what to say. I really didn't even know where to start. It was exactly as bizarre to see her as it was not bizarre at all. Of course she was here. She was my big sister. And yet it was like seeing an after-image come back to life.

"You look better," she said.

"That's not what Mom says."

"She's kind of a bitch sometimes, though."

She wasn't wrong. "True enough," I said.

"And a liar," Kitty added.

I frowned. "Not sure about *that*."

Kit went for a subject change: "How are you?"

"I'm not sure there are words in the world that can answer that question."

She shrugged, like, *Fair enough*, and tried a new angle. "How do you feel?"

"Physically? Or emotionally?"

"Either. Both."

But I didn't want to share any of that with her. Talking about things that tender required a closeness she had forfeited a long time ago. "What's with the suitcase?" I asked.

"I was thinking I might come stay here in the evenings. With you. You know: when Mom's not around."

I eyed the recliner chair. It was supposed to flatten into a bed, but I couldn't imagine how.

I shook my head. "No."

"No what?"

"No, you shouldn't stay here."

"Don't you want company?"

"Not yours."

She frowned a little. "Are you mad at me?"

I looked away. "It's just weird to see you. My life is weird enough right now."

"I want to help."

"Yeah, but you're not helping. You're making things worse."

She didn't answer. It was clear that hadn't occurred to her.

"Want to know who I've been staying with?" she asked then, brightly, even *chattily,* and before I could say no, she went on, "Fat Benjamin. From high school. Do you remember him?"

This was a classic Kitty trick: pretending things were fine until everybody forgot they weren't. She was trying to lure me in.

I didn't answer.

"Remember how he used to give me rides home in that Jetta with the broken back windows with Hefty bags duct-taped over them?"

"Did you just call this guy 'Fat Benjamin'?"

"Everybody calls him that."

"Seems kind of mean."

"He doesn't mind. He's the cute kind of fat. Anyway, he had a huge thing for me, but I never gave him the time of day because he was so doughy and had that mullet-y haircut? Well, he's not exactly fat anymore—more 'chubby.' He's cute now! He got cuter! Or maybe my standards went down. Anyway, I'm staying at his place, on the sofa bed, but I can tell he still likes me, and I'm sure I'll wind up sleeping with him before long if I don't get out of there."

I didn't meet her gaze. Was this her argument for why she should be here? So she didn't accidentally screw a guy called Fat Benjamin?

She shrugged. "I wish I could stay here instead."

"Don't ask me again."

"I'm not asking! I just said, *I wish*."

"We can't all get our wishes."

"I just think it would be a bad idea to sleep with him."

"Then *don't*."

She shrugged. "I'm terrible at saying no."

I met her eyes. "Well," I said. "I'm not."

She was not going to suddenly reappear in my life after three years and make me talk about *boys*, of all things. She could not just show up like this and expect to pick up in the same naïve place we'd left off.

"Anyway," I said. "I'm pretty tired, so . . ."

"That's fine," Kit said, rejecting the hint. "I brought some magazines."

I shook my head. "You need to go."

She stepped a little closer. "I'd really like to stay."

But I just shook my head. And then I turned my face away until she gave up and left.

Eight

THE NEXT MORNING, I learned something new about my hospital room: It had great acoustics.

This was after all the morning rituals: sponge bath, tooth-brushing into a bedpan, medicines, catheter change, bowel evacuation, breakfast of oatmeal and Jell-O, and OT with Priya for three breathless rounds of getting in and out of the chair and two failed toe-wiggling attempts.

My door was right next to the nurse's station. For the first time, I noticed I could hear voices talking about medicine and medical orders. I could hear someone typing on a keyboard. Someone was making a run to Starbucks. An orderly tried to flirt with one of the nurses, but she shut him right down.

Then I heard Nina's voice, a little louder than the others. "I need to talk to you about this schedule."

A man with a slightly nasal voice replied, "Okay, shoot."

"You gave Ian to this patient."

"Yes."

"I've made several notes in the chart that she should have someone else."

"I saw those notes."

"And you just ignored them?"

"Look, Ian's wide open right now."

"Yeah. There's a reason for that."

"Are you saying Ian is incompetent to work with this patient?"

"I'm saying he's not a good match for her. And I think you know it. I'm wondering if you might be kind of hoping it'll blow up in everybody's face."

"What are you saying, Nina?"

"Exactly what you think I'm saying, Myles."

Sheesh. This guy Myles was a wiener.

"You think I'm trying to bring Ian down? You think I'm sacrificing this patient's well-being so we can all watch him self-destruct?"

"Yes."

"Well, I don't have to. The man's a time bomb. He's going to self-destruct all on his own."

Nina wasn't having it. "Not with my patient, he isn't. She's right on the edge. She'd just gotten *engaged.* She just lost everything. You need to pair her with somebody kind and encouraging—April, or even Rob."

"I'm not redoing the entire schedule for one patient."

Nina's voice tightened. "She needs someone else."

"Everyone else is full."

"So switch somebody out."

But Myles—some kind of supervisor, maybe—apparently didn't like being told what to do. In the silence that followed, I could hear him bristle. "It's not your call. It's my call. And if you make trouble for me, I promise I'll make trouble for you. The schedule stays as it is."

He must have walked off then, because after a few seconds of silence, several nurses, including Nina, started talking trash about him, using words like "jealous" and "control freak" and "little Napoleon." I might even have found it funny, if I could find anything funny anymore. If it weren't so clear that the patient she'd been talking about—the one who had just lost *everything that mattered*—was me.

That's when I heard a Scottish voice out at the station. "I tried to switch, if it's any consolation. I talked to Myles yesterday."

"You didn't try hard enough."

"He never gives me anything I want."

"You never used to let him push you around like that."

"He never used to be the boss."

Nina's voice was all business. "You'd better be nice to her, Ian."

Ian's voice was, too. "Nice doesn't make you strong."

Two seconds later, the door to my room pushed open.

"Time for PT, Maggie Jacobsen," Ian said, not meeting my eye. He wheeled my chair close to the bed.

"It's Margaret," I said. When he didn't respond, I said, "I go by Margaret."

"You don't look like a Margaret," he said. He was dead serious.

"That's not really your call, though, is it?"

"Okay, Maggie. Whatever you say."

He grabbed the transfer board and lowered the bed, as well as the chair arm, and then he arranged the board as a little bridge between the two.

Then he turned and walked toward the door.

Wait—*what?* Where was he going? Had I made him mad with the Maggie thing? Was he really a time bomb? Was he about to self-destruct right now? "Aren't you going to help me?"

He paused but didn't turn. "Nope. Press the call button when you're ready."

Then I was alone—just me, a board, and a chair. Oh, and a catheter tube running out the waistband of my pants and taped to my hip on the side.

It was a problem to solve, I'll give it that.

I found the control for the bed and maneuvered it into a sitting position. Then I edged my butt closer to the transfer board. My yoga pants had a bit of a bell-bottom, and one cuff got caught in the bedrail, but I worked it out. Perched at the edge, about to shift myself onto the board where there'd be nothing below me but stone-hard hospital floor, I felt frightened for the first time since the crash. In fact, I felt *something* for the first time since the crash. I paused, out of breath, and wondered why my first feeling couldn't have been laughter. Or joy.

I edged a little closer, putting all my weight on my palms. The muscles in my trunk were atrophied, yes, but still functioning, which helped—but the dead weight of my legs threw me off balance. I wobbled a little, then hunched down until I was steady again. The chair was maybe twelve inches away, but it might as well have been a football field. I eyed the distance, ooched another inch, lost my balance, hunched down. Then again, and again. After a bit, I noticed that the fabric of my pants had two wet blotches on the thighs, and that's when I realized that I thought I'd just been *concentrating*—but instead, I'd been crying. Possibly for some time.

I decided to take a break, halfway across the board.

That's when Ian walked back in. "God, are you not finished yet? I had a cup of coffee and read the paper."

If he'd been someone else, it might have been okay. If we'd been friends, if I'd known he was on my side, if we'd built up a rapport—he might have been teasing me in a fun way. As it was, he was just a mean stranger.

I looked up, and when he saw my face—no doubt puffy and slick with tears—I saw the hardness on his falter, just for a second, before he came gruffly over and steadied my shoulders.

"I've got you," he said. "Keep after it."

With Ian there, it went much faster—and before I knew it, I was trailing along after him as I rolled myself down the hall toward the therapy gym. I tried to think of another time I'd been with another person and felt so alone at the same time. He didn't speak. He didn't look at me. You'd think he was out for a stroll all by himself.

He paused at a door to hold it open, which I thought was a nice gesture until he started speaking. "No," he said, as I rolled past him. "Your technique's all wrong."

He sounded irritated, like we'd been over this a thousand times.

"Well," I said, "I didn't know there *was* a technique, and this is my first time to ever do this, so—"

"Nobody's shown you how to use the chair?"

I shook my head.

"That's OT 101."

"I guess we're still doing prerequisites." Another sad little attempt at a joke.

He didn't smile. Instead, he bent forward to look into my eyes and then squeezed my biceps. Then, in a voice that sounded like he was about to impart vital, deeply insightful information, he said, "Arms are not legs."

I gave him a look, like, *Really?*

"What I mean is," he went on, unamused, "they can't handle the same amount of work as legs. You have to be careful not to strain them with overuse."

"I don't see that I have much choice about that."

"Not in the big picture, no," he conceded. "But in the details. Hence: chair technique." He put his hand over mine—it was warmer than mine was, I noticed—and placed it on the rim of the wheel. "Instead of ten little pushes," he said, "you want to do one strong push and then coast."

He stretched my hand down low along the back of the wheel and pressed it into a grip around the push rim. Then he brought it up and forward to push off, and I went zooming down the hallway fast enough to scare me, so I grabbed the rim to stop, and got a little friction burn.

Ian jogged up behind me. "You're going to need some gloves" was all he said.

Next we covered turning, rotating in place, and popping wheelies—though we didn't actually practice those. "Are wheelies really necessary?" I asked.

"Yes," he said, though he didn't explain why.

"Why?" I decided to demand.

"Because you need to know how to control your wheels."

"Why?"

"Because you need to know how to manage all kinds of terrain."

"Like for when I go off-roading in the Grand Canyon?"

He looked up. "More like for when you encounter steps. Or potholes. Or a curb." He turned away. "If you want to go anywhere, you need to know how to manage."

"I don't want to go anywhere," I said.

"You will," he said as he walked away, all tall and athletic and sturdy. There was something almost mean about how in shape he was, and the way his scrubs draped from his waistband over what any woman with a heartbeat would have to admit was an utterly perfect guy-butt. He was such a supreme physical specimen. I didn't compare myself to him, exactly, but just being near that kind of robustness made me feel extra weak and shriveled. I looked away.

Anyway, that little Wheelchair 101 moment made us a few minutes late arriving at the therapy gym, and so we signed in a little late, too, which seemed to irritate Ian. "Now we're late," he said, noting time on the clock, as if it were my fault.

As if it mattered.

I looked around while he gathered some equipment. If I'd been able to appreciate anything, I would have appreciated the gym. It had all kinds of machines and colors and games. It had a pop-a-shot basketball machine, and a ring toss, and two pinball machines—*Star Wars* and *Guardians of the Galaxy*. It had weights like a gym, and mirrors everywhere, as well as a set of walking bars, a standing frame, and a full-body harness. It had a fine-motor board with locks and latches and screws to work with, and a beanbag-toss game. It had a flight of practice stairs, a minitramp, and a row of recumbent bikes. It even had an entire car, painted a perky aqua, down at one end—I guessed for people to practice getting in and out. Also, up top: quite the speaker system, playing a relentless mix of lite-rock Eagles and Van Morrison tunes.

The old me would have felt tempted to boogie around a little bit, but the new me sat still as a sack of flour.

Ian wrote my name on a big whiteboard that had a slot for every patient on it, with "goals" written out, and smiley faces, and lots of little encouraging sayings. I watched the other trainers while I waited—without exception, an insistently cheerful, optimistic bunch. They laughed loudly, and high-fived, and called their patients things like "champ." They coaxed. They encouraged. They cheered. They sang along to the music.

One guy with a man-bun, who I would come to know as Rob, was working with an eighty-year-old lady on a walker—and while he wasn't exactly flirting with her, he was certainly paying her enough attention that she positively bloomed. A female trainer, April, was shooting Nerf hoops with her patient, a forty-something guy in a wheelchair, and high-fiving each swoosh. It was like a big fitness-and-recovery party. All around me, people were moving, and talking, and challenging themselves—and while the patients were more somber, the PTs were nothing short of jovial.

Except for my PT.

I looked over at Ian with his gray frown and his stiff jaw. He was so serious, so sour, so much the opposite of jovial that he practically had a little cartoon scribble of grumpiness above his head.

No wonder he has an open schedule, I thought.

"Late again, Ian," I heard then. The nasal voice. The same one I'd heard talking to Nina. I looked over to get my first eyeful of Myles, walking toward us. He turned out to have wavy, tight-cropped red hair—clashing boldly with the red sweatshirt he'd zipped over his scrubs—and tight, hard little brown eyes. He looked exactly like his voice.

Ian didn't respond.

"Hate to have to mark you in the book," Myles went on, almost glaring at Ian. "But rules are rules."

Ian held menacingly still, eyes averted.

"Just gotta watch that clock and stay timely."

Then, I didn't mean to stand up for Ian, but I did. "He was helping me with wheelchair technique in the hallway," I said. It just popped out.

Myles shifted his eyes to me. "That's not PT. That's OT."

"But he was correcting my technique."

"Not his job," Myles said. "Right, champ? Not your job."

Ian just worked his jaw.

Myles went on, "Wouldn't want people thinking you don't know what your job is."

I started to argue again, but Ian gave me a look.

Myles was baiting him. "Wouldn't want people thinking you have no right to be here."

Ian: Silence. Then more silence.

"Good talk," Myles said after another minute, clapping Ian on the shoulder.

Then he turned to point at me across the room and shout, "If you need any more advice, I suggest you come to me. I'm just right there in my corner office."

I saw Ian squeeze his hand into a fist and then stretch it out.

Then Myles pointed at Ian and said, in a pseudo-inspirational tone, "Go work some miracles."

Did that guy *want* to get punched? *I* even wanted to punch him.

"Sorry," I said, once we'd made it to the far side of the gym. "I was trying to help you."

"Don't help me," Ian said, shaking his head. "Don't do that again."

Then he walked off.

He stopped across the room at a mat table and looked exasperated to find that I hadn't followed him. He made a "get over here" motion, and I wheeled in his direction.

When I reached him, he handed me a transfer board and said, "You know what to do."

I hadn't let my armrest down on my own before, and it took me a minute to find the latch—during which time Ian kept his eyes focused out the window, breathing impatiently every so often.

"You could help me, if you're in such a rush."

"I'm not here to do it for you. You're here to do it for yourself."

"I didn't ask you to do it for me. I just said you could help."

"At this point, that's the same thing."

I could imagine one of the other trainers saying that in a playful tone, but Ian was about as playful as roadkill. He was silent, and tense, and now—since seeing that guy Myles—radiating hostility. I could sense it wasn't meant for me, but I was still collateral damage. The rancor fumed from his body—you could see it in his face and his gait and the way he held himself as stiff as an action figure—and I was just unfortunate enough to be stuck with him.

Just as I had that thought, Rob, the trainer with the man-bun, let out a whoop of a cheer over something amazing and inspiring his patient had just done. Then everybody in the room stopped to applaud.

Except Ian.

"Let's move," he said, urging me toward the mat.

I moved, and I got the armrest down, and I eventually dragged myself across the board onto the mat, but Ian's cranky, impatient, irritated nonhelp did not make things easier. Or faster.

By the time I made it, I was panting.

Before I'd caught my breath, Ian leaned over me and laid me back on the mat, careful of my burns, to start a whole series of exercises to take stock of my starting place—what I could and couldn't do right now. He did this without explaining first, and for a second I thought he was picking me up. I leaned forward just as he did and managed to smush my face into the corner between his neck and his collarbones. Just for a second, before I pulled back, I registered his scratchy, unshaven neck, firm with muscles, and the salty, linen-y smell of him.

It could have been a funny, slightly embarrassing moment, one we could laugh about—but Ian decided to make it humiliating instead. When I looked up, he seemed super annoyed. "Down," he said, pointing at the mat, as if he'd already explained this to me a hundred times.

I felt a sting of embarrassment. "Right," I said.

With that, we took stock of me: Could I sit up on my own? (Barely. With a lot of grunting.) Could I roll over? (Yes. Clumsily, but yes.) Could I lie on my back and lift my knees? (Yes, actually. But my thighs were weak and trembled like earthquakes.) Could I sit on the edge and straighten my leg out? (No. Not even close.) Could I lie on my stomach and lift my feet behind me? (About halfway.) Could I point, wiggle, or flex my toes? (No, no, and no.) By the end, we had the general idea. Everything above the knees seemed to work—though not always well. Below the knees was a different story.

The whole process seemed to go on for hours, and it left me breathless and shaky. I had known that my legs were not exactly working, but breaking it down into specifics—and by "specifics," I mean breaking the function of my legs and feet down by each specific muscle—made it more real. In a way, I didn't really want to know what I could or couldn't do. Observing this new, broken version of my body only seemed to give it a validity it didn't deserve.

But if Ian was aware of my unhappiness, he didn't seem to care much. He drove us on and on, testing everything: ankles, toes, thighs, hip flexors. He did pressure tests all up and down my legs, poking me with a little pin, and I saw him write down the word "spotty" in his chart over and over.

He was keeping a list of all the muscles that didn't work. It was far longer than I'd expected, but, to be fair, just the list of muscles in the legs was far longer than I'd expected. Ian's "not working" list included several leg muscles that had Latin names starting with "biceps," which I argued was needlessly confusing, since "biceps" made them sound like arm muscles, and my arms were fine. Ian totally ignored me and made his list anyway, which, in the end, looked like this:

biceps femoris
biceps semitendinosus
biceps semimembranosus
tibialis—anterior and posterior
peroneus longus
gastrocnemius
soleus
flexor digitorum longus

I wondered if I should ask what some of those muscles were, but as the list grew longer, I wasn't sure I wanted to know.

It was physically exhausting, and it was emotionally grueling, but I really think the worst part of the whole experience was, of all things, the *not talking.*

I'm a talker from a long line of talkers. My mom might be talking to you about the curtains and who should be sent to Guantánamo for choosing them, but she's talking to you. My dad might be placating my mom, but he's doing it with words. I don't think I have ever once, in my entire life, spent that much time one-on-one with another human being and spoken as few words as I did with Ian. Over the entire afternoon, you probably couldn't make one full sentence out of the words we exchanged.

It bothered me. Viscerally.

But I was too tired, demoralized, shell-shocked, discouraged, and numb to do anything about it. It was Ian's job to work the conversation, dammit. All the other trainers—and I had plenty of time to take stock—were doing the vast majority of the conversational grunt work, giving their patients the gift of conversational pleasure without the usual work, and leaving the patients free to concentrate on their tasks.

With Ian, I got the opposite of conversational pleasure. I got the cringe of uncomfortable silence. Plus the comparative disappointment of knowing I had the worst trainer in the room.

Silent, surly, and relentless. We didn't finish our session until all the other perky people were long gone and my entire body felt like Jell-O. I thought for sure Ian would help me back into the chair at the end, but he just slapped the board down and turned his gaze back to the window.

I gave a long sigh as I looked at it.

I didn't ask for help, because I knew I wouldn't get it.

I had to readjust my catheter tube, which had come untaped, and then I started scooting my butt sideways across the board.

But I was more exhausted than I realized, because just before I reached the chair, as I shifted my weight onto my lead arm, my elbow gave way and I went pitching forward.

I should have hit the floor, but almost as soon as I realized I was falling, Ian caught me. I would have bet you a hundred dollars that his entire focus had been out the gym window, but he must have been using his peripheral vision, because I was caught by his steady arms and settled in my chair before I even fully got what was happening.

"Thank you," I said, before I remembered that he was kind of the reason I'd fallen in the first place.

Before he stood back up, he checked my expression, meeting my eyes for the first time. "I've tired you out," he said.

"In more ways than one." I noticed his eyes were blue. Dark blue—almost navy.

"You worked hard today."

As mad as I was, it felt weirdly nice to have that acknowledged. *And you,* I thought, *stared out the window.*

He studied my face another second, and then he stood up and said, "Time to get you back to your room." I'd seen the other PTs pushing their clients' chairs—especially the elderly and the tired—at the ends of their workouts, and I just assumed that Ian would do the same.

Wrong. Of course.

He and his perfect butt just strolled off toward the exit, and I had no choice but to scramble after him in my chair.

At the door, Ian stopped at the patient whiteboard. Under my name was an empty box. Other patients' boxes had stars and smileys and hearts in them, but Ian marked mine with a solemn black *X*.

Which was about how I felt.

Nine

BACK AT THE room, a nurse I'd never seen before scolded us. "Ian, she was supposed to be back forty-five minutes ago."

I was? I narrowed my eyes at Ian, but he pretended to ignore me.

"She didn't want to quit," he said. "She's a machine."

"I need her now."

"She's all yours."

Just then, the new cell phone my mother had brought me rang. I'd never heard its ringtone—so loud and screechy—and it startled all of us. Ian picked it up off the side table and handed it to me.

"Hello?" I said.

A guy's voice. "Margaret Jacobsen?"

"Yes?"

"Neil Putnam from HR at Simtex."

My new job! Oh, God—I had forgotten all about it. Should I explain what happened? Did they already know? That interview felt like a hundred years ago in somebody else's life.

"I remember," I said, after a pause. Neil Putnam was the guy who'd told me that I unofficially had the job. "How are you?"

"Doing just great." His voice was overly bright, but I didn't notice at first. "Hey," he went on, like he'd just thought of something. "I've been asked to call and let you know that the guys upstairs have made an official decision about the position."

I held my breath. It was an impossible problem. I was twenty-eight and just out of business school, and I'd landed a dream job that nobody with my lack of experience had any right to, and it really was the offer of a lifetime, and at this moment, given that I couldn't even pee without help, it seemed unlikely I could make the most of it. What would I do if they wanted me to start next week?

I'd never in my life faced a challenge and given up. The non-quitter part of me could not imagine doing anything other than wrestling myself into an Ann Taylor suit and hauling my ass out to their corporate campus the minute they said *go.* But a much more vocal part of me—the part, shall we say, with the catheter sticking out—could not imagine ever even leaving this hospital room, much less dedicating my thoughts to "strategic and higher operational level engagement with the logistics environment."

My only hope was to delay. Maybe I could wrangle a start date later in the summer. How long was it going to take me to get myself back to normal? Two months, maybe? Four?

But as I opened my mouth to suggest it, Neil Putnam said, "They're going with another candidate."

"I'm sorry?"

"Someone with more experience."

"But you said I had it!"

"Unofficially. But then a better candidate came along."

I closed my eyes.

"They'll send an official letter, but we wanted to give you a heads-up."

"I see," I said at last. "Of course." Had they somehow heard about the crash? Did they know what I was up against?

"We wish you the best of luck, and hope you are up and around again soon."

Guess they did.

I pressed END and let out a long sigh comprised entirely of the word "Fuuuuuuuuuck."

When I looked up, Ian and the new nurse were watching me.

"I just got fired," I explained. "Though not really. It wasn't official yet. But right before the crash, they told me it was mine. The most amazing dream job ever. And I was going to rock it out."

"They can't do that!" the nurse said, all sympathy, like we'd been pals for years.

"Sure they can," Ian said. "That's how the world works." No sympathy there. Dry as chalk.

"Bad luck," the nurse said, and took my hand to squeeze it. It wasn't until she touched me that I realized how cold my own hands were. "I'm sorry about your bad news."

I shrugged. "It's okay," I said, and in a way, it was. A relief, at least. An impossible challenge that I didn't have to rise to.

I had enough impossible challenges these days.

But in a much larger way, it wasn't okay. I wanted that job, yes—but I also needed it. I had bought a fancy condo on the strength of my bright future. I had student loan payments and car payments and credit card payments. Plus, I had no idea what the medical bills were going to be like for this situation.

A panic about the future swirled inside my body like a dust storm. Another piece of my old life had just crumbled away.

Here's the weird thing, though, about all the emotions swirling through me right then: I felt them intensely—and, at the exact same time, I could barely feel them at all. I have no idea how that works, but I swear it's true. I felt full-out panicked and quietly numb simultaneously. I wondered if I'd ever feel things normally again—and then immediately hoped it would be a long, long time before I did.

Never would've been fine.

Ian was already back to business. "So," he said, rocking back a little, "let's recap. We basically made a map of your entire body today—and in the coming weeks, we'll strengthen what's working and try to wake up what's not." He spoke with his eyes on his clipboard, as if the topic in general, and me in particular, bored him to tears. "There's a great deal of mystery with spinal cord injuries, and we can't always predict who will see improvement and who won't. Your deficits are all at the patella level and below, and that's the area we'll focus on. Do you have any questions?"

As he waited for my answer, he looked out the window.

I shook my head.

"I'll be back tomorrow, then," he said, turning away. "And next time," he called over his shoulder, "you have to try."

The nurse and I watched him go. I could have been irritated with him, I suppose, but I was too tired to be mad. In fact, I felt all remaining energy whoosh out of my body like a sigh as he left. The day was over. All I had left to do was get myself back into bed. Then I could close my eyes and sink into oblivion.

But just before I turned to look for the transfer board, another figure appeared in doorway.

Kitty.

Again.

"I thought I told you no," I said.

"That was a long time ago," Kitty said.

"That was *yesterday*."

"I thought maybe you'd changed your mind."

"Nope."

"Fat Benjamin confessed to me after I got home last night that he still had a ponytail holder of mine from high school. And then he tried to put his tongue in my ear."

I faced her dead-on. "I have many problems right now," I said then. "But Fat Benjamin's tongue in *your* ear is definitely not one of them."

Kitty looked affronted. "I'm not asking you to solve my problems."

"Yes, you are. Like you always do." But not anymore. I didn't say it, but she'd lost the right to ask that of me.

"Not this time," Kitty insisted. "*I'm* here to help *you*."

"I already told you that you can't."

She blinked.

So I said it again. "All your being here can possibly do is make things worse."

"What if I bring you cupcakes?"

"No."

"What if I bring trashy novels and spring rolls from that Thai place you love?"

"No."

"Don't just send me away," she said. "Let's talk about it. Let's rap it out."

She was being cute, but I had no patience for cute. "I'm serious," I said. "Get out. Go home. Go back to New York, even. You are something I just can't handle right now."

"Can't? Or won't?"

"Both."

KIT LEFT, BUT she came back again the next night, just as I was finishing dinner. With cookies.

I sent her away.

She came after dinner the night after that with macarons, and I sent her away again.

And then, on the night after that, when she didn't show up after dinner, I noticed I was disappointed. I was waiting to see her. More than that: The idea of seeing her didn't seem weird and destabilizing anymore. In fact, it felt like something to look forward to. I was anticipating the sight of her with her crazy hair and tattoos, wearing a tutu or something equally nutty. Not to mention the cake pops she'd bring, or brownies, or doughnuts, or whatever.

I found myself worrying that she might have given up on me, and regretting being so cold.

When she finally did turn up at last, she was carrying one perfect, exquisite chocolate cupcake from my favorite bakery of all time, twenty minutes across town.

"Are you bribing me?" I asked, as she held it out.

"I am demonstrating," she said, "that I am not just here to escape trading sexual favors with Fat Benjamin in exchange for lodging. I am here to do whatever I can to make your day just a little bit better. Starting with cupcakes."

I looked at the cupcake. I took it.

"I also apologize for ignoring you for three straight years."

"Fine," I said, taking a bite and pressing the smooth icing against the roof of my mouth. Then, after swallowing: "You can stay."

"Really?"

I took another bite and savored it, then spoke louder for more authority. "But if you wind up making things worse for me, you're out."

"I won't," Kit said.

"For example," I said, throwing down the challenge. "It's time for bed now."

Kit glanced at the clock on my wall. "It's not even nine o'clock."

The cupcake was suddenly gone. We were done here.

"Yeah," I said, like, *Duh*, like it was past the whole world's bedtime. "Get your bed ready and let's hit the sack."

I watched her unfold the recliner and make it up with a sheet from the cabinet. She'd brought a pillow and blanket of her own—both plaid, which added a camp-out vibe. As I watched her work, her movements and her silhouette so familiar, my eyes kept trying to close on their own. I remember thinking I was so tired I'd never wake up. I remember wondering if she was going to sleep with that crazy nose ring in.

I WOKE A couple of hours later to Kitty at my bedside, whispering, "Hey. Hey! Wake up!"

I opened my eyes in the pale darkness. Kitty was leaning over me in a sleep shirt with R2D2 on it. I was out of breath.

"What's going on?" I asked.

"You were having a nightmare."

She wasn't wrong. "I was drowning," I said. "I was trapped in the plane—underwater."

"I figured it was something bad."

I squeezed my eyes closed and took a second to catch my breath.

My hair—what remained of it—was damp with sweat, and I was shaking. Kitty got a nubby white washcloth from the bathroom and pressed it to my forehead. Then, without a word, she crawled into my bed beside me—careful not to touch my neck. She was slender enough to fit. She curled on her side and stroked my hair. "Your hair's a mess," she whispered.

"The fire burned it off," I said.

"Well, that's kind of lucky," she said, "because guess what I've been doing since the last time you saw me?"

"Tell me."

"Cutting hair."

I frowned. "You're a barber?"

"A *hairstylist*. I'm famous. I have forty-six thousand followers on Instagram."

"You're famous?"

She nodded. "I also do tattoos. I have a place called the Beauty Parlor in Brooklyn. And we do piercings."

"You do the tattoos yourself?"

"Yep. Tattoos and haircuts. I'm amphibious. Guess what else? I'm sleeping with the manager. Or maybe he's sleeping with me . . . Either way, it's one-stop shopping."

The manager's name was Ethan, but he had a handlebar moustache that he waxed at the tips, so everybody just called him the Moustache. Even Kitty.

She told me all about him in soothing tones while I waited for my body to settle down and stop shaking—his motorcycle, and his cooking skills, and his favorite books.

At last, after letting her talk and talk, I asked, "Do you always use the article? Like, do you say, 'Hey, the Moustache! Come here!' Or, 'What's for dinner, the Moustache?' "

She thought about it. "Actually, to his face, we call him 'Stache, like it's a name. But when we're talking about him, we call him the Moustache, like it's his title."

"What does he call you?"

"I can't repeat it," she said. "It's X rated."

The last time I'd seen her, she'd been temping as a receptionist. She'd been wearing pumps and an ill-fitting gray suit that she'd refused to have altered. "You've really changed a lot," I said.

"For the better."

"Maybe. Except for that nose ring."

"You don't like it?"

"You look like Elsie the cow."

"But sexy."

My sister, the nose-ringed hairstylist. "Can you fix my hair?" I asked.

"Of course. I'll give you an adorable little pixie. It'll be cuter than what you had before."

It wouldn't, of course. But I was too tired to argue.

"Remember that time," Kitty said, "I cut that girl's hair at summer camp and made her cry?"

"That was actually a really cute little bob."

"I took like ten inches off, though."

I remembered. "She called her parents to come and take her home."

"I should send her a gift certificate. Now, I can make anybody look good." She nudged me. "Even you."

I knew she meant it as a joke. But I closed my eyes.

"I was kidding," she said, when I got quiet.

I said, "Mom can't even look at me."

"That's not about you. That's about her."

"My *face* is burned."

Kitty made a *pshaw* sound. "It's a sunburn. It looks exactly like a sunburn. Except for the blisters. Not a big deal. I'll show you tomorrow."

It was strange to listen to our conversation. It was like I was eavesdropping on it somehow. In one way, we sounded very much like we always did—the back-and-forth, the teasing. We'd only ever had one way of talking to each other, and it was playful and jokey. That way of talking didn't fit the situation now, but it was all we knew how to do.

So we did it. But it was in a minor key, just a muffled, gray version of itself.

Of course, that's how everything I said or did or thought felt now. Flat, and colorless, and altered.

"Kitty?" I asked, after a bit.

"What?"

"Stay here tonight, okay? I don't want to be alone."

"I am staying here."

"No, I mean right here. In the bed."

"Okay."

"I don't want to have any more nightmares," I said.

"I'll keep an eye on you."

"Thanks."

We let ourselves get quiet and start to settle, but then I had to say one last thing. "You can't be drinking here, by the way. I'm making that rule."

"Drinking?" she asked.

"'Cause you get crazy when you drink, and I just can't take any more drama—"

"I haven't had a drink in three years," Kit said. "Dad sent me to rehab."

This should have been thrilling news, but my heart was too numb to feel it. "That's great," I said. "I didn't know."

"Yeah, he thought he should keep that under his hat."

"That's why you went away?"

"That's part of it."

"And you stayed away because—*what?*—you were too fragile?"

"That's part of it, too. I'll give you the whole story sometime. But not tonight. Then you really will have nightmares."

Fair enough. "So . . . you quit drinking entirely?"

"Entirely. It was brutal, but I did it."

"I'm sorry."

"It's okay. We all have our struggles. I'm better for it, actually."

"Does Mom know?"

"I have no idea."

"You should tell her."

"Nah."

"It might help the two of you make up."

"Well, that's the thing, right there," Kit said. "I'm not sure if I want to make up."

She was offering up some answers to questions I'd carried around a long time, but somehow they were raising more questions than they were settling. What had happened that night she pushed our mom into the pool? What had they fought about? Who was mad at who, exactly? What on earth could have made Kit—who always longed so much for attention—shut us out for so long? I wanted to know, but I also didn't. It had to be something big, and I wasn't sure at this point I could even handle something small.

Wondering about Kit did offer a small distraction, and in the face of the wasteland my own life had become, there was something about a distraction that felt like relief.

Until Kit turned it all back to me.

"Can I tell you something comforting about your situation?" she asked, after a minute.

"No."

It hadn't been a real question, of course. It was just an intro. "Really? You don't want to be comforted?"

"Nope."

She wasn't buying it. "Everybody wants to be comforted."

How to explain to her that there was absolutely nothing she could say that would comfort me? Even the attempt would make things worse. There was no upside. There was no silver lining. There was no comfort.

But there was no way she could understand that. "Don't comfort me. Don't say a word. Just go to sleep before I kick you out again."

"Okay," Kit said.

So that's how we stayed, two in the bed, all night long: Kit patiently comforting me while I rejected the very notion of the concept.

As long as she was just breathing in and out beside me in that snoozy, wavy, sleepy-Kitty rhythm of hers—it was fine. I didn't believe in comfort anymore, and I knew for a fact that I would never, ever feel better. But having her with me like that? Not being alone? Well, it didn't make me feel *worse*. That counted for something.

Ten

KITTY WAS GONE in the morning when I woke up, and she'd folded the chair-bed back so neatly that it was almost like she was never there. For a second, I wondered if she'd left for good—until I noticed her stuff in a neat pile in the corner. Maybe she'd left early to make herself scarce to avoid running into my mom.

And so I launched into another day, all on my own—everything pretty much exactly the same until the very end, when Ian walked me back from another awkward, silent, antisocial session of physical therapy, and we found a nurse I'd never seen before waiting for me in my room.

She met my eyes with a bright smile. "How do you feel about good news?"

I glanced at Ian, who gave me a tiny shrug.

I hesitated. "I'm . . . for it?"

The nurse's smile got bigger. "Because I have good news for you."

I waited. "Okay." I wasn't sure I could muster the excitement she was clearly expecting. "I guess you'd better tell me, then."

Then she pointed right at my crotch. "We're about to take out that catheter."

* * *

THERE WAS NO guarantee the catheter wasn't going back in. The spinal surgeon had noted "sacral sparing" down in the nether regions, and he was optimistic that I had both enough sensation down there to feel when I needed to pee, and enough muscle control to make it happen—but there was no guarantee.

Only trying would tell.

The nurse put an absorbent pad on the bed before helping me get up into it, and then she slid the tube out with no ceremony at all. Then she helped me into an open-back gown for the night, "for easy access."

"When you feel the feeling and need to pee," she said, "move fast. Press the call button. Don't try to transfer on your own."

"Okay."

"And don't wait until you're about to burst!"

"I won't."

She'd be back soon to check on me. The question now was, would I feel that feeling? And if I did feel it, and manage to get to the bathroom without wetting myself first, would my urethra know what to do when I got there?

Safe to say, I had never adequately appreciated the sheer, elegant genius of the urinary system. Now it became a significant character in the story of my life. It was common for patients with injuries like mine to spend the rest of their lives catheterized, facing all the humiliations and discomfort that implied—not to mention chronic infections from the tubes. I found myself rooting for my bladder to impress us all.

After the nurse left, I lay in the silence of my room, eavesdropping on the conversations outside, waiting alertly to feel that delightful old sensation of needing to pee—what did it even feel like? I could barely remember—and rooting for my brave little-urethra-that-could to face this challenge and triumph.

Until I fell asleep.

I slept until Kitty arrived with Chinese takeout.

She poked me, saying, "Hey, are you sleeping?"

I put my hand over my eyes. "Don't wake me when I'm sleeping, Kit!"

"I brought dinner," she said, as if takeout justified anything, and she started unloading containers.

As I came awake, I noticed something. "Oh, my God. I need to pee! I can feel it!"

Kit looked at me like I was a little nuts. "Hooray?"

I pointed at the transfer board. "We have to get me to the bathroom."

Long story short: I did it. *We* did it—my urethra and I—without a hitch.

Except for the moment when I looked up to find Kit trying to take a picture of me on the toilet.

"Kit! What the hell? Don't take a picture of me peeing!"

"For Instagram!" she said, like that made it better. "It's photojournalism!"

Had she always been this crazy? We were barely back on speaking terms. "Shut it down."

"I'm kidding," Kit said. "But my followers *are* all rooting for you."

"That's rule number two," I went on. "No photos—ever."

"Not even selfies?"

"My hospital room, my rules: No comfort. No photos. And no goddamned selfies."

"Fine."

"Fine. Now help me back into the chair."

We worked me back into the bed, and once I was all tucked in, Kit laid out the Chinese food like a feast—fried dumplings and egg rolls and sesame chicken. All my favorites from childhood.

I knew what she was up to. "This isn't *comfort* food, is it?"

Kit narrowed her eyes. "This is just what I happen to like. You can't blame me if you find it comforting."

"I'll blame you if I want to," I said, but I gave her a little smile. Which felt shaky, like those muscles had atrophied, too.

Kit speared a chicken hunk with her chopstick. "Aren't you kind of glad I'm here?"

I was, actually. Far more than I would admit. "When you're not taking pictures of me on the frigging toilet."

I COULDN'T EAT much, but Kit could. She finished off all the egg rolls and every steamed dumpling, slurping dipping sauce and licking her fingers. Then, after she'd cleaned up, she said, "Now: the haircut!"

I wrinkled my nose. "I'm too tired."

"You just had a nap!"

"Yeah. My pre-bedtime nap."

"No!" Kit protested. "I planned us a whole girls' night." She started pulling items out of her purse and stacking them up on the tray table: a box of chocolates, a nail-painting kit with emoji decals, a bag of popcorn, Boggle, and a couple of naughty-looking romance novels. Plus a set of long computer cords.

"You've got quite the party planned."

She nodded. "Total debauchery."

"Glad you woke me now."

She nodded, missing the sarcasm. "I can hook my computer up to the TV. I've got *Grease* cued up."

I smiled for a second despite myself. We loved *Grease* as kids. We'd put on the soundtrack and dance around the house, climbing the furniture and singing the duets.

She always made me be Danny, though.

Kit stood up and pointed her finger in the air, striking a Travolta-on-the-bleachers pose.

Nothing from me.

"Come on. I'll let you be Sandy."

Too little, too late. "I don't want to be Sandy."

"Yes, you do."

"I don't feel like singing."

"You always feel like singing."

"Not anymore."

She narrowed her eyes at me. "When was the last time you sang?"

"I don't know."

"I read an article that if you have a talent and you don't find a way to use it, your life can collapse in on itself like a black hole."

I gave her a look. "Too late."

"That's the most depressing thing I've ever heard you say."

"Only because it's true." She was pushing, and all I could do was push back.

"No, it's not."

I felt my hackles lift just a little bit. If I said my life was a black hole, then it was an effing black hole. "We'll have to agree to disagree."

I could read her face so clearly. She thought I was being stubborn.

The longer she stared, the more I felt my body tightening in defensiveness. *Really?* She was going to stand there with her working legs and resent my less-than-sunny attitude?

"Looks like we've got kind of a role reversal going here," Kit said at last.

I waited, and lifted my eyebrow a bit, like, *Oh, really?*

"This may be," she went on, in a conversational tone, like we were just chatting about the weather, "the first time ever that I am the one trying to make things better—and you are the one trying to make things worse."

And just like that, I was mad. "I don't have to *try* to make things worse," I said, my throat tight and strangely sandpapery. "Things are already worse."

"Things can always get worse," Kit declared.

My reply was like a reflex—a shouting reflex. "Not for me!"

I'm always amazed at how fast siblings can warp-speed into a state of rage. It's like they keep everything they were ever angry about growing up shoved into an overstuffed emotional closet, and at moments like these, it takes about two seconds to swing open the door and start an avalanche.

"You have to try!" Kit insisted, in a tone like she'd said it a hundred times.

"I *am* trying!"

"You're not!"

This was the trouble with sisters. This was the trouble with family. I had barely cracked open the door to my life, and she'd just barged in and made herself at home—taking photos of me and judging my coping skills. We hadn't even officially made up yet, and she was ordering me around.

Just as I had that thought, she went on. "You," she said, pointing right at me, "need to sing."

With that, the anger lit inside me like a flame—so physical, I felt myself light up. "I don't want to sing!" I shouted.

It was like all the anger I'd been unwilling to feel—at Chip, at my mother, at the folks in this hospital who kept making me do impossible things—had been quietly gathering like some flammable gas. And Kit had just lit a match.

I slammed both my fists down against the bed. "I'm not going to sing!" My voice both too loud in that moment and not loud enough. "You can't make me sing! Do you really think it's that easy? You can't just come in here with Boggle and show tunes and make everything all right! Stop trying to fix things! Give me a fucking break."

Kit blinked. Then blinked some more. I wondered if she might cry, or run out of the room—but she just nodded.

In the long silence that followed, I deflated.

"Okay," Kit said after a while, in a quiet voice. "Okay, that's fair."

I sighed, long and slow.

"You don't have to sing," Kit went on, shrugging, and looking at me with new eyes.

I matched my voice to hers. "Damn right I don't."

"I hear you," she said. "I'll back off." But then she peeked up from under her eyelashes. "Can I at least do the haircut, though?"

AN HOUR LATER, hair was all over the floor. I'd transferred into the chair so that I wouldn't have to sleep in a bed of "hair fuzz," and we'd made a carpet of hair sprinkles all around the wheels.

Kitty fussed and fussed, and it took far longer than it should have, as all her genetic perfectionist tendencies kicked in. At last, she declared victory and handed me a hand mirror. I started to lift it, but then I hesitated.

"Take a look," she urged.

I wrinkled my nose.

"You don't want to see?"

I did want to see the haircut—but I didn't know how to do that without also seeing my face.

"You know what?" I said then, shaking my head. "I'm good. I'm sure it's fine."

"Are you afraid you look terrible? Because you don't."

Yes. I was afraid I looked terrible. Of course. When your own mother can't even look at you, you have to be a monster. But it was more than that. Once I knew what I looked like now, I would always know. There are things you can't unsee.

It would be like the time my aunt walked me up to my grandmother's open casket to "say good-bye" and I looked down to see an embalmed, flattened, just-plain-wrong version of the face I'd known and loved so long. For a long time after that, the only face I saw when I thought of my grandmother was that wrong one. It had erased the face I wanted to hold on to.

I didn't want to look in that mirror to find that I was gone.

Kit seemed to read my thoughts. "You look just like you. A little sunburned, and with a few scabby blister things on the jaw . . ." She touched her jaw. "And with the cutest haircut you've ever had—*you're welcome.* But still the same you."

I tilted the mirror a little.

"Don't be afraid," she urged.

But I was. My hands felt cold. *Don't think,* I told myself. It was time to face the future, whatever it looked like. I held my breath, and lifted the mirror, and tilted it, one centimeter at a time, until my whole face gazed back at me.

My same face. A little roughed up, but familiar as an old friend.

"See?" Kit said. "You're still the beauty."

A ragged sigh escaped my chest. "I don't need to be the beauty. I just want to be recognizable."

"You are," Kit said. "Just way more stylish."

I'd never had bangs, but this cut flopped down over my forehead in the front and was short and spiky in back. Pixie-ish. I'd never had anything but long hair—out of fear, really, that I'd cut it all off and then hate it and have to wait forever to get back to my old self. Also, my mother thought short hair on girls was ugly.

But this haircut wasn't ugly.

Kit was grinning wide now. "How cute are you?" she demanded. "This is the haircut you've been waiting for all your life!"

"I don't hate it," I said.

"You love it. Come on."

Next, I angled the mirror ever so slowly toward my neck. Seeing my face better than expected made me hopeful that the rest might be, too.

But the skin grafts were *worse*.

The side of my neck, from my jaw to my collarbone, was utterly unrecognizable. It was purple and gooseflesh-y and mottled like pepperoni. It was Frankenstein-esque. My face, if I didn't scratch, would heal. But the grafts, even healed, as Chip had so tactfully pointed out, would look like Silly Putty forever. I would forever be a person that other people tried not to stare at in the grocery store. I would forever be someone who made other people uncomfortable.

Now a new feeling cut through my haze: resentment.

I knew what it was like to hate parts of my own body—what woman doesn't? You "hate" that little bump of fat behind your knee, or that pointy little pinkie toe that doesn't match the others, or that one crooked tooth. Anything about you that insists on being flawed despite all your attempts to get yourself perfectly uncriticizable is fair game for hostility.

But this was different. Those grafts didn't even look human.

It was like some alien creature had laid itself down over my neck. Old dissatisfactions with my old self dissolved in the face of what it felt like to look at my shoulder. I'd "hated" my flabby parts before, and I'd thought things were "gross," but I didn't even know the meaning of those words until now. The sight of the grafts—puckered and gooey and shiny with Silvadene ointment—was so viscerally shocking, I felt a squeeze at the base of my throat like I might throw up.

I had to look away.

This was the feeling I'd been afraid of—but it was so much worse than I'd feared. It was like a part of the old me, sweet and vulnerable and shockingly innocent, had died. It's one thing to think about in a theoretical way—we know we won't last forever—but it's quite another thing to see it happen. Part of me had been *destroyed.* I squeezed my eyes closed and felt a wash of regret. Why hadn't I ever even appreciated that curve of my neck before, or the smoothness of its skin, or the pattern of its pale freckles? What had I been thinking that night, wearing a strapless dress? Why hadn't I been more careful? How could I have been the keeper of such a precious thing—my body!—and taken it so stupidly for granted?

"That could have been your *face,*" Kit said then, peeking at my shoulder through squinted eyes. "You're lucky."

Lucky again.

"That's what people keep telling me," I said.

WE DID NOT wind up watching *Grease* that night. The haircut and all that came after was more than enough for me. I did let Kitty set up my computer so I could check email—but then I shut it right back down again when I saw that Chip had posted a photo of me while I was still in the ICU, looking absolutely ghastly, to Facebook, of all places, asking for prayers.

"After a tragic accident," he wrote, "the love of my life is fighting for survival in the ICU."

"A tragic accident?" Kit demanded, when I showed it to her. "*He's* a tragic accident."

He'd posted the photo on his wall and tagged me. He'd also linked to a news clip and an article in the paper.

People were understandably alarmed. With every comment, Facebook sent me an email notification, so my inbox was flooded. People were "praying" and sending emoticons of hearts and kisses and angels. They made comments about how great I was and cheered me on. But the volume—there must have been a hundred—felt overwhelming to me.

I fixated on the photo itself, amazed that Chip had overshared so wildly by posting it. I didn't even want to see pictures of people's *pedicures* in my feed—much less bruised shots of tubes and vacuums and abject suffering. What had he been thinking? What was he trying to prove? In what universe would I want a picture of myself looking like a meatloaf posted for the world to see? I had barely summoned the courage to look in the mirror myself—and apparently, I was the last one to know. An ex-boyfriend had even left me a GIF of puppies and kittens licking each other.

This must have been how Neil Putnam at Simtex knew about my situation. The whole damn city seemed to know.

"I'm never going back to Facebook," I said.

"Of course not," Kit agreed. "Facebook's for grandmas. Just follow me on Instagram."

LATER, AFTER WE'D fallen quiet for a while, and Kit was already starting to make slow, snoozy sleeping breaths, I had to wake her up.

"Kit!" I whispered. Then, with no response, a little louder: "Kit!"

She startled and sat up.

"Great news!" I said, still whispering.

"What?"

"I have to poop."

She leaned a little forward. "That's great news?"

"Help me out of bed."

"Didn't you just go right before bed?"

I snapped my fingers at her, like, *Let's go.* "That was pee."

She got up and shuffled over.

"You know what this means, don't you?" I said, as we worked me across the board into the chair.

Kit only had one eye open. "What does this mean?"

"It means I can pee and poo on my own."

"Does it mean you're getting better?" she asked.

"Well, I'm not getting worse."

"Can I Instagram *this*?" she asked, as we positioned me onto the toilet.

"Say the word 'Instagram' one more time, and you're on the first flight back to Brooklyn."

"Noted," she said.

She waited outside the door for me a long while, Googling random trivia on her phone to pass the time. "Did you know that Ben Franklin invented the catheter in 1752 when his brother John suffered from bladder stones?"

"I can't say that I did."

"Did you know you can use urine to make gunpowder?"

"That might come in handy."

"Did you know that seventy-three percent of people with spinal cord injuries never void normally again?"

"Don't tell me that! That's depressing."

"Not for you."

"Where are you finding all this?"

"PeeTrivia.com."

I took my time. Kit hinted several times that she was ready to go back to bed, but I was not rushing this miracle for anything.

Eleven

AT LUNCH THE next day, we did not linger more than sixty seconds on the triumph of my newly returned toileting skills before my mother declared the topic "unappetizing" and got back to worrying about my relationship with Chip.

"Has he been to visit you?" she wanted to know.

My BLT suddenly lost its flavor. "Can we not talk about this?"

"I did some reading on the computer—" she said next.

I glanced at my dad. "Here we go," he said.

She continued, "—and I think maybe he's afraid of you."

"*Afraid* of me?"

"Of what you represent. Of how you've come to symbolize his weakness and foolishness."

"Have I?"

"Well, what other explanation can there be?"

"I can't psychoanalyze Chip right now." I had my hands full just making it through the day.

"Well, someone has to!"

"Looks like you're doing a pretty good job."

My mom set her sandwich down—a gesture that meant we were getting down to business. She started to speak, but then she caught herself, turned to my dad. "You know what, sweetheart? This sandwich is not very good."

My dad looked at the sandwich.

"I hate to ask, but would you mind going back and getting me a Caesar salad instead?"

My dad had just taken his first bite of his own sandwich. He looked back and forth between it and my mother for a second. "You want me to drive back to the sandwich shop?"

My mother nodded, then gestured at me with her head. "We could use a little just-us-girls time anyway."

My dad looked at me. Then he nodded and stood up with his sandwich in one hand and his keys in the other and left the room.

My mom leaned closer to me once the door closed, and kept her voice low. "I read an article last night called 'Sexual Functioning After a Spinal Cord Injury.'"

"Mom! Don't read that!"

"Because if Chip's enthusiasm is like his father's—or any man, really—that's going to be important to him."

I wrinkled my nose. "Please don't talk to me about Jim Dunbar's 'enthusiasm.'"

"I've been best friends with Evelyn for years, sweetheart. I know *everything*."

I was shaking my head. "Nope. Please. No."

"The great news is," she pushed on, "even though men in your situation often lose sexual abilities, women typically don't. Which means even if you don't walk again—which, of course, you will—you'll still be good to go in that arena."

Was it worse to talk about Chip's father's sexual functioning with my mom—or to talk about mine? Words cannot express how much I did not want to discuss "that arena." But she had momentum now.

She went on. "You can have babies and everything—typically. In fact, the only trouble most women in your situation have is finding somebody who's willing to—"

She stopped herself.

"Somebody who's willing to what?"

But she turned her attention back to her sandwich, wrapping it up like she might save it for later.

"Willing to *what*?"

She started again, more carefully. "Women's level of sexual activity does typically go down, but it's not that the injury prevents it. It's that nobody . . ."

She paused, like she couldn't say it.

"It's that nobody wants to fuck them anymore?"

She closed her eyes. "You know I hate that language."

If I could have walked out, I would have.

Instead, with no other option, I banged my head back against the pillow. "Is that the inspiring message you came with today?"

She did have enough self-awareness to be a tiny bit cowed. She folded her napkin and smoothed it on her leg. "I just read the article, and it seemed like information you should have."

"Why?" I asked. "What am I supposed to do with that? Root even harder for a miracle? Defy the laws of human physiology?"

"I'm trying to help," she insisted.

"By freaking me the hell out?"

"The point is," my mother said, "we have to be proactive. We have to face this thing head-on. All the healing and recovery you're going to do takes place in the first six to eight weeks after the accident—and you're already two weeks in."

"Are you saying I'm a slacker?"

"I'm saying you need to get your head in the game."

There was always a kind of backward logic to my mom's crazy. I got it now. She hadn't *accidentally* revealed to me that I was facing a possible lifetime of being unfuckable. She was doing it on purpose. She was attempting to motivate me. To get me focused. To rouse some unsinkable part of my soul that would stand up in outrage and simply refuse to give in.

The worst part was, it was working.

This was how she'd motivated me my whole life: fear of the worst-case scenario. She was trying to scare me into action. She was trying to generate a *Rocky* moment, trying to cue the music and shift me into a training montage.

Did I think that I could beat my spinal cord into submission? Of course not. Could sheer willpower overcome anything? Of course not. Was there a hazy line between determination and denial? Absolutely.

But what choice did I have? Sure, she was playing dirty. Sure, she was acting like a terrorist. But her heart was in the right place—and she wasn't wrong. I didn't want to spend the rest of my life in a wheelchair. I didn't want to give up everything I'd hoped for. I didn't want to lose Chip.

Wait—was that right? The old me didn't want to lose the old Chip. But now, thinking about it, I wasn't totally clear on how the current me felt about the current Chip. Of course, in the face of my mom's hyperbole, how I specifically felt about Chip was not exactly relevant. According to her, if I didn't pull it together I would lose all guys, period.

This was one of her signature moves. If a little teaspoonful of ice-cold terror could burn off the fog and inspire me to try, was that so bad?

My mother sensed me cratering from across the room. For a lady so tone-deaf to others' emotions, she could be remarkably astute. She put her half-eaten lunch back in its sack and came to stand by the bed and take my hand. "Sweetheart, I know you've had a shock."

I waited.

"We all have."

I waited again.

"Even Chip."

There it was.

"I'm worried about him. He seems to be—" She glanced up to find the word. "Faltering."

"Faltering how?" I asked.

"I think he's lost his way. His mother says he's been out drinking, coming in at all hours, not showering."

Chip always showered. He took three showers a day.

My mom squeezed my hand. "What the two of you had was special."

"I agree."

"Don't you want it back?"

"Have I lost it?"

"No," she said, so emphatically she almost sang it. "Of course not. But—has he been to visit you?"

"Some," I said. *Not really.*

"I'm just saying, it's time to get better and put things right."

Why was this all on my shoulders? Why wasn't it Chip's job to get better and start visiting me? "By 'get better,'" I asked, "do you mean 'walk again'?"

She pretended the idea had never occurred to her. "Well, wouldn't that be ideal? Isn't that worth a try?"

Worth a try? I felt like my eyeballs were going to start spinning. What did she think I was doing over here? Playing Xbox and drinking beer? I *was* trying. Every morning that I woke up and remembered the wreckage of my life, I was trying. Every breath I took, I was trying. Every second of being conscious all day long, I was trying.

I took a slow breath and held it. Then I said, "I'm just glad I can shit on the toilet."

My mother's eyes widened, but before she could respond, someone knocked on the door.

"Come in!" my mother and I both said at the same time, not dropping each other's gaze.

The door pushed open, and it was Kitty. Looking mad.

MY MOTHER HADN'T seen Kitty in three years. Hadn't seen the spiky-blond new hair, or the tattoos, or the piercings. I'm not even sure she recognized her at first.

But when she did, she went very still.

Kitty held her gaze and walked straight in, stopping on the other side of my bed. She was a little out of breath. From below, I watched them eyeing each other.

When my mom finally spoke, her voice was low. "I thought you only came here in the evenings."

"I wanted to see you," Kit said.

My mother lifted an eyebrow. "I can't imagine that's true."

"I have something to say."

"I think we've said it all."

"I haven't."

With that, Kitty raised my curiosity—but not my mother's.

"As you can see," my mother said, "I'm pretty busy right now."

"I want you to tell Margaret why I went away."

My mom looked at Kit dead-on. "No."

"She deserves to know."

"I disagree."

"She is angry at me for leaving. At *me*!"

"I can't tell her how to feel."

"But you can tell her why I had to go."

This was how they always were together—Kit pushing until my mother snapped. This time, it didn't take long. My mother leaned closer, her voice like a hiss. "Hasn't she been through enough?"

The tone right there would have shut me right up. But Kit was always the braver one. "I don't think it's her you're worried about. I think it's you."

"That's ridiculous," my mother said, looking away. In that moment, I knew that whatever it was they were talking about, Kit was right.

"Tell her," Kit pressed. "Tell her right now. This has gone on too long."

"I won't."

"Tell her—or I will."

My mother's eyes looked wild. She had not expected this moment to rise up so fast—out of nowhere, really, like a flash flood: Kit showing up and making these sudden demands. One minute, my mother was trying to manipulate me—solid, comfortable ground for her—and the next, Kitty was manipulating her. I could see my mom's mind spinning, trying to come up with a way to stop her.

Kit turned to me. "On the night I left, it was because Mom and I fought."

"Stop it," my mother said, her whole body tense.

"I remember," I said to Kit. "You pushed her into the pool."

"I pushed her into the pool because she wouldn't answer a question."

"Stop!" my mother said again, eyes on Kit. "What do I have to threaten you with? Never speaking to you again?"

"You already don't speak to me. I'm not sure you ever did."

But my mom was still searching. "Cutting you out of my will! Not giving you Grandma's ruby ring!"

"I don't need to be in your will," Kit said. "I don't need a ring. I need my only sister"—and here her voice rose to a shout—"to understand what the hell is going on here!"

My mother blinked.

Kit turned back to me. "Remember when I was working for that genealogist?"

I shook my head. "Vaguely."

"She had that business helping people find their ancestors and trace their family histories?"

I squinted. "Okay. Sort of." I did not see where this was going.

"She talked me into having my DNA analyzed. She had a bulk discount with a mail-in company. She was sending in several samples, and she had an extra kit, and so I just did it. On a whim."

I frowned. "I have no memory of that."

"I didn't tell you," Kit said. "I didn't tell anybody. Why would I? The results weren't going to be interesting."

True. We could recite our various heritages in that way that lots of Americans can. Our mom had a little bit of lots of places. Irish, English, German, Canadian, French, and even, rumor had it, some Huron. Our dad's family, in contrast, was all Norwegian. His Norwegian ancestors had immigrated to an all-Norwegian town in Minnesota where Norwegians just married other Norwegians for generations—until one day, my dad's dad moved their family to Texas and broke the trend.

"Huh," I said. "So you, like, sent in your blood?"

"Saliva, actually."

Then there was a pause.

Kit looked at my mother.

My mother looked at Kit.

"Did you learn anything?" I finally asked.

"Yes," Kit said.

My mother shook her head at Kit. "You don't have to do this."

"Yes, I do! Because you won't!"

My mother looked around the room, her eyes stretched and frantic in a way I'd never seen before—searching, it seemed, for some way to stop what was happening. But short of tackling Kit, there wasn't much my mom could do. "Whatever comes of this," my mom said to her then, "it's all on you."

"Oh," Kit said, narrowing her eyes, "I think it's at least a little bit on you."

Everything about my mother's expression and posture was pleading. She shook her head, like, *Don't.*

Kit tilted her head, like, *You leave me no choice.*

At that, my mom sucked in her breath and, without another word, walked out of the room, clacking her heels, and leaving her purse and her sandwich behind.

When she was gone, I looked at Kit. "Maybe you shouldn't tell me," I said. "Maybe we can agree that you had your reasons, and I'll just promise not to be mad anymore."

"You need to know."

I shook my head. "I'm not sure I do."

But she nodded. "It's time."

I sighed.

"When the results came back, they were surprising."

I could not even fathom how something as random as this could have driven such a rift between my mom and Kit. "Surprising how?"

"You know how proud Dad is of his Norwegian-ness?"

"Yes," I said. Anybody who'd known my dad five minutes knew that.

"Well," Kit said, taking a breath. "This lab breaks down the results by particular regions."

"Okay," I said.

Kit went on. "My results came back with everything you'd expect from Mom: England, Ireland, Western Europe—exactly what we already knew. But I also have Italy and Greece." She checked my expression.

I shrugged. "So?"

"Guess what I don't have? *Scandinavian.*"

I puffed out a little laugh at the idea: Kitty Jacobsen didn't have any Scandinavian.

But she just crossed her arms and waited for me to catch up. "I don't have *any* Scandinavian in my ethnic heritage."

Now I frowned. I shook my head. "That can't be right."

"Think about it," Kit said.

I couldn't think about it. My brain refused to think about it.

"If Dad is fully, or at least mostly, Norwegian," Kit said, "and I don't have *any* Norwegian in my genetic profile . . ." She waited.

I shook my head. "That's crazy. That's wrong."

Kit's eyes were very serious. "It's not wrong."

"They must have mixed up the samples!" I said.

"That's what I thought," Kit said. "So we sent another sample. Same results."

"This can't be right. This is insane."

"Next, I confronted Mom about it. At the Fourth of July party three years ago."

The conversation was starting to feel like a rickety old mine cart on a downhill track. "And what did Mom say?" I asked.

"What *didn't* she say? She told me I was crazy and wrong and spoiled and selfish. She told me to back off, and it was none of my business. She told me to drop the whole subject and throw the test results in the trash. She told me I'd ruined her life. Then she plastered a big, false, Stepford smile on her face and walked out to the backyard to continue hosting her pool party."

I blinked at Kit.

"And that was the moment when I knew for sure. Our dad is not my father."

Twelve

I RUBBED MY eyes. "That can't be right."

"I'm telling you," Kit said. "It is. The minute I knew, I *knew*."

She had a patient look, like she didn't really have to convince me. Like the facts would get me there, and all she had to do was wait.

"But!" I protested. This was impossible. "You have his same smile! And his same sense of humor! And you both love sailing! And *The Matrix*! And popcorn!" *Case closed!*

Kit gave me a look. "Everybody loves popcorn. That's not genetic."

"There has to be a mistake."

"Mom was livid that night. She denied everything, but she did it so viciously, I knew I was right. I, of course, drank the entire margarita machine after that, because that's what I used to do back then, and then I pushed her into the pool—not my finest moment. When she climbed out, sopping wet, I followed her and got in her face until she finally told me the truth."

I waited a long time before I said, "What was the truth?"

Kit looked right into my eyes. "I was a mistake."

I did not look away.

She went on, "I was an 'unfortunate accident.' With someone who was not Dad."

All the air leaked out of my lungs. I felt like a punctured tire.

When my chest started to sting, I sucked in a big breath. "Does Dad know?"

Kit shook her head.

I tried to put the pieces together. Our mom knew, of course. Kit knew, and had for three years. Now I knew. Everybody except our dad.

A long silence. Then at last I said, "That's why you left."

Kit nodded. "I told her she had to choose. Either she told the truth, or I was gone."

"That's a tough choice," I said.

Kit's eyes snapped to mine. "Are you taking her side?"

"I'm just saying that's tough."

"Not for Linda," Kit said. "She kicked me out in five seconds flat." For just a second, I saw Kit's expression sag—before she raised her shoulders, stood up a little taller, and said, "Whatever."

"Just think," I said. "She carried that secret all those years."

Kit nodded.

"It must have terrified her to be confronted with it."

"That's why she wanted me gone," Kit said. "I'm the evidence."

"Who was the guy?" I asked.

Kit shook her head. "She wouldn't say."

"Are you going to tell Dad?"

"Never!"

"But you told me."

"I told you because I needed you to understand."

It was a lot to process. My head was swirling. "Why did you wait so long?"

Kit sighed. "I kept thinking she'd tell you, but she didn't. I kept thinking she'd reach out and apologize to me, but she didn't. At first, I had bigger fish to fry. I had to get through rehab and that whole first year of being sober. Then I was getting the Beauty Parlor going, and the time kind of flew. But the truth is, I was really, really, really angry. I thought I would never want to see any of you again."

"But I didn't do anything!"

"No," Kit said. "But you got to be Dad's real daughter—and I didn't. I know this sounds crazy, but it felt like you'd stolen him from me."

"But I *didn't*!"

"My brain knew that," Kit said. "But my heart was a different story."

I tried to put myself in Kit's shoes. "You were just mad at everybody."

"Every*body*. Every*thing*. It stirred up a lot for me. Mainly about how I always thought she loved you better. Turns out, I was right."

"She does *not* love me better," I said, but now I wondered—and not, actually, for the first time.

Kit shrugged. "It's okay. It's hopeless with her. But I didn't want to lose you, too."

"So the crash made you miss me?"

"The crash made me want to stop wasting time."

"So you came home to see me."

"But then I just couldn't explain. It didn't feel like my secret to share. I wanted to give her a chance to say something, at least."

"Why today?" I asked. It was a fair question. She'd been here two weeks. Why come storming in now?

"I ran into Piper McAllen at Starbucks this morning. Do you remember her?"

I shook my head.

Kit shrugged. "A mean girl from my grade, now a show-offy mother of two. She told me everybody says I went crazy and was put into a home. She said that to my face! In *Starbucks*! Apparently, the whole world just thinks I lost my marbles. And that was it for me. I was like, *We're done here*. Time to set the record straight. I left my latte on the counter and stormed over."

I was about to suggest maybe Kit should go find our mom—she'd left her purse here, after all, and wouldn't get too far without it—when there was a knock at the door. When it pushed open, it was our dad.

In the instant I saw him I felt a rush of sympathy. He was my mother's high school sweetheart. They got married the summer after they graduated, and Kit was born a few months later. My dad had been all set to go to college in California, but he joined the marines instead. Of course, my mom gave up college altogether.

Neither of them had gotten quite what they'd hoped for.

These were facts I'd known for a long time, but they were only part of the story. What would my dad think now, if he knew everything? Would it change how he felt about his family? About Kit? About my mom? Would he leave if he knew? I couldn't imagine our family without him. He was the best thing about it.

Right then, I made a mental vow I would never tell him.

"Hey, girls," my dad said then, as he stepped into the room. "Look what I found!"

Out from behind him, of all people, stepped Chip.

CHIP LOOKED LIKE hell, just like my mother had threatened.

Even so, just seeing that face of his gave me jolt of pleasure. It was like some kind of Pavlovian response. See Chip; feel a thrill. Whether I wanted to or not. Whether he looked like hell or not. Whether he deserved it or not. It was quite a realization, and it reminded me of what Kit had just said. My brain knew one thing, but my heart was a different story.

Plus, my mother had spent our lunch hour scaring the hell out of me.

Chip hesitated in the doorway, sensing they had interrupted something.

He looked like he'd slept in his clothes. He hadn't shaved. He was holding a manila bubble envelope in one hand. He gave Kit a little wave, but then got down to business.

He walked a little closer to the bed, his eyes on me, and we all watched him.

"I just got this package from the FAA." He held it up. "They've closed their investigation of the crash. 'Pilot error.'" He put his head down and gave a breathy laugh. "We could've told 'em that."

"I thought it was a 'senseless tragedy,'" I said, and Chip blinked at me.

"What's in the bag, son?" my dad asked then.

Chip looked down at it. Back on track. "They're scrapping the wreckage, and I'll pay for the plane out of pocket. But they found this."

He pulled his grandmother's engagement ring out of the envelope and held it out for us to see. It was, to put it gently, a little charred.

"They found it," I said.

"They knew our story from the interview, so they knew what it was."

I didn't know what to say. It was so strange to see Chip at all—especially like this. He had always, always been perfectly put together, and in control, and groomed like a male model. This disheveled guy was like his antimatter.

As soon as I thought that, I wondered if he thought the same thing about me. Now that I was unfuckable—according to my mom.

"Hey," he said then. "You got a haircut."

I touched the spiky back. "Yeah."

Chip shrugged. "Don't worry. It'll grow back."

"Chip," I said then. "What are you doing here?"

He shrugged. "Bringing you your ring."

I watched in shock as he bent down on one knee, losing his balance for a second before getting situated, and then lifted the ring up to me like a kid playing King Arthur.

"Margaret—" he began in a thespian-like voice, but then interrupted himself: "Oh, shit! What's your middle name?"

"Rosemary," my dad offered from the wings.

Chip began again. "Margaret Rosemary Jacobsen, we've had a rough month. I have let you down in more ways than I can count. But I think this ring can be a symbol of a new beginning for us. I vow to be a better man. I know I can be a better man. So now I ask you, in front of your dad and your crazy sister, despite everything we've been through—will you marry me?"

I knew my line. But I didn't say it.

I took in the sight of this very different Chip for a good while. True, my mom had succeeded in stoking some of my insecurities and semi-convinced me that I might never get a better offer than this one, right here, from a disappointing, wrinkled, slightly soused version of the man of my dreams. If my mom were here, she'd be hissing at me to say yes and just lock it down right now before he sobered up.

But I couldn't.

Did I want to marry him?

I'd wanted to marry him for years—so long, I almost didn't know how to *not* want to. Part of me still did, as bad as ever—maybe worse. But another part was having massive second thoughts.

He was looking at me. Waiting. *Well?*

The answer could have been easy. But easy didn't exist anymore. If it ever had. "I don't think so, Chip."

His Shakespearean expression fell away, and he stood up. "No?"

"You said yourself it's been a rough month."

"I'm trying to make it better."

"I get that, but I'm not sure this is the way."

Chip's face crumpled. There was no other word for it. "I'm so indescribably sorry about that night. I never meant for this to happen. I would give anything—anything—to change places with you."

"This isn't about the accident," I said.

"What is it about?"

"How many times have you been to visit me here?" I asked. I genuinely didn't know.

He looked fuzzy, too. "I'm not sure."

"Three," my dad offered, "if you count right now."

I looked at Chip. "Three times in two weeks. Do you think that's enough?"

"It's just—" Chip's voice caught. "It's that every time I see you—all burned and messed up—I feel so guilty, knowing it was all because of me, knowing that I ruined your life. It's like I'm suffocating."

Really? I thought.

"Okay," I said. "One: The jury is still out on whether or not my life is ruined. And two: Fuck you. You should have come anyway. I don't care if you feel guilty. You should have been here every minute of every day. You should have been sleeping here and waking up here and buying me stuffed animals in the gift shop and bringing me Chinese takeout. *Kitty* has been a better friend to me in here than you have."

Kitty shot a glance over at my dad.

Chip looked down. "I'm sorry."

"So you can see why the idea of marrying you, the idea of 'in sickness and in health,' doesn't make a lot of sense to me right now."

Chip looked down and nodded.

"It's not the accident," I said. "It's everything since the accident."

"But it's not off?" he asked then, looking up. "The engagement's not *off*?"

"Well, it's not frigging *on*."

"Can it just be, like, *on hold*, then?"

I felt all six eyes in the room on me. I wanted to punish him. I wanted to tell him it was off—one hundred percent. I wanted to make it clear, to everybody, that insult to injury would not be tolerated.

Instead, I sighed. "It can be on hold."

Chip broke into a smile. "That's something. I can work with that."

He did not deserve to be smiling right now. But I couldn't have said no, and we both knew it. I wasn't ready to give up on Chip. He'd just failed a test of love, yes. But I couldn't—wouldn't—decide it was the only test that would ever matter.

"And will you wear the ring?" Chip pushed.

Did I want to wear that charred, bent ring? Not really. It was a bit too close to forgiveness. But I let him slide it on my finger anyway. I was too tired to be strong about this. And, more than that: Letting go of my past and my future at the same time felt like more than I could bear.

As he nudged the ring into place on my finger, Chip gave a relieved burst of laughing and crying at the same time, and at this range I got a sour whiff of alcohol. "It's a little bent," he said.

"It fits better now, though."

"Can I kiss you?" Chip asked.

I nodded, but I couldn't meet his eyes. I felt, more than saw, him lean in. I held still and braced for impact. When his lips touched mine, I tried like hell to feel something. And I did, in a way, but it was not something any kiss had ever made me feel before. It felt like a reminder of exactly how life used to be—followed by an ache of sorrow that it might be gone for good.

Thirteen

AT THE KISS, Kitty and my dad took off, assuming, as you might, that Chip and I wanted to be alone.

In truth, what I really wanted was time to talk to Kitty. And to give my dad a little hug for wounds he didn't even know he had. And to figure out where the heck my mom had disappeared to.

But Chip did not remove his face from mine for a good while.

Something about him kissing me made the burns on my face itch. I tucked my hands under my blankets to remind myself not to scratch.

While I was waiting for him to finish, Ian walked in.

"Smooching hour is over, folks," Ian said.

Chip pulled away, and we both turned toward Ian.

Ian always looked annoyed, but now he looked extra annoyed. "Time for your therapy, Maggie Jacobsen. Maybe your man can help with your transfer while I grab a coffee."

I shook my head, like, *Definitely not*. "He hasn't had any practice."

Ian raised his eyebrows. "Well, there's nothing to it."

Chip turned to me. "What did he say?"

"He's Scottish," I said. "He wants you to help me transfer to my chair. He says there's nothing to it."

Chip frowned, like this was another test he was bound to fail. "Maybe you could show me," he said to Ian.

Ian frowned. "You want me to show you?"

Chip nodded, and, as ever, I read his face so well. He thought getting a lesson would get him out of having to do it himself.

Ian shrugged. "It's not rocket science, man, but if you want a lesson, let's go. For Maggie's sake, if nothing else."

Chip looked at me. "Did he just call you Maggie?"

I shrugged. "He can't pronounce Margaret." I turned back to Ian. "I don't need help."

Ian shook his head. "You do."

"That's not what you said before."

"Before, I was teaching you a lesson."

"What?" I said. "That you're kind of an asshole?"

Ian blinked, and I could not read his expression. "A lesson that you *can* do it yourself," he said. He looked over at Chip. "But that doesn't mean you should have to."

Chip looked at me. "I can't understand him at all. It's like a speech impediment."

Ian didn't take his eyes off me. "Watch yourself, little man."

There was a knock at the door, and then my dad's voice. "Is everybody done kissing?"

"Yes," Chip and I called flatly, at the same time.

My dad stepped in—with my mom trailing behind him, looking dazed. "Look who I found! At the candy machine!"

"Where's Kit?" I asked.

"She had to go," my dad said. Then, in a stage whisper, "She's got a date with Fat Benjamin."

My mother, a few feet behind my dad, held an unopened Hershey bar and looked shaken and pale. I made a stab at mental telepathy, trying to promise *I'll never tell him* from my brain to hers. But I don't think it worked.

My dad was as jolly and unaware as could be, and that just made it sadder all around. He put his arm around my mom and gave her a little squeeze. Then he said to Ian, "I'd like to see how to do a transfer, too."

"You heard that conversation?" I asked.

"Sure," my dad said. "You can hear everything out in the hallway. That's how we knew you and Loverboy were done making out."

"Then why did you ask?"

He lifted his eyebrows like, *Duh*. "To embarrass you."

Ian coughed. Then he reached behind me to grab the transfer board and lower the bed.

I regarded Chip for a second. Seeing him next to Ian, he suddenly did look like a *little man*. I'd always thought of him as "trim" or "sporty," but standing next to Ian gave him a slightly shrimpy vibe.

"The trick to the transfer," Ian told us all then, "is letting Maggie do as much for herself as she can. But stay close by. There's a temptation," he added, "when someone you love is struggling, to want to help too much. Keep in mind that the struggle makes her stronger."

I gave Ian a look. I might be in danger of many things, but "getting too much help" was not one of them.

Ian wasn't looking at me. He was looking right at Chip. "The most important thing," he said, "is being there."

When he'd finished staring Chip down, he patted the board and crooked his finger at me, like, *Come here.*

I pulled back my covers, and then we all beheld—because I was wearing a gown for the whole using-the-potty project—my bare legs.

Chip had seen those legs a thousand times, and caressed them, and kissed them—even shaved them once, in an exercise in erotic suspense that worked much better in theory than in practice. But these weren't the legs that he knew. They'd atrophied so much even in the short time I'd been here, they were like a newborn calf's legs—spindly and soft and splayed.

The sight of them made me feel deeply ashamed. I hated them. I wanted to beat them with my fists. I wanted to pummel them into bloody bruises on the mattress.

Ian was unfazed. "You're going to need some pants for the therapy gym, lass."

I pointed my mother toward the cabinet, and she found a pair in a gym bag, along with my last clean bra—hot pink with tiger stripes. She also grabbed one of the several T-shirts we'd cut at the shoulder.

Ian gently helped me into the sweatpants, edging them up, and when it was time to pull them under my butt and around my hips, he leaned down so I could circle my arms around his neck. I pulled up just enough that I inhaled the most delicious scent of him. Kind of gingery. Sweet, cookie-ish spices mixed with a microscopic hint of salty manliness.

I can't even put it into words, but you know when they bring the dessert tray around at a restaurant and you immediately just know what you want—like, *That one. Right there!* I had that reaction to the smell of him. That one.

But we were on to the dressing-the-top-half phase, and so my mother asked the men to leave the room.

"Even me?" Chip asked.

"Especially you," I said.

Minutes later, when the men got the all-clear, I was all decked out in my *Flashdance* look with the bra strap on the burned side tucked down under my armpit. On a normal person, this outfit might have been provocative. On me, it was just sad. My mother promised to bring me something normal tomorrow.

Ian began his lesson, but I didn't even listen. I was too busy trying to catch another whiff of him.

LATER, IN THE gym, on the mat, as Ian worked my legs, I said, "I'm sorry I called you an asshole."

Ian didn't meet my eyes. "You called me 'kind of an asshole.' That's different."

"Not really."

With a normal person, that might have been the start of some kind of conversation, but Ian just let it die. As we continued to work, first on one side, then on the other, then doing some actual sit-ups, I watched the other therapists talking to, encouraging, and playing around with their patients, and I couldn't help it: I felt a little shortchanged.

Every attempt at talking fizzled out like a spark going dark.

"Are you married?" I tried.

"No."

I waited for more.

Nothing.

Uncomfortable pause.

Me again: "Any kids?"

His jaw went tight. "No."

Pause.

Me: "Hobbies? Things you do for fun?"

Another pause so long I thought he wasn't going to even answer at all. About as conversationally agonizing as I could imagine. Finally: "Triathlons."

"You do triathlons. For fun."

"For a challenge."

"Is there anything you do for fun?"

"Challenges *are* fun."

I'd say, on the whole, he seemed about as excited to talk to me as he'd been to talk to Myles. But, dammit, I wasn't Myles. I wasn't taunting him like that. Or provoking him. Or out to get him.

But maybe I was, in a way.

I didn't realize it at the time, but the fact that Ian was so reticent might have been good for me. With some people—not all, but some—when they run away, it makes you want to chase them. That was Ian: so withdrawn, it coaxed me out.

I tried again. "Thanks for the transfer lesson, by the way."

Nothing.

"My family's all a little freaked out right now," I attempted.

Not even a nod for that one. He was working my ankles and just kept his head down.

Finally, I tried this: "Did you know you can drink your own pee?"

His head popped up, and he was all surprise, and he flashed a shocked smile for half a second before dropping his head back down. "I didn't know that, no," he said, getting back to work.

But now I knew that smile existed. I wanted another one.

"Some tweed coats are dyed with it."

Nothing.

"Romans used to brush their teeth with it to whiten them."

When that didn't get a response, I peeked around at the side of his face to see if he was stifling a smile. He was.

He was hooking giant rubber bands around my ankles now, for resistance. Then he rolled me over onto my stomach and told me pull against them until I could touch my heels to my butt. Apparently, it would strengthen my hamstrings, which were still working.

"You want me to touch my heels to my butt?"

"Just try."

"Do I have to actually touch?"

"No."

"Are you saying trying is more important than succeeding?"

"Always."

Another long silence while I tried, and failed, to touch my butt with my feet.

"Not a big talker, are you?" I said.

"Not when I'm working."

"Other people seem to be able to do both."

"I'm not other people."

"Apparently not."

"We're here to get you stronger. Not joke around."

Just then, a group of other PTs burst out laughing at something one of the patients had said.

I met his eyes. "Okay."

But I couldn't leave it alone. I have never, ever, been comfortable with silence. I can't get a massage, or a manicure, or even a pelvic without making constant chitchat the entire time. I cannot be in the presence of another human being, especially one I don't know very well, and not talk—whether they want to or not. I surveyed the other PTs, chatting away so solicitously with their patients. If I'd had one of them, I might've stayed more passive and let the conversation come and go—but being stuck with the king of quiet stirred up all the compulsive-need-to-talk chemicals in my body, and I just started yammering on like a nut-job.

Anything, I had apparently decided, was better than nothing.

Hence this monologue, delivered on my back, to the ceiling, as Ian made me push against various objects with my legs:

"Did you know I got engaged on the same day this injury happened? You probably do. Everybody seems to. The nurses keep talking about it. I hear them in the hallway. They feel very sorry for me. They can't imagine what it must be like to be me. Which is funny, because I can't either. The best day of your life and the worst day are the same day. How does that bode for a marriage? If it even happens. If your once-charming prince doesn't turn into a seedy alcoholic and die in some gutter somewhere. And now I'm wearing this ring—and I don't even want to. Or maybe I do. I don't know who I am. I used to be a runner. I ran three different marathons. I didn't place or anything, but I knew how to push myself, and I knew how to be dedicated. When things got tough, I went for a run. I ran in the rain. I ran at night sometimes—or at four in the morning. What am I going to do now? Go for *a roll*? I can't move. I can barely breathe. But then I think, who am I to complain? There are girls who've been sold into slavery. There are children being beaten. Half the world is worse off than me—probably more. Half the time I feel petulant and whiny, and the other half, I think I've suffered something beyond human imagining. And I can't find an in-between. All I know is that my life as I knew it is gone. Nothing is the same. Food doesn't even taste the same. Voices don't sound the same. Things I used to love, I hate. Things I used to hate, I hate. I don't want to see anyone, I don't want to talk to anyone. My cell phone has like fifty messages. I hate myself, and I hate everybody else. I think about dying. It seems like it would be easier. But then I don't want to die. I just don't want to live either. My mom says the only way I can get better is to believe I will get better—to be such a determined maniac that even the laws of nature can't stop me—but then I look at these noodles I have for legs and I can't believe it. It's like asking me to believe the sky is green. The sky is just not green—you know?—and I can't pretend that it is. All I know is, I don't feel anything at all—not even hope."

Somewhere in my soliloquy, I'd closed my eyes. By the time I ran out of words and fell quiet, I noticed Ian had set my legs down and was no longer touching me. Had he walked away? Gone for a coffee? Left for the day? I knew he wasn't listening, but something about the idea that he wasn't even there stung a little bit.

I opened my eyes, and that's when I saw that he'd stood up and was leaning in to take my hands. "Sit up," he said, not looking at me, in a way that gave the distinct impression I was just another annoying obligation in his day.

I took his hands, but he did not pull me up. He just held them while I worked my way to a sitting position.

Once I was steady, he let go.

Then he bent down in front of me and met my eyes for the first time all day. He looked straight into my pupils until he had my full attention. Then he said, "Whether you walk again or not, I'm going to tell you the one thing I know for certain."

I blinked. "What's that?"

He took a deep breath. "It's the *trying* that heals you. That's all you have to do. Just try."

And he did not say another word for the rest of the day.

Fourteen

LATER, I FELT embarrassed about it.

I had *assaulted* him with my talking. He clearly didn't like to talk, and he certainly hadn't asked to be subjected to my whole pathetic story. He was utterly robotic that whole time, and afterward, he was even more determined to stay poker-faced.

That said, "It's the trying that heals you" really stuck in my head.

The next morning, for whatever reason, I woke up ready to try.

That day, after all the morning routines, I spent the "rest hour"—that I'd been using to stare into space—researching spinal cord injuries. My mother wasn't the only person in the world who could read articles. I started at Christopher Reeve's foundation and worked my way down, reading about expectations, therapies, strategies, equipment, clothing, and experimental theories. I learned terms like "axonal sprouting" and "neurogenesis," and I memorized the names and numbers of all the vertebrae. I studied anatomic charts of the spine and the body. I did Google searches for the phrases "spinal cord injury" and "miraculous recovery," and then I read every article my mother had found and then some. I made a choice to get inspired. I made lists of reasons to feel hopeful. I forced myself to look at the sky and see green.

During those moments, whether they were in the late afternoon when my muscles were twitching from everything Ian had forced me to do, or in the wee hours of the night when I'd woken and couldn't get back to sleep, I felt the tiniest bit like myself again. Because this was how I had conquered every challenge in my life—with impeccable organization and driven focus. I got Kit to buy me index cards and file folders and a new pack of ballpoint pens. I had my dad set up a printer, and I started printing out articles, organizing them into different folders, and color-coding them with highlighters.

My mother had made a good point: There wasn't time to grieve. Everything I read confirmed what she'd said. There was a window of opportunity for recovery, and after that, it would be foolish to hope for more. I'd wasted two of my weeks in a stupor, and insurance would sponsor exactly four and a half more. So I had a month. A month to try every single possible thing I could think of to get my life back.

I read an article that said to talk to your body and tell it what you wanted, so I did. Another said to massage your limbs to wake up the nerve responses, so I did. One article said to make a list of tangible goals, and to check them off as you met them, so I did that, too.

- wiggle toes
- point toes
- flex toes
- rotate feet 360 degrees at ankles
- strengthen calves and arches
- strengthen core
- extend legs from knee out
- take a step
- stand for 5 minutes alone
- walk again—like a boss!

Of all the things on that list, I could sort of do exactly one: I could stand with my knees locked for two minutes—but only if I had a bar, or a person, to hold on to. Still, being able to lock my knees was huge. Lots of people couldn't do that.

But of all the advice I found, and all the mental tricks I tried, my favorite was the article that told me to visualize my ultimate goal over and over. Want to know my ultimate goal? To wheel myself out of the hospital to go home for good on a breezy spring day and run into Chip.

In the visualization, I'm wearing my favorite jeans and a gray-blue collared shirt that covers all my scars, and he's headed in to pick me up—but he stops still when he sees me because I look so much better than he'd expected. Out of the sickening hospital lights and away from the mauve décor, with the sunlight on my skin for the first time in far too long, I have a new radiance. He sees me now, suddenly, not as an invalid that we all feel so sorry for, but as the real me. In that second, as he's struck by the sight, I push myself up and stand—then I take one step toward him, and then another, and he's so astonished, he can barely breathe.

That's it. That's the grand finale. I'm the old me again, but so much better. Because now I've astonished us all. Now I've done the impossible. Now I've returned from hell—wiser and stronger and grateful as shit for all my ordinary blessings.

Chip feels a surge of awe for me, followed quickly by desperate love—and here's the best part: In the fantasy, identifying with Chip, I get to feel those things, too. Which is such a profound relief, because all I can feel for this mangled, malfunctioning body of mine these days is contempt. Wait—no: "Contempt" is too simple. It's more than that. It's disappointment. It's disgust. It's *loathing.*

But in the visualization? All that's gone. All viciousness is replaced with admiration. I can see it on his face so clearly that I can feel it, too, and it's bliss. It hooks me and makes it irresistibly fun to return to the moment again and again. Chip is amazed at my strength and determination and power. And then I arrive at his arms, and he kisses me, and

I've aced another challenge. Even my hair is restored to just the way it was before—only better—because *why not*.

This wasn't self-indulgence, the article assured me. This was therapy. I had to see what I wanted. I had to *want* what I wanted. I had to create a vision to move toward. The more time I could spend making that vision real in my head, the stronger its pull would be. So I let myself long for my old life to the point of aching, on the theory that the more I longed for it, the more strength I would conjure to go after it.

Was centering my image around Chip a little bit antifeminist?

Maybe.

You could argue it either way. You could read it as a rescued-by-the-prince fantasy, I suppose—though, in truth, Chip didn't rescue me. He didn't do anything but behold my awesomeness. I did it all myself. Would my women's studies professor from college point out, though, that my accomplishment wasn't significant or meaningful or emotionally resonant until it was appreciated by a man? Sure. Okay. That's fair. Maybe that was something to work on someday in therapy. But I had four and a half weeks left, and that visualization was addictively powerful. I'd take any power I could get.

Getting focused made me feel in control. It cleared my head. It's possible the worst thing about those first two weeks in the hospital was being so directionless, so passive, so lost.

THEN, ONE NIGHT, Kit came in with a stack of articles on the health benefits of singing and slapped them down on the rolling tray.

"I spent the day online," she said, "researching why you should sing."

I eyed her stack. "I'm not going to sing, Kit."

She lifted up the top third of them. "These detail the emotional benefits of singing."

"Not interested."

She lifted up the second third of them. "These are the social benefits."

I shook my head. "Don't care."

"And these"—she held the final third up like the Statue of Liberty—"are the physical benefits."

I sighed.

Kit started counting off on her fingers. "Singing helps release oxytocin and dopamine and endorphins. It decreases anxiety and depression. It reduces stress and helps regulate the endocrine system. It creates better oxygenation in the blood and leads to better sleep. It increases antibodies and strengthens the immune system. And—" She stepped closer for her grand finale.

"Do not say it makes you happy—"

"It makes you happy."

I dropped my head back against the pillow. "I don't want to be happy."

"Fine. Don't be happy. But sing anyway. Because it's good for your health in just about every possible way."

"Does it reduce inflammation in the spinal cord?"

"There's no study showing it doesn't."

I had to hand it to her. She was ready for me. That girl was going to get me singing or die trying. She described study after study. She told inspirational stories. She barraged me with statistics and inspiration. A study in Denmark—or was it Holland?—had tracked three hundred cancer patients, half of whom joined choirs and sang at least three times a week, and half of whom, the control group, did not. The singers were more likely to go into remission, and stay there—and the singers increased their life expectancy by six months over the nonsingers.

When I started to protest, she said, "I know, I know. You don't feel like singing. Well guess what? You seem to believe that you can only sing if you're *already* happy. But I believe that singing *makes* you happy, and science appears to be backing me up. Plus, an endorphin or two wouldn't kill you."

"Look, I just don't think I can be happy anymore."

"Well, I think you can."

"Why do you keep pushing this?"

"Because you love to sing."

I *used to* love to sing. "I love to sing exactly as much as everybody else."

"False. That's Mom talking."

I squinted at her like she was nuts. "Mom doesn't talk about singing."

"That's right. Or encourage it or value it. Or recognize your talent."

"I am not a talented singer. I'm just a normal person."

Kit nodded, and added, "With perfect pitch."

"I don't have perfect pitch."

"You can harmonize to *anything*. Anything at all! Do you think everybody can do that?"

I shrugged.

"No. *Nobody* can do that."

"Big deal."

"It is a big deal. You never should have left it behind. Now, are you going to start singing, or should I?"

But she didn't even wait for an answer. She just moved fast, so I couldn't shut her down, and then when she finally ran out of ammunition, without even pausing, she tapped her phone, where she had "Let It Be" already cued up, and hit PLAY.

She knew I couldn't resist that song.

She started singing along while I watched her, with my mouth clamped closed and my arms crossed over my chest. Then she started deliberately getting the words wrong, singing things like "And when the broke and hardened people . . ."

"Broken-hearted people!" I couldn't help but correct.

She went on, "For though they may be partying—"

"Parted!" I shouted. "They're not *partying*. This is *not* a song about partying."

But she was having fun now. She mutilated the whole rest of the song, changing "whisper" to "whistle," "cloudy" to "crowded," and "light" to "blight," while I shouted out protest after protest. Finally, we neared the end.

"You know I've got it on repeat, right?"

And so, when it started up again, those deep and soulful piano chords we remembered from my dad's old records, I leaned my head back against the pillow, fixed my gaze on the ceiling, and let myself give in. I did love that song. It was the comfort food of Beatles tunes. Would it really kill me, I decided, to take a little bite?

"Fine," I said, "but sing it right this time."

"You're the boss."

So we did.

And, yes, I harmonized a little bit.

Did it make me happy? It didn't make me miserable, I'll give it that.

When the song ended, we sang it again.

Fifteen

AFTER THAT, WE fell into a schedule.

My official first order of business every morning was to try to wiggle my toes—which I never could. After that, it was: sponge bath, bandage changing, Silvadene application, and OT with Priya, who was very pleased with my progress in the areas of chair transfer, tooth-brushing, toileting, putting on sneakers and tying them, putting on and taking off socks, and wriggling into yoga pants. I was progressing well in the wheelchair obstacle course next door to the therapy gym. I could navigate both tight turns and cobblestones without tipping, and Priya was starting to eyeball the final frontier—curbs and steps. Next, she wanted to take me to the OT kitchen so we could bake a batch of cookies for practice.

Also, she insisted that I take up knitting.

"Knitting?" I asked.

"It's good to have a hobby," she said.

"Can I pick my own hobby?"

She shook her head. "Nope."

Midday was always lunch with my parents, who nodded with bright, optimistic faces as I recounted inspirational stories I'd found online about people like me.

And then followed PT with Ian, who continued to bring his not-talking-at-all A-game. We worked our way through the therapy gym, using the bike and mat almost every day, and rotating through other things like the parallel bars and the monkey rings. He even put me on the standing frame a couple of times, which meant getting buckled into a body harness and hanging from a metal frame above a treadmill. I would bring my thighs forward, and Ian would help position my feet and move them through the motions of walking.

The idea was that the spinal cord, and even the muscles themselves, had their own sense of memory. Walking, in theory, was such a fundamental human activity that it might not need the brain to direct it. So, like a reflex, the neurological signals for walking could reroute themselves and leave out the brain altogether, if they just had enough inspiration.

There was improvement, for sure. My knee joint was significantly stronger, and I could lock it now. My whole upper body was stronger now, in fact, and muscle mass I'd lost was coming back.

But the truth is, though everything above the knee was making progress, everything below was not.

Even with all my reading, and charts, and highlighting, and goals. Even with dreams almost every night of walking through the woods, or along the beach, or even just across an empty parking lot—dreams so convincing that I sometimes wondered if my dreaming life was actually my real one and vice versa, improvements were slim.

Below the knee, at least.

One day I thought I wiggled a toe, but nobody else could see it. Another day, on the bike, I felt like I'd pushed off with the ball of my foot, but when I tried to repeat it, it just dragged.

My mother brought in some literature that said plateaus were normal as the body adjusted to previous improvements—and so "plateaus are normal" became my internal mantra.

Ian became quite the subject of discussion during my evenings with Kitty. She always wanted the Grouch Report, and I was under strict instructions to chronicle all hidden smiles, uttered words, and human moments. We spent so many hours trying to psychoanalyze Ian that we finally came up with a broader theory that we must somehow be doing deep psychological work. Maybe, we decided, women talked about men as a coping mechanism. A distraction from the real troubles in their lives.

No doubt, it was more fun to fret over Ian than to fret over myself.

Maybe we should have wanted to talk about Chip instead. But there wasn't much about him that appealed to me right then.

Despite promises to the contrary, since his re-proposal, he'd managed only three short visits in three long days, standing the entire time for them, as if waiting to be dismissed. His timing was uncanny for the worst possible moments: just as an orderly was arriving for my sponge bath, or as Priya was forcing me to practice taking my sweatpants on and off, or as I was wheeling toward the bathroom. He'd stay for an obligatory thirty minutes or so, checking his texts over and over, and then give me a stiff kiss and head out. I half-waited to see him all day, kept my peripheral vision on the door in hopes he'd show up, but then, when he did come, I found myself wishing almost as fast that he'd leave.

I was muddled, to say the least.

Ian was a much juicier topic. He was almost a mysterious fictional character. Chip and his shortcomings were all too real.

After much discussion, Kitty developed a detailed theory about Ian, that there was a fun person trapped inside him, clawing against his ribs to get out. She labeled it her Beauty and the Beast theory and insisted that something terrible had happened to him in the past. But I disagreed. My theory was that he'd been left unattended too long as a baby in some remote Scottish orphanage and had missed a critical window for developing social skills and human empathy.

"Is he an orphan?" Kitty asked.

I shrugged. "No idea."

Whatever Ian's deal was, as strange as it sounds, he turned out to be good for me.

I really didn't talk much during the rest of the day or with many of the other hospital personnel, but when Ian showed up, I unleashed every thought, theory, observation, dream, or opinion I'd held in since the day before. Partly this was my fear of conversational silence, but partly, I came to notice more and more, it was just fun to mess with him. It was like trying to provoke a guard at Buckingham Palace. The fact that Ian didn't respond made me want to make him. I tried shock. I tried surprise. I tried every joke I knew. His blank face became more and more irresistible. He didn't react, but he listened, and as the days went on, I found myself Googling crazy things in anticipation of seeing him, just so I'd have good material.

"Did you know," I'd say, "that octopuses have three hearts?" And when that got no response, I'd move on to "Did you know there's an underwater postal box in Japan?" And when that got silence, I'd plunge ahead with "Did you hear about the guy who had to be fed intravenously for a year, and he lost all of his taste buds after going so long without using them? They disappeared. His tongue just got all smooth, like a porpoise."

It was the only time all day when I felt anything like my old self. It was the only time when the fog lifted. The game of it was so engaging that I'd forget myself—to the extent anyone ever could when trying, and failing, to walk the parallel bars from one end to the other.

It should have been my worst time of day, as I fell short on challenge after challenge. But somehow it was my best.

That same week, I got my bandages off the donor sites under my collarbones, and now I had two meaty red scabs like fat strips of bacon adding to the horror show that was my body. But my face was better, at least. A few penny-sized blisters on my jaw had scabbed over. Scabs are far more noticeable than blisters, but I was moving in the right direction, certainly, and the rest of my face barely looked burned anymore. It did, as the doc had promised, itch like hell—but I never scratched it.

Kitty continued to show up at night with a wide array of meals from both our favorite restaurants and ones I'd never heard of, leaving no cuisine undigested: Indian, Thai, Tex-Mex, Italian, Cajun, Japanese, Vietnamese. She made it a goal to surprise and delight me.

She'd also jumped on Priya's knitting bandwagon, insisting I knit a scarf while we watched all her favorite musicals: *South Pacific, Singin' in the Rain, Meet Me in St. Louis.* I didn't even fight her on the singing anymore. I jumped into every song without protest, quietly at first, but going full Judy Garland by the end.

The scarf they were making me knit was terrible. I thought I'd picked a stormy-sky blue, but it turned out to be just plain gray. It looked like a mutant slug with tumors.

"We'll make some pom-poms for it," Kit said. "No problem."

The truth is, some parts of my personality came back to me fairly quickly. I still found human beings—and conversation—to be the best possible distraction. When I had somebody to talk to, I focused on the talking, and compulsively joked around, bantered, and chatted. Those moments felt—if not *good,* at least better than usual.

But there were lots and lots of quiet, lost, nebulous moments when I felt the opposite of good. I don't want to leave them out. Most were like that, in fact. Everything that happened—every PT session, or sponge bath, or viewing of *Auntie Mame*—was set against a background of just trying to keep my head up. The minute I was alone, or the second I saw something on TV that reminded me of the life I'd left behind, or the moment I came awake each morning and remembered where I was, the grayness would rush back in. The rule, not the exception.

ONE AFTERNOON, DURING the lull between PT and dinner that I had come to regard as a sacred napping period, I had an unexpected visitor. Chip's mom, Evelyn.

She arrived while I was sleeping, and noisily scooted the visitor chair around until I opened my eyes.

"Oh," she said, "were you sleeping?"

She knew I was. "Yes."

"You seem surprised to see me."

I was. I hadn't seen anyone outside a very small inner circle since I'd been in here. On purpose. "I have a no-visitors policy."

"I told them I was your mother-in-law. To-be."

"Guess that worked."

She hadn't seen me since the ER. "You look much better." Her words were kind, but her eyes were critical as she took me in. The way she was studying me made my face start itching. She went on, "Except for those scabs on your neck, and—oh, God!" She'd caught a glimpse of my skin grafts. She looked away and tried to regroup.

"Did they have to shave your head?" she asked after a while, like of course the answer would be yes.

"No," I said. "It's just a pixie cut."

"I'm sure it'll grow out again soon."

"I'm going to keep it this way. I like it."

"Oh, don't!" she said. Then, "It's a little masculine."

"I think it's cool."

"I'm sure you'll change your mind once you're back to your old self."

Chip's mother was a lot like my mother. Overly put-together. Overly focused on how things looked instead of how things felt. Overly hard on both herself and others, but too gracious to say it in polite conversation.

Still, sometimes it leaked out in funny ways.

I'd known her long enough to know what she was thinking. She and my mother played tennis together, and got pedicures together, and had a genuine friendship that they each treasured. They'd lived next door to each other for ten years, and in that time I don't think they'd ever had a disagreement. It was a remarkable coincidence that two such women should wind up neighbors. They shared the same thoughts on almost everything, and the principal gist of every conversation was to validate each other's worldview. What are the odds?

Of course they were rooting for Chip and me. Of course they wanted us all to be just one big, happy family.

Which is why I didn't see it coming when she frowned, pulled her chair a little closer, and said, "I want to talk to you about Chip."

It was funny to hear his name. He had started showering again, I noticed at his last visit, which felt like progress. He'd also sent several flower arrangements, and even though I'd left instructions for all flowers to be sent down to the children's wing, the ones from him managed to make it through.

My mother liked to arrange and rearrange them on the windowsill.

He was making an effort. I had to give him that.

"He seems better," I said to Evelyn. "He's showering again, I think."

"Yes," she agreed. "And he's not out all night at bars anymore."

"Progress," I said.

"But," she said then, taking my hand and squeezing it, "I don't think he's happy."

Happy? Was that an option? I was just shooting for "conscious."

"That's why I'm here," she went on. "I'm worried about him."

"I'm worried about all of us," I said.

But she had something to say, and she was going to say it. "He's been so crushed by what happened. It really has torn him to shreds. He has to force himself to come here every time he visits. Every time he looks at your poor face, the guilt is just overwhelming."

"Are you asking me to feel sorry for Chip?"

Her voice took an indignant turn. "It's been hard on him, too, Margaret."

"I'm sure it has. Hard on his liver, at the very least."

"Not everyone is as strong as you are."

"I'm *not* strong. I'm just trapped. My body keeps breathing against my will."

She wasn't having it. "Don't be dramatic."

I leaned back against my pillow and squeezed my eyes shut. I was giving up my nap for this.

Evelyn took that moment to get herself back on track. "Chip's father and I have talked about it, and we'd like to ask a favor of you."

I opened my eyes. "A favor?"

"You know how loyal Chip is. You know how important it is to him to do the right thing. You know he would never, ever let himself call off your engagement."

"I'm not even sure that we are technically engaged," I said. Had we settled that?

"You're wearing my mother's two-carat diamond. I think that counts."

"If you say so."

"I'm just not sure what your expectations are—given your situation."

Where was this headed? "My situation *that Chip caused*?"

"You wouldn't want him to marry you out of guilt, would you?"

"What are you saying?"

She sat back a bit. "He's in a very strange predicament."

"Aren't we fucking all?"

"Please watch your language."

"Are you kidding me right now?"

She blinked at me for a second. "We're all coping the best we can."

"Some of us better than others." My thoughts started spinning. "Hold on—did he send you here? Did he send *his mother* to break up with me?"

"He doesn't know I'm here."

"So you just decided this was *any* of your business?"

"My child is my business."

"He's *not* a child!"

She sat up a little straighter. "A marriage—starting a lifetime together—needs a strong foundation of . . ." She seemed to cast around for the word. "Desire."

Desire? Were we talking about *sex* now? "Desire?"

"Among other things."

A strange, acid anger started burning in my chest. She did *not* just walk into this room and creepily tell me her son no longer wanted to screw me. "Oh, he's got plenty of desire," I said. She really wanted to get into this? This was where she wanted to go? Fine. We'd go there. I could go there all day.

"He's got desire in the golf house at the club," I said. "And in his childhood bedroom. And on the garden bench beside your weird little cherub statues. And in your master-bath Jacuzzi when you're on vacation. And even in the kitchen pantry during Christmas dinner. Your 'child' is a tenth-degree horn-dog. He's got more than enough desire. I think he'll find a way to manage."

I wanted it to feel good to attack her like that, but it didn't.

Evelyn stayed still as stone. "That was before," she said at last. "Things have changed."

"Yes they fucking have."

She turned her face away at that word—*again*. "Chip's father and I feel that he's looking for something else now. Something he can't find in you."

I crossed my arms over my chest. "Do you?"

Her face was solemn. "He says he wants to be with you, but we can plainly see his actions."

"What actions?"

She closed her mouth as if I'd asked some wildly inappropriate question. As if she wasn't the person who had brought the whole thing up in the first place.

"You're not going to tell me?" I demanded. "What actions are you talking about?"

I could see that she realized she'd said too much.

I leaned forward. "Tell me," I said, my voice menacing.

She turned away.

As she did, we both caught sight of a figure in the doorway.

Chip.

If I could have slapped him across the face right then, I would have. "Did you send your *mother* to break up with me?"

Chip looked at his mother. "What are you doing?"

"I'm trying to help you." Her voice suddenly got wobbly. "Your father and I are very worried." She lifted her hand to her face, and I realized she was wiping away tears. All at once, she looked very fragile—and I regretted, a little, how many times I'd just said "fuck."

A son can't be angry with his crying mother. His voice got tender. "Mom," he said. "You can't help me. Don't help me, okay?"

He came over, helped her stand, and steered her out of the room. As he did, he held up his hand at me to say *five minutes*. I guessed he was going to walk her back to the hospital valet and send her home.

Once they were gone, I noticed my breathing was ragged, and my chest stung a little, as if the imaginary acid had burned some kind of sad, hollow hole. I spent several minutes trying to tell myself that it was good to feel *something*, at least, before deciding that was bullshit. Why was it that the only emotions that seemed able to penetrate my fog were the worst of the worst?

When Chip made it back, I noticed then that he looked—for the first time since the accident—just exactly like his old self. Here was the Chip I'd fallen in love with. Here was the Chip who had it all together, ready to confidently stand at the helm of anything and everything. He looked picture-perfect. He'd gotten a haircut. He was wearing a crisp polo and pressed khakis. He'd brushed his teeth—and even possibly flossed.

It was a powerful thing to see him again. It was like the real Chip had been gone all this time, but now he'd finally come back, and all that toughness and resistance I felt about the new Chip disintegrated as soon as I saw the old one again.

"Are we engaged?" I asked him then, my voice soft. "Did we ever settle that?"

He gave me his famous Chip Dunbar smile. "You know we are, on my end at least." He was flirting with me! "Your position's a little less clear. But you're still wearing the ring."

"Your mother thinks," I said, making air quotes, "that you don't 'desire' me anymore."

He let out a honk of a laugh and then sat in the chair his mother had just vacated, grabbing my hand in a very similar way. "I do. Oh, my God, I still do—so much—"

I felt myself release a breath I didn't even realize I'd been holding. I felt a pinch of hope that things might turn out okay for us, after all.

Until he went on. "The old you."

What?

"I think about her all the time." Chip pressed his forehead down against my hand, and his shoulders started to shake. "I miss her so much," he said, all muffled.

"You miss her? She's not gone," I said, not even trying to disguise my astonishment. "She's literally right here."

Was Chip crying? "I miss her hair," he went on. "And how she walked in heels. And the way her jeans hugged her hips."

That was just mean. "You realize you're talking about me in the third person," I said.

"I'm sorry," he said.

"Your mother thinks you're going ahead with the engagement out of guilt," I said next. "She thinks you don't want to marry me anymore, but now that you've, you know, *paralyzed me,* you feel like you have to."

"No." He shook his head as he lifted it. "I still want to marry you. I want that more than anything."

"Her? The girl you miss? Or me?" As if we weren't the same person. "The old me or the current me?"

"Any you I can get my hands on."

That made me smile—a little. I wanted that sunshiny feeling back again. "So you do still want to marry me?"

"More than I can possibly say."

It felt good to hear it. I won't lie.

Chip sat up straight then and let go of my hand to wipe his face. He took a deep breath, as if he might be about to shout something, and then he held it a second. When the words came out at last, they just seeped out in a whisper. "I want to marry you, Margaret. But I think I can't."

I held still.

He lowered his eyes. "I think," he went on, "in the end, you're not going to let me."

Then, like a premonition, I knew what he was about to say. I knew exactly what "actions" his mother had been talking about. Yet again, I found myself several mental steps ahead of Chip.

Now I had a decision to make.

I could end this conversation right now, and let him off the hook, and never hear for certain what he was about to say. If I did that, we could continue on. We could keep muddling through, trying to patch things up. I could chalk everything we'd said or done up to "the tragedy" and forgive it all and stay focused on my impossible odds.

I could so easily take that route. It was wildly tempting.

But I didn't. "Chip. What happened?"

He kept his eyes on the bedspread and shook his head.

"Chip," I said, more pressure in my voice. "Tell me."

He held very still.

"Tell me!"

Then he did tell me. But he closed his eyes first. "I slept with someone."

I HADN'T BEEN wrong. I knew that's where he was headed. But the words, once they were spoken, meant the end. They severed us. That was it. He'd made a choice, but I'd made a choice, too. I'm sure I felt many things at that moment, but the only one I remember is loneliness.

"Who?" I said.

"It doesn't matter."

"It does fucking matter."

Chip stood up then—too fast—and knocked his chair over. It clattered to the floor. He didn't pick it up, just paced around the foot of the bed. "Tara," he admitted at last.

"Your old girlfriend, Tara? The one you call the Whiner?"

He nodded.

"You don't even like her!"

"I know."

I didn't even know where to start. "Chip." It was more of a sigh than a word.

"She saw my post about you on Facebook, and she got in touch. She started coming by to check on me. She brought soup."

"She brought *soup*?"

He shrugged. "I wasn't eating. She was concerned. And then one thing led to another."

"Don't tell me." I felt it like a gasp: I didn't want to know.

But now I'd gotten him going. "She came by one night and found me crying—"

"Am I supposed to pity you?"

"—and I just couldn't pull it together. And so she just kind of put her arms around me—"

"Stop."

"—and kind of cradled me—"

"Chip. Shut it down."

"—and the next thing I knew, we were kissing—"

"Stop! I'm fucking serious! Stop!" I didn't realize how loud I was shouting.

Right then, the door to my room pushed open, and Ian walked in.

He eyed Chip for a second before turning to me. "Everything all right?"

"Get the hell out, man," Chip said. "We're talking."

Ian kept his eyes on me. "I wasn't asking you, prick."

I looked up at Ian. He was motionless with suppressed tension. I knew in an instant my dad had been right, that the acoustics between my room and the hallway went both ways. I could hear them out there perfectly—and they could hear me just as well in here.

Ian had just witnessed this whole, humiliating, life-crushing conversation. Enough of it, anyway.

"Can I do anything for you?" Ian asked me then, his voice as tender as I'd ever heard it. "Get you a glass of water? Beat the crap out of this wanker?"

I gave a microscopic smile, but Ian caught it.

I shook my head.

"Can we finish our conversation, please?" Chip asked, though I couldn't tell if he was asking me or Ian.

"Maggie?" Ian said, never shifting his gaze from mine. "Is this a conversation you'd like to continue?"

I shook my head again. "I think we're done."

"That's it, prick. Beat it."

But Chip wasn't ready to go. "Margaret—"

In a flash, Ian was right up next to him, looming a good six inches above. "You heard her. Get out."

Chip put his hands up and backed away. "Okay." He took several steps back, without turning, seeming to consider his options, and then, because he really didn't have any, he turned to leave.

Just as he did, I called, "Chip! Wait!"

He turned back, and I pulled off his grandmother's engagement ring and threw it at him with all the force I could muster.

He ducked, and I missed.

The ring bounced off the wall and then skittered under the empty bed next to mine—so Chip had to get down on his hands and knees to crawl after it. It was just enough humiliation to give me a twinge of satisfaction.

But only a twinge.

AS SOON AS he was gone, the fog closed back in.

It was like suffocating in plain air.

I started panting, but in deep, swooping breaths, pushing them out and then sucking them back in. For a second, I couldn't see. The room didn't go black—it went white. It blurred out of focus until there was nothing.

Except Ian's voice. Ian was still there. "Slow it down," he said, near my ear. "Take it slow. Count to four going out. That's it. Now four going in. Good."

As my breathing slowed, the world came back, and I felt Ian's hand on my forehead, stroking my hair. I opened my eyes, and there was his face, just a few inches away.

"You're all right," he said. "You're okay."

"Ian," I said next, when it felt safe to speak. "I need you to do me a favor."

"Anything," he said. "Of course."

"I really, really need you," I said, "to get me the hell out of here."

Sixteen

IAN STOOD UP and evaluated me for a minute. Then he reached over to pull back my covers.

"Right," he said. "Scoot to the edge of the bed."

I dangled my legs over, and he bent down in front of me and backed up. "Climb on."

"What? *On* you? Like a piggyback ride?"

He nodded. "Pretend I'm a horse."

"A Clydesdale, maybe."

"Move it, lass. Make it happen. Squeeze with your thighs."

The good news was, I could do that. My thighs worked just fine. It was everything below them that didn't. I leaned forward until my chest fell against his back, and then I wriggled my legs into position around his waist. I wrapped my arms around his neck.

"Not a choke hold, though," he instructed. "Low, on the collarbones." He moved my hands down.

He stood up. "Is this okay?"

A piggyback ride. When was the last time I'd had one of those? "Yes."

"We're not touching your donor sites? Or pulling on your grafts?"

"I'm good. I should travel like this more often."

He pulled the quilt off my bed and grabbed a pillow, and then he walked us out past the nurses' station—where every single person stopped what they were doing to gape at us going by. As we passed, without even slowing down, he grabbed a bag of Milano cookies off the reception desk.

He took long steps and moved fast. He really was a Clydesdale. He didn't walk, he strode. I hadn't moved that quickly through any space in weeks, and despite everything, it gave me a tickle of a thrill in my stomach. I felt an odd urge to laugh, but I held it back.

He walked us to the elevator, and we rode up to the top floor, then got off and strode to the end of a corridor, directly toward a door with a push handle that said NOT AN EXIT—ALARM WILL SOUND.

"Hey—that's not an exit." I said, as we barreled toward it. "Hey! 'Alarm will sound'!"

We burst through the door anyway, though. No alarm sounded.

"It's disabled," he explained, as the door swung closed behind us. "It's where the nurses go to smoke."

Then we were outside. I caught my breath. It was a crisp, clear March evening—with the most stunning orange and purple sunset I'd ever seen. Or so it seemed. It would have been breathtaking in any situation, but I literally had not been outside since the night of the accident. How long had that been? We were ending my second week in the inpatient wing, and I'd spent a week in the ICU before that, so: three solid weeks without seeing the sky, or feeling the breeze, or breathing fresh air. No wonder I was feeling so crazy.

That, and everything else.

Ian took us across the roof to the far edge, which had a view of downtown Austin and the capitol building. With me still on his back, he laid the blanket out flat and dropped the pillow and the cookies. Then he got down on his hands and knees and backed up to the blanket like a dump truck and tilted up so I could slide down onto my knees. The whole thing gave me just a smidge of vertigo, and I rolled onto my side in the middle of the quilt. He brought the pillow around to prop me correctly so I could lie back to see the sky without damaging my grafts.

The sky. The wind blew across me and fluttered my hair back. I felt a little cold, but it was okay. It made me aware of all my edges—where I stopped and the rest of the world continued. I was still alive, I thought then. It hit me out on that roof for the first time.

I was alive.

In the next second, I felt Ian lay his fleece sweatshirt over me, and then he flopped down beside me and got settled on his back. Then he lifted a cookie up into my field of vision, and I reached up and grabbed it.

Nobody spoke, and for the first time ever—maybe in my entire life—that was okay. We listened to the wind, and the muted traffic ten stories below, and the crunch of cookies as we chewed. We watched the sky darken as the sun sank out of view. So much of life is just grinding through. So many moments just exist to deliver you to the ones that follow. But this moment was a destination in itself.

Did I feel happy right then? Not exactly. When you feel happy, or joyful, it's kind of like a brightness in your chest, and my heart was too numb for brightness.

If you think of human emotions as music, then mine were like an orchestra with no conductor. I felt a lot of different sounds, but I didn't know quite how to read them or combine them in ways I understood. And yet there was no doubt that the instruments of my body were playing—my skin under the wind, my lungs drawing in crisp breaths, my eyes taking in the vast and brilliant sky. There was music—good music—even if it wasn't a melody I recognized.

Given the context, it seems odd that I should have felt such good feelings right then, and I guarantee it didn't last. My brain still knew that my entire future was ruined—that Chip's confession marked more than just the end of our relationship: It meant the end of my life as I'd known it.

But the physical pleasure of being outside for the first time in so achingly long was too real to deny. Later, there would be fallout—moments of rage, and bleakness, and grief over everything I'd lost—as I tried to understand what Chip had done and why. But not yet. Not tonight. Ian had given me this impossible gift—a little pause from it all. An experience so viscerally alive that nothing else could compete.

It was just us, and the wind—and now, suddenly, the stars starting to appear—for a long, quiet while.

Then I heard Ian's voice, surprisingly close to my ear, say, "Myles'll fire me for this, for sure."

I turned my head. There he was. Starting a conversation. Of all things. "Will he? Seriously?"

He was gazing up, an arm behind his head, and the pose was so casual, so unguarded, so *friendly*, it was shocking. "Maybe not. He didn't see it with his own eyes, after all. The nurses might not rat us out."

"But don't the PTs take patients out all the time?"

"Sure. On educational excursions. In groups. Not up to the roof alone."

"What does he think you're going to do to me?"

A classic Ian-style silence followed that question—but rather than feeling uncomfortable I suddenly started thinking of all the things that Ian could potentially have been doing to me, right that very moment. The longer the silence lasted, the more vivid my thinking became. He was just inches away. He could so easily roll onto his side and put his face down alongside mine. He could so easily take one of those big hands and run it along my side. The thought took hold of my thinking. I could almost feel it happening—the weight of his hands, the roughness of the stubble on his jaw, the warmth of his mouth.

I drifted off into the fantasy of being kissed by Ian, but then his voice pulled me back out. "There are all kinds of ungentlemanly things I could do to you on this roof," he declared at last. "And I'm sure Myles would accuse me of them all."

It's a little odd—and a bit embarrassing—to confess that I had a vivid, unrequited, thirty-second, highly sexy, totally unauthorized fantasy about my physical therapist not an hour after I'd thrown my engagement ring at my ex-fiancé. But it's important to mention. Because in those seconds, something happened. I felt a swell of some very potent, very enthusiastic, very *physical* feelings in response to that kissing fantasy.

Which meant—and this was big news—I could feel those feelings.

Suffice it to say, my time in the hospital had not been the most erotic experience of my life. On my scale of worries that month, my future sex life rated comically low. Probably, if I'd had a choice between a future with walking and a future with sex, I'd have picked walking. But I wasn't given that choice. That said, since all my sensation down there was, as I'd been told over and over, "spotty," I'd known there was a good chance that I'd lost that part of my life forever. Though, even if I'd been thinking about it enough to check, I likely would have been afraid to check. Part of me didn't want to know. *Don't go looking for trouble.*

But now, suddenly, thanks to this roof, I knew.

My body could feel things. Enthusiastically.

True, my body had just felt those things about a man who—most days, anyway—didn't even want to be in the same room with me, but I wasn't going to quibble over details. This was great news, dammit, no matter how foolishly I'd come across it! I could *feel the feelings*! One of life's greatest pleasures was still on my menu!

Did I feel joyful about it? No. "Joy" didn't seem to be an option anymore. I wasn't really sure I could access "happy," either. The best I could do right then was "pleasant." I felt *pleasant* about it. And—maybe more than that: relief. Relief I didn't even know I'd been waiting for.

The sunset was completely gone now, replaced by a deep blue night sky full of stars. I tried to sit up then, but lost my balance partway, and Ian lost no time helping. He sat up, too, and cradled me into a sitting position. "You okay?" he asked.

"Uh-huh."

"You look a little nauseous."

Reading that so wrong. "I'm fine."

"Do you want to go back?"

I turned and met his eyes. "I *never* want to go back."

He gave a little shrug and then said, "Okay."

"Tell me about your nebbishy boss," I said then, as we watched the lights of the city skyline. "What's going on there?"

"Only if you put on my sweatshirt."

"I'm fine," I said.

"Put it on."

"Bossy," I said. But I put it on, and as I did, I got a great waft of that delicious Ian smell. It was so overpowering in that moment, it was all I could do not to press my face into it and gulp down a big breath. But I covered well. I pretended like the zipper was stuck. Then I looked at Ian to prove that I was waiting for him to start talking.

When he didn't, I prompted: "So? You think Myles would fire you for taking me up here."

"Myles would definitely fire me for taking you up here."

"Even though you don't like me like that." It was the kind of statement girls sometimes make in honor of the one percent chance that the guy might contradict it.

Ian did not contradict it. He kept his gaze straight out on the horizon. "No. I don't like you like that."

"So you're safe."

He looked off. "I am far from safe."

"What's Myles's deal with you, anyway?"

"That's a long story."

The wind kept blowing one lock of my hair into my face. I tried to tuck it behind my ear, but it was too short. "I truly have nothing but time."

Ian sighed. "I used to work here before. That's why I moved to Texas, in fact—to take a job at this hospital. I started young and worked my way to manager of the PT gym. Myles came about when I did, but I got promoted over him again and again."

"Why?"

"Because he's a rule-obsessed wanker, and a petty tyrant."

"Sounds about right."

"Anyway, then a female PT got hired to work in the therapy gym. Her name was Kayla. We hit it off right away, and we started seeing each other."

It was pushing, but I couldn't help it: "What was she like?"

He gave a little shrug. "Lovely. Feisty. She had no patience for foolishness. She could be so mean." He said it with great admiration.

I watched him think about her. After a bit, I said, "What does this have to do with Myles?"

Ian let out a long breath. "Myles liked her, too. He would say that he saw her first—and I stole her away."

"Did you?"

"He might have seen her first," Ian said, shrugging. "But she never liked him. I couldn't steal something that was never his."

"Of course not."

"But that fact was not—still is not—relevant to Myles. He liked her, and that was all that mattered."

"That's why he hates you?"

Ian nodded. "That's why he hates me. I ruined his life, and now he is determined to ruin mine."

"But she wasn't into him!"

"He feels, very strongly, that he could have won her over."

"But you're not still with her?" I asked, to confirm.

"No."

"You broke up?"

Ian seemed to hold his breath. "In a way."

"So what's his problem?"

"I've wondered about that a lot. I think Myles is the kind of guy who needs an enemy. He needs an enemy to fight so that he can feel like a hero."

"But he's *not* a hero!"

Ian looked over and gave a little shrug. "I might be a villain, though."

I waited.

"I wasn't very nice to him. I gloated a bit when I won her. I wish I could go back and change that. It wasn't kind of me."

"Okay," I said, "but Myles is totally the kind of person who makes you want to gloat."

"Maybe," Ian said. "But I should have been the bigger man."

I didn't say anything to that. I knew all about regrets.

Ian went on. "Kayla and I had been together about a year when I had this idea to strike out on my own from the hospital. I wanted to start a rehab gym for people who are beyond the critical phase, but who still want to work to get better—people who insurance won't cover. There's all kinds of great research out there about ways to stimulate the nervous system, get the brain and spinal cord to rewire and communicate with the body in new ways. I wanted to make use of that research."

"That's brilliant."

"And so she came with me. We took out loans, found a facility, worked out a business plan, printed up T-shirts, and sank everything we had into it."

He gave me a look. "I poached all the best people from the hospital and talked them into coming with me. I filled their heads with ideas about the fun we could have and the path we could forge. We could change people's lives. We could change the face of recovery."

"And Myles?" I asked.

"He wasn't invited."

"Because he's a wanker."

Ian nodded. "He's toxic, really, in so many ways. Narrow and vindictive and peevish. Not the kind of guy you want around. I didn't want to work with him. I kept the whole plan a secret from him—but he got wind of it somehow, and he started asking to join. I rejected him over and over. I was cocky about it. When he demanded to know why I didn't want him, I laid it all out in no uncertain terms."

"Like, you said he wasn't right for the job?"

"I told him he was an idiot and everybody hated him."

"Okay. That's laying it out."

"After we all quit, there was almost nobody left. So they promoted him."

"And now Myles is the boss."

"Which was fine with me, until—"

I looked over. "Until what?"

"Until the business crashed and burned. And then I found myself with no savings and no job. Then a spot opened up here. Somehow, in some circle of hell, I wound up working for him."

"The business crashed?"

Ian nodded.

"How? Why? You had all those great people! And such a great idea."

He shook his head, and I could tell we weren't going to travel far on that topic. "Lots of reasons."

I watched him a long time, but he didn't offer anything more.

Finally, he went back to Myles. "He's had it out for me since the day I came back—just a few weeks before you showed up. He's actively looking to get me fired."

"And it's torture for you to work with him."

He gave a nod. "He goes out of his way to make everything harder. If I don't play things exactly by the book, I'm out. But I've never been very good at playing by the book."

"Could you go work somewhere else?"

He shrugged. "Nowhere else is hiring."

"Maybe in some other city?" I suggested, hating the idea even as I said it.

"I haven't wanted to look in other cities. But I might have to start."

Suddenly, I became aware that my shoulder was leaning against his shoulder. I leaned away—but that felt abrupt. Partly to cover, I said, "So you weren't always so grouchy."

A faint smile. "No."

"Did you used to joke around?"

"Of course."

"And listen to oldies rock?"

"That's a job requirement."

"I've decided it's good that you've been mean to me."

"I haven't been nearly as mean as I intended to be."

I looked over. "Why not?"

He looked away. "Something about your eyes, I think."

I had to ask. "What about them?"

"Let's just say being mean to Myles makes me feel better. Being mean to you made me feel worse."

I didn't know what to say to that, so I just let the wind blow.

"Thank you for telling me about your troubles," I said after a while.

"It wasn't very professional of me."

"Professional is overrated."

He turned to take in the sight of me, as if I'd just said something so true, it surprised him. Then he said, "We should get back."

I shook my head.

But he nodded. "It's late. You need rest."

I suddenly felt tears in my eyes. I wiped them on his sweatshirt. "I don't want to go back."

Ian helped me get up on my knees so I could climb onto his back. "I'd offer you a cookie, but we ate them all."

"Promise me we'll come here again," I said, as I climbed on.

"I promise."

"Soon."

"Soon," he said, and as he stood us both up, the view—and the breeze, and the feel of his back against my chest, and the endlessness of the sky above us—made me so dizzy, I had to close my eyes.

Seventeen

I WENT THROUGH a period of—shall we say—disillusionment after Chip's confession. Once I returned from the roof to my inpatient cell, I had nothing to distract me from the realities of my life—every awful one of them—and I kind of lost sight of the meaning of everything.

To sum up: My motivation for physical therapy, and everything else, was rather low.

There was no way to deny, at this point, that everything I cared about was destroyed, or broken, or had self-destructed. Even my own personal goals. Because that one inspiring fantasy of walking to Chip that I'd used to push back the fog had disintegrated the minute I found out about Tara and her soup.

I would never walk to Chip again.

I would never walk again, period.

In some ways, if I'm honest, giving up felt good. It certainly took the pressure off. Staying hopeful was exhausting.

In life, I'd always had tangible goals. I made good grades so I could get into a good college. I worked hard in college so I could get into a good business school. I worked hard in B-school so that I could get a great job, make great money, be a leader in the business world, break a few glass ceilings, and make my parents proud. Those weren't the only things I wanted, of course. I wasn't totally shallow. I wanted love and friends and babies and laughter. I wanted to be a good person and help take care of the world. But I'd spent my life working toward specific goals.

What was I suffering for now? What was I working toward now? To get a little more movement in my legs? To *not* get an infection in my skin graft? To approach some vague approximation of the person I used to be? To make it through the day without freaking the hell out? I couldn't motivate for goals like that.

Somehow, the presence of Chip in that recovery fantasy had been the lynchpin holding it all together. Without him, the whole thing fell apart.

My mother had fed me false hope, and I'd swallowed it whole like a baby bird with an open beak. I hadn't questioned it enough because I hadn't wanted to—but there was a fine line between determination and delusion.

Some things really were impossible.

My grandfather had been shot in the eye with a BB gun as a kid. He lost the eye and spent the rest of his life with a glass one, taking it out every night and—I swear this is true—putting it in a glass of water on the bedside table. Kitty and I used to sneak in before he was awake sometimes and steal it out of the cup—and then, totally game, he'd stumble down in his robe and PJs at breakfast time, a hand clapped over his face, saying, "Somebody stole my eye!" We'd cackle until he found it—and he never complained. But no amount of wishing or determination or denial could have grown that eye back.

I hadn't let myself think about that until now.

Now, all I did was just keep breathing, and even that felt like a lot. One breath after another. Easier on some days than others. But let's be clear: I had nothing—nothing—to look forward to.

The day after our lovely night on the roof, for example, Ian showed up for PT, and I just refused to move.

He was all business, of course. None of the warmth from the night before. He walked in as brusque and formal as if he had never carried me piggyback through the hallways, never made me wear his sweatshirt, never told me about his mistakes. From the expression on his face, I could have been anybody—one face in a parade of wheelchairs. Which was how I felt about myself, as well.

He got the transfer board ready, but I didn't sit up. I just stared out the window.

"All right. Let's go," he urged.

I didn't say anything. Didn't look over.

He came around to peer at my face and double-check I wasn't sleeping. "Maggie," he said. "It's time."

I wasn't trying to be rude. Responding just seemed like it would take too much energy.

"Let's go," he urged again.

But I just kept breathing.

"Are you not coming, then? Is this what I get for busting you out of jail?"

I was locked in a stare out the window, but I heard my voice. "I just don't see the point."

"You don't have to see the point. You just have to come with me."

"Not today."

"Maggie," he said, lowering his voice. "Can you look at me?"

I couldn't. I was stuck in that stare, and everything else seemed far away.

Ian leaned his face down in front of mine, but my eyes didn't refocus. He was just a blurry head. "You have to take care of yourself. You can't let him win."

"Who?" I asked, still unfocused.

"The prick who broke your heart."

But I wasn't sure I had a heart anymore. It felt like maybe it had burned away in the crash. I just lay limp. One breath in, then out. Then another in, then out.

"Are you refusing physical therapy?"

It hadn't occurred to me that I could refuse. I kept my eyes on the window. "Yes. I guess I am."

The next day, I refused again. The day after that, too.

My family was concerned. Ian reported me to the supervising physician, who passed the reports on to the social worker and psychologist on staff, as well as my parents. The professionals agreed that a "dose of depression" was normal, even healthy, in my situation, but my parents, and even Kitty, disagreed.

It threw our family ecosystem into disarray. I had always been the hardworking, cheery, rule-following achiever, and Kitty had always been the source of all our problems.

Simple.

What did it mean—to any of us—for *me* to be the problem?

It led them to desperate measures. I later found out that despite all the tension between Kitty and my mom—worse now—Kitty and my parents arranged a secret rendezvous within forty-eight hours of Chip's confession to figure out how to fix me.

They were all business—coming together for the greater good, focusing on the task at hand, meeting in the coffee shop of a Barnes & Noble and then scouring the self-help books to find some inspirational reading to get me back on track. Kitty and my mother wordlessly agreed to set aside everything that had gone down between them, and they wound up spending a hundred dollars on titles like *Why Me? A Daily Guide for Getting Back to Normal* and *The Joy of Suffering.*

My dad suggested that Kitty should be the one to bring the books to me because I'd be less likely to view her as a foe.

"I'm not a foe!" my mother protested.

But she was outvoted.

IT WAS NICE for them to have a project, in a way, Kitty admitted later. What purpose would it have served to rehash all their conflict and strife, anyway? They left things unresolved but moved on to the more important pressing problem of me.

"Didn't the two of you at least apologize to each other?" I asked, when Kit confessed what they'd been up to.

"Apologize? What for?"

"Well," I said, "you, for telling me Mom's biggest secret against her wishes. And Mom, for pretty much your whole childhood."

Kitty shook her head. "There was no apologizing. Have you ever heard Mom apologize?"

Fair enough. Apologizing wasn't Mom's thing.

I refused to read the self-help books, of course. They should've seen that coming. When Kitty tried to read some excerpts aloud, I plugged my ears and sang Aretha Franklin. So, late at night—or rather, after 9:00 P.M.—after I'd fallen asleep, Kitty read the books herself with a flashlight.

If I wouldn't help myself, by God, she'd do it for me.

It was the time pressure that got to all of them. I had three and a half weeks left before the window of improvement would slam closed for good, and, in the wake of my depression, my improvement had stalled.

In truth, my improvements had stalled before Chip's confession—the whole week before had been significantly absent of improvements, as well. We all just noticed it after the breakup. Before, when I still believed in my fairy tale, I viewed the stall as a natural plateau—an adjustment period on the way to more inspiring success.

Now, I saw the slowdown as part of a different narrative: the beginning of the end.

I didn't say that to anybody, but I guess it was obvious.

Then my parents decided I needed a "tutor."

My mother brought it up at lunch. We were eating Vietnamese noodle salad from their favorite spot, and my dad was enjoying it so much, he was smacking.

"So," my mother said brightly, holding a forkful of noodles, "you're starting your your last three weeks here—"

"And a half," I added.

"After insurance runs out," my dad said, "you'll come home to live with us."

I snorted. "I am *not* coming home to live with you."

My parents looked at each other. My dad asked tenderly, "Where would you live, sweetheart?"

"At my place," I said, like, *Duh*.

My dad proceeded very gingerly. "Your place is three stories high. With stairs."

I closed my eyes. "I'll stay on the ground floor."

He was almost whispering now. "There's no bathroom on the ground floor. Or kitchen."

I knew that, of course. "I'll figure it out."

We all knew I wouldn't. What would I do—climb the stairs on my knees? Actually, maybe that could work.

"Nonsense," my mother said, in her most authoritative voice. "You can't keep that place. I've already spoken with a real estate agent. He says now's a perfect time to sell. You stand to make a good profit." Then she added, "He also loves your décor."

This from the woman who'd told all the neighbors I'd be good as new by summer. "I am not moving in with my parents," I declared. "I am not a child!"

"Just temporarily," my dad said, ever the spoonful of sugar.

But I pointed at my mother. "Do not talk to agents! Do not sell my place! You said I'd be good as new!"

It was such a childish accusation, in one way—to get mad at her for my misfortune, the way little kids sometimes do before they've come to understand that, in so many big ways, parents are just as powerless as they are.

At the same time, it was a declaration of independence. My whole life, I'd turned to my mother for instructions on what to do, and where to go, and how to get it done. My mother had insisted to me, and the doctors, and, apparently, all our neighbors, that I was going to "beat" this paralysis.

She'd always interpreted my life. Though to be fair, I'd always let her.

But maybe that wasn't her job anymore.

In the strangled silence that followed, we all felt the shift in my thinking like a little, earth-trembling rumble of plate tectonics. Even if we didn't know what it was.

Faced with this Kitty-like behavior from me, my mother dropped it. She put up her hands in surrender. "Fine. We won't sell your condo."

"Of course not. If you don't want to," my dad said.

"I don't want to." How could anybody possibly think that I would? Hadn't I given up enough?

"The point is," my mom said, getting back to business, "you are running out of time here."

"I'm aware of that," I said, stubbornly leaving my lunch untouched.

"And so we're thinking," my dad said brightly, "why not do everything possible right now to promote healing and recovery?"

I looked back and forth between them for a good long minute before I said, in a low voice like a growl, "My whole life is 'doing everything possible.' I don't go five minutes without 'promoting healing and recovery.'"

My mom leaned in. "Did I forget to tell you that I just read the most inspiring story? About a girl—a former ballerina—in just exactly your situation? She tried very hard for weeks, and got nowhere at all—and then one morning, out of the blue, her right big toe wiggled. Then, the next morning, her left big toe wiggled. The morning after that, she could wiggle them all. The morning after that, she could bend her knees. And by the end of the month, she could do a *pas de bourrée*!"

Quietly, then—secretly—I tried to wiggle my toes.

Nothing.

I wasn't even entirely sure I remembered how.

I'd been thinking I hated these inspirational stories, but that wasn't quite right. I *loathed* them. "What is your point?"

My mom blinked. "We think you might need a tutor."

A *tutor*? I frowned at my dad. "What is this?" I said. "The SAT?"

"Someone to give you a little extra practice," my dad said.

"That's not a thing," I said.

My dad shrugged. "A personal trainer, then, if you like."

"Someone to help you—physically—do more than the bare minimum that insurance requires."

Bare minimum struck me as deeply insulting. Spoken like a person who had no idea what it was like for the bare minimum to be your own personal ultimate maximum.

My mom went on, "We just want to be sure you're doing everything—while you still can."

"I *am* doing everything I can!" I said.

My mom gave me a look, like, *Come on*. "I saw you study for finals, and the SAT, and the GMAT. I know you're capable of more than this."

I heard my voice get very quiet. "You have no idea what I'm capable of."

My dad jumped in. "I think your mother's just trying to say that we want to help. However we can."

That wasn't what she was trying to say. I suddenly saw it very clearly. She wanted to help—but only in the ways that she had already chosen. My mother was always very helpful—when you did exactly what she wanted.

A lifetime of following my mother's every piece of advice ticker-taped through my head. A lifetime of never questioning her type-A standards, and working like a dog to meet them, and internalizing them without question. In that moment, possibly for the first time ever, it occurred to me: She didn't know everything. She didn't have it all figured out. I'd followed her instructions for life to the letter, and look where it had gotten me: right here, trapped in this bed, enduring stories about ballerinas. She said take advanced calculus? I took advanced calculus. She said major in business administration? I majored in business administration. She said get an MBA? I got an MBA. Top of the class. Always. Every time. Like a chump.

Sitting there, I tried to scan back for even one time—one tiny time—that I'd rejected her "help" and done my own thing. That's all Kitty had ever done, by the way—reject my mother's advice—and it had made her teen years in our house pretty miserable for everybody. But had it made Kitty's *life* miserable? Sure, she'd been through some rough times, and she had a crazy hairdo, and way too many piercings, and a defiantly funky lifestyle—but she was always, unapologetically Kitty. She knew who she was. She did what she loved. Who was I? What was I good at, besides keeping my apartment neat, and keeping myself groomed, and acing tests? What did I like? What was I passionate about? What would it feel like to do what I wanted instead of what was expected?

I had no earthly idea.

"No," I heard myself say then.

My mother blinked at me.

"No thanks, I mean. I don't need a tutor."

"I'm not sure you see the time pressure here," my mother said.

"I think I do."

"In exactly three weeks, your window of opportunity will slam closed."

"Maybe not *slam*," my dad amended.

But my mom was irritated now. "Don't you want to get better?"

"I can't believe you would even ask me that."

"Because right now it doesn't seem like you do."

I looked at my dad for help.

He jumped in. "Maybe we just need to redefine 'better.'"

"'Better' doesn't need to be redefined," my mom said. "It is what it is. It's *better*."

"Unless," I said, "it's you applying it to me. Then 'better' means 'fixed.' As you've promised all the neighbors."

She held her position. "Don't you want to be fixed?"

"That's not a relevant question."

But she lifted one eyebrow the way she always did when she was about to win. "It's the only relevant question there is."

Sure, she had a point. There were some real, physical issues here that I needed to address in a timely way, and now might not be the best moment to give up. But I realized then—possibly for the first time ever—that my parents telling me what to do was making it harder, not easier, to figure out what to do. It was just a glimpse of a feeling, but I now grasped that it was my job—and only mine—to try.

"I don't want to talk about this anymore," I heard myself say.

"Fine," my mother said. "We'll take a break."

I shook my head. "At all. Period. I'm not going to discuss any of this with you." My voice, I noticed, sounded just like my mother's when she was declaring the case closed. "If you want to come have lunch every day and see me, great. But the topic of my recovery is off-limits."

My mother looked at my dad.

"If you try to bring it up," I went on, "I will scream until you leave the room." In my old life, I might have left the room myself—but now that wasn't an option. "And if that doesn't work," I said, adding the thing my mother hated the most, "I will burst into show tunes."

I could almost see her shiver. "Fine," she said.

"I have to figure this out," I said, my voice a little softer as I looked over at my dad. "You can't do it for me. I have to do it myself."

I could see a hundred protests forming in my mother's head. Most notably: What if I did it myself—and did it *wrong*? She had a point. Even I wondered if this was really the best moment to thrust myself out of her nest. Weren't the stakes a little high? Shouldn't we start with what to eat for dinner and work our way up? But I let the questions go unanswered. For the first time ever, I didn't care. This was bigger than me.

This was my mangled body and my hopeless soul, stepping up at last.

Eighteen

STANDING UP TO my mother was surprisingly elating. In a life as out of control as mine was at that moment, little things can be big.

When Ian showed up for PT, I went with him willingly. He didn't talk, and neither did I, but as we worked our way through stretches, and the stationary bike, and a machine I called the "Thighmaster," I did everything he asked with a new kind of determination.

Neither one of us talked this time, and the vibe was decidedly different than it had been. Instead of babbling incessantly to fill the silence, I concentrated on my task at hand. Instead of staring out the window, he watched my form and—of all things—helped me.

"Good," he'd say, as the weights on the machine went up. "That's it."

"Are you *encouraging* me?" I said, not looking over.

I felt, rather than saw, him give a little smile. "Nope."

Even Myles couldn't slow us down. He passed by several times to correct my form and then demand to know why Ian wasn't paying better attention. He also pointed out that Ian's scrubs weren't regulation blue—even though they were barely a shade lighter than the ones Myles himself was wearing. At one point, Myles came by for no other reason than to let Ian know he had been "missed at the staff meeting this morning."

Ian didn't look at him. "I was not told about that meeting."

Myles gave him a look, like, *Please.* "Pretty sure you were. There was a staff-wide email."

"I didn't get it."

"You're saying every single member of our team got that message but you?"

"Looks that way."

"I think maybe you just don't like meetings."

"I *detest* meetings," Ian said, standing up to full height and looking down at Myles. "Especially bullshit meetings that waste everyone's time. But I never miss them—unless someone deletes my address from the recipients list."

I caught a flash of *busted* cross Myles's face. Then he regrouped. "I've started taking roll," he said then. "So you'll want to be sure to make it to the next one. On time."

"With pleasure," Ian said, turning away.

"Did he delete your name from the email list?" I whispered, after Myles was gone.

"No comment."

"How are you going to make it to the next one if he doesn't tell you about it?"

Ian met my eyes. "I've alerted my network of spies."

AFTER PT, I was so tired I could barely transfer back to the bed.

I took a coma-like nap, and when I woke, around the time Kitty usually arrived for supper, I was ravenously hungry. I was also ready to report on how I'd both stood up to our mom and rocked it out in PT—and then psychoanalyze how those two things might be related.

But when the door opened, it wasn't Kitty.

It was Ian.

My first thought: He was quitting. He couldn't take me—or Myles—anymore.

He walked close to the bed and stood there, a bit uncomfortable.

I decided to jump the gun. "I'm sorry I've been so difficult lately," I said.

"Your situation is difficult," he said then. "Not you."

That was nice of him.

"I think you're coping remarkably well, actually," he said.

"You do?"

He nodded. "You worked hard today."

"I did?"

"Could you feel the difference?"

The question sparked a realization. This might have been the first time in my life that I did something difficult not for how it would matter to somebody else, but for how it would matter to me.

It was a strange, new feeling, but it felt like a little nudge in the right direction.

"It was different," I agreed. "But I'm not sure why."

"You've got a lot of strength, Maggie," Ian said then. Such a serious face. Practically *mournful*. "Much more than you realize."

"I hope so. I'm going to need it."

"And I think we could be doing more."

Where was he going with this? "Okay."

"That's why I'm here."

"Here now, you mean?"

"Your father hired me for extra sessions in the evenings."

My dad hired *Ian* as the tutor? Hadn't I just put my foot down about that? "Well, I told him I didn't need a tutor."

"He told me that."

I shook my head. "The thing is, I just had this really triumphant moment with my parents where I told them to stop running my life, and then I made a grand step toward—you know—being my own person and making my own choices from the inside out, and that extra gumption you saw in the gym today was me claiming my own long-lost power, so if I just give in now and let them take back over, I'm kind of surrendering after I've already won the battle."

There was no way he'd followed that.

But he nodded. "I understand."

"You do?"

"I absolutely think you should"—here, he slowed down to get the words right—" 'claim your own power.' "

He wasn't going to fight me. "Thank you," I said.

"Except," he said then.

"Except what?"

"As good as it feels to win a battle, I want you to win the war."

"What does that mean?"

"It means your parents are right."

I gave him a look, like, *Really?* "That's not exactly helpful."

"You *could* benefit from extra help. There are all sorts of things we could do that are outside the range of typical PT."

"Like?"

"Like anything. Swimming. Yoga. Horseback riding. Massage. Reflexology. Cold and heat. Acupuncture. Anything we can think of. In the gym, we're limited to a specific insurance-approved list. It's not a bad list, but it's certainly not everything."

Why was he here right now? Why had he said yes to my dad? Why on earth would he stay in this hospital one second longer every day than he had to? "Are you saying we're desperate?"

He shook his head. "Not desperate," he said. *"Creative."*

I stared at him. I was tired and hungry, and ready for the day to be over, and pissed at my dad for siding with my mom. "Why would you do this?" I asked. "I know my dad. The money couldn't be that good."

"This is what we did at my gym," he said. "This is the part I loved—the creativity, the challenge, the thinking outside the box."

Did I want to give Ian a chance to do what he loved? Of course. But, after finally tasting the sweetness of what it felt like to do something for me, I did not want to backslide and agree to extra PT just so Ian could have better job satisfaction.

Until he said these words: “Plus, I could get you out of here.”

“What do you mean, out of here?”

He shrugged. “If you’re doing therapeutic horseback, we can’t exactly do it in this building.”

“You mean, you could check me out?”

“For therapy, yes.”

“Often?”

“If you had the energy for it.”

“You wouldn’t get in trouble with Myles?”

“I’m in trouble with Myles either way.”

And voilà! An internal motivation! Doing something that would make my parents happy or give Ian job fulfillment might blur my newly drawn lines, but there was nothing blurry about getting the fuck out of here.

“Sold,” I said. “I’m in.”

Ian stifled a smile. “Great,” he said. “Let’s go.”

“I can’t go now,” I said. “My sister’s bringing dinner.”

“Oh,” he said. “That’s all right. I’ll wait.”

“Are you hungry? Do you want to eat?”

“That depends on what you’re having.”

“Italian, I think.” Then, as if to confirm, Kitty walked through the door with a bag from Napoli’s.

“Who is this?” she asked, breezing past him.

It was so weird to think she’d never met him. But his shifts were during the day—and she was all about the night.

“Kitty, this is Ian, my physical therapist. Ian, this is Kitty, my sister.”

“Your black-sheep sister,” Kitty corrected, and then she looked Ian over. “You didn’t tell me he was gorgeous.” She reached out to shake hands. “You can call me Kitty Kat.”

“Do not flirt with my physical therapist,” I said.

“He looks like he can resist me,” Kitty said. Then, to Ian, “Want a soda?” She pulled a can of full-sugar Coke out of her purse. I looked at her, like, *I can’t believe you drink that stuff,* and she shrugged at me, like, *You’ve gotta have some vices.*

"No, but thanks," Ian said.

Kitty turned to me like a kid who'd just spotted a candy bar. Then she whispered, "He really is Scottish."

I nodded.

"Yum."

"Do *not* flirt with my physical therapist!"

"Hello? *He's Scottish.* All rules are off."

"Dad hired him to be my walking tutor. Against my wishes." At the memory, I tried to wiggle my toes. Nothing.

Ian said, "I really do think I can help you."

"Well," I said, "you'd better. My mother wants me to be perfect again, and she won't accept anything less."

"Amen to that," Kitty said.

But Ian was looking at me. "Were you perfect before?"

I shrugged. "I tried like hell," I said, just as Kitty said, "Yes."

"That sounds like a lot of work," Ian said.

"You have no idea," Kitty said.

"What did you do for fun?" Ian said, looking at me.

I looked at him back. "I worked really hard all the time."

"That doesn't sound like fun to me."

"I'm not sure you're qualified to judge, triathlon guy."

"I'm fun," Ian protested.

"You are the opposite of fun," I said.

"You might not say that after tonight." He raised his eyebrows a little, as if to say, *Listen up.*

I squinted with suspicion. "What happens tonight?"

"I'm taking you swimming."

I stared for a second. "There's a pool?"

"A therapy pool." He nodded. "In the basement."

I looked around the room. "I don't have a swimsuit."

"Yes, you do," Kitty sang out. "Mom packed you one."

Ian nodded at me. "Sounds like you do."

"But you could also just skinny-dip," Kitty suggested.

Suddenly I remembered my donor sites. And the third-degree burns on my neck. "Wait! *Can* I swim?" I gestured at my whole collarbone-neck-jaw area. "With these?"

Ian just gave me a little shrug. "Let's go find out."

AN HOUR LATER, I was wearing my least favorite swimsuit—a retro polka-dot two-piece that I hadn't worn in years—and sitting on the edge of the pool with my spaghetti legs dangling in. It was something I'd done thousands of times before, but it was different now. For one thing, my sensation was spotty below the knees, so I could feel the cold water in some places, but not in others. For another, I could not kick my legs, so they just draped like wet towels over the edge.

The therapy pool was deserted at nine-thirty at night, and it reeked of so much chlorine it was like sniffing a straight bottle of bleach. The fluorescent lighting gave it a slight public-bathroom vibe. I had a distinct feeling we were not supposed to be here.

I was waiting for Ian while he changed, wondering if he kept a swimsuit at work for last-minute swims just like these.

No, it turned out. He appeared in just a pair of regular cotton cargo shorts. No shirt. The sight of his naked shoulders and his torso was so shocking, I could only stare.

"You're going to swim like that?" I asked.

"I could skinny-dip, if you prefer."

"Did you just make a joke?"

"I never joke," he said. Then he cannonballed into the far end of the pool. When he surfaced, he shook out his hair like a dog and then freestyled over to me.

I put my hands out as he approached. "Don't get me wet."

"No," he agreed. "It'll be weeks before your donor sites heal up. Check with the doc, but I think it might be up to a year before you can swim after a graft like that."

"A *year*?" I had not gotten that memo.

"But that doesn't mean you can't use the water, if you're careful."

"I'll be careful, Cannonball Run. *You* just be careful."

He frowned like he didn't get my obscure American reference to my dad's favorite Burt Reynolds movie, and then he went on. "The great thing about water is it makes everything easier."

"What are we going to do?"

"We're going to walk," he said, like it was the easiest thing in the world.

I suddenly got the feeling he was about to pull me into the pool. "Be careful!"

He read the nervousness on my face. "Listen. This is the shallow end. It only comes to your waist."

"But I can't stand up."

"You might be able to in the water."

"What if I fall in?"

"I'll catch you."

"But what if you *don't*?"

Ian lifted an eyebrow. "If I suddenly have a heart attack and die while we're in the middle of the pool, I might not catch you. If that happens, float on your back to the edge, and then scream your lungs out until someone comes to help you. Because you are in a hospital, you will get medical care quickly, and because you are on massive antibiotics already, it's unlikely you'll get an infection, but if you do, again, you're already at the hospital."

"What about you?"

"I'm dead already. Just leave me in the pool."

I stifled a smile. "That would traumatize the other patients."

"Toss me in the bin, then. Whatever."

I took a deep breath and geared up for going in. Ian went to put his palms on either side of my ribs, right on the skin, just under my two-piece top—and watching it happen gave me the giddy anticipation you get when someone's coming to tickle you.

I sucked in a breath.

He stopped short of touching me. "What?"

No way was I explaining to him how visceral the anticipation of his hands on my body was. That was need-to-know information. "I'm ticklish," I said.

He nodded, like, *Noted,* and then continued.

"I've got you," he said—and all of a sudden, out of context, he was different. He was the Ian from the roof. He was not the guy in the PT gym with the cartoon scribble of angst above his head. He was not the guy who answered my questions with one-word nonanswers, and grunts, and total silence. He was a guy who had just cracked a joke—possibly two! He was looking into my eyes, and paying attention, and promising me I could trust him.

"Are *you* ticklish?" I asked.

He gave me a look. "Do I *look* ticklish?"

I felt a strong temptation to find out, but I was scared I might fall into the water. "Who are you?" I said then, peering at him.

He frowned, as if the question made no sense. "I'm the guy who's going to walk you across the pool."

With that, he pulled me toward him in a little nudge, and I popped off the edge—and instead of floating down gracefully, I squealed and grabbed him tight around the neck in what could only be described as a very clingy hug.

I didn't mean to. I was just going to bob into the water, like always.

But this wasn't always. My burns felt extra-naked, and I didn't trust my legs to work any better in the water than out. I didn't entirely trust Ian, either. And so: the chicken version of a leap of faith—one that involved clutching his neck with my face buried into the crook of his wet, post-cannonball shoulder.

"Too fast?" he said.

I nodded into his neck, liking the way the skin felt.

"Push back a little. Otherwise, it's not therapy. It's just hugging."

"Hugging could be a type of therapy."

"Not the type your father's going to pay me for."

"He might if I asked him to."

"You can do this. Take a breath."

So I did. Then I pushed myself back until there was half a foot between us, and worked my legs into position as if they were foreign objects. He kept his hands at my rib cage, and I braced mine on his shoulders. Then there we were, waist deep in the water, standing. Right then, I felt it for the first time—almost like an electrical pulse: a tiny flicker of joy.

He saw it. He saw me feel it. There was nowhere to look but straight into his face, and he read me in less than a second.

I couldn't help but smile.

He smiled back. A real smile. The first one of his I'd ever seen. And I felt another electrical pulse.

"You're standing," he said.

"You're smiling," I said.

"I'm not," he said. But that just made him smile more. He threw his head back and said, "Focus! Focus!" To himself, as far as I could tell.

For a flash, as I noticed all those muscles and tendons crisscrossing under the stubble on his throat, I forgot all about myself, and why we were here, and the impossible thing we were trying to do. For a second, he was just a guy in a pool in wet cargo shorts—and I was just a girl, being held.

But just for a second.

Then he brought his face down and got serious. "Okay," he said. "When I take a step backward, you take a step forward."

But it had been too long. I shook my head. "I can't remember how."

"Don't overthink it. Your body remembers. You know how to bring the knee up. Then let the water help the foot follow."

When he took a step back, I brought my knee forward. Then my foot followed behind, carried by the current. Then I set it down.

"I did it!" I whispered.

"Good. Do the other one."

So I did.

It was slow, but it felt so good to work that old, familiar pattern. One foot, then the other, side to side, in that ancient human motion. It was bliss, and heartbreak—both. It was *just enough* of what I wanted to remind me of what I wanted—who I'd been, what I'd lost. That must have been the aspect that made me cry, because by the time we made it to the far side, my face was cold with tears.

But I was smiling. Crying and smiling both. As sad and happy as I'd been in a while. Not numb, that was certain.

"We made it all the way!" I said. Then, because nothing else seemed like it could possibly be more interesting, I said it again. "We made it all the way!"

"Aye. We did."

"I want to high-five you, but I don't want to let go."

"Don't high-five. We're going back across."

I felt like I could go all night, but he said that was just the excitement. He promised I was working much harder than I realized.

"The thing is," I said, as we moved back across. "I don't think my muscles are bringing my foot forward. I think it might just be drifting in the current behind the knee."

"That's okay. The theory is, the more your body does it, the more it will remember what to do. Going through those motions helps spark memories in your body. That's the hope, at least."

"Thank you for not letting me fall."

"We're not out yet."

"Thank you for being so nice to me today."

But Ian didn't have a reply to that, and once again, he got quiet.

Nineteen

ONE NIGHT, A hospital volunteer showed up just after Kitty arrived with Moroccan lamb tagine. She was perky and big-eyed, and she carried a little clipboard. She was recruiting volunteers for a crafts fair that week in the children's wing, and I was just drawing breath to shoo her out when Kitty said, "What kind of crafts?"

"Oh, everything," the volunteer said. "Rock painting, finger knitting, friendship bracelets, balloon rockets, beeswax sculpting, sand candles. Also: anything with googly eyes."

Kitty looked at me. "They are having a lot more fun in the children's wing than we are."

"Would you like to sign up?" the volunteer asked.

"Yes," Kitty said loudly, just as I said, "No."

The volunteer looked at Kitty. "Great."

"Can we sign up for knitting?" Kitty asked. "My sister is knitting a slug."

"Ooo, bring it!" the volunteer said. "The kids will love it."

Kitty wiggled her eyebrows at me. "Maybe we can steal some googly eyes."

After the volunteer left, I said, "I'm not going."

"Yes you are. You just signed up."

"*You* just signed up."

"What else do you have to do?"

"Stop trying to cheer me up. You know it makes me feel worse."

"You feel worse, anyway."

"Yeah. But you make me feel guilty about it."

"Look, I just saw a very inspiring quote on Instagram that said, 'Our struggles lead us to our strengths.'"

"Say the word 'Instagram' one more time and I will burn this building down."

"Fine, but every single article in the entire world says you need to learn to appreciate what you have and not dwell on what you don't."

"Are you *kidding* me right now?"

She hesitated. "Okay, that sounded a little flip."

I rolled my eyes to the ceiling. "It's been four weeks!! Four weeks since I lost everything I cared about. Can I get five minutes to adjust?"

"Yes! Of course! And in the meantime, let's go teach a bunch of hospitalized children how to knit a slug."

"Dammit, stop trying to fix me!"

Ian showed up in the doorway then, but that didn't slow us down. Kitty flung her arm in his direction. "Ian gets to try to fix you!"

I glanced over at him. "It's his job to fix me."

"So?"

"So! A job is different."

"That's better?"

He was right there, listening, but I was hell-bent on making my point. "Yes! Because in less than three weeks, I will never see him again. He won't think about me, he won't worry about me, and he sure as hell won't spend the rest of my life telling me to cheer up. He will feel a wash of relief as I roll out the door to go live my tragic life, and then he'll be done."

I was about to go on, but Ian stepped in closer. "That's not true."

Kitty and I both turned toward him. "What's not true?" I asked.

"I will think about you after you're gone. I expect I'll think about you often."

Was there more? Nope. A man of few words.

But just enough, as we stared at him, to stop the fight in its tracks.

"Want some Moroccan tagine?" Kitty asked after a bit, peeling the lid off a container and holding it out.

Ian said no.

"Maggie's knitting a slug," Kit said then. "Want to see?"

She got him to smile. I loved when he did that. "I'd love to see," he said.

"Hey," I said to Kit, "don't—"

"*Shh.*" Kit held her finger out. "For a scarf, it's terrible. For a knitted slug, it's divine. Just go with 'slug' and be proud." She thrust it at Ian.

He held it for a second, looked back and forth between us, and then said, "That's a fine knitted slug."

Kit turned to me. "Does *everything* sound sexy in Scottish?" Then, back to Ian, "If you were a kid at the craft fair, wouldn't you love to see that?"

He looked up. "The craft fair?"

"Yeah, they're holding one for the kids, but Cranky McCrankypants doesn't want to volunteer."

I gave Kitty a look.

But I did have to give her credit. He seemed to like it when she teased me. His eyes crinkled up at the edges in an expression that was almost warm. And then, like just a normal, friendly, healthcare professional, he shook his head all wryly and said, "Now you make me think of my mother."

Kit and I both frowned. "Your mother?"

"She always said, 'When you don't know what to do for yourself, do something for someone else.'"

WE WENT TO the fair. What choice did we have? Neither of us had the guts to disobey Ian's mother.

The fair turned out to be the most fun I'd had since my incarceration.

There, surrounded by kids of every variety, I felt more relaxed than I had been in all these weeks. In the rehab gym, the focus was on how we could fix what was broken about me. In my room, I was, well, in a hospital room. But in this rec room in the children's wing, it was just bright colors and helium balloons and yarn animals and sing-alongs and face painting. Noisy? Yes. Chaotic? Totally. As I sat at my finger-knitting station with Kit, teaching kids what to do when they came up, and chatting with Kit in between, I felt noticeably peaceful.

"These are your people," Kitty said.

"They do seem to get me," I said.

"You're craftier than I realized," Kit said next, eyeing the long yarn snake I'd been making.

"I'm craftier than *I* realized," I said with a shrug.

It was here, among all this chaos and peace, that Kit decided to give me two pieces of information.

One: She'd booked her flight back to New York. She was leaving on the morning of the same day I was getting discharged.

"You're not going to come home with me?"

She looked at me like I was crazy. "No."

"Not even for a couple of hours? To help me get settled?"

"No. This was the cheapest flight, and I took it."

"I can't believe you're leaving me."

"It's not for two weeks."

'Two and a half," I corrected.

"That's, like, ten years in hospital time."

"Now I have to dread it."

"I did everything I came here for," she said then. "I cleared things up with you. I confronted Mom. I went on an erotic journey with Fat Benjamin."

"Did you come here for that last one?"

She squinted. "I guess Fat Benjamin was a surprise."

"And *did* you clear things up with Mom?" I asked.

"As much as I ever do," she said.

"'Cause it seems like we haven't talked about"—I didn't know how to describe it—"*your information* since the day it all came out."

Kit shrugged. "Yeah, well. We've all been kind of busy."

True, we'd been busy. But this was also a classic Jacobsen-family technique for responding to big, earth-shattering news: pretending it didn't exist.

There was probably a more delicate way to ask the question, but I said, "Don't you want to know who your real dad is?"

Kit got quiet at the sound of the words out loud.

"Our dad *is* my real dad."

Had I hurt her feelings? "Of course he is," I corrected. "I just I meant your *biological* dad."

She thought about it. "I've thought about it. I am curious. But as long as Dad doesn't know, it feels disloyal to take it any further."

"And Dad will never know."

We agreed.

Two: Kit's other piece of news was she had decided to throw a party on her last night here. In the rehab gym.

"They'll never let you do that," I said.

"It's closed at night. No one has to know."

It was a "Valentine's Day party," even though it would happen on the first of April.

"Details," Kit said, making a *pshaw* motion. "Love can happen anytime."

"Do you know that's April Fools'?"

"Only you would notice that."

"You realize what happened to me the last time it was Valentine's Day," I said.

"Yes," she said.

Of course she knew. We all knew. But I said it anyway. "I was in a *plane crash*."

"Duh. I'm aware of that. I'm giving you a do-over."

I shook my head. "No."

But she had a fire in her eyes. "I'll do everything. You don't have to do anything. I'll talk to the nurses, hang the decorations. I've got a vision! Little heart-shaped chocolates everywhere, punch that we'll call 'love potion,' and Fat Benjamin's got a chocolate fountain that he stole from a catering gig. Streamers, and karaoke with nothing but love songs, and I've got that old disco ball in my high school bedroom. I love stuff like this! Let me do something for you. Yes?"

Maybe it was because the kids' craft fair was so unexpectedly charming, but I let out a long sigh, and as soon as my shoulders sank, she knew she'd won.

She held up her arms in victory.

"Who would you even invite?" I said. Then I pointed a warning at her: "Nobody from Facebook. No normal people, okay?"

"Just injured people. Just the folks on your floor. And the nurses. And anybody else good. Plus Fat Benjamin, of course."

"Why do you have to do this?" I asked. "Let's just eat tacos and watch TV."

"I need to go out with a bang," she said. "And guess what? So do you."

That's when it hit me. "You've already started planning this, haven't you?"

She wiggled her eyebrows at me. "It was supposed to be a surprise, but you know I can't keep a secret."

"You sneaky weasel!"

"I dare you to be mad," she said, "when you're drinking straight out of the chocolate fountain."

Twenty

THE NEXT NIGHT, Kitty showed up with some astonishing information: I'd been granted a furlough.

She held out a box of spanakopita with a triumphant flourish and said, "Great news!"

I was knitting a new slug. "What?"

"We have an amazing birthday present for you."

I had to think about it. Sure enough, my birthday was coming up on Sunday. "I forgot about my birthday," I said.

"You are not going to believe how great your present is."

"My face is back to normal?"

Kit frowned and then squinted at me. "Not quite," she said. "But close."

"What, then?"

Kit stretched up taller. "We are about to blow your mind."

"Who's 'we'?"

"Mom and me."

"Since when are you and Mom a 'we'?"

Kitty's expression darkened. "It's a fragile, don't-ask-don't-tell truce."

I frowned. How was that possible?

"Never underestimate Linda's ability to compartmentalize," Kit said. "Or mine, either."

"So you're not talking about anything?"

"Nothing but you."

"Okay."

"She hates everything about how I look, though."

"Of course she does."

"Especially the tattoos."

I gave Kit a look. *Of course she does.*

"It was her idea, actually. This whole thing."

"What whole thing?"

Kit pretended to blow a trumpet. "Announcing the greatest birthday news ever!" she announced. "We are giving you a night out."

"A night out?"

Kit dropped her voice back to normal. "Mom thought you might like to have spaghetti and cake at home."

Our traditional birthday dinner. Spaghetti and cake. The thought of it made me sad. "I don't want to go home."

"I know." Kitty looked pleased with herself. "I told her that! And Dad backed me up."

"I don't have to go to Mom's?"

"No. Better."

"Where?"

Kit did a little shimmy. "The lake."

"The lake? Our lake?"

She clapped.

But it was no good. "I can't go to the lake," I said. It was my grandparents' old fishing cabin. Rustic, to say the least. Hardly wheelchair accessible.

"You can! It's all set up!"

"They'll never let me out of here for that."

"Mom got them to okay it. It's all official. I was waiting to tell you until it was certain. We'll spend Saturday night at the lake. Which means you will wake up on your birthday *not* in the hospital."

"But . . ." I wasn't sure what to think. Kit wanted me to be excited, but it just seemed like such a terrible, awful, exhausting idea.

"We figured it all out. Mom's been down there all week, cleaning so it shines. Fresh sheets, dust-free: the works. Plus a ton of groceries to stock the kitchen."

"Is Mom coming, too?"

"No! That's just it! I said, 'Mom, Margaret is a young person! She wants to spend her birthday with young people!' And Dad backed me up."

"So who am I spending it with?"

"Me!"

This sounded worse and worse. "Kit, you can't take care of me. You can barely take care of yourself."

"Rude. And untrue. And I *can* take care of you, because I talked your boyfriend into coming with us—and he's going to do all the hard stuff."

My boyfriend? "Who—*Chip*?" I hadn't seen or heard from him—absolutely nothing—since the night we'd ended it. It was like he never existed.

Kit shook her head. "No. Your *Scottish* boyfriend."

I put my hand over my mouth. "You didn't."

"I did!"

"You asked him?"

She nodded.

"And he said yes?"

"I might've implied I could accidentally kill you."

I leaned back against the pillow. "No."

"Anyway, that's your real present. Now you can have forbidden sex with your secret love." Then she frowned and leaned in to whisper, "Your vagina still works, right?"

I put my hand over my eyes. "No secret love. No forbidden sex. Come on, Kit!"

"You think I'm an amateur? You think I can't read that sexual tension? Sexual tension is my primary language!"

"Kit, look at me. Look at my life."

"So?"

"This is not junior high. I'm a month into a total shit-storm of utter devastation."

"All the more reason to have a little fun."

"I hate fun. I don't even believe in fun anymore."

"You do when you're with Ian."

"We are not doing this."

"It's all arranged. He's taking a personal day and everything."

"So me, you, and my physical therapist are going to the lake for my birthday?"

Kit nodded. "And Fat Benjamin, too. For a little forbidden sex of my own."

"What about the Moustache?"

"We're nonexclusive."

I'd grown up spending long weekends and summers at this little fishing cottage, scampering around the yard, swimming for endless hours, only breaking for lunch and dinner, and exploring the lake in the rowboat. I'd spent my childhood there, never even imagining—of course—that I'd end up like this. The idea of facing any normal thing now, with my life so changed—even the grocery store or a movie theater—seemed heartbreaking. But a place so happy? A place so densely layered with memories of my other life? A place where the future had always been something to look forward to?

It broke my heart to even consider it.

And yet. It was all arranged. I did want to get out of here. I did love that lake. The cottage was only a hundred feet or so back from the shore, and when you woke, the first thing you saw was morning sunlight glittering on the water. I did want to see that. I longed to be someplace beautiful.

Kit went on, "We're going to eat camp food and make s'mores."

My stomach felt like it was filled with pebbles. I wanted to go exactly as much as I wanted *not* to go.

But I didn't know how to refuse. It was happening. Plus, Kit wasn't wrong: I did believe in fun when Ian was around.

* * *

IAN AND I had become quite the ninja rehab team since he'd become my tutor. I stayed motivated and focused, and Ian finally caught on to the notion that people do better when you encourage them. We worked every day in the gym, and then we worked again after dinner.

In fact, he was the only person I'd told about my morning toe-wiggling attempts, which had become quite a ritual for me. I never started a day without giving my toes a little pep talk and then trying to rev them up.

"What do you say to them?" he asked, when I told him about it.

"To my toes?"

He nodded. "In the pep talks."

In the name of healthcare, I told the truth. "I say, 'Come on, little guys. You're a lot stronger than you think you are.' "

"What do they say back?"

I gave him a look. "They say, 'Right back atcha, lady.' "

Some nights, I was tired, and he just hung out in the room with Kit and me, working my lower legs in a low-key way, with texture therapy, or stretching, or massage, and talking in a far more relaxed way than I ever saw in the gym. In the gym, with Myles never far off, Ian was always all business. He scowled less now, maybe, but he still scowled a lot.

But after-hours Ian was different.

First of all, he was jazzed about our activities. In the rehab gym, he had a going-through-the-motions vibe, but on his own, he was full of energy and surprises. When I wasn't too tired, we went to the pool, where he had a whole array of inflatables to cheer the place up—surfboards and noodles and blow-up unicorns. Other times, he'd show up with an acupuncturist friend, and do acupuncture right there in my room while Kitty ate sesame chicken and looked on. Now and again, he brought a reflexologist who also dabbled in aromatherapy. Once, he had a chiropractor friend in tow—which was a little alarming because I did not want her even *touching*, must less adjusting, my back—but she just used a handheld ultrasound machine to stimulate my calves and feet.

Was it helping? Who knows? It wasn't *hurting*.

The rehab gym was all work, but tutoring became play.

Some nights, we played Pop-A-Shot outside the rehab gym until bedtime. The first time we ever tried it, after I explained in detail how much I sucked at basketball, I beat Ian's score by thirteen points. He wasn't thrilled about that. After that, I beat him every time we played. I'd sit in front of the basket as Ian handed me basketballs, and I'd make swish after swish after swish until the timer went off. Then Ian would take a turn. Sometimes he made baskets, sometimes he didn't. I'm sure he was fine at it. But, to everyone's surpirse, I was remarkable. I never missed. And this drove Ian crazy—especially since I had never even seen a Pop-A-Shot game before now.

I liked driving him crazy.

The first night he'd showed up for tutoring, he'd stood the entire time, like an at-ease officer, and waited for Kit and me to eat. Now, he'd long since given in, and he and Kit sat in visitor chairs on either side of me, the bed lowered to table height, dinner spread out all over it, wedging containers between my ankles or up against my knees.

Maybe it was the food, or the easy rapport between me and Kit, or just being far enough from Myles—but sometimes Ian seemed like a different guy entirely. An easygoing, smiley, *likable* guy. The more we saw that guy, the more we wanted to see him. It became a game.

Kit and I ganged up on Ian a lot, trying to make him smile, or blush, or laugh out loud—ideally all three. Embarrassing him worked like a charm. We cursed. We talked about shocking "lady" things. We made him teach us Scottish insults. Turns out, there were plenty, and they were delightful. Both words—"clipe," "dobber," "scrote," "roaster," "numpty," "jakey," "walloper"—and phrases: "Shut ye geggie," "erse like a bag o' washin'," and "yer bum's oot the windae." Not to mention "baw," meaning "testicle," which apparently goes with just about anything: "bawbag," "bawface," "bawjaws." Plus, just words for regular things were awesome: "oxter" for armpit, "cludgie" for toilet, "blootered" for drunk, and "puggled" for out of breath.

Ian gave us the shocking news that the Scottish accent was not as universally adored in the U.K. as in the U.S.

"They're just jealous," Kit said.

"Should we not make fun of your accent, then?" I asked. It was one thing to make fun of an accent that was unassailably cool—and quite another to kick an accent that was down.

"You can make fun of Scottish," he said, "if I can make fun of Texan."

Kit and I looked at each other. "*Can* you make fun of Texan?"

Ian pointed at me. "You say 'tumped' for 'fell over.' You know that's not a word, right?"

"It *is* a word," I said.

Ian shook his head. "Only in Texas."

We loved to try to copy his accent, but we were bad at it. We also gave him American words to try, especially Native American place names that Kit Googled on her phone, like the Caloosahatchee River, Lake Tangipahoa, and Quittapahilla Creek. It cracked her up to hear him try, and it mesmerized me. I'd watch his lips forming those sounds, pulling back, and pouting out, and making that classic Scottish *o*. Sometimes I forgot to laugh. Sometimes I got hypnotized by it.

He turned out to be remarkably game. We got started to bring him out of his stoic shell, but it always got us going, too. We laughed so hard at dinner sometimes that we couldn't even finish our food. It was the kind of goofy, uncontrollable laughing you almost never do in grown-up life: Things weren't just funny, they were *hysterical*—even things that were objectively not even funny: the noise of a scooting chair, a veggie dumpling that got dropped on the floor, a nurse coming into the room to investigate the noise.

It's strange that I could have laughed so hard under those circumstances, during that very dark moment in my life. But I've decided sorrow can make things funnier. Endure enough hardship, and you start really needing a good laugh. I remember my dad and his brother, on the day of their own mother's funeral back when I was a kid, in the car, driving to the cemetery, making fun of all their relatives and cracking each other up. They were in the front seat, and Kit and I and our mom were in the back, and I watched those two grown men, now motherless, having just lost forever a woman they both truly loved, not just chuckle a bit but *howl* with laughter.

I was maybe ten at the time. “What are you doing?” I demanded of my dad. “How can you be laughing?”

“Sweetheart,” my dad said, “if we don’t laugh, we’re gonna cry.”

That’s what this laughing was like. It took us over. It made our faces hurt. And it happened not despite all the sadness, but because of it.

Kit was bolder than I was. She begged him to wear a kilt to work one day.

“Wear a kilt to this building,” she said, “and I’ll give you ten thousand dollars.”

“She doesn’t have ten thousand dollars,” I whispered to Ian.

Ian smiled. “And I don’t have a kilt, so we’re even.”

Mostly, it was Kit and me egging Ian on, but one night, eating sushi, he picked up a teaspoon-sized wad of wasabi with his chopsticks, held it up so we could see it, and then said, “Do you dare me to eat this?”

I looked at him like he was crazy. “The whole thing?” One tenth of that wasabi ball would be enough to send steam out his ears.

Ian nodded.

“No,” Kit said. “I won’t dare you. Not even I am that crazy.”

“I’ll dare you,” I said—and before I could take it back, Ian had popped the whole thing in his mouth, swallowed, and thrown his arms up in victory.

Kitty and I both gaped at him.

“Not so bad,” Ian said, but the words were barely out before tears started running down his cheeks, and his face turned red, and he started panting and hissing like a feral cat.

He grabbed his water and drank the whole bottle in one go. Then he grabbed my water and drank it all. Then Kit’s, too.

“Whooo!” he said, pacing around the room. “Fuck—that stings.”

“Curse in Scottish!” we called out.

But he was jogging in place now. “Not my best idea.”

“Say ‘bawjaws’!” Kit suggested.

"Call yourself a 'numpty jobber'!" I jumped in.

"Dobber," he corrected, while bent over at the waist, panting. Then he banged his head against the foot of the bed. Then he realized he was drooling, and took the wad of Kleenex I was waving at him.

In all, it took half an hour for him to recover, and that's when he threw us a bone and gave us a little Scottish. "I *am* a dobber," he said. "What was I thinking?"

"You were thinking," I said, not even bothering to hide the affection in my voice, "that you'd entertain us."

It was like we had all made an unspoken pact to choose to have fun.

"That's backed up by science," Kitty, Queen of Googling, said, when I noticed how much just the idea of dinner with her and Ian was impacting the rest of my sad days. "Anticipating a reward lights up the same region of the brain as actually getting a reward," she said. "That's what a dum-dum the brain is. It doesn't even know the difference."

There was nothing, truly nothing, fun about any other part of my day. But I anticipated the hell out of dinner.

Twenty-one

THE MORNING OF my furlough was a usual morning—bathing, cleaning, failed attempts to wiggle my toes—and my parents came for their usual lunch. But then, instead of heading off to the rehab gym, I transferred to the chair, and my parents wheeled me down with a little overnight bag to where Kit was waiting in my father's sedan.

I felt surprisingly anxious about leaving the hospital.

I would have said I'd be thrilled, elated, ecstatic to leave. Instead, I just felt shaky. I didn't trust Kit to drive my dad's big car. I didn't trust all the idiot drivers texting their way through intersections. I didn't trust the big, bad, chaotic world outside my controlled little hospital biosphere.

Even in the car, I couldn't relax. If I'd been a cat with claws, they would have been impaled in the dashboard. Every turn, every red light, every touch of the brakes made me wince with anxiety.

"You have got to chill," Kit said.

I nodded. "Yes. Good advice. Chill."

But I had no idea how to do that. How do you *make yourself* chill?

By the time we made it to the cabin, the tension in my neck was migrating to my head. I felt woozy and headachy, and Kit declared I had to take a nap.

Of course, the house was not wheelchair accessible. Why would it be? We got me into the chair and across the gravel drive, but then we had to pause for a while to puzzle out how to get me into the house.

"I knew this was a bad idea," I said.

"Hush," Kit said. "If nothing else, your Scotsman can carry you in when he gets here." She tromped off to examine the back porch to see if it might make a better point of entry, calling back, "Would that be so awful?"

"Just go," I said, closing my eyes.

Being back here was exactly as bad as I'd feared. Everything was the same as it had been since my grandparents had bought the place in the sixties. The screen porch door still squeaked and slapped. The gopher hole by the back steps hadn't moved. The pear trees my grandmother had planted still rustled in the breeze.

The only thing different was me.

It created such a visceral wash of grief through my body, I had to lean over and put my head between my knees. "We never should have come here," I heard myself whisper.

I was going to throw up. I felt that salty feeling under my tongue you get just before it happens.

But then I heard tires on the gravel of the driveway.

I looked up to see a brown vintage Bronco. With Ian in it. And then the door was slamming. And he was walking across the grass toward me with a duffel bag on his shoulder. In jeans, of all things, instead of scrubs. And brown leather shoes instead of sneakers. And a plaid flannel shirt.

I forgot to throw up.

"This place suits you," Ian said, as he got close.

"Really? Because I was just about to throw up."

"Carsick?"

"Heartsick, I think."

"Does it make you sad to come here again?"

I nodded.

"But happy, too, I hope?"

I shook my head. "Not yet. But I'm glad to see you."

"Why are you out here alone?"

"Kitty's trying to figure out how to get me in."

Ian nodded. "I can help with that," and as he said it, he dropped his duffel without a thought, kneeled down, pivoted, and backed up to me all at once. "Let's go," he said, jerking his head for me to climb on.

So I did. He hooked his arms under my knees, and I gripped with my thighs, and held on to his shoulders. Just for a second, I got another intoxicating whiff of him, and then we were off, rounding the side of the house, looking for Kit.

Ian stopped for a second when he caught sight of the lake—blue and bright and bigger than I remembered. The lawn sloped down to it, and from where we stood, we had a perfect, clear view.

"This is your lake?" Ian asked.

"This is our lake," I said, and when I spoke, my cheek brushed his neck.

"Will you take me out on it?" Ian asked.

"Of course."

Just then, Kit rounded the corner. "We're just going to have to wait for—" Then she saw us, and looked Ian over, in his flannel shirt and jeans. "The Brawny paper-towel guy."

I DIDN'T WANT to go back after that. It's not that Ian showing up made everything okay—it didn't. It made everything a little better, though. My heart was still humming a mournful tune, but it was like Ian arriving had introduced a little countermelody. It hadn't stopped the sad song, but it had altered it.

I needed to pee—we all did, after the drive—so after Kit opened the doors, Ian carried me to the bathroom and set me on the toilet with all my clothes still on.

"Do you need help?" he asked.

Even if I had needed it, no way in hell was I asking. "I've got it," I said.

The wheelchair turned out to be fifty percent useless at the lake. The ground was too grassy and gravelly for it to roll well, and the doorways inside the house were too narrow. Upside: Ian carried me a lot.

It was almost my birthday, after all.

It was a crisp, sunny day, and my next order of business was to sit in an Adirondack chair in the sun near the water while Kit and Ian unpacked. I couldn't expose my grafts to sunlight, so Kitty brought me out a pink dotted umbrella. I positioned it carefully to cover my burns but leave the rest of me—toes, legs, right arm—gloriously exposed. How long had it been since I'd felt the sun on my skin? I closed my eyes and drank in the feeling. The breeze was cool, but I felt warm.

Despite everything that had happened, and everything still to bear, this moment right here was pretty nice.

I don't know how much time passed, but my headache had gone by the time I heard footsteps crunching down the gravel path toward me.

It was Ian. "Kit wants me to bring out the boats," he said, not breaking stride.

I nodded, and went back to sunning, but I didn't close my eyes again.

Ian unlocked the boathouse and dragged boat after boat to the shore: a rowboat, two kayaks, two wakeboards, a clunky old paddle boat for fishing, and a canoe that my grandpa had painted with Cherokee designs. Back and forth he went. Mesmerizing.

After a bit, Kitty joined me, and before she'd even sat down, she said, "Now that's a gorgeous hunk of man, right there."

"He's not a man, he's a physical therapist."

Kit did not shift her gaze. "Pretty sure he's both."

"Where's *your* man?" I asked.

"Which one?" she said, looking sly.

"The chubby-but-cute one," I answered.

She looked a little offended on principle. A little protective even. "He's on his way."

We watched Ian line up the last boat and then turn toward us. I guess boat dragging must be hard work, because he took off his flannel shirt as he walked, wadding it up to wipe the back of his neck, and leaving only his white undershirt.

Kit let out a low whistle.

"Kit!" I said. "Don't objectify him!"

"That's not my fault," she said, gesturing. "I can't be held responsible for that."

When Ian made it to us, he dropped the flannel shirt on the grass. His eyes were on me. "Want to show me the lake?"

"Yes," I said, too quickly.

"Actually, she wants to take a nap," Kit said.

I swatted Kit. "I do not!"

"I thought about the kayak," Ian said, "but I'm worried about it tipping."

I was worried about my neck, too. The water in this lake was certainly not as chlorinated as the therapy pool.

"The canoe's fine," I said.

"Can I come, too?" Kit asked.

"No," we both said.

Ian carried me and my polka-dot parasol down to the water's edge, and then I waited on the grass while he moved the painted canoe into the water. Then he lifted me again and sloshed into the lake, jeans and all, and set me carefully in the boat.

The canoe wobbled as Ian climbed in, and I felt a little jolt of fear. I hadn't worn a life vest in this thing since I was a little kid, and this was the kind that wrapped around your neck like an airplane pillow. Of course, I couldn't put anything around my neck—I was still wearing all my shirts with the shoulder cut out—so I just wrapped it awkwardly under my arms and snapped it tight.

"I look ridiculous," I said.

Ian shook his head. "You look—" He stopped himself for a few attention-grabbing seconds before continuing on. "Resourceful."

"I get that all the time," I said, putting on my sunglasses, wondering what he'd been about to say.

It wasn't the busy season yet at the lake. It felt like we had it all to ourselves.

"Where to?" Ian asked, and I pointed to the far side.

I was totally okay not talking. The paddle lapped the water, the canoe sloshed and slapped, the wind whispered. I remembered this place so well—it was so much a part of the fabric of who I was—that I could almost put myself here without being here.

But actually being here, out on the water, alive like this—just the fact of it was breathtaking.

I directed Ian to paddle past a hundred-year-old house, the first one built here, and I told him every ghost story I'd ever heard about it. Next, we passed the decade-old unfinished mansion that some hedge fund guy had started and then abandoned. "That one's haunted, too," I said. Later, we passed the spot where the sailboat races happened every July, and then the giant floating trampoline all the kids liked to row out to, and the little hamburger joint that had no parking at all for cars—only docks for boats.

I leaned closer to the water and let my fingers dangle in. I'd dangled my fingers in this very water in this very boat in weather just like this a thousand times. The houses were the same, the clouds were the same, and even the beach where I'd been supposed to get married was the same.

Through it all, Ian paddled a steady pace, and I let myself feel just exactly as happy as I was sad.

I marveled at the feeling, because it really wasn't either-or. It was both, equally strong at the exact same time.

If you'd asked me before the crash, I'd have told you that feelings were like blocks of primary colors: You felt blue for a while, then yellow, then red. But now I saw the emotional landscape quite differently—more like the pointillism of a Seurat painting: each color made up of many other colors. Look closely, and it's dots. Stand back, and it's an afternoon on the lake—all the colors relying on each other for texture and meaning.

Maybe that would turn out to be an upside, I found myself thinking. Maybe I'd see the world like an artist now.

I could have just closed my eyes and given in to the drift. But I had a question for Ian that had been nagging me, and now that I had him alone, I had to ask.

"Tell me something," I said, keeping my voice casual.

"Okay," Ian said, still rowing.

"Why did your business fail?"

I could sense him tensing up at the words.

But I was already in, so I kept going, keeping my eyes out on the water. "What happened?"

Ian didn't answer. Just kept rowing.

"I mean, it was such a brilliant idea."

Ian was quiet for so long, I finally turned to look at him.

"I didn't manage things very well," he said at last. "I neglected it too much."

I shrugged, like, *Okay*. Like that was all the answer I'd wanted.

But, of course, his answer just created more questions. Why would a guy with such a great idea go to all the trouble of setting up a business—inventing an entirely new business!—and then neglect it?

I could tell just from the angle of his posture that he didn't want to talk about it.

I let it go.

We weren't here to be unhappy.

We were here to try, at least for a little while, to be the opposite.

BY THE TIME we got back, the sun was going down, and Fat Benjamin, who was far more "tubby" than fat, with a plump body like a dumpling and a bushy hipster beard, had arrived. He and Kit were building the bonfire. Ian piggybacked me over to the fire and got me settled in a chair, and I watched Kit and Benjamin flirt. He couldn't seem to stop his hands from touching her—and she didn't seem to mind.

Kit made us a vegetable stew in a pot on a grate over the fire. ("He's a vegan," she apologized, when the guys went to get more wood.) As the sun went down, the air cooled, and Ian went in for blankets. When he came back out with a stack, he also had something else under his arm.

A ukulele.

"You *are* musical!" Kit said when she saw it.

Ian shook his head. "I haven't played in years. But I can play 'Happy Birthday.'"

So he did. Serenaded me with it, really. I wrapped my blanket around everything but my burned neck, and after that, we all sat around the fire while Ian played requests and let us sing along. He messed up over and over, but nobody cared but him.

"Don't apologize," I said. "You are the best ukulele player I've ever met."

Ian gave me a half-smile. "Am I the only ukulele player you've ever met?"

"You bet."

He knew a little Bob Dylan, a little James Taylor, one Van Morrison, and a whole lotta Beatles.

That's how my birthday bonfire turned into a nonstop Beatles birthday luau. We sang and sang and sang. And ate vegan stew. And then, for a birthday cake, made cast-iron skillet brownies with melted marshmallows over the fire.

"I thought we were making s'mores," I said.

"We've made a million s'mores," Kit said. "Time for something new."

I'd cooked many meals in this fire pit before, and I'd celebrated many birthdays here, but I confess, as familiar as it all was, I'd never done it quite like this. Everything felt a little bit new.

I found myself wanting to stay and stay—or, at least, not wanting to go inside.

Ian kept checking with me to see if I was ready, and I kept shaking my head. I got cold, in my sundress, but I still didn't want to leave the fire. Kit and Benjamin cleaned up the stew, and took the pots and pans inside to wash, and then disappeared to get up to who-knows-what kind of mischief, but I didn't care. I loved looking at the fire. I loved feeling cold. I loved being out in the world. I loved calling out songs for Ian to play. He sang, and I sang, and I loved listening to our voices twist and wind around each other.

Tomorrow, it would all be over. We'd wake up and drive back to real life in an ugly hospital with fluorescent lights and mauve curtains. The sooner I fell asleep, the sooner this would all be gone. And I just didn't want to let that happen.

Finally, Ian said, "You've got to be cold. I'm freezing my arse off."

"I don't care."

He peered in. "Your lips look a little blue."

He set down his uke and came closer, and when he took my hands, he said, "Good God, Maggie. You're frozen solid."

In one swoop, he picked me up—this time, not piggyback, but cradling me in his arms. He tucked my good side against his chest, and I did my best to be easy to carry by hooking my arm around his shoulder and resting my head down against the crook of his neck. That intoxicating Ian smell. I let myself breathe it in and savor it. Then I wondered if I could just brush my lips across the nape without him noticing.

He marched us across the yard and then into the warm, bright house, through the kitchen, and up the stairs.

Inside was quiet, like it was empty, and I wondered if Kit and Benjamin had gone for a walk. Ian nudged lights on as he went. At the top of the stairs, he hesitated. I could feel the pulse in his neck beating.

"Which room?" he asked.

"At the end of the hall," I said.

Ian felt around for the hall light with his elbow, but he didn't find it, so he just moved on ahead through the dark. It wasn't impossible to see. There were shadows and outlines. He stepped carefully, but without too much hesitation. The door to my room was open, and the bed was just beyond it. It was lit by blue moonlight reflected off the lake.

He moved toward it, stepped through the doorway—and then he tripped on a little rag rug at the threshold.

He pitched forward, and then dropped to his knees. He clutched me tight to him as it happened, and then, intent on not falling forward and landing on top of me, he managed to fall backward.

Which meant I landed on top of him.

Fully on top. Smack-dab on top, you could even say.

At first, after impact, we were all about figuring out if anyone was injured. Had he hit his head or twisted anything? *No.* Was my graft okay? *Yes.* My back? *All fine.* Was anybody in any pain? Apparently not.

That's when we took stock of our situation: alone, in a moonlit room by a tranquil lake, on the floor, a little breathless.

My face was just inches from his, and we held there, frozen, for a few very long seconds, breaths churning, eyes alert. His were so dark blue, they looked black.

So I did a crazy thing that seemed like, really, the only thing to do: I leaned down, pressed my mouth against his, and kissed him.

Boom. I wasn't cold anymore.

I pulled back then, to check his expression and see what he thought—but he reached his hand up just as quick behind my head to bring me back. Another kiss. This one deeper and warmer and slower. I'd eyed those lips so much in the past weeks—and longed to touch them, even just with my fingers, to see if they were as soft as they looked. To see if they tasted as good as he smelled. And now I knew. Yes.

"You taste like brownies," I said, through the kiss, my mouth still touching his.

"You taste like marshmallows," he said back, and then he dove back in, brushing his tongue past mine.

"I love your accent," I said, a minute later, pulling back a little.

"I love yours," he said, leaning forward to catch my mouth with his.

"I love your ukulele," I said another minute later.

"I love yours."

"I don't have a ukulele."

"I don't care."

I wriggled around to get a better angle, and he wound up solidly on his back, me straddling him, and my palms flat against the floor on either side of his head, bodies pressed together.

"Are you sure you didn't get hurt?" I asked then, still kissing him.

"I got a little hurt."

"Where?"

"Doesn't matter."

"Does it hurt now?"

"Nothing hurts now."

What was my goal here? Was I trying to seduce my physical therapist? I wasn't even sure if I had been cleared for that type of thing! All I knew was, I wanted to get closer. I would have climbed inside his rib cage, if I could have. I wanted to devour him and be devoured back. Whatever tangled forest of feelings bloomed in my body every time I saw him—I just wanted to get lost in that forest and never find my way out.

I did get lost. I brought my mouth down to his neck, nuzzling in and biting a little, and he ran both his hands up my back, stopping short, bringing his hand around on my nonburned side to guide my mouth back to his.

For a moment, the two of us, just like that, made up the entire world. Nothing but longing, and closeness, and warmth.

That's why I didn't hear Kit and Fat Benjamin clomping up the stairs. Or trundling down the hall. Or turning the squeaky old door handle.

No. The first I noticed Kit and Fat Benjamin, they were pushing open the door and flipping on the lights and discovering the two of us down on the floor.

"OMG!" Kit said, slapping her hand over her mouth to cover a giggle. "This room appears to be taken."

"Get out, Kit!" I said, in a classic annoyed-sister voice.

"Sorry!" Fat Benjamin said, giving us both a little salute of apology.

They stepped back out of the room and slammed the door shut behind them, leaving the overhead light on.

"Wait!" I heard Kit say on the other side of the door. "Were they hooking up?"

With that, all the moonlight disappeared.

Ian blinked at the doorway where they'd just been, like he was waking up from a dream. I still sat astride him, trying to catch my breath, wondering how to get the moonlight back.

But he was up on his elbows now. "Oh, God, Maggie," he said, twisting sideways to move out from under me.

I shifted onto the floor beside him as he stood and turned to scoop me up.

He lifted me to the bed.

I held on to a doomed little hope that maybe we were just moving to a more comfortable location.

But once he had me securely settled, he turned away and walked to the window. He touched the curtain idly for a minute, delivering his signature silence. Finally, when he spoke, he said, "Maggie, I'm sorry."

"What are you sorry for?"

"I shouldn't have done that."

"You didn't do anything. *I* kissed *you*."

"I shouldn't have kissed you back."

"Because," I guessed, "messing around with patients is against your code of ethics?"

Ian was pacing a little bit now.

I tried again. "Because if Myles ever finds out, you'll lose your job?"

"If Myles ever finds out, I'll lose my *license*," Ian said. "But that's not it."

"What, then?"

"It wasn't fair to you."

There was nothing I wanted more than to be back in his arms. "I think it was fair. I think it was very fair."

Ian shoved his hand into his hair. "You're not qualified to judge."

"I'm not *what*?"

He turned to look at me for the first time. The overhead light seemed awfully bright. "You're not in a fit state to judge."

"You're saying I don't know the difference between what's fair and what's unfair?"

"I'm saying—"

"Because my fiancé crashing a plane that I didn't even want to go anywhere near and paralyzing me while he walks away without even a Band-Aid? Obviously: *unfair*. You coming here and playing 'Happy Birthday' on the ukulele and giving me the best kiss of my entire life? I'm going with *fair* on that one."

"That's just it. It wasn't the best kiss of your entire life."

I raised my eyebrows in disbelief. "It wasn't?"

"You just thought it was."

"Pretty sure that's the same thing."

But he shook his head. "When a person goes through something like what you've just gone through, when your whole world is ripped apart, it takes a long time before you can see things clearly again. Months. Years, even. The trauma leaves you vulnerable in ways you can't even feel. I know all about this. I've been trained on it—read textbooks, taken tests. It's against my code of ethics for a reason, Margaret—a good reason. To protect you."

I was Margaret now? I noticed tears on my face, but I had no patience for them. I smeared them off with my sleeve. "I don't care about any of that."

"But I have to. For your sake."

"But you—" A big, shaky breath interrupted me. I hesitated to go on, because it felt like a big thing to admit. But I had to try. I had to at least speak honestly. I took another breath, and said it: "You are the only thing I look forward to all day long."

He closed his eyes in what looked like a wince. Not the effect I'd hoped for. "That's exactly what I'm trying to tell you," he said.

"I don't understand."

"The things you feel about me mean that you are not safe. I shouldn't have come here. I knew there was a risk this might happen."

So he knew I liked him before he came. I pulled in a ragged breath. "Don't you like me at all?"

Ian shoved his hand into his hair again. Then he walked to the bedroom door, turning those navy-blue eyes to settle them right on me. "I hate everybody," he said. "Except you." He pulled the door open to leave, then added, "And that's another reason you're not safe."

"Are you leaving?" I asked. He was clearly leaving the room. But I meant, "Are you going back to town?"

"No. Of course not. I'll stay the night to look after you."

"I don't need looking after."

"You want me to leave Tweedle Dum and Tweedle Dee in charge?"

Not really, I supposed.

He continued. "I'll make sure you get back safe tomorrow."

"You're not going to switch me to some other PT, are you?"

"That's up to you."

I couldn't even imagine anybody else. "I don't want another PT."

"Then I'll stay."

"Are you still going to come for tutoring?"

"Yes, if you like. But I'll come after supper—just to keep things clear."

"No goofing around?"

He shook his head. "It's best."

What could I say? It's not best, it's *worst*? There was no way to win. He had decided I wasn't qualified to know what was right for me. And from the sound of things, he didn't trust himself too much, either. Was he rejecting me? Was he uninterested? Could you kiss a person like that and not feel something, at least? I knew there was longing there—but maybe it was just a general longing for anyone at all. Maybe he was so lonely, any live girl would do—even a broken one like me.

He was still standing at the door, staring down at his hand on the knob. He looked up. "I brought a present to give you tomorrow," he said then. "But maybe you don't want it now."

I turned my eyes to the window. "Just throw it away," I said.

I heard the door click closed behind him, and then he was gone.

I stayed awake for a good while after that—waiting to hear Kit creep back to her bedroom, because I needed to pee and I'd be damned before I asked Ian to take me. Maybe I'd be better off without him. He certainly seemed to think so. But in all that time of thinking, I could not for one second imagine how.

Twenty-two

THE NEXT DAY—my actual birthday—did not shake down the way I expected.

I expected to wake up and work my way through an awkward breakfast with Kit and Benjamin all lovey-dovey while Ian stared out the window with a face of stone.

But that's not what happened, exactly.

When I opened my eyes and tried to move my toes, as I did every morning—one of them did something utterly shocking.

It moved.

It *wiggled*.

The big toe on my right foot, to be exact.

Part of me thought I might still be asleep.

I tried again, and it moved again.

"Hey!" I shouted. "Hey!"

In seconds, all three of my lake housemates came bursting through the door in a hilarious potpourri of pajamas that made it clear I was definitely the first one up. Kit was in a hot-pink negligée, a sight I'd never seen before, and Fat Benjamin had a remarkable, gravity-defying bed-beard situation going on. Ian, I did my best not to notice, slept in blue cotton pajama bottoms. Only. Also, his hair was even more unruly than Benjamin's beard—but to be honest, it just made him cuter.

None of that mattered, anyway. "Am I dreaming?" I demanded.

"The sun's not even up," Kit said, in her best big-sister voice.

"I need to know if I'm dreaming right now. Am I?"

Fat Benjamin ventured, "Of course, if you were dreaming, then we wouldn't really be able to give you a straight answer."

Ian stepped closer. "What's going on?"

"Look," I said, pointing at my toe.

Everybody looked.

I pushed it down, then pulled it back.

"No! You! Did! Not!" Kit shrieked, turning around to hug me.

"What?" Benjamin said. "I missed it."

"Do it again," Ian said.

I did it again.

"Does it happen every time you try?" Ian asked.

"So far," I said.

"Can you do the other one?"

I tried. Nothing. I shook my head.

Ian did a little mini-evaluation right then, even though he didn't have any of the right equipment. Or a shirt. We didn't learn much, except to confirm that—one—the toe was, in fact, wiggling on command, and—two—I was not dreaming.

"What does it mean?" I asked Ian.

"It means there's more information getting through than there used to be."

It wasn't an unreasonable answer, but it wasn't what I'd wanted him to say.

Or Kit, either, apparently. "It means she'll walk again!" She started jumping up and down. "Right?"

We all looked at my toe again.

I wiggled it, showing off.

But Ian wasn't jumping. He stared at the toe somberly. "Not necessarily," he said, like a buzzkill.

"But it's not a bad sign," I said.

"It's a hell of a birthday present," he said. "I'll give it that."

DESPITE THE TOE-RELATED excitement, I managed to have several childish and ungenerous thoughts about Ian on the drive home. What a downer he was, for example. How he refused to let himself—or anyone else—be happy. How he squandered opportunities for joy. Maybe I *should* work with a different trainer. Somebody who knew how to motivate and inspire. Maybe Ian's intolerance for hope was holding me back.

Kit was absolutely spazzy with excitement about the whole outing.

"I never knew your toe was such a genius," she said on the drive. "It's, like, the Neil Armstrong of toes. Or maybe Abraham Lincoln."

As far as she knew, the weekend had been better than perfect. She had many topics she wanted to cover, but number one, for sure, just as soon as we finished our discussion of which famous person from history best represented my big toe, was "What the hell was going on between you and Braveheart when we walked in on you last night?"

I wanted to tell her. Badly. I wanted to give her the slow-mo replay of every single significant moment and spend the rest of the car ride and even the next several days analyzing the data into submission. I could see many vastly different, totally contradictory interpretations of Ian's behavior (and choices, and tone of voice, and facial expressions), and I had no clue which one was right.

But I couldn't tell her.

Kit had no real sense of privacy. I tried to chalk it up to exuberance—if she had the goods, she just had to share—but she was a little gossipy, too. She also gabbed on the cell phone all the time with no sense of who might be nearby listening. And do not get me started on her issues with Instagram.

I did not doubt that Myles would try to take away Ian's license if he ever got wind of what had happened. I'd seen him menacing Ian in the gym every day for weeks. I'd watch him trying to provoke Ian, needling him, pushing his buttons, hoping to goad him into doing something stupid, and I'd think, "That's a lot of anger."

I felt a little sorry for Myles, and the way something in his life compelled him to seek vengeance instead of just moving on. But I felt sorrier for Ian. Myles really was a revenge-driven prick.

Mostly, that was a problem for Ian, but it was a problem for me today, because it meant I couldn't do the one thing I wanted more than anything in the world to do right then: tell Kitty everything.

She was waiting. "Were you hooking up, or what?"

"Sadly," I said, "no."

"No? What were you doing on the floor?"

"He tripped," I said with a shrug, like, *No big deal.*

Kit squinted her eyes like she did not believe me at all.

I had to ramp it up. "You know those little rag rugs Mom has everywhere? He tripped on one at the threshold. And, seriously, then he managed to heroically catch me on the way down."

Kit studied me out of the side of her eye. "Bullshit."

"I swear," I declared then, "on my wiggly big toe."

That did it. "Okay," she said. "So what was going on between you? Because the romantic tension was so thick you could wear it like a sweater."

I told myself it wasn't lying, exactly. It was just mushing up the truth. "At the bonfire, I confessed some feelings to him."

"Yum," Kit said. "I love confessed feelings."

"I told him I had a huge, all-consuming, heart-wrenching crush and that he was basically the only thing I looked forward to all day."

"Besides gourmet takeout with your sister."

"Of course."

"And what did he say?"

Now I was grateful to him. Because this shit was too good to make up. "He said: No, I didn't."

"No, you didn't what?"

"No, I didn't have a crush on him."

Kit looked straight at me. "What the hell?"

"Eyes on the road, please."

"Explain!"

"He said I only *thought* I had a crush on him, and that this kind of thing happens all the time, and my life has been pulverized and so I'm grasping at any straws of happiness I can, but once I get through this, I'll realize that it was all in my head and I never had any real feelings for him at all. Not really."

"He did *not* say that."

"He did. Then he cited a whole bunch of studies from his training and basically told me that I was a teenage girl with Boy Band syndrome—thinking that some kindhearted prince was going to come in and take all my sorrows away."

I was a better liar than I thought. Though that kind of was what he'd said.

"Is he right?" Kit asked.

"No!" I said. "Nobody can take these problems away. Unless this toe thing turns out to be a surprise miracle."

"He didn't return your feelings at all? Nothing?"

"Nothing," I said. "He basically told me that I have all his best wishes as a healthcare professional, but to shut the fuck up and go to bed. Then he tried to make me do just that, tripped on a rag rug, and got crushed under my dead weight. Insult to injury."

"He's lying," Kit said. "I see the way he looks at you."

I couldn't help it. "How does he look at me?"

"Like you're a waterfall in a desert."

Did he? The idea of it made my stomach flip. But I had to keep obfuscating. "Guess what else? He knew how I felt before I even told him because I've been mooning at him for weeks, and he didn't discourage me because he thought it might help my recovery."

"Narcissist!" Kit shouted.

"Yeah," I said. "But the thing is, he wasn't wrong. You know you always work harder for teachers you have crushes on."

Kit nodded, and just from knowing her face almost as many years as I'd known my own, I knew I was in the clear. She'd bought it.

"I guess now," she said, "you'll just have to work hard for yourself."

"I guess I will," I said.

And that was true—whether I was lying or not.

THE BIG-TOE MIRACLE turned me into quite the celebrity. Doctors who had lost interest were suddenly popping by several times a day. Other patients on the floor wanted to get the story firsthand. Kit even drew me a homemade card that read, "Toe-tally excited about your big breakthrough!!"

It was such a busy flurry that the shenanigans with Ian seemed distant very quickly. I had bigger fish to fry, I let myself think. I'd get walking again, and then I'd grow my hair out, and then I'd pop by the hospital one day, pretending to look for—what? A lost earring? A book I'd lent out?—and he'd behold me in the hallway, tall and fierce and perfect and invincible. He'd say a sad hello because he'd know he'd missed his chance, and I'd give him a little wow-we-really-could-have-been-something smile, and then I'd flip my hair, walk away, and let him choke on the dust of his own regret.

I will never, ever divulge how many times I partook of that particular fantasy. But I will confess that for some reason, in it, I was wearing the exact same shiny hot pants and high-heeled Dr. Scholl's that Olivia Newton-John is wearing in the grand finale of *Grease*. And I had her fantastic butt, too.

All to say, when I saw Ian again in the therapy gym for the first time since our trip to the lake, the sight of him took me by surprise. He was back in his usual blue scrubs, with his hair in its usual slightly spiky configuration, but what caught me off guard was his new demeanor. He wasn't the hostile, sullen Ian I'd first met, but he sure as hell wasn't the warm, goofy Ian I'd allowed myself to swoon over.

This new Ian was *just not there*. I couldn't quite find the word for it, but he was just gone. His posture was blank. His shoulders were blank. His eyes were blank. He was like a pod person.

He still did everything he was supposed to. He still walked me through all my paces. He showed up on time. He even went the extra mile to bring in experts to consult and make sure we were doing everything possible. But he never smiled. He never relaxed.

And not once after we came back from the lake did he call me Maggie again.

BY THURSDAY, WITH exactly a week to go until my insurance ran out and I had to go back to live with my parents, I couldn't stand it anymore.

We'd all been on Toe Watch for days now, waiting for some new development—that hadn't come. If anything, that one superstar big toe had become less reliable. Was my improvement stalled because Ian was being weird? Either way, it couldn't be helping. Time was running out. I didn't want a robot for a PT.

That night, when Ian came to tutor, I told him I wanted someone new.

I'd hoped for some kind of reaction—a flash of disappointment across his face, some human curiosity about why, even irritation would have sufficed. But nothing.

"Okay," Ian said, with all the emotion of a glass of milk. "If you think that's best."

"I should probably change trainers in the gym, as well," I added.

No reaction there, either. "I understand," Ian said. "If you wouldn't mind letting me arrange the switch, it might give Myles one less reason to fire me."

"That's fine," I said.

"I'll find you someone good." His poker face broke my heart.

"Great."

Ian headed toward the door, but I called his name. He turned back.

This might be the last time I'd see him. I couldn't stand the idea that he'd always remember me as a pathetic, lovesick, delusional girl. I didn't want to be the only one who cared. If he could be a robot, so could I. "Thanks for your restraint at the lake, by the way. I cannot imagine what I was thinking."

Ian gave a sad smile. "What restraint at what lake?"

And we left it at that.

LATER THAT NIGHT, with a week minus one day until Kit's first-of-April Valentine's Day party, I asked her to call it off.

"I can't," she said. "I've rented a karaoke machine."

I held my hands out, like, *So?* "Unrent it!"

She mirrored the gesture. "Nonrefundable deposit!"

We were eating enormous taco salads in bowls made of taco shells.

Kit went on, "Plus, I've got a batch of kids popping in early to cut construction paper hearts, I've got a guy named Rodrigo bringing his garage mariachi band to play for free, I've bought the decorations and over a hundred heart-shaped cookies, I've invited everybody on the floor and all the nurses, and I frigging love Valentine's Day. And so should you."

"It's *not* Valentine's Day," I said.

"That's a bad attitude, right there."

"Damn right it is."

"You don't have to like it," Kit said. "You just have to come."

"I'm not coming."

She stopped chewing. "You have to!"

I shook my head. "I have one week left. There's no time for parties. I am not screwing around."

"But it will be my last night—and yours!"

"That's why you should cancel the party and spend it with me."

SHE DIDN'T CANCEL the party. I spent the following days meeting my new PT, working with my new PT, and doing tutoring in the evenings with my new PT—and Kit spent them cutting heart decorations out of construction paper.

The new PT was Rob-with-the-Man-Bun—the one I'd wished for early on. Without a doubt, he was the perkiest and flirtiest of everybody. He had huge energy and a laugh like a trumpet blast. I'd heard it a million times in the background in the gym, and I'd always assumed he was laughing like that because something was wildly funny. I had often wondered how he and his patients had managed to generate so much comedy from activities like riding the stationary bike, and I confess I'd mentally criticized Ian for being so serious.

But now, in this final week, working with Man-Bun-Rob, I came to realize something: That laugh was fake.

He was *over*laughing. He was pretending things were a thousand times funnier than they were. I'd crack the tiniest little nonjoke, and he'd throw his head back and absolutely bellow. That was worse—far worse—than not laughing at all.

Within hours of first starting to work with Rob, I grew to hate that laugh so much, it drove me to silence. I didn't want to do anything to provoke it. But even that didn't work. When he couldn't get anything out of me, he'd turn to other patients and other trainers—and pretend to laugh at *their* unfunny jokes.

Out of the frying pan into the fire.

But at least I wasn't tragically, unrequitedly in love with him. At least he had never given me a life-altering kiss and then said, "You know what? Never mind."

At least I knew I didn't like him.

Simple.

I could just concentrate on my recovery. Or lack thereof.

Every time I went to PT now, I worried Ian would be in the gym. Usually, he was, working with someone else—which, no matter if it was an elderly bald man or a postmenopausal lady, made me jealous. I'd steal glances at him over and over, but he never looked at me or even seemed to notice I was there.

I guess that's what happens when you push people away.

Though, to be fair, he pushed me first.

The person in the gym who did notice me was Myles.

He checked on me much more often now that Ian was across the room.

"Doing all right?" he'd say, materializing from behind a post.

"Fine, thanks," I'd say, not making eye contact.

Sometimes he prodded me about Ian. "Didn't work out with you two, huh?"

Was he tricking me when he did that? Was he trying to goad me into getting Ian in trouble?

"It worked out great," I said, thinking fast.

"So well," Myles pressed, "that you requested another PT?"

"It was Ian's idea," I said. Lying.

Myles tilted his head like I was the biggest liar ever. "Really?"

Here's where my obsessive study of medical journals brought its big payoff. "Yes," I said. "Because Rob has more experience with functional electrical stimulation, and Ian thinks I'd be a good candidate."

Suddenly, Myles wasn't so cocky. "You couldn't have wanted to stay with him, though. He was so unfriendly to you. Borderline hostile—"

I started to say, "I wouldn't call him *hostile*—"

But Myles went on, "When he wasn't standing outside your room listening to you sing."

I turned to face him. "What?"

"Oh, you didn't know he did that?"

I shook my head.

"Yeah." Myles lifted both his eyebrows. "Creepy, right? I had to issue him two different warning slips."

I looked around for Ian. He was helping a very elderly lady out of her chair onto the raised mat.

"Anyway," Myles said, pulling my attention back. "If he bothers you anymore, just let me know." He pointed a finger gun at me, gave me a nod, and pulled the trigger.

MAN-BUN-ROB AND I worked like dogs all week, both during scheduled PT and tutoring sessions, but made no progress. Ian had left a tutoring spreadsheet—even though he detested spreadsheets—detailing exactly what we were supposed to do, in order, in sections, counted to the minute. Rob and I followed it diligently—but nothing changed.

I did everything I could think of—took my vitamins, got plenty of sleep, drank extra water—and I tried to wiggle my toes about a thousand times a day. The hullabaloo over that toe had set up a strong expectation that a breakthrough was inevitable. But the longer that breakthrough refused to happen, the more I accepted the cognitive dissonance: I might get better any minute, or I might never get better at all.

That said, I was improving in lots of other ways. My shoulder was healing "beautifully," the dermatologist had said, and the scabs on my face had left no scars. The stitches on my neck were starting to dissolve, and, if I didn't look in the mirror, parts of my body felt almost normal.

Just not normal enough.

It wasn't that I hadn't made any progress. I could rattle off every muscle in the lower extremities like some kind of med student. My core strength, Rob said, was "phenomenal," and I could do sit-ups all day long. My arms and shoulders were "beasts." I had the gluteus muscles "of a champion," and my adductors, hip flexors, gluteus medius, rectus femoris, sartiorius, and deep gluteal muscles were all in excellent working order. I could even stand pretty well—twelve minutes was my record—but only if I held on to something, or someone.

The problems were all with the muscles responsible for extending the foot forward when taking a step. They were falling down on the job. Aside from that one delightful big toe (thanks to one feisty flexor hallucis longus), everything below my knee, to use the technical term, was "flaccid."

I preferred "floppy," personally.

Either way, it wasn't good. The tibialis anterior, tibialis posterior, popliteus fibularis longus, fibularis brevis, plantaris soleus, and gastrocnemius were all, um, pretty limp. Particularly frustrating were the semimembranosus, semitendinosus, and biceps femoris, which are the muscles that work to extend the leg. I could bring my thigh forward (thanks to a "boss" iliopsoas), but I couldn't straighten it.

Still.

That's why I wasn't going to the Valentine's party. That whole final week was a slow realization that, where walking was concerned, at least, despite the trying, and the determination, and all those hours of tutoring, and the many impressive gains I could claim—I was still going to fail.

I never failed. I'd never failed anything. Not even a spelling quiz.

It kept me from sleeping. Over and over that final week, I'd doze off for a few minutes at bedtime and then startle awake, restlessly shifting under my covers. Several nights I just couldn't take the anxiety, and I wound up transferring to my chair, careful not to wake Kit, and then sneaking to the gym. There, I'd hoist myself up onto the walking bars, brace with both hands, and pace back and forth until I was on the verge of collapse.

It was probably a bad idea, going to the gym at night. I would no doubt have done better to let my body rest. But I couldn't seem to stop myself. I kept thinking if I just pushed a little harder, I could break through. The prospect of failing this challenge—possibly the only one that ever really mattered—left me too panicked to think straight.

The night before Kit's party, I went to the gym again. My arms were sore from all the laps on the bars, and I could hear Ian's Scottish voice saying "arms are not legs," but I didn't care. It wasn't my arms I cared about. I went back and forth, back and forth—ten times, then twenty, willing my lower legs to swing forward, willing the balls of my feet to push off, willing for something, anything, to spark to life.

Then, just short of thirty, my arm just gave out.

It happened fast. I crumpled, smacking down on the mat hard, and lay there, panting. And there, with my face against the mat, smarting like I'd been slapped, it truly hit me: I wasn't going to walk again.

I really wasn't.

I wasn't going to overcome this. I wasn't going to be good as new. I wasn't going to show them all. I wasn't going to be the exception to the rule. I wasn't going to give an inspirational talk that would go viral on the Internet.

Every single thing I'd experienced, or thought about, or hoped for up until this moment seemed cartoonish. This whole experience had been so frantic and dreamlike it was almost like nothing at all had been real. Until now. Alone, on the floor, I finally, really got it. The only thing that was real anymore:

I was going to spend the rest of my life in a wheelchair.

I'D BARELY FINISHED the thought when I heard a voice—a Scottish voice. "What the hell is going on?"

I didn't move. Just lay there and calculated the odds of another Scottish person happening to pass through the rehab gym in the middle of the night.

Unlikely.

Then I heard Ian's sneakers squeak the floor—fast, like he was running—and then he was saying my name, urgently, like I might be in danger:

"Maggie, what happened?"

I couldn't lift my face from the mat. "You don't call me Maggie anymore."

Then he was down on his hands and knees beside me. "What happened? Tell me."

"Why are you even here?"

"Working late. What happened?"

He was perched to call for help. But I didn't need help. I put my hand out to keep him right there, and then I explained everything the only way I could.

"I failed," I said.

"Were you in here using the bars? By yourself? Jesus, Maggie, you're not supposed to come here alone."

But it didn't matter. Nothing mattered.

"Are you hurt?" Ian asked.

"No."

“Can you get up?”

“No.”

“Let’s get you back to your room.” He gathered me into his arms.

“No,” I said. “Just give me a minute.”

Ian hesitated.

“Please,” I said.

Then Ian rocked back, without letting me go, and sat on the mat, still holding me.

Probably, all his medical training told him to get me back to my room, and check my vitals, and attend brusquely to my physical health. But he went against it. He believed me that I was not hurt. He trusted that I didn’t need to be hauled back out into the bright hallway. He understood what I’d been doing. He knew as well as anybody that I hadn’t made enough progress. He got it.

And so he didn’t ask me any more questions. He just held me there, against his chest, on the mat, in the dark gym, stroking my hair.

I MUST HAVE fallen asleep, and Ian must have carried me back to my bed in his arms, because the next morning, I woke up in my room with Kit still snoozing away—but I didn’t remember going back.

I went through the motions that day. This was it. This was really it. Everything was exactly the same, except for one crucial thing: There was no hope anymore.

Kit stayed with me the whole day, cutting hearts for the party and making organizational phone calls, but I didn’t tell her. I didn’t want her to argue with me. There was nothing to argue about. She popped out for a bit in the late afternoon while I had PT with Rob, and when I came back, she was still gone. I fell asleep hard that afternoon, and I didn’t wake until supper: hospital food. There’d be nothing delicious tonight. Kit would be at the helm of her epic party, and I would be in here. Alone. Eating Jell-O.

As my meal came into focus, something across the room came into focus, too. A dress, hanging from the television stand, with a note on it in Kit's writing—big, in Sharpie:

Genuine vintage roller-disco diva dress
off the (right) shoulder!
JUST YOUR SIZE!
$5 at Salvation Army! (I washed it for you!) Come to the party!!!!!!

It was a pink-and-gold, one-shoulder, polyester maxidress with ruffles. It was hilarious, and also strangely lovely.

But I still wasn't going to the party.

I lifted the yellowish plastic cover on the dinner plate. Some kind of gray meat, rehydrated mashed potatoes, and canned green beans.

Nope.

I poked at the Jell-O. I listened to the nurses joke around out at the station. One of them had a little thing for Man-Bun-Rob, and she'd heard he was going to be there.

Guess that meant there would be no tutoring for me tonight, either.

Fine. It was pointless, anyway.

On the tray, dessert was a chocolate chip cookie, which seemed like a stroke of luck—until I bit in and discovered it was oatmeal raisin.

Things seemed quieter than usual. Everybody, I guess, was in the rehab gym.

Then the door pushed open, and it was Kit.

"I need you," she said.

"What?"

"The mariachi band is terrible! The children are crying!"

"It can't be that bad."

"Oh, yes, it can!" she said, pulling back my covers. "Go pee. Brush your teeth. Put on your dress! You're doing a love song medley in ten minutes."

I shook my head. "I don't think so."

She put a hand on one hip. "How many times have I been there for you when you needed me?"

"Are we talking recently, or our entire lives? Because I think you started with a deficit."

Kit pulled on my arm. "I need you. The kids need you. Valentine's Day needs you. Ian's mother needs you!"

What? She got my attention with that last one. "Ian's mother?"

She pointed at me, and repeated the favorite saying of hers Ian had told us once: "When you don't know what to do for yourself, do something for somebody else."

SHE GOT ME with that.

I did go to the party—although, when I showed up, the mariachi band was totally normal, not one kid was crying, and it was clear that Kit had tricked me.

I glared at her. "Not cool."

"Just try to keep that scowl on your face while you eat one of these cookies," she said, handing me a heart-shaped one with sprinkles.

It wasn't oatmeal raisin, I'll give it that.

Kit had gone all out. There was a craft table, a disco ball, the world-famous stolen chocolate fountain, and hearts and streamers everywhere. She had even hung a ball of mistletoe off the end of a stick to dangle over people's heads and force them to kiss. Rob was doing the honors for her, bursting out with that foghorn laugh every time it worked.

Confessions: It *was* a lovely party, I *did* love wearing my diva dress, I *did* sing a love song medley, and everything about being there was better than being in my room alone. It was, in truth, an effective distraction.

As sad as I was, I felt a little happy, too.

I stayed and stayed. We sent the children to bed at eight o'clock, and we all continued eating cookies and singing our hearts out.

My best song of the night by far was my last one: I absolutely belted out "Best of My Love," and halfway through, I looked up and saw Ian across the room, watching like he was spellbound. That, of course, made me sing harder and better, and I poured everything I had into the rest of it. At the end, I got the cheering equivalent of a standing O, and when I rolled across the room for cookies afterward, Ian followed and met me there.

We both held still for a few seconds too long.

"That was a hell of a song," he said at last, his expression focused and warm and non-robot-like. The sound of the real Ian filled me with longing.

"Thank you."

"I've never met anybody who could sing like you do."

Now I smiled. "Thank you."

"It's good to see you," he said.

"You could have seen me all week in the gym, if you hadn't been ignoring me."

"I wasn't ignoring you," he said, frowning. "I was—" But then he stopped. And he didn't start again.

"Kit said you weren't coming to the party."

"I'm not."

"But you're here."

"I'm just stealing cookies."

"I see."

He gestured back at the hallway to the offices. "I was working late."

"You do that a lot."

"I've been researching your injury, actually," he said, looking a little embarrassed about it. "Trying to think of some way to help."

I had to hand it to him. That was nice. But I said, "It's a waste of time. It's over."

"What's over?"

"My recovery."

He shook his head. "There are all kinds of ways to recover."

I looked away.

It would have been a good time for him to escape, but he didn't. Instead, he attempted to start up some chitchat. He nodded at the room. "Looks like you're all having fun."

"Not on purpose," I said. "Kit forced us."

He glanced over at Kit, who noticed us talking. When he turned back, he let his eyes take me in. "Great dress."

"I think I'm going to become a one-shoulder-dress person," I said. "You know, even when I have the option of two."

"You should."

"It can be my signature thing. Then, when I do something truly amazing that history needs to commemorate with a statue, they'll have no choice but to put me in this." I flipped one of the ruffles.

Ian smiled then—a genuine smile. Hadn't seen that in a long time.

He was about to say something else when Kit showed up next to us and said, "Mistletoe bomb!"

Ian and I looked up. She was holding the mistletoe over our heads.

"Mistletoe is for Christmas," Ian said.

"Ask me if I care," Kit said.

"She's been forcing people to kiss with that thing all night," I explained.

"You're going to force me to kiss your sister?"

Kit gave a shrug. "Kinda looks that way."

"He can't kiss me," I told Kit. "It's against the rules."

"Which rules?" she asked.

"All of them," I answered.

But Ian was considering his options. "What happens if I refuse?"

Kit leveled a don't-mess-around look at him, and then, like it was a challenge, she said, "Then I guess you'll waste a chance for a kiss."

"You don't have to kiss me," I said to Ian, and then to Kit, "Cut it out! You're going to get him fired!"

But Ian squatted down in front of my chair. He flipped up the foot rests as he lifted one foot, then the other, setting them flat on the floor. I was barefoot and I could feel, in places, how cool the surface was. Then Ian leaned close for me to put my hands on his shoulders, like he'd done so often in the pool, and he placed his hands on my hips to steady me, and I leaned forward, and I locked my knees, and I moved toward him—and we stood.

"It's bad luck to ignore mistletoe," Ian said.

Those blue eyes. His face so close. The air tingled in my lungs. Was he going to do this? "Nobody in this room needs any more bad luck," I said.

His gaze was locked on mine. "Very true."

"But you can't kiss me," I said, hoping like hell he wouldn't agree.

"I can't?"

"What if somebody reports you?"

"I don't care."

"You don't?"

"Want to know the only question I care about?"

I nodded.

He looked into my eyes and said, "What do you want?"

I held my breath. What did I want?

What the hell kind of question was that?

I wanted him.

I wanted to drag him up to the rooftop and stay there all night.

I wanted to be the girl I used to be. The one with the hair, and jeans, and hips. The one with at least a chance of being wanted back.

But no way was I saying that.

I might never get the things I wanted. But at least I was the only one who had to know.

I shrugged.

Ian studied me, as if he could tell by looking.

Then he glanced up at the mistletoe one more time and shrugged right back.

He pressed closer, and he tightened his arm around my waist. I stretched my arms up around his neck, and as I did, I ran my eyes over his collarbones at the V of his blue scrubs, then up along his jaw, to let my gaze rest on his mouth.

Then he leaned down toward me. It felt like slow-motion, with Nina crooning "Midnight Train to Georgia" in the background. Inches away, he slowed down and lingered, like he was savoring the moment. Like he was taking it in. I hadn't noticed how much Kit had dimmed the lights until suddenly the disco-ball light seemed to fill the room with stars, and it felt like the only steady thing in the world was Ian.

Everything about him felt solid and sturdy and like something I wanted to cling to. There he was, so close up, then closer—and then, impossibly, he lowered his mouth to mine.

Maybe he shouldn't have done it. But oh, God, I was so unspeakably glad he did.

And there was his mouth again, the same but better, like something lost forever and then found again, and everything suddenly swirled too much for me to see anything at all. I sank into the warmth and comfort and electricity of that moment, knowing it couldn't last long, but wishing it could go on forever.

Until the music suddenly stopped.

And the lights flipped on, bright as searchlights.

The room froze. The karaoke machine even went dead. We turned to figure out what was going on, and we both saw the same thing at the same time: Myles.

Myles had walked in.

He was halfway across the room, staring straight at us. "What the frick is going on here?"

"It's a party," Kit said, no idea who she was dealing with.

But Myles didn't look over. "Did I just walk in here to see one of my PTs *kissing* one of my patients?"

"You sure did," Kit volunteered. "I just Instagrammed it!"

"Congratulations," Myles said to Ian then. "You just got fired."

The crowd gasped.

"Say good-bye to your job," Myles went on, enjoying this moment far too much. "Say goodbye to your PT license. And I'll have to brush up on my immigration law, but I'm pretty sure you can say good-bye to this entire country, as well." Myles took a step closer and waved his fingers tauntingly at Ian. "Bye-bye, work visa."

But Ian had turned away from him. He was looking at me now, running his gaze over my face, studying the details. I could tell from Ian's expression that Myles wasn't wrong. Ian had just lost his job, and possibly much more.

My knees chose that moment to start to quiver—though Ian

anticipated that, somehow, and he was already setting me back down in my chair. As he got me settled and moved to stand back up, he squeezed my hand, and it felt like good-bye.

"Do you think I'm fricking joking, man?" Myles walked closer. "Because I am dead serious. You just lost everything."

Myles's beady little face was red and sweaty, but Ian seemed to go the other way and get calmer and cooler.

Ian turned to face him. "Actually," he said, "I know what it's like to lose everything—and getting sabotaged by a weasel like you doesn't even come close."

"You sabotaged yourself, friend."

Ian seemed to consider that. "Maybe I did." Then he looked up. "But don't call me friend."

"Who is this guy?" Kit asked the room. Then, to Myles, "It's a Valentine's party. Chill the hell out, dude. Have a cookie."

Myles looked over and noticed her for the first time. "It's not even Valentine's Day."

"Why is everybody so fixated on that?"

"Ian—" I started.

But Ian had not even turned his head before Myles barked, "Do not approach the patient!"

Ian gave him a look, like, *Really*? "I'm just going to walk her back to her room."

"You are *not*," Myles declared, crossing over to us. "Take one step toward her and I will throw you out of this building."

Ian turned to face him dead-on, and at this range we could all see that Ian was a good head taller. "You and what army, you bawfaced prick?"

At that, Myles decided to throw a punch. But Ian somehow blocked it, and then he grabbed Myles's two wrists to hold them still in the air. "You don't want to do that," Ian said calmly. "I'd hate to kill you by accident. For my sake more than yours."

If the expression on Myles's face had been a sound, it would have been a whimper. He was in over his head, and he knew it. He knew Ian could crush him—and he also knew he'd just made certain that Ian had little to lose.

Myles opened his palm in a gesture of defeat. "Okay," he said.

Ian released his grip. They both stepped back.

Then Ian took a few more steps backward, and I realized he was leaving.

He looked around the room, taking it in for the last time.

Then he turned to me, and said, "Maggie!"

Though my eyes, and everybody else's, were already on him.

Don't say good-bye, I found myself thinking. *Don't say good-bye.*

He looked right at me, gave me a nod, and then said, "Happy Valentine's Day."

Twenty-three

THE NEXT DAY brought a few beginnings—but mostly endings.

It was the day Kitty was leaving for New York, and the day I was leaving the hospital. The plan was for my parents to arrive late morning, and for my dad to drive Kit to the airport while my mom stayed with me to help pack up. As we waited, I tried very hard not to mope.

"I can't believe you're leaving me alone with them."

Kit wasn't having it. "Just in the nick of time," she said. "It's a miracle we got through this whole month unscathed."

She wasn't wrong.

Though some of us were less scathed than others.

When her suitcase was zipped and sitting by the door, she said. "Now can I please tell you the comforting thing I've been wanting to tell you?"

"You can tell me," I said. "But I won't promise to find it comforting."

"*I* find it comforting," Kit said. "That's enough."

"Spit it out, then."

"So I saw this TED Talk, and it was this researcher from Harvard—"

She paused. "Or was it Stanford? Actually, I think it was MIT. Anyway, a total brainiac—"

"You've lost me already. Just know that."

She pushed on. "He researches mathematical probabilities or something, and in his talk, he mentioned that people have, like, a set point for happiness."

"How does that relate at all to mathematical probabilities?"

"The point is, he had these great statistics. People who win the lottery, when you check in with them a year later, you'd think they'd be super happy, right?"

She wanted me to say it. "Right," I said.

"But they're not happy. They're just as miserable as they were before."

I tilted my head. "Were they miserable before?"

"And people," she went on, "who have terrible things happen to them—loss of a spouse, bankruptcy, disfiguring accidents—"

"That would be me?"

At that, Kitty nodded. "Exactly!" She pointed at me. "He specifically mentioned paraplegics."

I had not heard myself described that way before, and the word gave me a little start. But I pushed past it. "I still don't see what this has to do with math."

"There was a specific study on people who had lost the use of their lower limbs—people in wheelchairs—and those findings totally hold true. One year after the accident, they're exactly as happy as they were before."

I stared at her.

"Isn't that great?"

"*That's* what you've been waiting to say all this time?"

"Yes! You're going to be okay. Aren't you glad to know that?"

"Undecided."

Then, as she came in for a final hug, she said, "I just need you to remember that, okay?" She squeezed a little tighter. "There are all kinds of happy endings."

* * *

NEXT, MY PARENTS showed up at the door—with a top-of-the-line wheelchair with a bow on it. Literally: a bow. Like I'd just turned sixteen and they'd bought me a convertible.

I just stared. "This is the worst best present ever."

My dad came over for one of his signature hugs. "The titanium was developed by NASA," he said. "It has razor-thin inverted wheels, like all the basketball players use."

"Dammit," I said. "Now I have to join a basketball team." I thought about Pop-A-Shot with Ian, and wondered if I just might.

My dad wanted to walk me through all its features and do a little demo, but I shut that right down.

"He loves that thing," my mother said. "Spent all day yesterday scooting around in it."

My dad rubbed one of his shoulders and confirmed, "Arms are a little sore."

They were both so *excited*. My mother loved its compactness—how trim it was. "From just the right angle," she said, "you can barely tell there's a chair there at all."

"So I'll just look like I'm weirdly floating down the street with my legs bent?"

But she pooh-poohed me. "You know what I mean."

Everyone was civil. Everyone was elegantly polite. You'd never even know that we'd all just bounced back from being estranged. And then something weird happened: Just before Kit headed to the airport with my dad, she stepped in to hug my mom good-bye.

And my mom just didn't let go.

How long does a normal hug last? Five seconds? This one went on for five minutes. So long that Kit wound up opening her eyes to look at me like, *What the heck?*

Nobody said anything, either. We just stood there, in silence, and let it happen.

It was the first hug my mom and Kit had shared in years.

When my mom finally let go, there were tears on her cheeks. She wiped them away and turned to my dad. "She's going to need something to eat in the airport."

My dad sensed what was coming. He looked at his watch. "You're sending me to the sandwich shop?"

This was becoming her signature thing. Sending him for sandwiches. Especially when she wanted to have girl talks.

My dad shook his head. "We don't have time."

"We do!" my mother said.

Kit nodded then. "Actually, we have plenty of time."

My dad looked at my mother like, *Really?* Then he sighed, set down Kit's suitcase, and headed out—while Kit and I frowned at each other.

My mother watched him go, and only after he'd boarded the elevator at the end of the hall did she turn around to face us. Her expression was solemn. She took a deep breath and swallowed. Then she closed the door and took a step toward Kit.

"His name," she said, "was Derin Buruk."

Kit held her breath. She glanced at me, then back at my mother, who glanced back at the door, as if confirming the coast was clear.

"He was Turkish. An exchange student. Devastatingly handsome. Black hair and green eyes rimmed with black lashes. He showed up on our first day of senior year, and he was all any girl could talk about for months. I didn't talk about him. I ignored him. I was dating your dad—since ninth grade—and I wasn't looking for dates, but I couldn't help but notice him. He had a movie star quality. He was magnetic. And for some reason, he fixated on me. He passed me notes, flirted with me in the hallways, snuck flowers into my locker. I told him over and over to knock it off, but he said he couldn't. He stared at me constantly in the cafeteria and at football games. He called me almost daily. He professed love—obsessive love—and begged me to break up with your dad and go out with him."

I looked at my mother's hands. They were trembling.

"Turkish men are famously persistent," she went on, "did you know that? They are very determined about love. Your dad—your wonderful dad, the love of my life—he's not really like that. That steadiness, that easygoing nature—they don't lend themselves to mad passion. He was kind, he was good-hearted, but he was also a high school boy. He got a lot wrong. He knew next to nothing about romance, or wooing, or how to make a woman flutter. We were the best of friends. But I had never come up against a force like Derin. I had no defenses. I did my best. I pushed him away and pushed him away, but he just kept coming back—harder and stronger. The truth was, I liked it. I liked that he noticed me. I liked that of all the girls in love with him, I was the one he chose. I never understood why he picked me. I still don't know why."

My mom looked very shaky. I patted the bed down by my knees. "Come sit down."

Absentmindedly, she did. "That year," she went on, "over Christmas vacation, your father went away to visit family. He was gone for a week. Somehow, Derin heard that he was gone, and he started climbing the tree outside my window at night and tapping on the pane. I turned him away two times, but on the third night, he said he was leaving to go home soon, and he had to tell me something before he left." She closed her eyes. "God forgive me. I let him in.

"For the rest of the week, I let him in every time he knocked. He would stay until just before dawn, and then sneak away. The night before your father returned to town, I forbade Derin to ever come back—and he never did."

"What did he need to tell you?" I asked.

My mom frowned. "You know what? I don't remember."

Kit let out a long sigh.

"When school started up again," my mom went on, "Derin had gone back to Istanbul. I never saw him again. By spring break, I had figured out that I was pregnant, and by summer your dad had figured it out, too. He assumed the baby was his, and I didn't correct him. It could have been. He was so happy about it. He proposed, and I accepted, and I pretended that Derin Buruk never existed."

"Until I had my blood tested," Kitty said.

My mom shook her head. "Until the moment I first saw you. Right then, I knew."

"Do you hate him? The guy?" Kit asked then.

"No," my mom said. "I don't hate him. Not anymore."

"Do you hate me?"

"No!" my mother said.

"But when you look at me, do you see him?"

"Sometimes. You got his eyelashes."

"You always said they were Huron."

My mom gave a little *sorry* shrug.

"Does it make you feel guilty?"

"Sometimes. Or afraid."

Kitty nodded. "That Dad might find out and not love me anymore."

My mom shook her head. "That he might find out and not love *me* anymore."

I nodded at Kit. "You never did anything wrong."

My mom agreed. "He's adored you from day one."

"Mom is a little trickier."

My mom let out a nervous laugh.

"Well, he's not going to find out," Kit said then, looking at me.

Was it morally wrong to collude against him? I didn't really care right then. "I'll never tell."

"Neither will I."

My mom looked physically deflated now, as if releasing all those secrets had emptied her out. She kept her eyes on Kit.

"You're kind of his favorite, you know," I said.

"I know," Kit said. "Just barely."

"He always took your side over Mom's."

"I know."

"I'm glad for that," our mom said. "I'm glad you had each other."

Then, in the little pause that followed, we heard a voice out in the hallway, just outside the room.

"Can I help you with something, sir?" a voice asked.

At first, there was no reply, but then a man cleared his throat. "No," he said. "No. I just . . . forgot my keys."

My mom's eyes went wide. Because it was Dad.

The nurse bustled on past him into the room, leaving the door open behind her, and all three of us turned to see my dad, frozen still at the threshold of the door, eyes not quite focused, gazing uncomprehendingly in our direction.

"I'm so sorry," he said after a minute, a little breathless, his face blank with shock. "I came back to get the car keys. But I found myself eavesdropping instead."

Twenty-four

MY MOTHER RAN to him, a sob like I'd never heard escaping her throat, but he blocked her and stepped back.

He didn't meet her eyes.

"Come on, Kitty," he said, not meeting hers, either. "You've got a flight to catch."

"Cliff—" my mom started.

"No!" my dad barked, and she caught her breath.

Then, in slow motion, he reached down for Kitty's suitcase, walked over to slide the car keys out of my mom's purse, and left the room without a word.

My mother's legs collapsed from under her, but Kitty caught her and steered her over to the bedside chair.

"I'm sorry—I'm so sorry," Kit said. "I'll talk to him."

My mom lifted a trembling hand to her mouth.

"It's going to be okay," I said. "We're going to fix this. He loves you."

Kit had a flight to catch. She met my eyes. "You've got this, right?"

I nodded, though I wasn't at all sure that I did. "Don't miss the plane."

Kit came my way and squeezed me tight. "Call me if you need me."

"Not if," I said, "*when.*"

"At least you're not bored," Kit said then.

"Maybe we'll all be better for knowing," I said. But as I glanced at my mother, now catatonic in the face of what had just happened, it was hard to imagine how.

MY FATHER DID not come back for us after the airport. In my whole life, he had never ever not been there when I needed him.

But I got it.

He sent a car service instead.

It took my mother twice as long as anyone could have predicted to pack up and dismantle the décor, and the driver waited in the hall in his driving cap.

My mother, it's fair to say, couldn't seem to focus.

I tried to issue suggestions and encouragement from the bed, but she wound up walking around the room, picking things up randomly and setting them back down. She'd pack a few things, only to lose focus and leave others behind in the cabinet.

Meanwhile, nurses and patients popped in and out, saying good-bye.

I didn't expect to see Ian, of course. Myles probably had security set up around the perimeter. But, despite all the pressing drama of the day, I couldn't stop looking for him. I hadn't gone a day and a half without seeing him since we'd met.

The day was a parade of all the faces I'd come to know these past six weeks: farewells from the social worker, and the hospital psychologist, and Priya, and Nina. I saw the spinal surgeon and the dermatologist, and the insurance rep, and two of the orderlies. It was almost like I'd been at summer camp, and now it was time to say good-bye until next summer.

It took forever to go. Then we hit warp speed.

Next, I was rolling over the threshold of my parents' house, over the new ramp my dad had built for me, mentally thanking him and praising his workmanship while trying to staunch the flow of despair in my chest.

But when I rolled my way into the living room—there was my dad.

He froze when he saw us, and dropped his gaze to the floor. We froze, too.

He had an unzipped duffel bag in one hand—his pajama cuffs and part of a toothbrush sticking out, like he'd been trying to get out before we made it home.

"Hi, Cliff," my mother said, almost in a whisper.

But my dad just turned his head away and waited for her to leave.

She did, moving past us back toward their bedroom.

Once she was gone, he met my eyes.

"How ya holding up, kiddo?" my dad asked, squatting down in front of me.

I looked at my dad's duffel bag. "You're heading out?"

He gave a nod. "I hope that's okay."

"I get it," I said. "I do."

"I just need a few days. Clear my head."

Of course. That didn't surprise me.

But pretty much everything else about that day did surprise me. How much I missed Kitty already, how strange it felt to be "on the outside" again, how simultaneously comforting and terrifying it was to hear the front door close behind me.

My childhood bedroom was a surprise, too. After my dad left, my mom wheeled me right to it, as if to move on to brighter topics. She had redecorated. She pushed open the door and voiced a quiet "Surprise!"

She'd replaced truly everything—my trundle bed with the pink dust ruffle, my floral upholstered chair, my curtains, my rug. Everything old was gone—stuffed animals, photo albums, books, clutter, posters.

"Where is everything?" I asked.

"In storage tubs," she answered. "All the keepsakes, anyway. The furniture I set out on the curb—and it was gone in two days."

It was good and bad—both at the same time. She'd taken away the comfort of all those old familiar things, but she'd also taken away their ability to remind me of my old life. This new room was like a hotel. Roman shades in linen, a chaise longue by the window, a hundred pillows on the bed. A mirrored chandelier. Spare, and done in tones of her favorite color, "greige," a cross between gray and beige. It was tranquil and sophisticated and utterly unfamiliar. It looked like a magazine.

"A new room for a new start," she said.

I had to hand it to her. She had great taste. "Well, this is definitely a best-case scenario."

"And Dad can bring all your old junk in for you to sort through whenever you like," my mom said. Then she remembered and took a shaky breath. "If he comes back."

"He will," I said. "He just needs some time." Then, because it made it seem like we were almost doing him a kindness, I said, "We can give him that, right?"

She nodded. "We can give him that."

My mom lingered at my bedroom door for a good while then, unsure if she should leave me alone. "Well," she said, after a long silence. "I guess I'll let you get settled."

I sat very still for a long time. Twenty minutes? An hour? Maybe I was in shock. All I know is, I couldn't grasp how on earth my life's path had led me back here. I couldn't think about the past, but I couldn't see a future, either.

When the doorbell rang, I wondered if it was my dad.

But a few minutes later, my mom clicked down the hallway, swung open my door (without knocking), and presented—of all people—Ian.

I think she said something prim, like "You have a visitor." I feel like she might also have offered Ian a wine spritzer, which he declined. All I remember was the sight of him.

Because as soon as I looked up, I was alive again.

Ian Moffat was in my bedroom. In a blue T-shirt and button-fly jeans.

"Hello," he said, after my mother left, hooking his thumbs in his pockets and looking around. "Nice place."

I didn't know what to say. I had no idea why he was here.

"I've come to apologize," he said then, shifting his weight. "I think I've made your life harder, not easier—though that was never my intention."

I waited.

"I just wanted to help you get better—as much as you could."

Okay.

"I should never have let myself care for you the way I did."

I looked up. "You let yourself care for me?"

But I suddenly felt like I'd focused on the wrong part of that statement. Ian didn't answer. He studied the rug.

Right then, a foolish little hope lit up somewhere in my heart. Maybe that's why he'd come. Maybe now that I wasn't his patient anymore, we could—*what?* Hang out? Kiss again? Date? Be together?

"I'm also here," Ian added, "to share the news that I'm officially fired. Myles submitted it yesterday."

"Is that a good thing or a bad thing?"

"Both."

I smiled.

He went on, "I will miss it, though."

"Are they going to take away your license?"

"Yes."

If he lost his license, he lost his visa. "Does that mean you have to leave the country?"

He paused a second on this one, walking over to sit down on the bed beside me. "I think so. Yes."

I blinked. "They're making you leave? The government is going after you?"

He shook his head. "Myles is going after me. And he'll win, too."

"You're not going to fight him?"

"There's nothing to fight. It's over. Your sister posted it on Instagram."

"Oh, my God." I put my hand over my eyes. "Kit."

"It's not her fault," he said. "I kissed you in front of a hundred people in that room. It was hardly a private moment."

"But it wasn't your fault! It was the mistletoe!"

Ian shook his head.

"It was a pity kiss!" I went on. "You were just being nice! I'll testify!"

Now he smiled at me like I was deluded—but in a cute way.

"You weren't even technically my PT anymore!"

"Doesn't matter. I worked there. You were a patient."

It seemed insane. "That's it? One kiss, and you're exiled?"

Ian gave a half-smile. "Apparently."

Ian suddenly seemed very close. Just inches away, really. Having him right here—so near—made the idea of his leaving feel excruciating. "You can't go," I said.

He gave a shrug. "I can't stay. My visa was for a particular job that requires a particular license."

"What will you do?"

"Go home. To Edinburgh."

I felt a cramp in my chest.

He went on, "I've got four brothers there. Two of them are doctors. One's already found me an interview at a hospital."

I tried to keep my voice steady, like we were just chatting. "That's good."

But he didn't answer. He just reached out and took my hand. At the touch, I drew in a shaky breath. Then he let it go.

"The interview's on Monday," he said.

I blinked. "*This* Monday?"

He nodded.

"So that means you're going—when?"

"Tomorrow morning."

Panic. I genuinely could not imagine my postcrash life without Ian in it. It was too pathetic to say out loud, but he was just about the only thing in the world that made me anything even close to happy. My whole life was in black-and-white until he walked into the room—and then everything bloomed into color.

Losing Chip? I had barely blinked. Losing Ian right now? I could barely breathe.

"You're going to be all right, you know. You're a lot stronger than you think—"

But before he could finish, I did something that shocked the hell out of both of us.

I said, "Marry me."

His mouth opened, but no words came out.

It was kind of a great idea. "Marry me," I said again, "and then you can stay."

"You want me to marry you?"

I nodded.

"For a green card?"

"You want to stay, don't you?"

"Yes."

"It's sunny here, and the people are friendly, and we have tacos. Do they have tacos in Scotland?"

"They do have tacos in Scotland," he said, "but they're not the same."

Why were we talking about tacos?

I went on. "I had this great idea a few weeks ago about opening a summer camp for kids in wheelchairs." I was thinking fast now. It was all coming together in my head. "Maybe we could do it together—build it and run it, I mean. We could be partners. You could mastermind all the PT stuff and do your thing and get all outside-the-box, and I could do all the fund-raising, and we could create, like, just, a utopia for kids who've seen so much pain—with a garden, and a wheelchair racecourse, and a splash park, and movie nights, and popcorn, and juggling classes, and cookie baking, and Pop-A-Shot, and therapeutic horseback. And a choir!"

I was on fire now. I went on, "We could have classes for adults, too, in the winter, and hold retreats, and sponsor art fairs and teach adults crafty things, like how to knit slugs, and help create a source of light and hope and connection for people who really, really need it. I know you kind of lost interest in your other business, but this would be different."

I had some momentum now. I could see this idea really working.

Plus, and this is not a minor point, I was utterly, breath-stealingly in love with him. It suddenly seemed like I needed to tell him that. Whether I was ready to or not. If he was leaving the country in the morning—if I was truly never going to see him again—how could I let him go without stepping up and speaking the truth?

I'd done a hundred brave things since the crash, but I swear, not one of them was as scary as this.

"Ian," I said then, my breath swirling cold in my lungs like water. "The thing is, I'm in love with you."

Ian held very still.

I watched his face for some kind of response. Was this good news to him or bad? Was it something he'd been hoping to hear—or hoping *not* to hear? Most likely, of course, I was just a sad, shriveled client to him. But those kisses—those heartbreaking kisses of his—had given me a spark of hope I couldn't ignore. I had no idea how he really felt, but there was no time to guess. He was too good at being unreadable.

Without a response, I just pushed on. "Like crazily, swooningly, heart-burstingly in love. Like the kind of in love I didn't even know was possible. The kind of in love that makes every other emotion look tiny and dollhouse sized. The kind that feels like sunshine and fills you up with excitement somehow—even when there's nothing to be excited about. The kind that makes everything better—no matter how bad it is—and even utterly ordinary things like brushing your teeth feel tinged with magic."

It was hard to know how strongly to state my case. I could also have said, *I think about you at night when I can't sleep.* Or, *What I felt for Chip never even came close to what I feel for you.* Or, *You are the best thing in my life.*

The longer he didn't respond, the more I felt like I should push even harder. The more I felt like begging. I came very close to saying, *Please, please marry me. It wouldn't have to be love!* I'd take him for less than that. I'd take him for friendship. I take him for anything—just to keep him close.

But I never said any of that, and later, I was glad. As the expression on his face finally came into focus, I stopped. If any part of me had been hoping for a yes, that was the moment when it disappeared.

He was holding his breath. He let it out, and stood, turned away, and shoved a hand into his hair, all at once.

"I didn't 'kind of lose interest' in my business," he said.

A huge confession of love from me, and that's his talking point?

He went on. "The business was great. It was working out—growing, even. It was one of those impossible moments in life when everybody got to win. I was happy, my employees were happy, our clients were happy. Kayla was happy. We had moved in together. We were talking about getting married." He took a shaky breath. "Then, one night—it was actually the night the Oscars were on—Kayla stopped by the store on her way home to pick up a box of microwave popcorn, because she had this rule that you couldn't watch the Oscars without popcorn." Ian paused. "And a boy—a teenage boy—walked into the grocery store with an assault rifle and opened fire. For no reason. Nobody ever figured out why—why that store, why that day, why that moment. He shot a security guard, two checkers, and two people standing in line. And the last person he shot, before he shot himself, was Kayla."

I knew the rest without his even saying it.

There are facial expressions you can fake. You can fake a smile, for instance, or a frown. You can even fake tears. But certain expressions are so true and so directly connected to the heart that they are beyond description. That's what I saw in Ian then. The most desperate, unspeakable, agonizing, indescribable despair.

I held still and quiet. What could I say? How on earth could I respond? It was beyond anything I had words for. At last, grasping for something—some acknowledgment of what he was telling me—I whispered, "I am so sorry."

He nodded, staring at the floor like he was seeing something else.

After a while, quiet as I could, I said, "When was that?"

"Three years ago," he said. "Three years, four months, six days."

I suddenly understood. "That's why you lost interest in the business."

He nodded, lost in the memory. "She died at the scene. She never had a chance. He got her twice—one bullet through her right breast and lung, and one through her ear and out the back of her head. Only one person survived. The store was closed during the investigation, but then they reopened. Mopped away all the blood and opened the doors within two weeks. I've never gone back. I can't even drive down that street. It's so strange to me that people shop there now. They don't even know. They buy their Doritos and their beer and stand in line on the very spot where she took her last breath. She died alone on a cold industrial floor. It all ended right there. Everything she'd ever worked toward, or hoped for, or loved."

I watched his chest rise and fall. At last, I understood his silences. How words must truly fail him in the face of it all. My mind skipped backward to all the times he stood at the gym, holding so still, seeming like it took every ounce of his will to tolerate the world and everyone in it. I guess it really had.

For the first time since I'd known him, I didn't push against the quiet, or try to fix it, or try to fill it with noise. I just let it surround us, and I stayed right there.

After a while, he looked up, seeming to remember I was there.

"I want to thank you," he said then, meeting my eyes. "You are the only good thing that's happened to me since that day."

Context changes everything. My green card idea seemed so foolish now, knowing everything. I had the idea to grab on to that foolishness and make a little joke. "My offer of a sham wedding is still open," I said.

I'd hoped for a smile, and I got one, just for a second. "I can't marry you for a green card."

I watched his profile at the window, and I felt the most acute longing. Knowing what he'd been through made my problems seem small in comparison. It forced me to step back and see my own situation in a broader context. It forced me to notice that I was, if nothing else, still alive. Witnessing even a glimpse of what he'd lost made me feel both embarrassed by my declaration of love for him—and a thousand times more committed to it.

He must have sensed what I was feeling. "And you're not actually in love with me, by the way."

With that shift in topic, the light in the room seemed to change—just barely—as if somewhere not too far away the sun had come out from the clouds.

"Um," I said, "I think I would know."

"We talked about this already," he said. "It's not real."

I tilted my head. "Feels pretty real."

"Listen," he said, "you know how kidnapping victims can fall in love with their captors? That's what this is."

"You're saying I have Stockholm syndrome?"

"I'm saying you have a version of something like it."

"Are you saying you *kidnapped* me?"

He turned back. "I didn't kidnap you, but I have been one of your captors. You have been held hostage—robbed of your old life, isolated from your old friends, and at the mercy of others. You have faced adversity that most people never see. In response, you've created an imaginary bond with one of your captors—to feel safe, and to create hope, and to feel less alone. It's a classic form of self-preservation."

"Sounds like you've thought about this."

"Am I wrong?"

Actually, I didn't know. I guess that was one way of reading the situation. "*Is* the bond imaginary?" I asked.

Ian didn't answer.

"Do you feel it, too?" I pressed. "Or did I just make it up?" My brain could list a hundred reasons why a guy like him would not even remotely be interested in someone like me. Of course! It defied all logic to think that he might. And yet—I didn't *think* it. I *felt* it. I felt it over and over.

"I am fond of you," Ian said then.

"How fond?"

Ian didn't answer again.

"Because, honestly," I finally said, cracking the silence, "if you don't also feel what I'm feeling, then it doesn't matter if what I feel is real or imaginary, does it? If you have no interest in me—and I have no idea: sometimes I feel like you really do, and sometimes I feel like you absolutely don't—then this conversation is pointless. We don't have to talk about kidnapping, or theories of psychology. You just say you're not interested, and we're done here."

Ian didn't speak.

"Just say you're not interested, and you go home to Scotland, and I stay here with my mother and eat spaghetti for dinner, and we'll never see each other again. Easy."

Ian stared at the floor.

"Just say you're not interested," I whispered then, hoping with every cell in my body that he would say the opposite.

Finally, he turned to me, and something had shifted in his eyes. There was no softness there anymore. "I'm not interested," he said.

I sat back. I don't know what I was expecting him to say, but it wasn't that. Not in that way, at least. Not like it was *true*. "You're not?"

His voice was flat. "I am fond of you. You have been a pleasant patient to work with. Your situation is tough, and I've been impressed with your drive and your strength. But I do not have romantic feelings for you."

I took a few breaths in slow motion. Did I believe him? "And so that very passionate, Olympic-level kiss at the lake?"

He shrugged. "I guess I'm just a good kisser."

"How about that other kiss—when you publicly, in front of a whole room of onlookers, ended your own career?"

He looked up very carefully, straight into my eyes. "I must have let myself get too lonely."

"So," I said, putting it together, "it wasn't passion—it was desperation?"

He almost looked a little bored. "That's one way to put it."

"So," I tried again, hoping to make him deny it, "what you're saying is, you knew I'd developed a slightly overwhelming crush on you, but you didn't dissuade me because you were lonesome and horny?"

"That's another way to put it."

"Okay," I said, and then I felt a wash of shame.

Of course he wasn't in love with me. Why would he be? What had I been thinking? He could do and be and choose anything he wanted. He had the whole world ahead of him. All I had was a tiny little half-life. What was exciting or attractive or lovable about that? I'd forgotten what I'd become. If Chip, who had known me at my best, didn't even want me, how could I hope for anyone else? I was no longer lovable. *Note to self.*

"Okay," I said again. My chest started to ache as it all hit me.

There was no point in being honest anymore. There was no way to save face at this point, either. I just had to get him out of here. Fast, before the universe collapsed.

We were done. I turned away. "Hey—have a great trip back to Scotland."

But he lingered.

"I have something for you," he said, holding up a small box wrapped in kraft paper. "Your birthday present, actually. I brought it to the lake—but . . . I'd still like you to have it."

I turned away. "No, thanks."

He hesitated. "I could just leave it here for you."

"Don't leave it here. I don't want it."

He stood there.

"Time to go, dude," I said then. "Get out."

"I thought we might exchange contact information."

Why the hell would we do that? "Oh," I said, falsely pleasant. "I don't think that'll be necessary."

"I was hoping we could stay friends."

Fuck you. "No, thanks," I said. "I'm good."

"How will I know how you're doing?"

"I'll be fine," I said, still not turning back. "You said yourself I'm a lot stronger than I think."

"Maybe I could just—"

"Get the hell out," I said. "Please." We were so done here.

He got quiet. I heard him walk toward the door then. When he reached it, he turned. "I'm sorry, Margaret. I will always remember you."

"That's so funny," I said, glancing in his direction, but not actually meeting his eyes. "Because I've already forgotten you."

THE NEXT MORNING, lying awake in my new, greige bedroom, I noticed something on the table by the door. My birthday present from Ian. He'd left it, anyway.

It made me angry to see it. Hadn't I told him not to do that? Didn't I get any say in anything?

I resolved to throw it away in the kitchen trash.

I should probably have gotten up and gotten dressed. But I didn't. I found myself thinking about Kit's comforting thought. Kit's expert said to give it a year. Would I be back to normal in a year? It seemed utterly impossible.

But then I had a comforting thought of my own.

I'll give it a year, I thought, *and if I don't feel any better, I'll kill myself.*

It perked me up quite a bit.

All I had to do for one year was make it through the day. I'd ask my mother to get me a big wall calendar, and then, at the end of every day I successfully suffered through, I'd mark a big *X*. Things would get better, Kit's mathematician had promised. Great. I hoped so.

But if he was wrong, I had a plan B.

One bit of good news: It was not as hard to move back home as I'd feared.

Though my dad did not come home.

The "little time" he was taking turned into a lot of time.

My parents talked on the phone some, going through the details, my dad trying to get a handle on the story. Sometimes my mother cried and begged, which was disturbing because my mother never cried. Or begged.

But he didn't come home.

In fact, within the month, he called to tell her he was going to take a trip for a "personal project." He was going to donate his woodworking and construction skills to a help restore a historic whaling ship in a museum in Connecticut. He'd rented a little house up there, and he wasn't sure when he'd be back. If.

"Your father is moving to Mystic, Connecticut," my mother told me, before bursting into tears. "He's going to volunteer as a woodworker."

I had never seen my mother fall to pieces in the way she did in the weeks after my father left town. Her jobs died on the vine. She just didn't show up. She wandered the house crying, or staring into space. She'd forget to eat. Or she'd make a meal and then sit staring at it until it was cold. I'd find her sitting in my father's favorite chair, staring at the rug or rubbing at the chocolate stain he'd smeared on the arm.

"I snapped at him about this once," she said quietly, when she noticed me watching her. "I waited to reupholster that chair for years, and we hadn't had it back a week before he melted chocolate on the arm."

She didn't seem so mad about it now.

As bad as this time was, it was good, too. It let me see her differently. It let me see her story in a much wider context. It let me feel, for the first time ever, almost protective toward her. She had always been so strong, so in control, until now. I'd only ever seen her as invulnerable—but now she was the opposite.

There was another bonus to this time, too: Worrying about her gave me something to worry about other than myself.

I took to emailing my dad every few days, just "checking in" casually, trying to ascertain when, if ever, he planned to come back. I also called Kit with updates on the home front and—because she went out to visit him a couple of times in Mystic—gathered intel on his state of mind.

They never officially separated. My dad was just "taking time." Kitty promised us he wasn't dating anyone. And, she said, he didn't seem particularly out of sorts, either. Just eating way too much canned soup.

My time with my mom turned out to be a surprise. Something shifted in her after my dad left. At lunch, back in in the hospital, she had barraged me with advice and opinions and half-baked inspirational stories. She'd pushed me the way she'd always pushed me. She'd been relentless, and critical, and judgmental.

But now that the window had closed, and she'd accepted that, she'd become much calmer. If there was nothing I could do, then she didn't have to make me do it. She could relax and give us all a break. Of course, it turns out that the window never truly closes. I found a bunch of articles saying there's always potential for neurological plasticity, long after that initial healing period.

But my mom didn't know that. And I sure as hell wasn't telling her.

Adjusting the curve for how crushingly depressed we both were, life with my mother was surprisingly pleasant.

Once she'd recovered enough to get back to work, she reduced her workload by half. She made sure to be home for lunch, when she made us sandwiches and smoothies. In theory, I was responsible for dinner—but lots of nights we wound up getting takeout from the Italian place down the road. After dinner, almost every night, we worked puzzles and sipped wine, and half-listened to the news.

We were both miserable, and grateful for the company.

Of course, everything I might have expected to be hard was, in fact, hard.

It was hard to be back in that house as a broken version of myself. It was hard to compare the past to the present at every turn. It was hard to see my old clothes, shoes, keepsakes, photo albums, Rollerblades—not to mention a shelf of diaries filled with all my old assumptions about how my life would turn out. It was hard to glimpse ghostly memories at every turn of what it was like to run and skip and hopscotch and bicycle and shoot hoops. I even missed utterly ordinary things, like walking out the front door, or leaning on the kitchen counter, or standing in the shower. It was hard not to regret everything I'd lost. The abilities I'd taken for granted. The time I'd wasted.

I am not going to lie. Everything that happened in the hospital before I moved home? That was the easy part.

My situation didn't truly feel real until I was out of the hospital.

Without Kit, and Priya, and Nina—and, okay, fine, even Ian—it was like I didn't have anyone to keep me from sinking.

So I sank.

I went through a long, deep period of grief that involved bitterness, anger, mourning, judgment, rage, self-pity, fear, longing, and loneliness—usually more than one in combination, and often all together—as well as nightmares, insomnia, fits of temper, anxiety attacks, and dish throwing. In fact, after accidentally dropping (and smashing) one of my mom's favorite saucers, I got so enraged that I hauled a whole stack out into the backyard and smashed about ten more on the driveway.

Then I cried in the backyard until my mom came home and found me.

She should have yelled at me. But guess what she did instead?

She marched back into the kitchen and brought out her own stack of dishes to smash.

That weekend, she made a trip to Goodwill and brought back crates of unwanted dishes that we could smash at will. We didn't even clean them up afterward. Just left the shattered colors all over the driveway like a great mosaic homage to crazy-town.

"It's pretty, actually," my mom said one day.

In a way, it was.

Years before, I'd seen a video taken by a security camera that went viral on the Internet of some kids playing on a beach where they weren't supposed to be. The tide came roaring in, and the three of them got pulled into the waves. The beach was long and flat. Watching it, you just rooted for them to stand up, get balanced, and run back up to higher shore. But the tide was so strong, they couldn't get their footing. They just washed out to sea and then back in, over and over. They started to stand and then tumbled backward, lifted their heads for a good breath and got pummeled by a giant wave, tried to outrun the waves and were overtaken. You thought, "Those kids are going to drown five feet from dry land." In fact, even though you knew they weren't going to drown—because the title of the video was "Miracle of Survival"—you felt certain they were going to drown anyway.

That was me, during those early months after leaving the hospital. I was all three of those kids at the same time. A miracle of survival—but drowning anyway, all the same.

My old friends wanted to see me, for example, but I didn't want to see them. They wanted to "get together" and "grab a bite" or "have coffee."

Why would I want to do that? I dreaded the pity on their faces and the assumptions they'd make. I dreaded how sorry they'd feel for me. I dreaded every single reaction of every single girlfriend when she heard how Chip had ruined my life and disappeared. I wasn't going to feed their schadenfreude.

My mother read an article saying it was important for "people like me" to stay connected. She even tried to convince me to let her organize a girls' day at a spa. "It'll be fun," she tried to declare. "We'll get our hair done. Mani-pedis. You can roll home feeling great."

"I never feel great, Mom," I said. "That's not a feeling in my collection."

"I just read an article that said human connections help prevent Alzheimer's."

"Alzheimer's," I said, "is the least of my worries right now."

I tried not to feel bleak, but I felt bleak anyway. I tried to leave the house, but I always stopped at the door. I tried to count my blessings, but even just trying made me mad. Things went on like this for months—and months. No change in sight. I don't mean to gloss over it, but there just isn't much to report. Wake up. Feel angry. Avoid human contact. Smash dishes. Repeat.

And then, in late summer, Kit came home for a weekend.

Twenty-five

YES, KIT'S BOYFRIEND, the Moustache, had let the Beauty Parlor fall apart. Yes, things were far worse than she'd expected when she got back. Turns out, he had no interest in the boring, day-to-day activities of running a shop, like sweeping or taking out the trash or writing down appointments. Kit returned to angry customers, disgruntled employees, and a cockroach infestation.

We hadn't talked on the phone every day, as she'd promised—though she had found time to talk every day with my mom.

It was fine. My mom needed her more.

"If you'd just follow me on Instagram," she said, "we wouldn't *have* to talk on the phone."

"It's really not the same thing."

Kitty had the most contact with our dad of anyone, so she and my mom suddenly had a lot to talk about. They also had years of resentments, misunderstandings, disappointments, and blame to work through. But I had to hand it to them. They didn't just smile big and make nice. They went for it. They argued, they disagreed, they compared notes—on their lives and everybody else's.

When we did talk, though, Kit was very interested in my health, my progress, my daily routine. She asked tons of questions—sometimes so many we never talked about her at all. Specific questions, too, about how I felt and how I was taking care of myself. She started emailing me articles on spinal health, recovery, home rehab, functional electrical stimulation, and neurogenesis. Specific, highly technical articles, too—far different from the pop psychology we'd started with.

"Where are you finding these?" I asked her. "I thought you were repainting the shop."

"I broke up with the Moustache," she confessed.

"Because he drove your business into the ground?"

"Because I think I'm in love with Fat Benjamin."

"We're all in love with Fat Benjamin. He's adorable."

"Anyway, I have insomnia."

"Do *not* worry about me in the middle of the night!" I said. "Go back to sleep!"

"Nobody *chooses* who they worry about in the night," she said. "Just read the articles and shut up."

So I did. Or tried to. Actually, I just printed most of them off and put them in a stack. They were very dry. My guess was Kit herself only read the titles.

All to say, she'd hoped to visit in early summer, but she didn't make it until August. Which was fine. I wouldn't have been much fun before that anyway.

I wasn't much fun in August, either.

But being with Kit seemed to help.

She made me get dressed and put on lipstick and go out to hip new restaurants with her. She made me listen to disco and sing with her—and she filmed everything. One afternoon, she drove me to the ocean.

"I'm worried about you," she said, snapping my photo as we watched the waves. "You're living like an old person."

"I'm fine," I said.

She leaned over and sniffed me. "You're a little mothballish, even."

I swatted at her. "I am not."

"You do remember you're twenty-eight—not seventy-eight?"

"I think I'm doing okay," I said. I was alive, wasn't I? Maybe I wasn't doing yoga at sunrise, but I did get out of bed every morning. Usually.

"Why haven't you learned how to drive?"

"Where would I drive to?"

"Why haven't you investigated braces for your legs?"

"I'm fine with the chair. It's fine."

"I think you need to try harder."

She probably meant well, but I was tired of people meaning well. "I think you need to mind your own business."

But Kit didn't care. "You are my business," she said with a shrug. "You always have been."

She took a million pictures of me for her followers: me eating spaghetti, me getting my toenails painted rainbow colors, me sunbathing in heart-shaped sunglasses. She gave my pixie cut a freshen-up and Instagrammed that. She made me put on her retro 1950s lipstick and Instagrammed that. She even took a picture of the scars on my shoulder and Instagrammed that.

"Kit! Nobody wants to see my gross shoulder!"

"Everybody wants to see it. You're an Instagram star, lady. Just accept it."

But Kit just had to push me. On her last night, at dinner, in front of my mom, of all people, Kit said, "How's your summer camp coming along?"

It felt like an awfully private question to bring up in a place as public as the dinner table. I glanced at my mother.

"Summer camp!" my mom said. "You want to go to summer camp?"

Kit said, "She wants to *build* a summer camp."

My mom sat straight up. *Build something? Yes, please!*

She lobbed fifty questions at me at once, but I shut them all down.

"I haven't even thought about it in months," I said. Which was true.

But that night, as I was falling asleep, I found myself thinking about it again. Under the onslaught of real life in the real world, I'd almost forgotten the idea entirely. It was so like Kit to remind me.

Overnight, my head flooded with ideas, and the next morning, before I'd even had coffee, I wheeled into the kitchen in my pajamas to find some paper, and I made a list off the top of my head:

chair bowling
bonfires
gardening
singing
hand cycling
wheelchair kung fu
bungee jumping
pinball
Pop-A-Shot
racing
canoeing
zip-lining
ping pong
wheelchair obstacle course
horseback

"What is all that?" my mom asked when she came in, peering over my shoulder.

"Ideas for the summer camp," I said.

She nodded. "I've been thinking about it, too."

"You have?"

"If we built it," she said, "maybe the camp sign could be a mosaic. That would give us something to do with all your broken dishes."

That's how Kit got me to try harder. The same way she got me to sing. By tricking me. By playing a tune I couldn't resist. But I do have to give her credit—or maybe I have to give it to Ian's mom. Because the next thing I doodled on that paper was her famous quote: *When you don't know what to do for yourself, do something for somebody else.*

KIT LEFT THAT morning, but it was okay. I didn't have that same sense of panic I'd felt when she left the hospital.

Now I had a project.

Or maybe the project had me.

In the following weeks, I got consumed. I took over the dining table. I drew plans for buildings and consulted an architect. I made lists of ideas, resources, people to work with. I did real estate searches online—looking for land that was far enough out to be cheap but close enough to be accessible. I looked at other, nonprofit camps online to see how they did things and what they offered. I brainstormed names and investigated graphics. I made plans for a nature trail, a library, a ceramics studio, a yarn café, a bake shop, a butterfly garden. Everything would be wheelchair accessible—and everything would be architecturally beautiful. I had rolled my eyes so much at my mother decorating my hospital room—but after we'd taken it all down, I'd seen her point. The feeling of the room changed. Without her quilts and curtains and table lamps and splashes of color, it felt like the saddest place in the world.

I wanted this place to feel like sunshine. I wanted it to feel like hope. Warm, but cool. Bright, but shady. Alert, but calm. I wanted it to feel like magic.

"You could call it Hell on Wheels," my mom suggested one night at dinner.

"'Hell' might give the wrong vibe."

"What about Camp Magic?"

I gave a shrug. "Might sound like an academy for young magicians."

"Not a bad idea," she pointed out.

I pointed at her. "Yes. We should offer magic classes." Then back to the name: "It needs to sound fun enough for kids, but serious enough for grown-ups."

My mom grinned, "So the Margaret Jacobsen Center for Spinal Cord Recovery is out."

I gave her a look. "Too cutesy."

"What about Camp Hope?" she asked.

We let that idea simmer while we sketched out ideas for a camp T-shirt with the slogan THAT'S HOW WE ROLL.

It was both a lucky and a slightly unlucky thing that my mom was a contractor.

It meant that she knew a million workmen, plumbers, electricians, surveyors, real estate agents, bricklayers, painters, distributors, suppliers, A/C guys, and demolition experts. They knew the dirt on everybody and knew how to get the best deals. That was all in the "pro" column.

Under "con": If I really did this, I was about to spend a truckload of time with my mom.

And it did look like I was going to do this. I couldn't seem to make myself think about anything else, for one thing. I can't tell you what a pleasure it was to use my brain again—to use all my business training, and skills, and design sense, and creativity. The project brought together almost everything I loved to do.

More than that, it got me out of the house.

At a certain point, I had to start looking for land, and meeting with people, and talking with them about ideas and strategies, having lunches and coffees with potential contributors and partners. Leaving the house just for the sake of leaving the house had never interested me. But leaving the house to get a donation pledge of five thousand dollars? That I could do.

I dusted off my old pantsuits and my pearl earrings, and I gutted up and went to lunch.

Kit even made me set up a Kickstarter campaign, and then she posted about it to her now *sixty*-six thousand followers. Donations flowed in. Money piled up. The whole thing started to look like it might actually happen.

"They love you!" Kit said on the phone. "Send me a picture of you in that pinstripe Ann Taylor suit!"

Was everything suddenly all fixed and perfect? No. Did I get pitying stares in restaurants? Constantly. Did I still have profound moments—hours, days—of hopelessness, anger, bitterness, frustration, despair, self-hatred, and grief? You could say that. And did I one day run into Neil Putnam from Simtex HR, the guy who had hired-me-but-not-officially for my dream job before the accident and then nixed the whole thing afterward? And did he not recognize me at all? And when I finally explained who I was, did he say, "You changed your hair!"?

Yes. That happened.

But the tone of my life was different now. I had a purpose. I had a reason to take a shower every morning. I had a reason to take care of myself. More than that, I was figuring out how doing something for other people could—in fact—be doing something for yourself. Amazing.

It felt good to feel better, and so I started looking for other ways to amp it up. I got addicted to audiobooks. I joined a choir. I kept knitting, even though I never got any better. I taught myself how to make pastries from scratch. I let my mom sell my old condo.

By the time I put the three hundredth *X* on my suicide calendar, I had signed an earnest-money contract on a hundred-acre plot of land outside of town with a two-hundred-year-old oak tree, three hills, and a catfish pond. I used the money from the condo as a down payment. That night, even though my dad still had not come home after all this time, and even though my mom might well have been *X*-ing off her own set of impossibly strange and altered days, we celebrated with champagne.

Despite everything, I decided at last to bet on hope—and I stuffed my suicide calendar in the recycling.

If this is the rest of my life, I found myself thinking one day, *it's okay.*

It really was.

Twenty-six

THEN CHIP DECIDED to get married.

Married.

To that sneaky, soup-making ex-girlfriend, Tara, a.k.a. the Whiner.

In Europe, of all places. In a town in Belgium I'd never heard of called Bruges.

The invitation arrived on Valentine's Day, of all days. Which forced me to notice three things: One, it was Valentine's Day. Two, it had been exactly a year since the crash. And three, I had completely forgotten about Chip.

I also noticed something else: My mom, my dad, and Kit were the only names on the invitation.

My mother knew about the engagement, though. She was still friends with Evelyn. She just couldn't give her up. Although Evelyn never came to the house once I moved home. For a long time, my mother snuck out to meet her, saying she was "running errands," but I knew what they were up to.

"You can be friends with Evelyn," I told her one night after dinner. "It's okay."

"I'm not!"

"It's not disloyal to me. I'm fine."

"He cheated on you! He gave up on you."

"It was a messy time."

She didn't need to be mad for me. She really didn't. Hadn't we all lost enough?

I got it. I did. Best friends are not easy to come by. The two stayed friends, and they avoided talking about either one of us, until one day Evelyn just had to tell her about the upcoming nuptials.

My mom got the scoop: Chip had been promoted not once, but twice, and had risen through the ranks of his investment bank in exactly the way you'd expect a guy as handsome and WASPy and confident as Chip to rise. He was highly promotable. In fact, they'd transferred him to their Brussels office.

"Chip is living in Belgium?"

My mom nodded.

"He doesn't even speak French!"

I felt a flash of resentment—quick but distinct. Chip got promoted? To Europe? The crash sure hadn't slowed him down. Was his life really going to be that easy? I got that sour feeling that comes when you make the mistake of thinking someone else is beating you at life.

But then I took a mental breath.

So what? Chip was in Brussels. But I was genuinely okay in Texas. We had both moved on. We could both be okay at the same time. We weren't on a seesaw, for Pete's sake! There was plenty of okay to go around.

Just because Chip had gotten what he'd wanted so easily, without ever having to question it, without ever having to struggle—that didn't necessarily mean that what he got was *better*.

"I've known about the wedding for a while," my mother confessed. "Evelyn warned me."

"You didn't tell me?"

"I thought it would fall through," my mom said. "Apparently, that girl *followed* him to Brussels. She showed up at the airport with all her bags and announced she was coming along."

I shrugged. You had to give it to her. "Ballsy."

My mother closed her eyes. "Please don't talk about balls at dinner." Then she went on, "The good news is, it's in Europe, so no one could possibly expect us to go."

"Did you know they were going to invite everybody but me?" I asked, showing her the envelope.

From her face, she didn't. "That must be a mistake," she said.

That calligraphy did not look like a mistake to me, but before I could say so, my mom's phone rang.

It was Kit.

My mom put her on speaker.

"Did you hear about the wedding?" Kit demanded.

"We just got the invitation," my mom said.

"And I'm not on it," I added. "They invited everybody but me."

"I think it was an oversight," my mother declared.

"Maybe they're sending you a special one," Kit suggested.

I gave my mom a look. "Unlikely."

"Well," Kit said, in her determined voice, "you have to come anyway. You have to crash."

"Hell, no," I said, just as my mom said, "We're boycotting, like decent people."

"Listen," Kit said. "They invited Dad, too. Evelyn called him, since she knew he was 'on sabbatical.'"

"I hope he is boycotting, too."

"No," Kit said. "He's going."

My mom frowned. "Why would he go? He doesn't even like to travel."

"He's going," Kit announced, "because I talked him into it."

"Kit—"

"And I talked him into it because we're going to *Parent Trap* him."

My mother frowned, totally uncomprehending.

"We won't tell him you're coming," Kit went on, "and you'll show up looking *devastating*—and the shock of it will catapult him into your arms."

"There may be some logic flaws here," my mother said.

"He talks about you all the time," Kit insisted. "He misses you all the time. I think it's pride keeping him away. I think we need to give him a reason to get past it."

"You want to *surprise* him into forgiving me?" my mother asked.

"Shock and awe," I said, nodding. For a terrible idea, it wasn't too bad.

"Exactly," Kit said.

I shrugged. "It might be just dumb enough to work."

But my mom was shaking her head. "No. I can't."

"Yes! You can!" Kit said.

"It's too much," my mom said, and she suddenly looked remarkably old to me. Smaller, too. She'd always been so forceful—so certain and bulldozer-like about her choices. It was strange to see her hesitating and uncertain like this. It was disarming to see her hang back and hesitate. The little frown lines between her brows seemed deeper. As disorienting as it was to see her this way—so timid—I have to confess, it humanized her, too. It made me feel almost protective.

"Mags and I will help you," Kit offered then. "We'll go with you. We'll make it work."

My mother lowered her voice, like I might not hear. "I can't ask Margaret to do that."

"Hello?" I said. "I wasn't invited."

"Skip the wedding, then," Kit said, like, *Duh*, "but come to Belgium. Easy."

But would it be easy? Traveling so far might not be easy. Leaving the safe nest I'd built this year might not be easy. Facing a thousand unknowns had definite potential to not be easy.

But Kit was ready to make this happen. "Family trip to Belgium! End of discussion!" Kit said. "I'll organize everything. Hit the mall and find something heartbreaking to wear."

My mom squinted at me, like, *Is this a good idea?*

I gave her a nod, like, *Hell, yes.*

Was it a good idea? I didn't know. It actually seemed pretty risky—for everybody. I had just barely let go of my suicide calendar, after all. I hardly even had my head above water, and it wouldn't take much to wash me back under. Could I do this?

I suddenly thought maybe I could.

Especially as it hit me that Belgium was really not all that far away from Scotland.

It didn't seem like such a bad idea to help my mother get some closure with my dad—and then maybe just pop over to Scotland for a little closure of my own.

A terrible, heartbreaking, foolish idea—but once I'd thought it, I couldn't seem to unthink it.

The idea even woke me up from a sound sleep that night and gnawed at me until I Googled the distance. A nonstop flight from Brussels to Edinburgh took under two hours. Easy.

I could pop over for a day or two, maybe. Pretend to be in town "on business." Call Ian in a super-casual way, like I'd remembered him as an afterthought. We could meet for coffee. I could be near him again, even for a few hours. But, as I considered the idea, I had to think about what that might look like.

I'd be—as ever—in my wheelchair. It would be gray outside. We'd meet at some café with a door too skinny for my chair, so Ian would have to leave me outside while he ordered us to-go cups, if they even had things like that in Europe. He'd lead us to a bench nearby, and I would be utterly saturated with longing—like a starving person looking at fresh-baked loaf of bread—and he would be . . . What? Vaguely pleased to see I was still alive? Professionally curious about the state of my spinal cord? Polite? Even—oh, God—falsely friendly? Or worse! Maybe he'd be seeing someone by now, someone tall and able-bodied—a fellow triathlete—and he'd blithely bring her along so we could meet. You know, thinking that would be *fun for me.* I'd sit in asexual agony in my chair, watching the two of them on a bench with their able bodies side by side, smiling and stealing glances, but trying to keep it down for the desiccated, noodle-legged spinster in their midst.

It would be the worst circle of hell. My stomach cringed at the thought.

But I still wanted to do it anyway. Or maybe *needed* to.

Kit loved this idea—but then, terrible ideas were her favorite kind. She wanted details. "What are you going to do—show up outside Ian's flat and surprise him?"

"No," I said. "I'm going to surprise him on the phone, like a normal person."

"You mean, like—once you're already there. Like, around the corner, in one of those little red phone booths?"

I shook my head. "This is not a spy movie. I'll just tell him I'm in town on business or something."

"I love it. A sneak attack."

"I'd just chicken out otherwise."

"How will you even find him?"

"I have no idea." I thought about it. "Maybe I'll ask Man-Bun-Rob to get his address from the hospital."

Kit clarified: "You're going to ask a former PT to help you stalk his former colleague."

"In a manner of speaking."

"Perfect," Kit said. "What could go wrong?"

Twenty-seven

KIT ARRIVED IN Texas three days before the trip to get us focused.

We spent more hours than I can count strategizing over outfits for my mom—and me, too. Kit wanted my mother in green—my dad's favorite color—and she dragged her to four stores before they found the right look. After that, Kit insisted she get her hair and nails done and buy all new makeup.

"I don't need a new lipstick," my mother protested.

"It's crunch time," Kit said. "Go big or go home."

Me? I was trickier. Kit spent more time on me than on my mother, and I wasn't even going to the wedding. I could easily have just worn some clothes I already owned, but Kit wouldn't hear of it. Nothing in my "sad closet" would do. Kit wanted me in something "smart, sophisticated, and with a just a touch of go-fuck-yourself." But subtle. If I really was just going to "pop by" in Scotland to "say hello" to Ian, I'd have to meet the challenge of finding plausible business wear that could also "reduce a man to tears of longing."

"We might be setting our sights a little high here," I said.

"Hush. I'm working."

It took Kit two days to find my perfect look: a gray pantsuit with a crisp white blouse that cost four hundred dollars.

"Worth it," Kit declared.

She also forced me to buy my first lingerie in over a year. "What if you meet a handsome stranger in the airport?" she demanded, pulling a pair out of my dresser. "Are you going have your way with him in a sports bra and sad gray Jockeys?"

I gave her a look. "I'm not spending two hundred more dollars on uncomfortable underwear that no one will ever see."

"Don't be such an old lady," she said, holding the panties out. "I have to room with you. *I'll* see your underpants, if no one else. And this situation right here"—she dropped the pair in the wastebasket—"makes me lose my will to live."

In the end, she gifted me the lingerie. Against my will.

She also Instagrammed photos of our shopping day—but then she refused to post the final outfit. "You're too gorgeous," she declared. "You'd break the Internet."

I ALMOST CHICKENED out. This couldn't possibly be a good idea. But then I'd circle back around to the sad, quiet version of herself that my mom had been this whole long year, and my resolve would come back. I didn't honestly know if she could win my dad back. The plan seemed like a long shot with deep potential for crushing humiliation.

But it didn't really matter. I knew I had to help her try.

Besides, my mom had already spent all of her frequent flyer miles to get us an upgrade to first class.

Kit gaped when she told her.

My mom shrugged. "Go big or go home."

I looked at Kit. "We're going to need that on T-shirts."

The morning-of, I had a few more second thoughts.

"What was I thinking?" I demanded of Kit as we shotgunned our morning coffees. "How am I supposed to lug this wheelchair all around Europe? That place is one hundred percent stone steps! Stone steps and fashionable people. This is lunacy. They're going to stop me at the gates and send me home."

Kit wasn't having it. "You're not a quitter."

Maybe not—but I wanted to be. "It's going to be the worst thing ever."

My mom was walking by, and she paused to squeeze my shoulders. "No," she said. "You've already survived the worst thing ever."

And there was the crux of it. This would be my first flight since the crash. "I'm not sure I can do this," I said.

Kit drained the dregs of her coffee and clanked her empty mug down in the sink. "Loving the self-doubt," she said. "Let's definitely run with that. But let's get on the plane first."

FIRST CLASS WAS like a VIP party.

Not only had I never flown to Europe before, I'd never flown anything but coach before. Now I was ruined, because I found out what I'd been missing. First class greeted us with champagne and strawberries, and it only got better from there. It practically had a swimming pool and a DJ.

We had to fly direct to London, then hop over to Belgium on a second quick flight, then take a train out to Bruges. It was going to be a long day and a half. But I couldn't complain. They gave us warm blankets and steamed hot towels for our hands, like we were at a spa. We had our own little sleeping pods with seats that reclined into beds. Plus, our seats were in the closest row to the door, so it was easy to wheel right to my spot.

Still, no amount of luxury could change the fact that this was my first flight since the crash. Despite all my attempts to focus my brain on something else—and I was doing a valiant job—my body could not be fooled. My hands felt cold and quivery. My eyes darted left and right like a trapped rodent's. My heart stumbled around in my chest like it was being attacked. There was no point worrying about it, I knew. This was happening. It was out of my hands. I'd made my choice, and now I just had to survive it.

Once we were buckled in, when my mom reached across the aisle to squeeze my hand, it was ice cold.

She met my eyes. "Are you terrified to fly again?"

I wrinkled my nose. "Just a smidge."

Kit leaned over. "Remember that time we went to Hawaii—and you *lived*?"

"We all lived, as I recall," my mother said.

"Would you like me to distract you?" Kit asked, nodding as she said it to let me know that *Yes, I absolutely would.*

My hands were turning kind of a bloodless gray. "I really can't imagine any possible way you could do that."

Kit wiggled her eyebrows at me. "I can."

The engines were whirring into action. Our seats faced each other. I leaned forward. "How?"

She met my mother's eyes and gave her a little nod, like they shared a yummy secret. My mom fished around in her carry-on and pulled out a little wrapped box that I recognized instantly. It was Ian's birthday present to me.

"Hey," I said. "I threw that in the kitchen trash."

"I fished it back out," my mom said.

I stared at it.

"Do you want it?" she finally asked.

The captain was making final announcements over the loudspeaker. I nodded.

She handed it over, and I peeled off the paper and the tape. Then I lifted the lid off the box. Inside was a necklace—a delicate silver chain attached to each end of a small silver bar, and stamped into the bar, in tiny typewriter-like letters, was one word: Courage.

"What is it?" Kit asked.

"A necklace."

"What does it say?" my mom asked.

"Courage."

Kit and my mom looked at each other. "Well," my mom said, "aren't we glad I rescued it?"

As I fastened it behind my neck and felt the cool pressure of the silver bar against my breastbone, the plane started to back away from the gate.

I felt a surge of fear.

"I've got another distraction for you," Kit said, watching me. "A better one."

"What?"

"The address Rob got you for Ian is wrong."

Okay. That was distracting. "Wrong?"

She nodded. "That's his parents' address in Edinburgh, but he doesn't live there."

"How could you possibly know that?"

She gave me a mysterious *I've got so much to tell you* smile. "We're in touch."

I felt an anxious jolt of *Where is this going?* What could she possibly tell me that was that juicy? Without permission, my brain jumped to a worst-case scenario. "Please don't tell me you are dating Ian," I said.

"What? No! Gross! I'm back with Fat Benjamin."

"Why on earth would you be in touch with Ian?"

That smile again. "He found me online. He wanted to know how you were doing."

The plane stopped a second, then started rolling forward. "He did? When was this?"

"A few weeks after I went back. He asked if he could check in with me from time to time."

"Why didn't you tell me?"

"He asked me not to. He didn't want to freak you out."

I tried to absorb the idea. "Did he? Check in?"

She nodded. "He did indeed."

Off her tone, I said, "A lot?"

"About once a week."

"Once a week!" She was enjoying this reveal too much. "He called you?"

"Mostly just email. Also, you know all those articles I sent you?"

The plane sped up on the runway. "The ones I'm pretty sure you never read?"

"They were from him."

He'd sent the articles! That explained a lot. But why? "How did he sound?"

"Like a concerned professional."

"Did you ever talk about anything else?"

She shook her head. "Mostly just your health. Pretty dry."

The nose of the plane lifted. I nodded. "Okay."

"But my personal opinion? He still likes you."

"He never liked me."

"I disagree."

"He told me in no uncertain terms," I said. "He never liked me. It was all just me being delusional, and he let it go on so I'd have, you know, a reason to live. Trust me. If there were any possibility for hope, I'd have found it."

Kit shrugged, like, *Okay. Have it your way.* The plane left the ground now, rattling and shuddering as it rose. I touched my fingers to my necklace. *Courage.*

Kit said, "There is one other thing, though."

I looked up.

"He started following me on Instagram."

I took in a breath. "Is that why you always take a million pictures of me?"

She nodded, looking very pleased with herself. "And guess what else? He's never posted a picture, and he doesn't follow anyone else. He doesn't even have a profile pic. I am the *one* person he follows."

I tried to process the idea of Ian using Instagram. "He saw the picture you took of my scars?"

Kit nodded very slowly.

"And the one this morning in the airport?"

Kit nodded again. "Assuming he checks his phone."

"So he might know we're headed to Europe."

"He might."

"So much for a stealth attack."

"The upside is," Kit went on, "it makes it easier to find out where he lives."

"How so?"

"When we get to Scotland," Kit said, shrugging, "we'll just message him for his address."

I nodded at her. "It's almost too simple."

Kit patted me on the head. "Almost."

EVEN BEYOND THE white terror of flying, I was nervous about the travel in general. At home, I'd developed routines and ways of doing things that had lifted my confidence. In Europe, I had no idea what to expect. We had researched everything online, of course, and I had a folder of print-outs in my carry-on bag. You can call ahead for a ramp to help you board the train from Brussels to Bruges, for example, but you can't just show up and demand one. I'd also made sure to find a hotel with rooms on the ground floor I could get to. Kit had wanted us to take a boat tour around the canals, but we learned in advance that none of the boats in town could accommodate wheelchairs.

We were as prepared as we could be, but nothing could have prepared us for the actual experience of being in Bruges. It was like a fairy tale city. None of the normal twenty-first-century clutter, like neon signs or billboards. Just medieval stone and brick buildings with turrets and gables, a town square with a Gothic church, and chocolate shops, and cobblestone streets. And the canals! Every few blocks, stone bridges arched over the quiet water below.

Not to mention all the swans.

All my prep was worth it. There were tricky moments of travel—like when we boarded the train and found it packed with people, shoulder to shoulder—so full, folks had to move to the next car to make room for us, and Kitty sat on my lap in the chair to make space. But, in general, it wasn't as hard as I'd feared. I'd expected roadblock after roadblock, and humiliation after humiliation, as I tried to navigate a world set up for able-bodied, French-and-or-Flemish-speaking foreigners. But we got along with surprising ease.

We reached the hotel in the late morning, and our jet-lag guide said we only had to stay awake until 10:00 P.M., so we ordered room service—steak frites—and watched European TV. Before it got too late, Kit and my mom popped out to raid the chocolate shops, and came back with a full shopping bag of dark, milk, white, peppermint, and salted caramel chocolates in every shape under the sun, from hearts to starfish, and filled with creams and nougats, fruit purees, coffee, almonds, macadamias, and peanut butter.

Kit dumped it all out on her bed in a pile.

"You've lost your marbles," I said to them both. "We can't eat all that."

"Sure we can," Kit said.

"We'll get sick," I insisted.

"Not me," Kit said. "I've spent years building up a tolerance."

In the end, we ate it all. The more we ate, the more it felt like a challenge we had to win. We really did make ourselves sick. It was impressive debauchery. Afterward, my mom and I had to lie green-gilled on the bed, and Kit threw up in the bathroom.

"I think I'm just dehydrated," she said, climbing into her rollaway bed by the window.

But in the morning, Kit was sick again.

"Maybe I picked up dysentery in the airport," she said. The nausea got better by midday. By evening, Kit was exhausted—but luckily nothing worse.

When it was time to get dressed, Kit lay on her rollaway like a corpse.

"You're fine now," I tried to insist, as she adjusted the cool rag over her eyes. "You haven't barfed in four hours. You and Mom need to get going."

But Kit, her voice froggy, didn't open her eyes. "I don't think I'm going."

"Um," I said. "You have to go! This was your crazy idea!"

"I do not feel good at all," Kit said.

My mom clutched her purse. "Maybe we should just skip it," she suggested.

"You're not skipping," Kit said.

"Well, I'm not going by myself," my mom said.

"Mags can go with you."

"I wasn't *invited,*" I said.

"Go as me," Kit said. "We RSVP'd for three."

"But they don't want me there."

"Nonsense," my mother said. "It was an oversight."

I looked at Kit, who really did look awful, and then I looked at my nervous mother, who also looked awful. Kit clearly wasn't going anywhere. But no way was I making my mom go alone. I sighed to my mom. "Get me Kit's dress."

It was red—a "your-life-is-ruined crimson," Kit called it—and strapless, and kind of fifties-looking, with a crinoline underskirt. I worked my way into it while my mom fussed and tried to help. I also—fuck it—wore the new lingerie. I did my hair. I put on all the new makeup Kit had bought me, including red lipstick. Taking one last look in the mirror, I stopped to wonder if I should leave Ian's not-quite-formal-enough necklace on, before deciding *of course.* I'd be needing the word "courage" tonight.

Then I forced my mom out the door.

We were doing this.

Honestly, in the face of all the other things we'd survived this year, how hard could it be?

THE WEDDING CHAPEL was not far. Just around the corner.

My research had assured me that Bruges's terrain was very flat and that the cobblestones would be more of a nuisance than a barrier—both true. I also knew from my research that the chapel itself was right on ground level, so I could wheel in with no trouble. What I didn't know, until we got there, was how very tiny the chapel would be.

Seriously. It was like a little Christmas ornament.

Standing around outside, in a large crowd, were all the guests who couldn't fit in the building.

Surely, there were other churches that could have held us all. Surely, Evelyn Dunbar had not overlooked a detail like the size of the venue. But the longer we stood there, surrounded by others who couldn't get in, and craning our heads for glimpses of the action, the more it felt like Chip's mom—perhaps in a grand gesture of triumph to the watching world—had overbooked the wedding on purpose.

"Do you think she knew we wouldn't all fit?"

"I suspect she did," my mom said, nodding. "Better an overflowing church than an empty one."

We found a place in the stone churchyard to wait, but there was no place for my mom to sit, and so we were at different altitudes, not even talking, and I spent the next half hour watching her worry her hands at her waist.

"Why are you doing that?" I asked after a while.

She looked down. "Doing what?"

"Twisting your hands around. Are you nervous?"

"I'm not twisting my hands around," she said, stopping.

That's when I looked up to see that she wasn't peering toward the church like everybody else. She was searching the crowd.

That little moment right there made me glad I'd come all this way. She had something important to do, and I was helping her do it.

Ten more minutes went by. Then another ten. Finally, my mom decided to go check in with the usher standing at the door to see what the holdup was.

That's how we got separated. She disappeared in that direction, cutting right and left through the crowd—and she hadn't been gone five minutes before the church bells started ringing. Before she could come back, the chapel doors pushed open, and the bride and groom came striding out.

Of course they did. This was a wedding! Their wedding.

I felt myself hunch down, suddenly realizing in a new way that I was *crashing Chip's wedding.*

I had nowhere to hide, but as the little stone churchyard flooded with strangers in sparkly gowns and tuxes, the photographer called all the important people off for photos.

An usher directed everyone else to follow a little side street to the reception, but I waited for my mom—who never came back.

I was not positioned well, down low in my chair. People I recognized walked straight on past without seeing my face, and all I could really see was belts and handbags.

Finally, I wheeled up to the church doors to ask after my mom.

"I'm looking for a woman in a green dress," I asked the usher.

He shook his head. "There's no one left inside."

I looked around. Did she miss me in the crush? Did she go ahead to the reception, thinking I'd gone ahead, too? Was she waiting for me there, trembling and nervous? An image of my mother, twisting her hands through the reception, alone, appeared in my head.

Time to find her. I wheeled off, following the last of the migrating crowd.

IT DIDN'T TAKE long for me to lose them entirely.

My research swore that ninety-five percent of the streets in Bruges were manageable for wheelchairs, but this one street belonged firmly in the other five percent. These particular cobblestones were smaller and narrower, with deeper grooves between them. The "razor-thin" tires my dad had been so proud of on this chair were not exactly built for this terrain. In fact, I got stuck over and over—the wheel wedged between stones as I rocked back and forth, wrestling it out. Slow going. Frustrating. My hands got dirty. My fingers got pinched. At one point, the wind tangled the hem of the dress in the spokes.

Then the side street opened onto a better, smoother one, where I was able to pick up some speed and coast up over the crest of a stone bridge. That's where I caught up with all the wedding guests. At a taxi stand. Which turned out to be for a *water* taxi. The kind I knew from the Internet couldn't accommodate wheelchairs.

This was how we were all getting to the reception. Boats.

I stopped right there on the bridge and took in the scene. Two boats, filled to the brim with wedding guests, had just motored away from the dock, and a last boat was loading. Men in tuxes and women in gowns waited in a snaking line around wood turnstiles. I scanned the guests for my mom's green dress, but I couldn't find her. Then I eyed the boat. I might manage to board, if somebody would help me. But as I coasted over and arrived at the entrance to the taxi stand, I found a bigger problem: It was about twenty stone steps from the road down to the water.

Twenty steep, uneven, Escher-like stone steps.

I stopped still at the top. The steps were tall and narrow. I could navigate a curb back in the States, and possibly two low steps on a very lucky day, but not this. No way was I making it down this. Not without dying.

I watched couple after couple use their working legs and feet to walk thoughtlessly up to the boat and step in, and I felt a sharp stab of despair. What was I doing here? Kitty had bailed, I'd lost my mother, and now there was no way I could make it to the reception that I wasn't even invited to.

I felt a funny little pressure in my throat, like I might cry.

I took a shuddery breath. I should never have come. Time to give up. Long past time, probably.

That's when the boat driver noticed me.

"Est-ce que vous allez à la soirée?" he asked, in French.

He thought I was Belgian. How flattering! *"Non!"* I shouted back. *"C'est d'accord." No. It's okay!* High school French for the win. It didn't often come in handy in Texas.

But the driver was already gesturing at the two guys on the dock, both of whom looked about seventy, and then they were both clambering toward me, up the steps with determination.

"Non, non," I said, shaking my hands at them like I didn't need help. *"Mes jambons sont eclatés."* I was trying to say, "My legs are broken," but I didn't realize until later that I'd confused the word *jambe,* French for "leg," with *jambon,* French for "ham." I'd also accidentally switched "broken" for "burst"—and so I'd basically just told them that my hams exploded.

The two men paused to look at each other.

Then they kept coming. I clearly did need help.

Of course I wasn't just a passerby in wedding attire. *Of course* I was a guest at this wedding. Just because I couldn't make it down those steps didn't mean I wasn't going to.

Over my protests, one elderly but surprisingly strong dock worker lifted me and cradled me in his arms as if he carried women like this every day, and then we were off, teetering down the steps. The other guy folded up my chair and followed us, and before I knew it, they were stepping into the boat and depositing me there—in a seat up at the prow that faced backward toward the crowd.

Every other seat, as far as I could tell, faced forward—except the one I was in, and the empty one beside it. In the churchyard, absolutely no one had noticed me. Now, they all stared.

What could I do? There was no getting off. There was no changing seats. I stared back. I didn't recognize anyone. My chair and my wedding-crashing self were stuck alone on a boat full of curious strangers. A boat that wasn't going anywhere.

The taxi crew had switched back into Flemish, but I could tell that the driver wanted to leave, even though the dockworkers thought he should stay. He kept telling them to untie the boat, but they didn't think they were supposed to. Finally, one of them dashed back up those lethal steps again to get a look around, and he called something down and pointed out of view.

Was somebody coming?

And then I saw.

Somebody was coming, all right.

The wedding party.

Twenty-eight

THEY GATHERED BY the bridge at the top of the steps to the taxi stand like a pouty spread in *Vanity Fair,* at the very spot where I had just been. I got my first good gander, and it was so strange to see all the guys who would have been our groomsmen, Woody, Statler, Murphy, and Harris, paired up with a flock of female strangers. Just as I thought that, a breeze rose up and caused all the bridesmaids' gowns to billow in slow motion.

Then the group parted, and I braced myself for the appearance of the bride and groom. But the couple that appeared were not Chip and the Whiner, but instead, Jim and Evelyn Dunbar. Chip's folks.

I had seen Evelyn several times since the day we'd fought in the hospital, of course. She was our next-door neighbor, after all.

But I had not spoken to her. Not once, in all this time.

At first, if she popped by, I hid. I felt like I couldn't face her, and I gave myself permission not to. As time went by, I stopped caring about avoiding her. But by then, she and my mother had begun their secret rendezvous.

We didn't work to avoid each other. It just happened.

After a while, my mother insisted that Evelyn had "entirely forgotten" our little "tiff" at the hospital. But I suspected that she'd long ago made me the villain of the situation: the desperate, broken girl who'd tried to manipulate her perfect son into giving up his perfect life out of guilt. Evelyn had never been the kind of person to face her son's limitations head-on. She could be very selective about her facts.

Hence, the "omission" of my name on the invitation.

It was fine. I didn't care. Except for one thing: She was coming my way, and I had no escape.

As she walked closer in her pale blue mother-of-the-groom suit and pearls, I wondered how she would react to the sight of me.

Not well, it turned out.

I have a theory that we are at our meanest when we feel threatened. People really seem to do their worst when they think you're out to hurt them, or steal from them, or take something that's rightfully theirs. And I could tell the minute Evelyn Dunbar's eyes met mine that she immediately thought *all of the above.*

She must have thought I was there to ruin the wedding. In her shoes, I might have thought the same thing.

She stepped into the boat, and froze when she saw me. Mr. Dunbar walked on to chat with some guests, but Evelyn bent toward me in my seat and dropped her voice about an octave. "What are you doing here?"

Other guests looked our way. No way was I discussing the *Parent Trap* plan in public. I shrugged instead. "Kit got sick, so I took her place."

She glanced around. She arranged her face into a smile. "You were not invited."

"I noticed that," I said.

"We thought it would be awkward."

"It would have been."

"But here you are."

"My mother thought it was an oversight."

"It wasn't."

"I'm not going to cause any trouble," I said at last, lifting my hands in a gesture of innocence. I meant to deescalate, but that just made her madder.

"How can you do this?" she hissed.

It seemed like an overreaction. "Do what?" I asked.

"Come uninvited and sit there like a goblin staring at everybody. It's creepy."

Was that what I was doing? "Did you just call me *a goblin*?"

"Just what are you trying to achieve?"

"I still can't get past the word 'goblin.'"

"Chip is moving on, and you should do the same."

"I agree."

"But you still had to come here? You still have to make this day, of all days, weird for him?"

I hadn't come here to make anything weird for anybody. But anger is contagious, I guess. Now, I couldn't resist. "Chip has made every day of the rest of my life weird for me, so maybe we're even. Except we'll never really be even. Unless I paralyze him back."

Evelyn's eyelids stretched a bit in surprise, like she suddenly feared that might be why I'd come here: to paralyze the groom. "That's not funny," she said.

I looked at her, like, *Come on*. "It's a little funny."

"It's time for you to go."

Sometimes you have no choice but to fail. But now was not one of those times. I hadn't gone through all this just to give up at the end. I had a mother to rescue.

"I'm not leaving," I said.

But Evelyn leveled a *don't you dare* look at me. "You're leaving," she said. "Now." She snapped at the boat crew to come over and deal with me.

Was that how this night was going to end? Me being tossed back onto the dock by an elderly team of Flemish boatmen? I thought about why I was here. I thought about who I wanted to be, and I decided that I wanted to be stronger for my struggles. Wiser, too, if I could. I wanted to be someone who made things better, not worse.

"I'm sorry I cursed at you," I said to her then.

Evelyn blinked. "What?"

"Back at the hospital. Last year. I used some language that upset you."

Evelyn pursed her lips at the memory. Her expression didn't exactly soften, but I could tell I'd surprised her.

"I was hurting, a lot," I said, "and I lashed out. I guess I thought if other people hurt, too, I might hurt less. But it didn't make me feel better to hurt you. It made me feel worse. I regret it, and I want you know I'm sorry. I should have been kinder."

Now she blinked some more.

When the crewman she'd snapped at made it over to us, he did not look like he was there to do her bidding. Instead, he looked like he wanted her to sit down. He started insisting that Evelyn take her seat, gesturing at the line behind her.

The usual Evelyn wouldn't have stood for it.

But it was like I'd taken the wind out of her self-righteousness. Or maybe I'd just shown her that I came in peace. Whatever it was, she didn't fight them. Instead, she went all docile and let them lead her to her spot.

THE REST OF the wedding party filled the remaining rows, leaving only the two prime center seats—directly across from me—open for Chip and the Whiner, the guests of honor.

Whatever lagniappe of peace had come from my moment with Evelyn, it disappeared at the sight of them cresting the bridge and then descending the steps so glamorously they could have been in slo-mo.

I looked around to check where the boat driver had stashed my chair. As if I might use it to roll away before they could spot me.

Of course, there was no rolling away. Staying right here, trapped in a seat directly across from the two reserved for the bride and groom, was apparently my only option.

I didn't know what to do with my hands—clasped? loose?—or where to turn my head. Should I gaze out at the swans and pretend I didn't notice them? Or maybe I should bend my face into a pleasant smile and look right at them on arrival, like, *Oh, hello! I didn't see you there.*

Instead, I reached up to rest my fingertips on the silver bar of Ian's necklace. *Courage.*

Chip didn't notice me until after he'd sat down. For a second, as he draped an arm around the Whiner, man-spreading his legs wide and taking in the sight of the canal, I sparked a hope he might never notice me at all.

No luck.

When his gaze drifted to a stop at my face, he leaned forward and flat-out stared. "Margaret?"

At the sound of my name, the Whiner sat up and stared, too.

There she was. Chip's new me. With a spray tan and too much eyeliner.

Tara. A girl I'd only ever seen in pictures. A girl Chip had compared me to from time to time—but only to point out my superiorities. I made better coffee. I had a better sense of humor. I had more rhythm. Here she was, in the flesh.

She looked awfully pouty.

I gave a little wave and said, "Hey!" like I was just now noticing them. "Happy wedding!"

"I didn't know you were coming," Chip said, and in that moment I could just tell: He did not know that I'd been left off the list.

What he didn't know wouldn't hurt him. "We all came," I said, and then added, "Everybody." Safety in numbers.

Chip looked around for the rest of the Jacobsens but came up short.

"I've lost them all now," I said, like, *No biggie.*

Then he looked around for my chair but didn't see it. "Where's your chair?" he asked. "Do you still need it?"

If my life were a movie, the answer would have been "That old thing? I haven't seen it in months." It would've been my moment to rise from my seat like a goddess and triumph over Chip and the Whiner and every person who had ever doubted me, including myself: Stand. Triumph. Roll credits.

I had longed for an ending just like that. But that's not the story I wound up with. And this wasn't the ending, either.

I pointed toward a storage compartment. "It's there."

"So you're still . . ."

"Paralyzed," I said with a nod.

He leaned a little closer, cautiously—like I might be feral. Then he put a big, fake smile on his face, leaned in even more, and said, "How are you?"

That's when I knew. *He pitied me.*

The bride was leaning forward, too, now, her arms crossed over her chest, but it wasn't quite pity on her face.

I matched his expression. "I am super great," I said, showing all my teeth. "How are you?"

Before Chip could respond, the Whiner jumped in, pulling his focus. "Chip!" she whined (there it was). "What the hell?"

Chip let go of his smile and got serious with me. "Why are you here, again?"

"It's a long story," I said.

Chip pushed out a sigh. "Because I'm trying to start fresh here."

"That's great," I said. "I cheer you on."

"Is that sarcastic?"

"No!"

"I don't need you to cheer me on, okay?"

I gave another shrug. "Too late."

My read on the situation at this point: Chip was mostly puzzled, and pitying, and jumping to conclusions about my motivations. But his brand-new wife was only one thing: furious.

"Look," I said to them both, "I wish you both well, okay? I am not pathetically stalking you. I've moved on."

But neither of them believed me.

That's when Statler called out from the next row of seats back, "Here to ruin the wedding, huh, Jacobsen?"

It was a joke, of course—meant, no doubt, to deflate the tension—but I suddenly realized that's what they all must have been thinking: that I'd come here with tragic, ridiculous hopes of sabotaging the wedding.

"I'm just here to celebrate," I said, lifting my hands in surrender.

But Statler just laughed. I was clearly a broken ex making one last desperate attempt to—*what? Roll off with the groom?* There could be no other explanation. Fair enough. Out of context, flying three thousand miles to your ex's wedding might seem a little suspicious.

Before I knew it, I was trying to make them understand.

"It's been a rough year," I found myself announcing then, to Statler, and the happy couple, and the whole damned boat. "It's not the life I would have chosen," I went on, "and parts of it are absolutely brutal. But there are upsides, too. I'm wiser. I'm kinder. I've taken up knitting."

They couldn't possibly get it. Some kinds of wisdom can only be earned. I should have dropped the whole thing right then. But I just needed to stand up for myself.

"I am building a summer camp," I said next, "and I've started my own nonprofit, and I'm as busy and happy and productive as I've ever been. I've found my calling. I've found work that's so satisfying and thrilling, I wish I didn't even have to sleep."

I read their faces. They weren't convinced.

But it was okay.

Needing to find reasons to live had forced me to build a life worth living. I would never say the accident was a good thing. I would never, ever claim that everything happens for a reason. Like all tragedies, it was senseless.

But I knew one thing for sure: The greater our capacity for sorrow becomes, the greater our capacity for joy.

So I went on, "That's the thing you don't know—that you *can't* know until life has genuinely beaten the crap out of you: I am better for it all. I am better for being broken."

The truth of it both steadied me and left me a little shaky.

It felt like a real triumph.

Until Chip's bride gave me a look, like, *Please.*

Chip didn't seem too convinced, either. "You're saying you've moved on?"

Ugh. "Yes."

His eyes were like dares. "Does that mean," he asked, "that you're seeing somebody?"

Seriously? Was this the only definition of moving on? Was there no way to get better or be happy or live a great life that did not involve *dating*? Was being in love the only kind of happiness out there? I took offense at the question on feminist principle. I felt tempted to lecture him all night on the ways that women's lives did not need to be validated romantically by a man. Ridiculous! Narrow-minded! Conventional!

I almost said so. One more second, and I would have.

Twenty-nine

BUT THAT'S WHEN we all heard a person shout, "Wait! Hold the boat!"

At the sound, I noticed that the guys on the dock had already untied the ropes, and we were starting to motor away.

We turned in the direction of the voice, and one of the dockworkers shouted, in Flemish, what I presumed was "Hold up! One more!"

A lone man in a tuxedo was sprinting down the steps toward us.

A man who at first looked weirdly like Ian.

A man who in fact kept on looking like Ian, even as he got closer.

And then turned out to actually be Ian.

My Ian, of all people. Not in Edinburgh. Here. In Bruges. Running to catch the boat to Chip's reception, in a shawl-collared tux.

Ian. Here, apparently, to crash the reception, too.

I saw him, but he didn't see me. Too busy running and looking deadly handsome.

I would have told you my reaction to seeing Chip and Tara was visceral—but I did not know the meaning of that word until I watched Ian sprinting down those steps.

My lungs stopped working.

If I could have turned my eyes away, I would have looked for a place to hide.

But I couldn't turn my eyes away. I took in Ian's new haircut—a little shorter, a little spikier—and the fit of his tux, noting how European men seemed to wear their pants a smidge tighter than Americans, like they'd shrunk them in the wash.

In a really good way.

Then Ian was vaulting over the wooden turnstile, and then he was on the dock, running—no: sprinting, charging, *pumping*—along it, after us.

The boat had already edged away. It was three feet from the dock by now, but Ian didn't even falter.

He just leapt right off the corner of the dock and landed in a crouch on the one open spot of deck—about three inches from my knees.

It was a cool, badass, James Bond move like I'd never seen in real life.

Ian stood up then and faced the crowd. "This is the boat to the reception, I hope," he said to them all.

The *voice*. That accent—again, after all this time. I felt my insides melting like warm butter.

The driver shouted something angry at Ian in Flemish—I assume something like *Not cool, man! You're going to get yourself killed!*—just as the guests all broke into cheers. Ian brushed off his suit, apologized to the driver, and waved an aw-shucks thank-you at the cheering guests before looking around to notice there were no seats left.

That's when the boat driver pointed straight at him, like, *Sit down, pal!* Then pointed straight at the seat next to me.

Ian turned toward the seat, and that's when he saw me.

Our eyes locked.

If there was a moment for me to die of intensity, this was it. But I couldn't even do that. I couldn't breathe, couldn't think. And from the looks of things, Ian wasn't doing any of those things, either.

"Please take your seat, sir," the boat driver said, in English, at last.

But Ian did not take his seat. Instead, he dropped to his knees on the deck. In front of me. Kneeling at my feet.

"You're here," he said, a bit breathless.

All I could think of was nonsense. "I'm not here. *You're* here."

Every single person on the boat was watching us now, but as the driver revved the engine to pick up speed, the white noise of it gave us a little sound barrier.

"I'm sorry I'm late," he said.

Can you be late to a party you weren't invited to? "You're not late," I said.

Next, his eyes dipped down and caught sight of my necklace. "You're wearing my present," he said.

I nodded.

"I thought you might have thrown it away."

"I did," I said. "My mom fished it out of the trash."

"Good woman," he said. "Do you like it?"

Slowly, I nodded.

If it was good to hear the voice after all this time, seeing the face was just short of ecstasy. It made me woozy to be so close. I didn't have even one photo of him, and so I truly hadn't seen that face in almost a year. I drank in the sight—those dark blue eyes that always looked a little sad, the Adam's apple just above his tux tie, the jaw squarer than I'd remembered.

"What are you doing here?" I asked then.

"What are *you* doing here?"

"I'm here," I said, gesturing at the rest of the guests on the boat, "for a wedding."

"Your prick ex-fiancé's wedding."

"It hasn't been that bad," I said. Then I gave him a little grin. "It hasn't been that good, either."

He leaned forward and took my hands. "What could you possibly have been thinking?"

I shrugged. "My parents broke up, and Kit and I were trying to *Parent Trap* them back together."

Ian frowned. "At your ex-fiancé's wedding?"

"It was kind of a make-it-work moment." I met his eyes. "Plus, I'd never been to Europe."

"You should have come to Scotland."

I couldn't read his face. Did he know? "I was thinking about it," I said.

He seemed surprised. "Were you?"

"I thought I might pop over there when I was done here."

He studied my face. "Is that true?"

"Yes. Did you know that already? Did Kit tell you?"

"No. She didn't."

" 'Cause I know you've kept in touch."

He looked down. "I had to keep an eye on you."

"I'm pretty sure the last time I saw you, you told me you never cared about me at all, so I'm not sure you *had to*."

"I was lying."

"What?"

"I was lying to you when I said that."

I squinted at him to get a better look. "You *didn't* not care about me?"

He settled his eyes square on mine. "I didn't not care about you." He leaned closer. "I cared about you." Then he added, "Too much."

"Can you care about a person too much?"

"I'm still trying to figure that out."

I studied his face. What was he saying? "Maybe you're lying now."

But he shook his head and picked up one of my hands and pressed it to his heart. It pounded in his chest. "I'm not lying now," he said.

That was a heck of a confession. "Why did you lie before?"

"Because I thought it was better for you."

"Why? Why would it be better for you to break my heart?"

He frowned and leaned closer. "Did I?"

"Pretty much."

"I'm sorry. I didn't think that would happen."

"Because you thought I didn't really like you?"

Ian nodded. "I thought it was just the aftereffects of the trauma."

"Well, guess what? It wasn't."

"I thought I was doing you a favor, really. I thought I was the only one who would suffer."

I had to ask. "Why would you suffer?"

He held my gaze. "Because I didn't want to be without you."

I kept not breathing.

This didn't seem like it could possibly be happening—me in Kit's red dress, talking to Ian, in a tux, on his knees, holding my hand against his beating heart. And yet there was no denying the boat, the water, breeze, the churn of the current.

We motored under a stone bridge, lit underneath by hanging lanterns, but I barely noticed. Until I heard my name, just as the bridge passed overhead.

"Margaret!" The voice sounded very close.

I looked up.

"Margaret!"

Hands waving on top of the bridge. Two sets of hands.

"Margaret!"

It was my parents. Together, side by side, standing on the bridge at the top of the arch.

"Why aren't you at the reception!" I called up to them.

"We decided to ditch!"

"Did anyone think to tell me that?"

"Couldn't find you!"

That's when my dad put an arm around my mom. In that one gesture, I knew something. *She was okay.*

More than that: *They* were okay.

All that worry about her? I could let that go. They'd found each other, and they knew what to do. They'd either work it out or they wouldn't. But my job there was done.

THE BOAT DIDN'T slow. We kept moving ahead. My parents receded into the Bruges night, waving a little longer, then dropping their hands and turning to continue their stroll.

Ian watched them, too, for a minute, before turning back to me.

"Why are you here again?" I asked.

"I came to find you."

"You came all the way from Scotland to find me?"

He nodded.

"Why?"

"Because I miss you." The word sounded like "mess."

"You do?"

Ian nodded. "Every day."

I didn't want to break this easily. I wanted to hold out and be tough and stay mad. Maybe it was the thump of his heart against my hand, or those earnest eyes, or that tuxedo he was not just wearing but *rocking*—but I couldn't hold out. "I miss you, too."

"Even after so long?"

"I think it might be getting worse, actually," I confessed.

"I told myself I had to wait a year to find you again—give you time to settle and find your way. I consulted with my brothers, even, and everyone agreed—a full year at the minimum. Now, it's a year. I had just bought a plane ticket to the States when I saw Kit's post about you coming to Belgium."

"You bought a ticket to the States?"

Ian nodded.

"But then you came to Bruges?"

Ian nodded again.

"Did Kit know you were coming?"

"In a way, I suppose. She gave me the name of the hotel, and your flight schedule, and texted a photo of the wedding invitation." Then he looked at me. "Why were you coming to Scotland?"

"Oh, you know. Just general tourism. Visit Loch Ness. See a few kilts."

Ian smiled a little. There it was.

It was so strange, looking back, to feel on that crowded boat like there was nobody else around. The sound of the motor disappeared, and so did everyone around us, and so did the past and the future.

"Back when we met," Ian said, "I was supposed to be helping you—but it was really you who helped me. The way you teased me—the way you called out my bitterness—the way you surprised me over and over and showed me the world from different angles. It made me better to be around you. You made me laugh—probably more in those weeks we spent together than in my whole life beforehand. You taught me about goofiness. You showed me a different way to be in the world. You brought out some warmer, more hopeful part of my soul. Then, after I left, I had to go cold again."

He went on. "I moved home to the gray skies, and I took a job I didn't like. I didn't even try to look for something better, because all I could do was count the weeks until I could get back to you. I made a pact with myself to give you a year—but I almost broke it a hundred different times. My only exception was if you started seeing somebody else. Then I was allowed to go to Texas and fight for you."

I gave him a look like he was crazy. "Seeing somebody? Like who?"

"I think that carpenter working on the camp lodge has a thing for you."

"He does not."

"It wouldn't surprise me if the architect did, too. He's a bit too enthusiastic."

"That is bananas."

"And of course I keep expecting Chip to crawl back begging any minute."

"Unlikely. Since he's married now."

"Short of that, I had to wait a year."

"For my sake."

Ian nodded. "So you could get back on your feet."

I let out a long breath. "Not literally, though. Because it's not looking like that's going to happen."

Ian nodded. "Maybe not, but you've done great. I've been cheering you from afar."

Something about not just what Ian was saying but the way he was saying it—so intense, so unflinching—had me practically hypnotized.

"Do you understand what I'm saying to you?" he asked then.

Did I? I could barely think. "Are you saying you're glad I'm better?"

He shook his head, like, *Not quite it.*

"Are you saying it's been a tough year for you, too?"

Not it, either.

I shrugged. "You're going to have to tell me."

He'd been resting back on his heels a bit, but now he rose up on his knees and edged forward, leaning in close.

"I think about you all the time, Maggie Jacobsen. I can hardly sleep for missing you. I ache to see you and be near you. I love you with a longing that I can barely contain, and I fear it's going to drown me."

Those eyes again.

Maybe I should have leaned in to kiss him then, but I found I couldn't move. It seemed impossible that I could want something so badly—and also get it. I'd been holding back for so long, I didn't know how to let go.

Until he brought his hand up to the back of my neck and pulled my mouth to his.

Because at the kiss, I came to life again.

The world stood still, but the boat kept going. We drifted past stone houses with stairstepped gables and gardens with foliage so lush, it tumbled down to the water. We floated past boathouses with wooden shutters. We passed cafés with hanging lanterns and candlelit tables by the water. But we didn't notice any of it.

Even as the boat taxi pulled up to the reception site and docked, and even as the bride and groom, and his parents, and the wedding party, and all the guests averted their eyes as they climbed up out of the boat and off toward the reception, we didn't let go. We barely noticed them.

We just stayed lost in that one kiss we'd waited so long to find.

Epilogue

THAT WAS TEN years ago.

We never made it to the reception, by the way. Just rode the taxi back to the stand and made our way to the hotel from there. Ian kindly—and impressively—carried me piggyback to the hotel, my folded-up chair under one strong arm like it was nothing.

We decided we ought to take it slow, but then we didn't.

We went back to Ian's hotel room—just down the hall from mine—and stayed up all night. I spent much of the evening trying to explain to Ian why he couldn't possibly be attracted to me, and he spent just as much of it proving me wrong. Convincingly.

In the morning, at breakfast, we all ran into each other at the hotel buffet—Kitty, my parents, Ian, and me—and found a table together. None of us looked too perky, but Kitty looked the worst of all.

"I think we're going to need to take you to the doctor," my mother said, touching her hand to Kit's forehead. "You look like a wax figure at Madame Tussaud's."

Kitty wiped her hand away. "I'm fine."

"Wrong," my mother declared. "You are pale and sweaty." Then, giving her a look, "I'm pretty sure they have doctors in Belgium."

"I don't need a doctor."

My mom looked at me for help. "Reason with her."

"You do look"—how to say it nicely?—"*not yourself.* Why don't you just—"

But Kitty started talking over me. "I'm fine! I'm fine! I don't need a doctor—"

As I kept going with "—see somebody? Just in case?"

While my dad added, "It's going to be such a long flight home, and the last thing you need is—"

As my mom chimed in with "It could be Ebola, it could be a burst appendix, it could be some kind of *E. coli* situation—"

We all yammered over one another like the most ridiculous bunch of foreigners, right there in our lovely Belgian hotel's breakfast café, until, maybe just needing to put an end to the madness, Kitty shouted, "I'm not sick! I'm just pregnant!"

We all fell quiet.

"I took a test this morning. Actually, I took three."

"Whose is it?" I stage-whispered, after a good long pause. "Fat Benjamin? Or the Moustache?"

"I vote for Fat Benjamin," my mother said, in her normal voice.

"Me, too," my dad said, raising his hand.

Ian and I raised ours for Fat Benjamin, too. "Unanimous," I declared.

Kitty gave us a look like we were *the worst.*

Then she said, "Benjamin, okay? I have to throw up now."

THAT'S OUR STORY. In the decade since the crash, things have moved on for everyone, like they do.

My parents did get back together. My dad just wasn't a grudge holder, or the kind of guy who could stay mad. As he explained it to me once, when I asked, "Your mother has never been perfect. And I've always loved her anyway." I'm not sure what I would have done if I'd been in his shoes. But I think choosing to go back and work it out suited him. Leaving wasn't his style. He was a for-better-or-for-worse kind of guy.

My dad retired two years later, and about a month after he did, he got the news that he had lung cancer. Of all things. And he didn't even smoke.

"Too much sawdust," he shrugged, when he told us.

He fought it like a champ, and my mom sat right there with him at every appointment and through every treatment. She crocheted fuzzy socks for him and read him articles from *Reader's Digest,* and made steak, spaghetti, and meatloaf for him in a rotation. All his favorites, over and over.

To fill the time, in between treatments, when he felt good, he started volunteering reading books-on-tape for the blind. It wasn't long before he realized he had a knack for reading stories. For a while, he invented a job for himself as the bedtime story guy at camp, reading by the fire every Friday night to rapt groups of kids—doing all the voices and the sound effects. He loved it so much that even after he'd gotten far too sick to read, or even to walk out to the campfire, he still came out to listen to his replacements and offer them pointers. My mom drove him in a golf cart and brought folding chairs.

One night, near the end, when I was visiting him at hospice, he told me that those last years with my mom had been the best of all.

"Why?" I asked.

He smiled, a little sly. "She appreciated me more."

I flared my nostrils at him.

"I appreciated her more, too," he added. "And guess what else?"

"What?"

He gave me a half-smile. "I wouldn't change a thing." Then he squeezed my hand. "Be sure to tell that to your sister."

My dad didn't want to be buried, he wanted to be *planted.* So we dug a hole for his ashes on the bonfire hill and planted an oak tree there. My mother wants us to plant another tree over her ashes right next to it when it's her turn—so the two can grow together with their branches interlocked.

She brings it up a lot.

It's been three years now since he died, and my mom still seems lost. She keeps busy, though. That year without my dad changed her, and humbled her, and freed her in a lot of ways. She's easier on everyone these days—including, I suspect, herself.

She keeps the books for us at camp now, and helps with the kids, and not long after my dad died, she offered to take his storytelling place at the campfire. She also joined a feminist quilting group called Sew Feisty! that meets every week to sew and talk politics. She still worries too much and starts with *death* in every situation—but between me, Ian, and Oprah, we've got her keeping a gratitude journal.

She's trying. And trying always counts for a lot.

ARE YOU WONDERING if I ever managed to walk again?

I didn't.

We tried braces and walkers and electrical muscle stimulation, and one more surgery about two years after the crash, and then we called it quits. New technologies pop up all the time, and maybe science will catch up with me, but I'm not holding my breath. I no longer scour the Web for hope on that front. I've learned to look for hope in other ways.

I'm happy to report that my donor site scars did heal up, and after ten years of applying vitamin E, you can barely see them. That said, the grafts are a different story. Parts are smooth and parts are ropy and mottled, but no amount of vitamin E could make them anything less than tragic.

Which is why, on the five-year anniversary of the crash, I let Kitty tattoo the whole thing. She'd been begging me for ages, and she had a design all made up: a folk art flower garden "growing" from the back of my shoulder forward over my scar. She did the outline all on the first night, and she's been slowly adding colors ever since. Look at me from one side now, and I look like my old self. Look at me from the other, and I'm graced with flowers.

My mom said she was going to get a tattoo that night, too—but then she couldn't decide. She's still working on it.

I won't lie. Losing the use of my legs has been the hardest thing in my life. I don't want to downplay it. I don't want to pretend it has been easy. It's been the opposite of easy.

But there have been good things, too.

Ian wasn't kidding about being in love with me. I never could talk him out of it.

Guess what we did? We got married.

We dated for a while, long-distance at first, and then Ian came back to Texas. Now we run the camp together. Ian runs the PT side—Myles never did go after his license. Turns out, running Ian out of the country was enough revenge to satisfy him, and then Myles himself got a job in Orlando, left town, and—fingers crossed—forgot all about us. I run the business-y stuff and some fun stuff, too: finger-painting, slug knitting, origami, cake decorating, hay rides, *Sound of Music* sing-alongs.

Everything about Camp Hope turned out better than I imagined. We raised almost twice as much money as I'd been shooting for, due in part to all those followers of Kit's—but also due to my hard, tireless, obsessive work.

Yep. I give myself credit. I give us all credit.

Once my parents were back together, it took them about two minutes to get out the plans and start discussing the build, and my dad jumped in like a pro. I got to see my parents through new eyes, working as a team. My mother's relentless perfectionism, when focused on a project instead of on me, was powerful, inspiring stuff, and my dad's good-natured practicality was a nice counterweight. They collaborated, and even disagreed, in inspiring harmony.

I guess the design apple doesn't fall far from the tree, because my mom and I turned out to love all the same things: big windows, stone fireplaces, kitschy Western retro lamps, wagon-wheel fences, deep porches, ceiling fans, clean modern lines with classic farmhouse details, and whimsy.

We really got along okay.

The camp's been up and running for seven years now. It's a real, bustling, thriving place. It's sunny and warm, and the buildings are stone and stucco with tin Texas roofs, and big porches, and shady trees. We've got fields of wildflowers and nature trails. Everything is entirely ramp accessible—even the treehouse. We found all kinds of craftspeople to create magic with murals and sculptures and fountains. We made mosaics on the camp gates using all my broken dishes, and now we have a mosaic class where folks get to smash their own.

We run camps all summer for kids, and classes all winter for grown-ups. We have movie nights and cookie contests and charity projects for the sick. We have resource networks and referral systems. We offer classes for the newly injured as well as projects and support for their loved ones. We help people cope with where they are—but we also show them where they can go.

We don't fix everything, but we sure do make things better.

That's really become my whole guiding philosophy. I would never tell you that the life you wanted couldn't have been exactly as great as you planned. But you have to live the life you have. You have to find inspiration in the struggle, and pull joy out of the hardship. That's what we try to do—counterbalance the suffering with laughter, fuzzy blankets, hugs, sing-alongs, sunny-day picnics, chocolate chip cookies, and wildflowers. Because that's all we can do: carry the sorrow when we have to, and absolutely savor the joy when we can.

Life is always, always both.

And so: chili cook-offs, karaoke concerts, outdoor movie nights, inner-tubing, nature strolls, campfires, s'mores, skits, painted flowerpots, hayrides, and inspiration of all kinds. We chiseled Ian's mother's saying about helping others into a stone lintel above the office doors, and service to others has become a huge part of the program. Kids mentor each other, and teach crafts classes, and work in the garden, and help clean up. They make valentines for other kids who are in the hospital, bake muffins for the elderly, groom the horses, and work with service dogs to help socialize them. They learn through experience—kind of the only way you *can*—that taking care of others is a way of taking care of yourself.

And, of course, everybody gets a T-shirt that says THAT'S HOW WE ROLL.

Are you wondering what happened with Kitty and Fat Benjamin? As soon as we got back from Europe, he and his hipster beard came charging over to our house to beg Kitty to marry him.

Which she refused to do.

Not her style.

But she did allow a lifetime commitment ceremony, which is pretty much exactly the same thing. And she did tattoo his name on her arm, and they did move in together, and he did turn out to be the sweetest, most nurturing mate. And Kitty did give birth to the cutest little cupcake of a baby. Tragically, against all advice, they named her Pandora Snapdragon.

But you can't get everything right.

Somewhere along the way we decided "Fat Benjamin" was mean and changed his nickname to Sweet Benjamin, even though he insisted he liked Fat Benjamin better. Eventually, he became just Sweetie, which he likes even less.

Pandora got the nickname Dorie from us, which was the best we could do for her, and now she is ten and taller than her mom. Kitty and Uncle Sweetie turned out to be quite fertile, adding two brothers to the mix before Dorie was even five, and moving back to Texas after they were outnumbered.

Tragically, against all advice, they named their two boys Wolfgang and Socrates. But we do not tease the boys about it. Only their parents, late at night, when all the kids are fast asleep, and the grown-ups are playing board games and drinking wine—and we are begging Uncle Sweetikins to shave off that crazy beard.

OH! I WAS able to get pregnant, too. We were trying for one, but we got surprise boy-girl twins—and while nothing, truly nothing, about that has been easy, they're six now, and we hope we're through the worst of it. We named them Captain and Tennille.

Just kidding.

We named them after our four parents: Andrew Clifford and Elizabeth Linda. They play with their cousins at the camp all summer—swimming in the lake, and feeding the horses, and "helping" tend the garden.

Is everything perfect? Hell, no. Everything's a mess. A crazy, galloping, heartbreaking mess.

You can't fix everything. Not even close.

But you can look for reasons to be grateful.

More than that, you can work to create them.

That's what I've taken from all this. The crash all those years ago shattered the life I had, but the pieces wound up making a pretty good mosaic. That's what art is, I suppose: transforming things from what they were into what they could be. My life now, without question, is transformed. Maybe that makes it a work of art.

All I know is, we have as much fun as we can.

Every year on April Fools' we throw a giant Valentine's Day party, just so we don't forget. *Love happens all the time.* We made a mosaic out of that saying, too.

Do I ever think about the crash? Do I ever wonder what life would have been like if I had married Chip (who's already on Wife Two), or if I hadn't gotten hurt, or if I were still that perfect girl I used to be?

Not really.

I know better than to look backward. I know how to try, and how to fail, and how to try again. I know how to live from the inside out. I know to savor every snuggle, every morning swim, every tickle, every meal, every warm bath, every moment when somebody makes you laugh.

More than anything, I know that you just have to choose to make the best of things. You get one life, and it only goes forward. And there really are all kinds of happy endings.

Acknowledgments

This story required vast amounts of research, and I'm so grateful to all the people who helped me try to get it right. Hugs to friends who hooked me up with experts to answer my many questions: Vicky and Tony Estrera, Jennifer Hamilton, Eve Lapin, Mark Poag, and J.J. Spedale.

Much gratitude to all the healthcare professionals who took time to help me research Margaret's treatment. Dr. Darrell Hanson met me for coffee and walked me through exactly the injury Margaret would have had, explained in detail the surgery and recovery, and taught me the world *iliopsoas*. Dr. Forrest Roth walked me through the treatment of burns and skin grafts. Robert Manning, PT, kindly took a morning to show me around the ICU and rehab gym at Houston Methodist Hospital. Ross LaBove and all the guys at Project Walk in Houston let me spend a day with them learning about all the creative and inspiring ways they help people work to get better.

Thank you to Jeff Scott and Wesley Branch, who were both gracious enough to share their spinal cord-injury stories with me and to talk at length about the realities of life afterward. Also, I'm glad to have found two honest and inspiring narratives about life with spinal cord injuries: Mark Hall's book, *Across the Street from Hell*, and Pamela Henline's book, *Walk, Don't Run*. The Christopher & Dana Reeve Foundation was also helpful.

Many thanks to Mollie Gordon, who connected me with her dad, Alan Gordon—who very kindly took me up in his Cessna, flew me to Galveston and back, even let me "fly" the plane for a little while. Then, once we were safely back on the ground, showed me the best way to crash that plane. Thanks, too, to John Marino, who met me for coffee and told me of his harrowing—and yet somehow very funny—experience of surviving a plane crash.

A quick shout-out to my friend Sam Nichols for the night at the Cherry Blossom in Fishkill, NY, when he just about killed himself eating an entire blob of wasabi on a dare.

I've been inspired for many years by the resilience of my mom's friend Jan Myers, who, with her husband, founded a summer camp for children with health needs after they lost their young son John Marc to cancer. Camp Hope in this novel—its thoughtful and whimsical design and its determination to bring joy into people's struggles—is inspired by Camp John Marc.

I also need to thank friends who've supported me, talked books with me, and gone out of their way to help me either get my writing done or get the word out about it: Brené Brown and Steve Alley, Chris and Connie Seger, Jenny Lawson, Sheryl Rapp, Vicky Wight, Faye Robeson, Andrew and Katherine Weber, Bryn Larsen, Maria Zerr, Tracy Pesikoff, and Dale Andrews. And thanks to my fun family for always being so excited about what I do: Bill Pannill and Molly Hammond, Shelley and Matt Stein (and Yazzie), Lizzie and Scott Fletcher, and Al and Ingrid Center.

My amazing mom, Deborah Detering, and my rock-star husband, Gordon Center, always rack up a million points for helpfulness and selflessness as I try to get my writing done. (Special thanks to Gordon for mangling the French language so beautifully and inspiring the phrase "my hams exploded.") My kids, Anna and Thomas, also get a million points. Just for being sweet-hearted and hilarious.

Thanks, also, to all the folks at St. Martin's Press who have supported this book and been so great to work with.

Last, but not least: Heartfelt gratitude to my agent, Helen Breitwieser, who's advocated for and stuck by me now for a solid decade. And to my editor, the brilliant Jen Enderlin, who I don't think I can ever thank enough for taking me on. Thank you both beyond words.